When

Love Aint

Enough

When Love

Aint Enough

A novel by

Vivian M Kelly

GNE Books

GNE Books

Published by Gritz N Eggz Productions (GNE BOOKS)

Gritz N Eggz Productions USA Inc

Printed in the United States of America

First Edition

1 2 3 4 5 6 7 8 9 10

PUBLISHER'S NOTE

This is a work of fiction. Names, characters, places and incidents either are
the product of the author's imagination or are used fictitiously. Any
resemblance to events or persons, living or dead, is entirely coincidental.

BOOKS ALSO AVAILABLE AT WWW.VIVIANMKELLY.COM

"You can't stop the sun from shining or the rain from falling, so why try. What will be, will be!"

Dedicated

In loving memory of my best friend

Mr. Ronnie Sexton

Acknowledgements

First and foremost I want to thank God for his daily blessings. He has blessed me with a loving and supportive mother, Beulah and two siblings that I adore, Sharon and Cedrick. I thank my dad, Wilson who instilled in me, "every rat got have they own hole."

I want to thank my niece who is the apple of my eye and thinks the sun rises and sets on her "Teedy", Miss Indigo Kelly. I want to thank my best friend, Ronnie who stood by me for 17 years. It was truly a blessing from God that I should have a friend like him. He was my soul mate, my compadre and my dearest friend. I will miss him always. I also want to thank Rodney, James, Chris and Marty, Tracey Moore., Erica B, Nykki Middleton., my aunt Pearl, my uncle Myles, Teresa, Daniel, Portia, Vanessa B. and Keisha Simpson. Then last but definitely not least, I want to acknowledge Maxwell, who kept me going when I thought I'd give out.

When

Love

Aint

Enough

She loves me, she loves me

not, she. . . .

Prelude

When I was younger, I never understood what my mom meant when she'd say,

"Aint no sense like bought sense!"

Well I damned sho' do now! As I think back on all the hell I went through, I realize my sense cost me my heart, my soul and I damn near lost my mind!

It was 11am Monday morning. I should have been at the office three hours ago, but I was still in bed. I hadn't slept a wink all night from tossing and turning waiting on Jade to call.

At that point, my job was the least of my concerns. Now, all I could focus on was the two of them together doing God knows what!

In the midst of my agony, I cursed aloud at the devil for playing havoc with my mind, stealing my joy and forcing me to imagine shit I never dreamed could happen.

It was damn near 20 degrees outside, but I was burning up. I lay sprawled on my back, watching the ceiling fan spin violently, trying to hypnotize myself and escape to some far away place, any place, but there. For a moment, I imagined I was back home in Mississippi. Momma was in the kitchen cooking something that smelled good as hell and my brother was laid out on the leather chase flipping through the channels on the TV. My sister Chelle was locked in her room, hogging the phone, as usual. And me, well, I was just happy to be there, safe and secure from all the hell I'd been going through.

But my visit was short, as thoughts of Jade slithered to the forefront of my mind and her plans to marry NBA player, Trevaire Brooks. Upon realizing there was no escape from my awful reality, I moaned in despair,

"She's getting married!"

The thought ripped through my heart, cutting away at my soul. I felt as though I was sinking in a pit of quick sand. The more I struggled to pull myself out of its painful grasp, the more it sucked me in. Tears welled up in my eyes, burning like hot coals, as I fought back the urge to cry. I opened my mouth to speak but nothing came out! My mind frantically searched for something else to concentrate on, but it was no use. The moment one tear escaped and rolled down my cheek, the others quickly followed.

I cradled myself helplessly, in a fetal position, trying to stifle the pain that quickly consumed me. Slowly I rocked back and forth trying to regain control of my shattered emotions. My every being cried out for the one person who could console me, Jade.

Weary of the tears, I rolled over in the crumpled sheets and reached for the glass sitting on the night stand. Hungrily I pulled it up to my lips and gulped down its contents!

"Ahhhh" I sighed, greedily savoring the taste of watered down Cognac. It was good and quenched my thirst momentarily.

As the liquor slid down my throat, I squeezed my eyes shut still hoping to find that "high" I'd been searching for since I realized sleep was not an option. Carefully I balanced the glass on my stomach as I felt around the bed for the remote to turn off the music that had been playing all night. I'd left it on, hoping it would lull me into a much needed sleep. It was something I did as a kid, afraid of the dark at bedtime.

But the Luther Vandross CD had become annoying and only made me want to cry more. But this time, instead of crying, I lay dazed and wounded like a deer trapped in headlights.

Soon I gave up trying to find it and decided to go turn it off my damn self! I grabbed my glass, finished it off and sat up in the bed. As I looked around the room I was shocked at the mess I'd made. The room looked like a tornado had hit it!

During my many tantrums over the weekend, I'd trashed any and everything that got in my way, after not being able to concentrate on anything other than her. Papers and books lay everywhere. The clothes and shoes that I'd thought about putting on, but never did, were thrown about the furniture and floor. Pictures of Jade and I were thrown about the room like confetti. Empty beer bottles, filled with half smoked cigarettes and ashes, gave off a terrible odor as if I was in a café alley.

Displeased with the room, I jumped down from the bed only to land in a saucer filled with more ashes and cigarette butts. As if it were possible to be any more disgusted, I kicked

3

and rubbed the ashes off my foot onto the plush crème carpet and made my way out into the hallway, still clutching my empty glass.

As I walked through the hallway and down the stairs the music grew louder. My head throbbed from lack of sleep forcing me to squeeze my tired eyes shut, to release the pressure. When I got downstairs and looked around, it looked worse than the bedroom.

My eyes immediately gravitated to a bottle of unopened Cognac, sitting awkwardly by itself, in the middle of the marble floor. I stumbled over to it and anxiously looked around for a clean place to sit. Unknowingly, I'd left the patio blinds open all night. Now the blue gray sky spilled lazily through its partitions. Its light bothered me but strangely, drew me near. As I walked toward it, I caught a glimpse of myself in the door's reflection.

I looked worse than I felt! My powder blue pajama bottoms, looked gray from the abuse I'd put on 'em over the past weekend. My hair was a mangled mess, making me look like a crazy woman! I stared at my pitiful reflection and dropped my head. The sight repulsed me. I was broken! Slowly, I turned around and walked over to my favorite chair and plopped down.

It had been three days since I talked to Jade. Over and over I'd replayed our last conversation in my head. I'd been so sure about us. Now she was gone and I didn't know what to make of any of it. I desperately needed to hear her voice. If I could just talk to her everything would be okay again.

Though I'd called her a million times since hearing the news, with no success, I was determined not to give up. I was at a point of no return, my pride and everything else could go to hell! My soul was grieving and the pain was unbearable.

Anxiously, I grabbed the phone off the table and said a quick prayer before dialing her number. Every vein in my neck stiffened, as I listened to it ring. I jumped to my feet and paced back and forth waiting on her to pick up. My steps grew increasingly weaker after each unanswered ring.

"Please pick up," I whispered anxiously into the receiver. But she didn't. And slowly my heart sank again as the answering machine came on. I listened intently as though I was hearing the instructions for the first time. Suddenly breathing became a difficult chore and my heart beat violently as I waited for the beep.

Then it came! I quietly exhaled and began to speak,

"Hey Jade, it's me," I said, pausing momentarily still hoping she'd pick up. "Baby I really need to talk to you. I need to know what's going on with you. What's this all about? I've been calling you for two days and... you haven't returned any of my calls..." I whispered into the receiver as though trying to hide my begging from anyone else within earshot.

"Baby I don't understand any of this, its crazy!"
Then I grew really desperate.

"I thought you loved me Jade. I thought we were better than this?!" Baby I'm dying over here, please talk to me. Please baby, I love…"

The recorder interrupted my begging, announcing I'd reached my recording limit.

Slowly, I lowered the phone from my ear and stared at it incredulously. I plopped down on the nearby sofa and allowed the phone to drop to the floor. My face grew hot as tears welled up in my eyes and rolled down my cheeks.

"I can't believe this is happening. I've really lost her. It's really over!" I cried aloud.

In despair, I fell back on the sofa and hugged myself as my body trembled. My chest began to heave uncontrollably, as I frantically tried to breath. The floodgates had opened once again and this time I cried like a baby. And in the background, Luther sang on…

* * * * * * * * * * *

Now, as I reflect back over everything that led up to this, I realize how suddenly life can change for a person. In a matter of months my whole life had gone from sugar to shit! I tried frantically to grasp all of the pieces of the puzzle and make sense of it all. Though by no means was my life perfect, still, I was happy. I had a booming career, a beautiful new home and was crazy in love with my girl. Now all hell had broke loose.

"It's like a nightmare!" I thought.

A few months ago, Jade and I split up. She said she needed space and I guess I did too because I was more than willing to give it to her. She claimed she couldn't take the pressure I was putting on her to commit. She didn't want to be gay!

This in itself was a slap in the face because she spoke of it as if it were a choice she could easily make. Still I didn't sweat it. We'd broken up and gotten back together too many times for me to believe that this time was any different.

Then, a couple of days ago, I'd seen her and her ex-boyfriend at Claude's, our favorite restaurant. She'd look up to find me staring at them in disbelief, and then she looked away!

I stood awkwardly watching them, crushed by her betrayal. As I slowly came to my senses I walked out of the restaurant.

Adding insult to injury, my best friend, Kris, the owner of Claude's, had witnessed the whole thing. She followed me outside and tried to convince me to stay. But I couldn't. I was so humiliated that I couldn't even bear to look at her for fear of falling apart right then and there. And I damn sho couldn't stand to see Jade with someone else, acting as if I didn't exist.

Kris knew it was killing me. And I knew what she was thinking. It was the same thing she'd always say whenever Jade and I argued,

"Kick rocks on her ass man! Let her go if that's what she wants to do!"

But I couldn't. I loved that woman more than I loved myself.

I thanked Kris for coming out, but told her to go back inside. This was a battle that I would have to face on my own. She told me to call her once I got home and I promised I would. Numb, I jumped into my truck and drove away blinded by tears.

When I'd settled in, I remembered to call Kris. That's when she gave me the news. Jade and Trevaire had announced their engagement. For lack of a better phrase, you could have bought my ass on credit. I was done! Shocked shitless was a more accurate description! An endless number of questions swarmed around in my head,

"How can she do this, we just broke up three months ago?!" I yelled through the phone.

I was devastated! The bottom had just fallen out of my world and I had nothing to hold on to and no one to catch me.

"She don't want me!" I thought repeatedly.
The room started spinning and I grew weak.

"Man I'll call you back."

"Do you want me to come…"

"No!" I insisted. "I'm ok…everything's ok. I'll give you a call later" I lied.

"Alright…" said Kris reluctantly
I hung up and dropped the phone beside me. My chest started to hurt terribly. I put my hands up to my mouth and breathed into my hands, trying to quiet the panic attack I felt coming on. Numbly, I looked out into space and waited.

Above all, I had always believed Jade loved me, just as I loved her. But now I was lost. Anger soon took over, as feelings of betrayal crept in. I thought back to how hard I'd tried to prove my love was real. My actions embarrassed me now! Angered, I walked throughout the house destroying anything that got in my way, as even more questions ran through my aching head!

"How long has she been sleeping with him? Has she been fucking him the whole time she was dating me? Or is she doing this to show the world she aint gay cause she got a MAN?!"

"She got a man!!!" The phrase slithered through my brain like worms! If I had a nickel for every chic wanting me to screw her then later declaring she wasn't gay because she had **a** man, I'd have enough money to build-a-bitch! And I'm talking about a bad ass bitch at that!!!

****

Now, Jade was of that astute circle of women who "Had a man!"
And I, well I was left out in the cold, yet again! Why was I so unlucky at love?! What the hell ever happened to living 'happy ever after?" Does it even exist?! That was the question of the day! And if so, what about me! Where was my happy ending?

Slowly, I began reflecting on how I'd gotten to this point, my life, my dreams and past relationships, trying desperately to make sense of this present one.

PEEK A BOO... I SEE YOU

My childhood was like that of the average young child growing up in the south. I was the oldest of three children with a brother and sister pulling at my coat tails all the time.

When I was six, my father left, and followed his mother to Chicago. At the time, up north looked real good to the average black man looking for a quick fix. Evidently, during that time, a lot of men must have needed a quick fix because most of my friend's dads left for the Promised Land when their eldest child turned six.

At any rate, my mom was the head of our middle class household and she never let us forget it.

Momma was strict, but fair. Although we didn't get our butts whooped as often as we probably deserved, she had her moments when we were ordered to go find a belt or get a switch from the peach tree in the back yard, because she was fed up with our mess. And as she'd warned, prior to this doomful moment,

"When I whoop your butt it will be for all the things you've done!"

Not just the one thing that happened to break the camel's back on that unfortunate day.

When Love Aint Enough

My mom worked hard for her money. She was a nurse at a local health clinic and damn good at it. Often her job would require her to work long hours. And when she did, being the oldest, I was left with the responsibility of ensuring us kids stayed around the house, did chores, homework, and took a bath before night fall. It was a lot of responsibility, but I dealt with it. It didn't hurt matters any that my brother Darnell and I were more like best friends than siblings and my little sister Chelle idolized us both. The only thing she adored more was attention. And she tried to get it, most times, by ratting us out if we didn't let her have her way. Though mom would beg her not to be a tattle-tale, knowing Chelle as she did, but it was no use. Her response was the same,

"But I gotta tell you momma. I just gotta!"

During the summer time we kids would take our annual trip to visit my grandmother, Ida, also known as Miss Ann, in San Francisco. This was the highlight of my existence. I adored her. She was Lena Horne and Billie Holiday all rolled up in one glorious package. The fact that she lived in San Francisco only added to my illusions of her grandeur. She'd moved there after leaving my grand daddy, who still held out hope they'd one day get back together.

So, while I was there, I took it upon myself to accomplish two things: 1) reunite my grandparents and 2) convince my mom to move to California with the rest of her family.

11

As a child, I was painfully bashful with a vast imagination. So the gates of San Fran opened up a world of wonders to me. I felt at home from the first moment I stepped onto its sultry bay, at age tender age of ten.

I was rejuvenated by its aura and vibrant culture, which seemed to make room for everyone and anyone. There, a person was free to be whomever or whatever they desired and that definitely appealed to me. The possibilities seemed endless.

Each summer my shyness would shed like a well-worn cocoon, unleashing a beautifully crafted butterfly, anxious to see the world.

Those were happy times for me and very trying times for my mother, whom I pestered to move there each year at summer's end.

But mom was practical. She saw things I could never see. So Mississippi remained our home. I would have to settle for visiting the fair city and never living in it, as I so deeply desired. And my grand daddy, well, he and my grandmother never got back together, but they were friends. And that was good enough for him, so I was happy.

As I grew older, my objectives changed. Still painfully shy, I began on a self-enthused quest to find myself. My mom laughed when I first told her about my search for self and asked me,

"Do you remember the last place you put yourself?"

Though funny, I wasn't amused. I was growing into myself or something of the sort. And the realizations were shocking to say the least.

It was my freshman year of high school, when I started going with Mathew Sykes. He was tall, chocolate and very handsome. All the girls liked him but for some reason he chose me. And that was all she wrote. At his insistence, we both went out for the varsity basketball team and made it. When we'd go on road trips with the team, he would insist on my sitting with him on the way back home. This was our time to snuggle and share moments of passionate kisses, while covering our heads with blankets from the few onlookers who weren't engaged in it themselves.

Matt and I became a serious item. We'd sneak and talk on the phone for hours, late at night, while everyone else in our respective homes was fast asleep. After we'd been going together for a while, he started bringing up the subject of sex. He claimed making love would make us closer and always swore I couldn't get pregnant on the first time. Though he could be aggravatingly persistent and forever coming up with a reason why it was in my best interest to do it, I never gave in. Instead my response was pretty much the same each time he asked.

"I'm gonna wait until I'm married"

My mother, a devout Christian and true offspring of the old school had always instilled in us kids that sex was sacred and came after marriage. And I agreed whole heartedly. I was

damned determined to save my virginity for that special man
who would take me as his wife.

There was only one problem, lately I'd realized I was more
attracted to women, than men.

Though I cared deeply for Matt and we did all the typical
things teenagers did, like kissing and going to the movies,
something seemed to be missing. The most notable thing was, I
didn't feel a tingly feeling when we were together. It was a
fluttery tingle in the pit of my stomach I'd started having when I
was anywhere near my best friend Lisa!

The tingle was uncontrollable and hit me at the weirdest
times when we were together or just talking on the phone. At
first I didn't know why the tingle was there but I soon learned it
was due to my strong attraction for her. An attraction that felt as
common as the desire to have a drink of water when I was
thirsty. But still, I was terribly troubled by it.

Lisa and I had been best friends since the sixth grade. And we
were inseparable. We talked on the phone constantly, shared all
the same classes and even dressed alike!

Lisa was beautiful. She had a pecan tan and was a bit
shapelier than me. I in contrast, was tall, slender and flat
chested while she was short and already wearing a B cup! Matt
joking claimed to be jealous of her when he'd call and I chose to
talk with her, rather than hang up to talk to him. Looking back
now, I realize he had every reason to be, because I was crazy

about her. But back then, I justified it to myself and him, by saying, she was my very best friend.

During our sophomore year, Lisa got a boyfriend. This wasn't just any boyfriend. He was practically a man! His name was Don and he was a sophomore in college. Don was really popular and was the starting quarterback for his team.

Rumor had it, he and Lisa and had gone all the way. But I didn't believe it and denied the rumor every opportunity I got. But the rumors kept coming. Soon, Lisa and I began seeing less and less of each other.

Now when I called her, she was already on the phone with Don. She'd promise to call me back, but most times never did. I soon grew irritated with her and her new man! After all, even though I had Matt, I always managed to make time for her and felt she could do the same for me, since we were suppose to best friends! Then, whenever we did talk, her whole conversation was about Don! She was definitely changing.

One day during one of our rare phone conversations, I took the opportunity to tell her about the rumors I'd been hearing. After spilling my guts and telling her everything the kids at school were saying, I expected her to go ballistic! But she didn't. Instead she replied,

"People ought to mind their own damn business! They jus' jealous 'cause I have him and they don't!"

I was shocked! I couldn't believe what I was hearing. It was as if she was proud of the rumors! Nevertheless, I casually

15

agreed with her. And a little while later, made an excuse to get off the phone.

Afterwards, as I lay across my bed, I began to cry. I didn't know why I was crying. I just did, for a very long time. After that day, we grew even farther apart. I no longer understood her and she was too busy with her man, to miss me or realize we weren't close anymore.

I went through the depression of losing Lisa's friendship for months. During my senior year I was careful not to pick any of the classes she had. Matt and I were still dating and things were getting serious. So serious that on a couple of occasions I'd almost went all the way with him.

Still, whenever Lisa and I crossed paths or someone mentioned her name, I would get butterflies. The feelings were so intense I would be momentarily weakened by the sensation. Now, being a fairly intelligent person, I knew this was probably something different from what other girls were feeling for their friend girls.

"Am I jealous and want her for myself?

The idea of wanting Lisa for myself hit me like a ton of bricks! I had heard about "women like that" and the idea of me being one of them scared the hell out of me!

Discreetly, I researched homosexuality in the only resource I had available to me, the school library. I'd seclude myself in the back, carefully hiding the title, in hopes of getting information on the subject. I'd never check the book out and was careful not

16

let anyone see me pull it from the shelves. To do so was a dead give away to anyone watching, I was a homosexual.

Unfortunately the books available were few and far between. But what I did find described homosexuality as a "mental disorder", an act of depravity and most definitely frowned upon by God.

As I hid in alcoves of the library, reading and rereading theories about homosexuality, I cringed in despair because nothing I read was positive. Nor could it tell me why me, out of all people, was like that! In fact, after my research sessions, I was more frightened and confused than ever before.

My feelings of self-hatred became overwhelming. I can remember locking myself in the bathroom and staring intently in the mirror trying to reconcile the perfectly normal looking person looking back at me, with the pervert living inside me.

When I could no longer stand the thought of it, tears filled my eyes and I'd cried until my head hurt. All the while, my sister was outside, beating on the door, begging me to let her nosey butt in.

From then on, I was on a mission to keep my deep-dark secret from my family. I vowed I would never tell my mother or anyone else for that matter that I was "funny." This was a secret I would take to the grave!

At night, I'd lie awake in my bed praying, begging God to take the feelings away, to make me normal like everyone else. I prayed that my love for Matt would generate the type of feelings

17

I felt when I saw an attractive female. And when it didn't happen, I was convinced if I didn't leave home soon I'd turn into a man like creature that everyone hated and talked about. Then my family would hate me!

The only thing I knew to do was leave. And that's where college came in.

College Daze

College, proved to be my most revealing time. I never thought I would amount to much, being "funny" and all. I wanted to study law but my mother had her heart set on me becoming a doctor. She loved medicine. But it wasn't all her idea. When I was younger, I'd told her I wanted to help sick people, like she did.

It was only natural that she would think her brilliant daughter would follow in her footsteps. But that was not to be the case. I soon realized the sight of blood made me faint and my knees ached terribly. Momma thought it was funny and it even became the family joke, much to my dismay. Still, I wanted to make her proud of me, since I was failing her as a person. That's where Melbourne College came in.

It was a private, historically black college, renowned for its Pre-Med program and the high number of its students accepted to medical school each year. My mom even told me she wished she'd had the opportunity to attend Melbourne. But it was expensive. And back in the days when mom went to school, the opportunities simply weren't as plentiful as they were to me. So, when the school offered me a scholarship, I took it. It was

19

my chance to make up for the disappointment she'd certainly feel if she ever learned my terrible secret.

My first day of orientation was scary as hell. I'd tried, unsuccessfully, to convince mom to let me stay home until after I'd celebrated my birthday with the family but failed. So off to campus we went.

As we took the short drive to Jackson I stared out the passenger window overwhelmed. Even though was I with my mom I'd never felt so alone in my life. Still, I tried to keep a stiff upper lip and comforted myself with the knowledge leaving home was best for all involved.

When we arrived at the entrance of the campus it was introduced by a humungous white iron arch, bearing its name. As mom drove through the gate, I got a sinking feeling in the pit of my stomach. It was a feeling I'd I get each time I entered the gates, during my freshman year.

Our first stop was Ruston Hall, the freshman dormitory for women. Ruston Hall was a large, white antebellum structure, as were most of the buildings. Before the civil war, the campus had once been a vibrant plantation. It came equipped with a mansion and family living quarters. My dorm was one of those former living quarters. As we rode up the winding gravel road, lined with weeping willows and oversized magnolia trees, I pulled my welcome packet out of my backpack.

Our first stop, according to the instructions, was to check in with the RA, residential assistant, who would direct me to my dorm room.

The parking lot beside the dorm was jammed packed with cars and people moving about. Mom squeezed our '81 Chevy Camaro as close as she could to the side entrance as I peered out reluctantly at the people walking around the campus.

Most seemed of them so confident and relaxed. Some were with their parents but most were socializing. Yet all of them seemed happy. I didn't see anybody I thought I could identify with.

Weary, I got out of the car and gathered my luggage. Along with most of my clothes, I'd brought Hannibal, my red and white teddy bear.

After checking into the dorm, we walked across the street and down another winding path, to an old red and white building with the picture of a large Eagle painted above the entrance. It was the gymnasium. As we made our way inside, upper classmen greeted us, instructing me to sign in and pointed us to the registration tables. There, I was assigned a mentor to guide me though the process.

The butterflies in my stomach seemed to be dancing a tango as I made my way through each line and finally to the Finance officer's make shift office, on stage. Mom, being her ever sociable self, struck up a conversation with another parent whose

21

daughter was also a freshman. They introduced the two of us in hopes that we'd hit it off just as they had.

Well, that wasn't to be. I could tell from the looks of her we weren't the same speed. Though she looked shy I could tell she wasn't. Still, for appearance sake, we talked and I learned her room was only two doors down from mine.

When I'd received the last of my paperwork, we went to the chapel. There we sat through speech after speech and introduction after introduction as mom beamed with pride.

Afterwards, as mom prepared to leave, my mentor, who'd followed us to the car, reassured her I'd be fine, promising she'd be there to help me for the rest of the week.

"Be good and call me later" she said with a slight crack in her voice revealing the tears she was fighting back.

"I will," I responded fighting back my own as well.

As I reflect back on it now, I realize, momma cried because her baby was leaving the nest. But I cried out of pure fear!

"What the hell have I gotten myself into," I thought.
But I braved a stiff upper lip and kept it together, at least until she was out of sight, then, I fell to pieces.

After dinner everyone was invited to a "back to school dance" in the union. I made an excuse not to go and instead, hid out in my room. The thought of being around all those people scared the hell out of me and was a bit more than I was willing to deal with, being homesick and all.

22

When Love Aint Enough

The next couple of weeks I walked around the spacious wooded campus feeling like a fish out of water. At first I attended all of my classes diligently. But the more I went the more displaced I felt. A month had passed and I still hadn't made any friends. When I think back on it, I know it was mostly my own fault. I isolated myself because I was afraid of anyone getting too close and finding out my secret. I stupidly thought my feelings on the inside showed on the outside. I craved "*normality.*" And if achieving it meant being alone, it was a sacrifice I was willing to make!

After a while I stopped eating in the cafeteria. Instead, I utilized my supply of canned goods I'd brought from home. When I grew tired of canned spaghetti and canned wieners with crackers, I treated myself to a Mel-Burger, at the campus grill. It opened at nine pm and closed at midnight. It was my safest time. Few people were out at that time of night, aside from frat boys and sorority girls who were too busy doing their own thing to notice me. I didn't know them and they didn't know me.

One day, during second semester, I opened my door to find a short dumpy girl who lived a few doors down. She quietly announced I had a visitor in the lobby and swiftly walked off. She didn't give me a chance to ask who it was as she slipped neatly back in her room and quickly closed the door.

I grew irritated, figuring it was Mathew, who lately, had a knack for "*just showing up!*" To tell the truth, his surprise visits were starting to get on my nerves. But for all it was worth, he

23

gave good face, meaning, he was hella fine and most of the girls couldn't help but flirt with him and envy me.

When I walked into the lobby I looked around but didn't see him. I was about to walk outside when a voice stopped me cold in my tracks. It was my mom.

"What is she doing here?"

I turned and smiled as I walked over to greet her. I casually searched her face wondered what was up with the unannounced visit. Her face gave no clues and my radar was reading improperly that day, so I miss read her, thinking she was tired from work. She told me to follow her to the car and I did, assuming she'd brought the food replenishments I desperately needed. I should have thought something strange about her being parked by the Deans office instead of behind the dorm where she normally parked, but I didn't. Like I said, my radar was definitely off that day. When we got to the car I peeped in for my stuff but didn't see anything. I looked up in time to see her getting in and telling me to do the same.

"Maybe God's answered my prayers and she's come to rescue me from this dreadful place?" I uneasily joked to myself.

Once settled in the car, momma opened her pocket book and pulled out a sheet of paper. I recognized it immediately. It was my grade sheet. Naively I'd thought I'd be able to intercept it, I didn't know they mailed the damn things to your house. Hell I thought they'd give it to me like a report card or something. And

24

I didn't know it was time from grades to be posted in the first place. But I guess I might have known if I'd been going to class.

Momma held the paper in the air as if it were an official decree and began reading aloud my grades in a high pitched voice! With the proclamation of every failing score, I sank deeper and deeper into my seat. When she was finished, she stared at me.

The iciness of her stare pierced me like a knife and I seriously feared what would happen next. Nervously I looked out onto the campus praying for something to come to my rescue. The tension in the air was so thick I thought I'd choke on it. The silence in the car was deafening and seemed to last an eternity.

As we sat silently waiting on the other to speak as a chill filled the car from the cold outside. Birds of all kinds had descended upon the campus for winter and they were busily sweeping in and out of the gigantic old oak trees, creating a fanning noise which momentarily seduced me into a false sense of safety. The sound was hypnotic. But as quickly as I'd been entranced by their movements, I was snatched back to my current abyss. It was momma and she back in full force.

The sound of her voice made the hair on the back of my neck stand at attention! Calmly, she told me she'd also received a call from my Calculus instructor. She'd told her I was failing math and barely came to class.

25

You could have stuck a fork in my ass 'because I was done!
My brain was shot! I didn't know what in the hell to say!

"You're going to lose your scholarship if you keep this up, did you know that?
My mind raced to think of something to justify my behavior but I'd drawn a blank. That always happened when I needed to tell a good lie. Soon my body grew painfully stiff from all the anxiety.

"Do you hear me talking to you Casey?
I nodded my head awkwardly as I stole a quick look in her direction.

"Don't nod your head at me!"

My tongue fell to the back of my throat as I choked back my tears. I knew she was disappointed in me and for my teacher to have the nerve to call her really took the cake! Calmly I tried to speak but could only muster up a weak,

"Yes ma'am"

"What do you have to say for yourself?
Again my mind went blank!
Momma stared at me awaiting my reply but I couldn't say anything, I was busted!

"Well let me tell YOU something! YOU will go to class and YOU will pass them with flying colors and I do mean all of them! Do you hear me!!" she snapped.

"Yes Ma'am." I sniffed as I dared not look anywhere else but the car floor.

"I could understand it if it were any other class than math, but math Casey?" She yelled. "You're excellent in Math!! I want to know what's going on and I want to know now!!"

"Oh God," I thought.

My heart was racing now and my legs were now numb. I thought I would surely pass out at any moment. Still, in a weird way, I was glad she was there, cause now she knew something was wrong. But I still couldn't bring myself to tell her what was bothering me.

Momma continued to rant and rave while I "yes mam'd" in agreement to all her demands. Finally there was silence again. This time it was even more eerie. As the silence persisted I shifted in my seat to glance inconspicuously in her direction. She was looking out the window. Her face was filled with anguish and confusion. My mom, a beautiful caramel colored woman, who always seemed to know what to do and what to say, sat in frustration, agonizing over what could possibly be wrong with her daughter of whom, she had such high hopes.

Now this tall, slender woman sat slumped in her seat with a look of defeat plastered across her face. Today, she looked small and weak. Her fine, brown hair lay sprawled on her neck from the Afro that had long since fallen, from all the head shaking. Though I felt terrible for disappointing her and causing her to worry I still couldn't summon the nerve to speak aloud the words that were going through my head,

"I'm sorry momma...I am so very sorry!"

27

After another mini eternity of silence, she told me to get out of the car and we walked me back to my room. I breathed a sigh of relief as we walked in to find my roommate was still out.

She was a small town girl with city girl dreams. She was then what's now called a hoochie. Only she was a country hoochie. She knew most of the guys on campus and attended all the frat parties. When she dressed it was more like she was going to the club instead of class. I, on the other, hand was conservative and dressed the part. I wasn't dorky but I wasn't wildly cool either. Having her there now would've only add to my humiliation because I got the feeling that she didn't care for me much. And I damn sure didn't want her around to hear what momma had to say.

Inside the room, we continued to talk about my grades and class. I made several weak attempts to explain why I hadn't been going to class but none of my answers justified my actions. As we talked I made up my mind to never give her cause to feel this way again. I was determined to work my butt off to make her proud of me even though I wasn't proud of myself.

After she left I grabbed Hannibal, threw myself on my bed and cried. Again I cried out to God to release me from this heavy burden, to make me normal so I could live a normal life and not be an abomination to my family. Finally, in despair, I drifted off to sleep.

GETTING IT TOGETHER

In the weeks that followed, I worked my butt off to catch up on my classes. When finals came, I passed with flying colors. I was damn proud of myself! And momma was happy too. Now she could finally stop worrying about me and return her attention to other things.

Summer came and went, throwing me into my sophomore year of college. This time I was assigned to a co-ed dormitory. I attended classes faithfully and even made a few friends.

One Friday evening, after my last class, I decided to walk down to the campus park to do some reading. It was a secluded little area with a couple of picnic tables hidden behind the baseball field. I'd discovered it during my freshman year quite by accident. I figured it would be empty since most people were leaving for the weekend to go home, but not that day.

As I approached, I saw a guy sitting at one of the picnic tables. Now, normally, I would have turned around and went back to my dorm, but for some strange reason, that day I didn't. I guess the smell of chicken or something like it drew me near. Anyway the guy was sitting there drinking a beer and smoking something that smelled like fried chicken.

Some time later, he confessed when he saw me coming he wanted to dump the beer and put out his joint but he was too

29

high to move. He claimed it was fate we met like that, him high as hell and me looking like little Orphan Annie.

As I walked past him to go sit at the other table, he called to me. I don't remember exactly what he said but as a result, we struck up a conversation and introduced ourselves. His name was Lionel Gray. He offered me a beer and a pull of his joint. I gladly accepted the beer but was reluctant to pull off the joint with its pungent chicken odor. When I told him it smelled like chicken he laughed.

"I work at the Wing Shack. It's been in my pocket all day" he said awkwardly, a little embarrassed about the odor.

"I see"

We laughed like crazy and that was the beginning of a long and beautiful friendship.

Lionel, a music major, was very outgoing. He was a fulltime student and had a part time job. And if that wasn't enough, he played piano for the school choir and was openly gay. But most importantly, he was the only one of my new friends who had wheels. Having an automobile at Melbourne made a person very popular, very fast, since the campus was located in a remote part of the city and to get anywhere from it you needed a ride because public transit didn't come out that far.

In those days, there was only one store within walking distance, Mabel's, a small mom and pop store with a couple of pinball machines and a ragged pool table. If a person wanted to go anywhere else you had to have a ride. Fortunately for me, I now had a permanent one with Lionel. Soon he and I were inseparable.

And even though Mathew and I still dated and talked on the phone, things were changing. We were growing apart. Our conversations, instead of being filled with the events of our lives, were now filled with arguments. I even stopped running home every weekend to see him, but instead, hung around the yard with Lionel.

It seemed like there was always something to do. Lionel knew everybody and was constantly introducing me to someone new. Most of them were either gay or gay friendly. Initially, I had a problem with it, but after many a late night reality checks by him and his crew, I became more accepting of others.

"Hell, it doesn't mean I'm gay because my friends are," I rationalized.

Soon, I began relishing the time I shared with my compadres in our little part of the world.

I'd known Lionel about two months when he introduced me to the club scene. I'd never been to a club of any sort in Jackson.

So when my boy told me we were going to a hotspot, I was ready, waiting and willing! But what I didn't know was it was the "Bar" a gay club nestled in the middle of the downtown area. You could have bought my ass on credit when I'd jumped clean as a "lean dick dawg" ready to shake my booty and ol boy dropped the bomb on me!

31

"What?! What if somebody sees me? They gonna think I'm gay or some shit?"

"And…"

"And my ass!"

"Blanche (a playful nickname he called me whenever I was working his nerves) stop tripping! If anybody you know see you, you might want to ask them what the hell they doing there! That's if it matters that much to ya!!!"

"You know what I mean! I just don't know about this…" I said shaking my leg nervously, clutching the door handle with one hand and picking imaginary lint off my well fitting 501 Jeans, that just happened make me look fine as hell"

"Ms Thing you tripping for nothing, aint nobody gonna bite you up in there!"

"I didn't say they would. I just don't feel comfortable going"

"Well look, if you going lets go, if not…then oh well cause tonight is beer bust night and I don't want to miss it. Besides, I thought you had gotten over your gay phobia. Hump, but I guess not"

"Man I can't afford for that mess to get back to my family"

"Alright then see ya! Wouldn't want to be ya!"

I stared at Lionel thinking his ass was cold as hell when it came to my feelings. Then I looked out into the blackness of the empty yard. It was Saturday night, I was clean as hell and if I didn't go out all I had to look forward to was going back to that dead ass dorm. I swallowed hard, let go of the door and said,

"Let's go."

And that was the beginning of my clubbing days.

On the other side of the world, Mathew was growing more and more agitated with our relationship. From time to time I contemplated breaking up with him but always decided against it, thinking the relationship would add balance to my life and deter me from going in the homosexual direction. So, I mechanically resigned myself to being his girlfriend and him being, "my man."

When spring break came I reveled in it like a flower bursting through its bud at the first sign of a warm breeze. Even though I'd become more acclimated to college life, I still had my spells where I missed my family and looked forward to spending time with them for a change. My bed at home, lined with stuffed animals, was calling my name. And though I knew it meant seeing more of Matt too, I was so anxious to get there, I caught the first thing smokin', the Dean's secretary, who was from my home town.

When I got home, Darnel and Chelle met me at the door like I was a long lost friend. Later, when mom got home, we all sat around after dinner playing "remember that time..."

"Remember that time you stuck your hand in the orange juice jar to stir it up and you're hand got stuck in the jar? I reminded Chelle "Then you called me instead of momma cause you knew she was gonna whoop your butt" I kidded, rolling over with laughter.

33

Chelle tried to top me by telling one of my embarrassing moments, but it was no use, we were killing ourselves laughing as I described the stupid look she had on her face when I found her standing in front of the refrigerator with her hand stuck inside the jar. We reminisced for hours, just happy to be together.

The next week was filled with hanging out in the mall with Chelle and cruising the streets of my hometown at night with Darnell.

"Have you talked to Matt since you been home" asked Chell one day out of the blue.

"Not really, every time I call he's busy."

"Yeah, I bet!"

"What's that supposed to mean?" I asked

"I'm not going to say nothing"

"Then why did you bring it up"

"I just heard something about him that's all"

"What"

Chelle went on to tell me the town gossip, Matt was supposed to be seeing this older chick. They were even saying he'd gotten her pregnant!

But I only half listened, knowing to take anything traveling through the town's grapevine with a grain of salt. And if he did, then hell, maybe he was justified. After all, it wasn't like I was able to give him what he wanted. So why be selfish!

When Love Aint Enough

Still, I knew my sister only was only looking out for my best interest. So, I listened attentively to what she had to say. And as she expected, I got pissed. But not with Matt, with the silly gossip mongers that had nothing better to do but preoccupy themselves with other people's business. They made me sick. The ominous "they" didn't care who they hurt or talked about, any and everybody was fair game for them.

"Who is '*they*' Chelle?"

"Everybody"

"Well I could care less what '*they*' got to say. I know my own man!"

"I didn't say you didn't"

"I know" I added softly.

Chelle looked away awkwardly into oblivion. Realizing I'd hurt her feelings, I added,

"Besides, I know Matt. And though he's arrogant as hell, but he'd never do anything to intentionally hurt me."

Or least that's what I thought. Still, I couldn't help but wonder where the truth lie in what my sister was telling me.

Friday, Matt called and we did our usual, went to the movies and later parked on a secluded back road on the way back home. As soon as he turned the motor off the arguing began.

"Are you seeing somebody else" he asked genuinely.

"No Matt" I said, tired of his constant accusations.

"Well what's wrong then?"

"There's nothing wrong."

"You can tell me Casey."

"There's nothing tell, why do you keep trying to make something out of nothing. Is there anything you want to tell me?!"

"No, of course not," he said defensively.

"Then why are you so defensive?"

"Maybe because we never spend time together anymore."

"But I'm here now aren't I" I said, moving closer to him and laying my head on his shoulder.

"Ye-ah but …"

"Yeah but what Matt?" I said hoping he would just shut up and hold me so I could secretly test his desire for me.

"I don't know baby, I just miss you. When you go back can I take you?"

"Sure, don't you always?"

"Not really…, most times it's Lionel"

Matt was well aware of the fact that Lionel and I were just friend. That's a subject we'd gone over a thousand times. But I fall short of telling him Lionel was gay because I didn't want to throw suspicion on myself, plus, I rationalized,

"It wasn't his business."

"You know me and Lionel are just friends, so don't trip" I said getting angry and sitting up abruptly"

Matt pulled at me to come back beside him. I ignored him and turned to look out into the quiet night"

"I wasn't saying that! Damn I can't say nothing to you no more without you getting an attitude."

"I don't have any attitude but I am tired of this conversation. Did you bring me here to argue?"

Seeing that I wasn't going to come back over to him, Matt slid over to me and wrapped his arms around me.

"Is it okay if I say I miss you?"

I looked at him. He really was trying. So I tried back. I leaned into him and kissed his full lips softly. Matt responded by softly pushing me down onto the seat to lie on top of me and smother me with his hot, passionate kisses. I could feel his excitement growing on my leg as I etched my tongue inside his mouth and parted my legs slightly to accommodate his long body. Slowly, we moved, rhythmically, kissing and hunching each other, working up a steamy sweat. Him, hoping it would bring about other things and me, hoping I would feel the desires for my man that I was felt for women. But still, there were no butterflies.

That night we did things we'd never done before, but fell short of making love. Instead I pacified him by touching it, holding it and caressing it until he came. For now he was content but I knew he wanted and needed more for me. I grew more despondent at the thought of never being able to please him as he and I both wanted. Later, I snuggled close to him, inhaling the soft smell of his Calvin Kline cologne, as we drove to my house.

37

When we arrived, we sat in the quiet driveway, talking to each other, instead of at each other, for the first time in a long time. Also for the first time in a long time, I didn't want him to leave him and I could tell he felt the same way.

The idea of him being with someone else pained me, but in actuality I knew he had needs, which was evident by the stiff lump in his pants that readily brushed up against my elbow as I leaned on him. Still, if he and I were to be together we had to do it right, wait until marriage. And if we weren't going to do it, I damn sure didn't want to hear about him doing it with anyone else.

Saturday was yard day. After helping Darnell mow the yard, I decided to sit out front to rest up. As I watched the cars go by, enjoying the beautiful spring day, a familiar one came roaring around the corner. It was Lionel! His white Z-24 roared into the driveway like a baby elephant in search of shade.

"What's up - Blanche?" he shrilled as he peeled his 6'5 frame out of the car.

"Nothing dar-l-ing," I drawled giving my best drag queen impersonation.

After exchanging hugs and kisses, we leaned back on his car talking and laughing, oblivious to everything else.

Lionel, from the coast had come up for the weekend to meet a trade-boy or piece of trade as he called it, in Vicksburg, impulsively he'd decided to stop by and see if I was home.

"Child go out wit-me tonight"

38

"Tonight? What's happening tonight?"

"You, if you go," he said, doing a mean shimmy and flashing his trademark grin.

I looked at him conspicuously hoping he wasn't going to be flaming like that during his entire visit. Because you could never tell who the hell was watching you and I didn't need anybody talking crazy.

"I don't know if I can."

"Why not"

"The club don't start jumping 'til midnight and by that time I'm expected to be in the house or returning to the house if you know what I mean!"

"I heard some 'Gurls' from Memphis gonna perform tonight, high class drag queens baby! So you know the crowd is gonna be cute! And you know what that means?!"

"What?" I asked dumbfounded

"Some pussy for you and dick for me!" He sang.

I instantly gave him a look that would make brimstone melt, warning him to hold his voice down!

"Nigga please!" I whispered, looking around to see if anybody heard him. Hell my mom had 20/20 vision and could hear a mouse pissing in a cotton patch when it came to her children. Lionel nodded apologetically then lowered his voice.

"Girl you know how bad you need to get –you-some! I see how your dick be jumping when you there!"

Vivian M Kelly

While I'd learned to ignore his smart ass comments, unfortunately this time he was dead on the money. The more time I spent with him the more receptive I'd become to the idea of being with a woman. In fact I wanted to, badly. And the club didn't make it any better. Hell, the women in there were gorgeous. After a night of clubbing my stomach hurt like crazy from all the butterflies that swirled around inside me. Lionel, the self proclaimed "Mack" of all times was constantly egging me on to talk to them while giving me his so called "Mack pointers." But I relented. Secretly it wasn't that I was ashamed of who I was anymore. In fact, inside the club I'd begun to feel safe. I was free to be me. Hell, like Lionel always said, we all have our reasons for being there. And I wasn't any different. Still, I was very apprehensive about what my family and people would think. My attraction to women had grown wild and I didn't know how much longer I could hide it from the rest of the world or deny it to myself for that matter.

Lionel continued to rant on about the guy he'd met and hoped would be at the bar tonight. I, on the other had, drifted into a sea of what ifs.

"What if I do meet someone, what in the hell am I going to do with her. What would I say, How do I…"

"Blanche! Oh Blanche! Did you hear what I said? "

"What?!" I answered snapping back to reality.

"Girl you need to get some quick," he said smiling his devilish smile.

40

When Love Aint Enough

Finally, after being thoroughly convinced missing tonight would be a terrible mistake, I summoned the nerve to ask my mom. Lionel was like a part of the family now, she liked and respected him. Still, I told her I was going to a house party in Jackson at his sister's house. Lionel assured her I would be fine, explaining we'd be staying in the apartment over his sister's garage.

After some discussion, she said okay but cautioned me to be careful and call when I got to Jackson. I quickly grabbed an outfit and got out of the house before she could change her mind. We jumped into his car and drove off into the sunset for a night of partying.

We arrived at the club around eleven. It was located in business district of the illustrious capitol city. The outside of it looked innocent enough. It was a two-story brownstone of about 6000 square feet. There weren't any signs or anything that gave it away as being a gay bar. To its patrons it was simply called "The Bar." To onlookers it might very well have been a warehouse.

Surrounding the club was a large parking lot about the size of a football field. Its patrons tended to park back there if they wanted to enter the club discreetly or needed a little privacy after meeting someone.

Entering the club was always like entering into another world. The seductive techno music met you at the door creating an excitement for the forbidden. Back then it only cost two dollars to get in. Lionel reached into his tight, "Husband stealing jeans" and pulled out the cash to pay our way in.

For some reason I was always nervous when I first walked in. And tonight was no different. I walked silently behind him, careful not to look at myself in the mirror lined foyer, which led to the open space. The first thing you saw when walking out of the foyer was the gigantic octagon bar sitting in the middle of the floor. This of course was a welcomed sight once you had the nerve to actually pay your money and come inside, you needed a drink. The lights from the disco ball beamed off the wine glasses that twirled magnificently above the bartenders head. Inside the octagon were two topless, male bartenders. Both of which were white which was something I found strange since the patrons of the club were mostly black. But both had beautiful glowing tanned chest, as though sketched by an artist.

The laughter of the patrons and the music was an exhilarating force to be reckoned with. If you were depressed when you got there you'd soon get over it after being there for a couple of minutes.

As we made our entrance, Lionel stopped several times to meet and greet friends and potential lays of the night. This was a Mack Rule, "Always be sociable, nobody really cares for a snob, not even the snob," he'd say. I on the other hand stood at his side like a trusty sidekick, admiring the crowd and taking inventory of the women in attendance.

As I stood waiting on Lionel I grew impatient. He was taking way too long with his meet and greet so I whispered I was going to find us a good table. After a little searching, I found a spot off to the left side of the stage. It was away from the crowd and dark there. The spotlight was sure to hit it when the performers came out, that's probably why it was vacant. Still I grabbed it. Normally I didn't like to be so close to the spotlight but since there was going to be visitors in the show I didn't want to miss a thing. About twenty minutes later Lionel strolled over with a couple of beers. He complimented me on the seats and I flashed a big smile, feeling very proud of myself.

For the next half hour we sat there talking and scoping out the room. A constant stream of people continued to stop by the table to speak, most came to see Lionel. His popularity never ceased to amaze me. He was a good looking guy with honey brown skin and a low fade. He was the clean cut type without being prissy. Rumor had it he was packing. Though he wasn't arrogant he was very sure of himself and people loved him.

When a popular number began to play we jumped up and ran down onto the sunken dance floor. Lionel, always the show off, would not be outdone by my rendition of the robot, flounced around like his pants were on fire. He was high as a kite. The way he was buzzing around you would have thought he would take off flying any minute. I could hardly contain my laughter as he buzzed around drawing a crowd of onlookers.

43

We had been at the club for about two hours when the bunny rabbit song came on. The bunny rabbit song was a signal to clear the dance floor because the show was about to start. As the lights dimmed, the first performer came out. He was wearing a white western outfit with fringes down the sides of his chaps and long sleeves. Beneath his white cowboy hat were long tresses of hair cascading loosely on his shoulders. Adorning his waist were two silver pistols, tucked away in their shiny white holsters. The outfit was "hot talent" as the queens would say.

The performer lip-synced "I want to ride that pony" the crowd roared as she turned around showing her exposed cocoa brown butt! The patrons rushed in droves to the long stage to stuff a dollar in those tight fitting pants. Not eager to fight thru the crowd, I sat back and watched. Lionel on the other hand was in full effect. He was up mingling again with queens hovering all around him. I shook my head in amusement. Then I returned my attention to the show.

As I sat enthralled by the performers, I felt someone walk up to the table. I didn't bother to look up, assuming it was someone else looking for Lionel.

"Is this seat taken," inquired the female voice.
Surprised, I looked up to see a longhaired diva looking back at me.

"No, ah, well, it is, but he's gone for the moment, do you…but you can sit down" I stumbled.

44

When Love Aint Enough

"Ok" she said smiling as she sat down neatly in the seat, crossing her legs almost immediately as her butt hit the seat. The young lady was wearing a pair of shades which was odd since the club was already dark. She was petite and stood no more than five foot three with a hazelnut complexion.

As she began speaking she removed her glasses revealing her eyes. She was flawless! Everyone once in a while a hint of light would reflect off her glimmering dark brown eyes. Her hair, the color of black coal, hung straight down her back. When she smiled a dimple showed in her left cheek. I was immediately attracted to her.

"My name is Nahdia," she said, "What's yours?"
In awe that this beautiful Nubian had chosen me of all the people in the club to speak to, I replied back slowly,

"Casey"

"Casey?! Um... okay", she said.

"Why, what's wrong?" I asked nervously.
She laughed.

"Nothing," she said "I never met a black girl named Casey before. It sounds a bit Angolsaxonish to me don't you think?"
I looked at her amused. I was surprised she didn't say I sounded like a white girl. That was the normal response I received.

"What's up with the name Nahdia that ain't the typical name for a sista?"

"Well, my mom is Indian and my dad is black" she explained.
"Oh really, what tribe"

"Muslim", she replied watching my expressions in amusement.

"For real?!"

"Yeah for real!"

I regretted having to ask the next question because I knew how small minded it sounded but it came out anyway.

"Are you from Mississippi?"

"Yes," she answered in a matter of factly sort of way.

"Oh, okay," I said trying to figure out how to let that conversation go and get down to some serious Macking.

We then turned our attention to the show, which was still going strong. As I watched the performer, my mind raced for something to start up a conversation. And as I did Nahdia beat me to the punch.

"Would you like another beer?"

"Damn!" I thought. *"Why didn't I think of that?"* I looked at my bottle and realized I was sucking on an empty bottle.

"Yeah," I said reaching into my pocket for some money.

"I got it, I'll be right back," she said waiving me off.

This is crazy. I didn't even think to offer her a drink.

Nahdia smiled as she got up and walked toward the crowded bar. I, on the other hand, waited at the table like the little girl I was turning out to be.

The butterflies in my stomach were driving me crazy. Try as I might I couldn't think of nothing to say or worse yet any thing to do. I craved privacy. I quickly devised a plan of attack to get her to walk outside with me.

"Then we would go to the car and... the car!" I thought alarmed.

"Man I hope Lionel ain't in it. This is one time I really need it," I thought. Anxiously I rose up in my seat and looked around the club to find him. I must have been looking pretty hard because I didn't hear or see Nahdia when she returned with the drinks.

"Here," she said handing me a beer and sitting back down.

"Damn," I thought, startled, as I lowered myself back into my seat.

"Thanks," I said as I raised my beer to my lips to take a much needed drink.

As the music began for the final performer, Nahdia jumped to her feet and reached into her pockets for money to tip the singer. Then I saw my opportunity to be a Mack and quickly gave her a five-dollar bill. She smiled and sat back down as we waited for the performer to come on stage.

The lights dimmed and a single spotlight, the size of a quarter, beamed in the middle of the black curtain. The crowd roared as Miss Ava Bouvier, the reigning Ms Gay Jackson, poised angelically, was revealed behind the parting curtains. She stood motionless singing the first chorus of "Come Share My Love" by Mikki Howard. As the music played on she sauntered across the stage reminding me of Bugs Bunny when he dressed in drag to fool the angry farmer!

47

Her long slender body was dressed in a formal beaded white pearl gown that flowed to the floor and white gloves that came just above her elbow. Her make up was impeccable. Her lips were painted with a hot red lipstick that glowed like rain drops on her fair colored skin. Her hair was molded high on top of her head in a spiraling cone adorned with a brilliantly sparkling Tiara, accentuating her mystically slanted Asian eyes.

The song was a club favorite, a true anthem of mythical proportions. As Ava mouthed the lyrics, people rushed the stage to tip her.

I glanced over at Nahdia and extended my hand to her. She took it and the two of us walked, hand in hand, to the base of the stage. As if on cue, Ms. Bouvier looked down and began singing to us. I blushed at the attention and tried to steady my nerves. Nahdia smiled and handed her the five then walked away dragging me gently behind her.

Instead of going back to the table she led me out of the bar. And happily I followed. As we walked out into the warm spring air neither of us said anything. I allowed her to lead me to a blue Toyota Corolla that was parked in the far back corner of the parking lot. She introduced it as being hers.

I leaned back on the car as she stood in front of me. I rubbed her arms mechanically as I searched her eyes for what was to be my next move. I desperately wanted to taste her lips, to feel her softness on mine but instead I took her hand and traced the inner markings in her palm. She watched curiously as I did so.

Gently I lifted her hand to my lips and softly kissed the back of it. She sighed then leaned forward pressing her lips on mine.

When our lips touched it was like a soft summer rain. Her breath was hot as she gently pushed her tongue into my mouth and I eagerly nibbled at her lips sucking her tongue deeper. We moaned in unison, as I thought I'd faint from the sheer pleasure of her soft touch. She sank into my arms, pressing her small frame into mine as I wrapped my arms around her waist pulling her so close we looked like one person.

My butterflies were working over time now. I felt lightheaded as we searched within each other mouths, unleashing our desire. We stood kissing and softly grinding into each other for what seemed like an eternity. I was in heaven. Slowly, I pulled back and looked deep into her eyes. In the moonlight she was even more beautiful than before.
I thought naively to myself,

"Does she really deserve to get Macked?"
I lifted her face and gave her another short sensual kiss. We looked at each other and I knew the answer to my question. I knew that what ever was going on with us was much more than making out behind the bar.

It was late and neither of us wanted to go back in. Instead we stood outside talking, hugging and laughing having a truly fabulous time in each other's company as if we'd known each other for years.

REVELATIONS

After that night Nahdia and I became an item. Nahdia attended school at a nearby private Christian college in Jackson. I'd originally received a scholarship there myself, but in the end, turned it down in favor of Melbourne. It had been three months since we first met and we still hadn't gone all the way. I guess you can say we both were hesitant.

I was fast realizing my relationship with Mathew was at an end and knew it was only right to tell him so. But, as I expected, he refused to accept the break up over the phone and insisted on coming to the campus. I agreed to it rather than having him pop up unexpectedly and catching me off guard or worse yet with Nahdia. But more importantly, even though I didn't want to be with him romantically I did respect him and thought we could salvage our friendship.

So, I agreed to meet him in the dorm lobby after my last class. I anxiously paced the hardwood floor, avoiding conversations with everyone, focusing on what I'd say to him.

Though Matt was persistent, I didn't anticipate any real drama. I knew our break up would be a blow to his massive ego and he'd be hurt. Still I was determined to convince him this was the best thing for both of us.

Around three pm Matt finally arrived. By then I had relaxed enough to sit down near the big picture window and stare absently in the direction of the television. I heard him before I saw him, whistling as he came into the lobby. He strolled up to me wearing his typically tight fitting 501 button fly jeans, a blue and white western shirt and a pair of rattlesnake cowboy boots I'd bought him last Christmas.

I stood up, preparing to walk outside with him. He smiled his crooked grin and we hugged awkwardly. The grin on his face told me he was more than confident he could sway me to his way of thinking. His arrogance showed as he opened the large double doors that led to the yard. His expression made me slightly nervous, but I dismissed the feeling knowing this was one time he would not get his way.

The yard was empty except for a few students who were busy packing their cars for the weekend. I'd decided to stay at school to spend time with Nahdia. And I was anxious to get this over with so I could see her.

As we strolled up the walkway, I pointed to a bench where we could sit and talk. It was right off the street in full view of everyone. I plopped down and sat quietly watching the cars go by, wondering how to start.

Matt saved me by going first.

"Damn it's quiet today." he said awkwardly.

51

"Everyone's gone or leaving for the weekend." I said somberly.

Again we sat in silence. This time I spoke.

"Matt, I know you came up here to try to talk me out of it but I want you to know I've given this a lot of thought.

Matt's demeanor quickly became defensive.

"But why?! That's what's puzzling me."

"It's just not working for me," I said apologetically.
He turned to face me with a look of determination on his face and took my hand in his.

"Not working for you. Baby you won't let it work! How many times have I asked you to let me come up here for the weekend, huh, how many? He pleaded.

"Your coming up here on the weekend isn't going to make it work. I just don't want to be involved right now."

"But why? Have you met someone else or what?" he asked somberly.

Up until this point I hadn't planned on lying. I was trying to be as honest as possible but it looked like I might have to lie. I looked away and gently pulled my hand from his. His constant rubbing of it was becoming annoying. In fact his whole presence was beginning to annoy me for some reason. Suddenly he stood up and started pacing in the small area of dirt before me. I watched him for a minute then, in an effort not to play into his dramatics, looked away.

"For months I've been asking you if there was someone else and you been saying no. I even asked if you wanted to break up and again you said no! Now all of a sudden you tell me you aint feeling it! Why aint you feeling it?!" he demanded

I looked up at him and my face grew hot at his presumption of my guilt. He had no idea I knew he was cheating on me. But he felt his shit didn't stink. I took a deep breath and released it quietly.

"Are you accusing me of cheating on you?" I asked annoyed with his self righteous attitude.

He stared at me bucking his eyes in his usual cocky way. So I continued,

"Cause we both know who is doing all the cheating, ain't that right Matt? I mean, after all, don't you have at least two other women in Edwards that call you their man? And on top of that, isn't one of 'em pregnant!"

His mouth dropped as if he'd been slapped! I could have bought his ass with a biscuit! My revelation of his sneaking around hit him hard. Sensing his defenses falling, my courage grew.

"So while you're sitting here acting like I've done something to you, you can squash that shit because we both know you ain't right in the first place!"

He stood looking at me incredulously. He had no idea that I knew about his little dirty deeds nor had I ever spoken to him like that before.

Visibly shaken, he sat down and tried to explain.

"Matt," I interrupted calmly, "I don't want to hear it. I only agreed to your coming up here in hopes that we could possibly save our friendship. But guess what, I don't have to have it. As a matter of fact I don't even want it!"

"But babe, let me talk to you…"

"There's nothing to talk about."

I stood up and nervously started to walk away. He called after me but I didn't bother to turn around. By now I was shaking and my objective was to get away before I started crying. As he continued to call my name I walked faster. Faintly, I heard the pounding of feet behind me and then he grabbed my arm stopping me cold in my tracks. I swung around violently pulling my arm from his grasp and stared at him. I hoped he would realize just how mad I was and back off.

"Baby you said what you wanted to say now please give me a chance to say something"

I looked around self consciously to see if anyone was watching. Except for the yardman, we were alone. I folded my arms waiting to hear what he had to say.

"Can we go to your room for a minute?" he asked

"For what? You can say what you have to say here!"

"I just want to talk to you privately Casey"

"I don't think that's a good idea"

"Please, I promise I'll leave when you ask me too. I need to sit and talk to you for a minute."

When Love Aint Enough

I studied his face hoping it would reveal what I should do. The look on his face showed his pain. I knew he was hurting but I didn't want to pretend anymore either. I figured it wouldn't hurt to let him come up, say his piece then send him on his way. Since it was a coed dorm there wouldn't be a problem with him coming in. As he continued to plead his case, I gave in.

My roommate had long since left for the weekend so I figured we would have the room to ourselves and he and I could get this over with. I closed the door and sat down at my desk by the window. Matt sat on the bed beside me.

"First of all", he began "I don't have two other women, its only one."

I glared at him. *Did he really think having one instead of two made a difference to m*e? I wondered. I breathed a deep sigh and looked out the window.

"Yeah I cheated but you got to understand..."

"What should I understand? That you lied and cheated on me!

Matt was quite and sat staring at me.

"Or," I continued, "that a man has needs or some crazy crap like that? Which one is it Matt?"

Matt shook his head defensively and bent forward to touch me. I moved out of his reach by turning slightly in my chair.

"See that's what I'm talking about! You won't even let me touch you!"

55

"No Matt I wont let you fuck me, that's the real problem. I wouldn't and she would!"

"There you go again," he said exasperated. Then standing up, as he began to pace in front of me.

"What do you want to hear Casey that I slept with her? Okay, I did! But you weren't there for me or don't you remember that? Every time I tried to spend time with you where were you? Shit you pushed ME away!"

"Okay," I thought. *"This aint- gonna- work! Now he's trying to blame me for his fuck ups!* I crossed my legs and tried to give off the appearance of being calmer than I felt. I looked at him and responded,

"Is that supposed to excuse it Matt?"

"No, but I'm being honest."

"Well I appreciate your honesty, but it really doesn't make a difference now. I don't want this anymore!"

"See you ain't trying to hear shit I'm saying to you!"

"What is it I am supposed to hear to make me change my mind, that there was only one girl not two and that you did it because I wouldn't have sex with you? You're tripping!"

"Casey, you've changed. Your whole attitude has changed!"

"No, that's not it. It's that I 'm no longer willing to do something I don't want to do just because someone else wants me to do it! And since we're not getting anywhere with this, I need to go to the library before it closes."

Matt stopped pacing and stood in front of me.

"Why are you being a bitch about all this?"

"A bitch?!" I repeated shocked that he would call me that knowing how I felt about the word!

"Yeah a bitch!!!"

"Matt, this is getting ugly, I want you to leave."

I stood up and walked toward the door. Matt followed and grabbed me by my waist. We struggled as I yelled at him to let me go. Ignoring my screaming, he dragged me over to the bed and threw me down. I flung my arms wildly trying to get up but each time he'd push me down again. As he stood over me, he leaned forward, placing his face in front of mine, so close I thought he'd kiss me but instead he snarled!

Before I could assimilate my thoughts he jumped on top of me. Again we struggled. I clawed and beat on his back with my fist. But it didn't bother him. I could feel him becoming aroused as he pulled at my blouse, ripping it open and exposing my breast.

"I'm gonna show you're ass something! You ain't gonna lead me on and drop me like that!"

My heart was racing a mile a minute as perspiration collected on my forehead. I'd never known him to be violent! I knew it was only a matter of time before he'd have my pants off. My mind raced frantically.

I watched terrified as he reached down to unbutton my pants, pinning me to the bed with his weight while squeezing my wrists together over my head with the other hand. I struggled violently beneath him, bucking and biting at him until I thought I'd pass out from exhaustion.

The idea of Matt raping suddenly hit me full force! I'd read before that men didn't rape for sexual pleasure but more so to dominate the victim. My mind went blank trying to think of something to do or say to make him stop. I was exhausted mentally and physically from our struggle. And I wanted to give up and say

"Fuck it! Take it if it will make you happy!"

When he tried to force his mouth on mine I turned my head from side to side to avoid him. Tears rolled down my face onto the thick comforter as he continued to grope between my legs and in my pants. The button on my khakis was not cooperating with him as he pulled and jerked at it. Finally, I yelled out,

"Matt I love you! Why are you doing this to me?" lying, hoping it would snap him back to reality. But he was like an animal out for the kill. Nothing was registering with him. My pants were open now. I repeatedly called his name begging him to stop. His breathing grew heavier as rubbed up and down between my legs then roughly pushed my panties to the side and squeezed my vagina.

With all the strength I could muster I started bucking again as I felt his fingers enter so deep into my body that my stomach begin cramp. I winced from the pain and started to cry. Slowly he pulled his fingers out of me and quickly unbuttoned his pants.

I could feel myself drifting off. Everything around me grew still as all I could hear was the moans he made as he felt on his self. Silently I cried out to God as I felt the warmth of his erect penis on my leg.

Then all of a sudden, I stopped resisting. I was paralyzed emotionally and physically. I allowed my head to fall to the side and looked out into space. I was resigned to let him do what he wanted to do. Maybe I did owe him. Maybe I had been a bitch to him and deserved whatever he decided to dish out. Yeah, he could have it but he still couldn't have me!

So when he pressed his lips to mine to kiss me, I lay motionless and allowed it. He raised his body up a bit and started running his hands down between my legs as he continued to press me down on the bed. Our bodies, both half naked, were touching now. Unsuccessfully he tried to push his fully erect penis inside me. I continued to stare out in space but the pain from his intrusion burned at my soul like hot coals and I couldn't help but scream out. Quickly he put his hand up to my mouth and ordered me to stop. I wanted to but I couldn't, it hurt too badly!

After several minutes of him trying to force himself inside me, he suddenly stopped and sat beside me on the bed. I took the opportunity to jump up too, pulling at the comforter to cover me.

"Casey I'm so-o-o sorry baby. I never meant for this to happen," he mumbled and shyly slipped his arms around me and the comforter. "I don't know what came over me."

I sat silently replaying the episode in my head. I wanted to run for the door but I was afraid it would stir him up again. I sat on the bed clutching the comforter with my pants down around my ankles. I prayed silently as he continued to talk.

"Baby did I hurt you?" he asked as tears rolled down his face.

I quietly looked away and nodded my head, still too afraid to speak.

Matt excused his behavior by saying he only wanted to make love to me. He felt that if we could only share that intimacy it might make me realize we were meant to be together. I sat damn near in shock of what he had to say. I wanted to ripped off his clothes, throw him around and then invade his body with my fingers to see how close that would make him feel to me.

Instead, I sat silently on the edge of the bed, clutching the comforter as though it would shield me from any further attacks. I was certain if I said anything he would be all over me again. In fact, I was convinced that at any given moment he would try to finish what he started.

Matt turned to look at me. I looked down at the floor and stared at the button that had been ripped from my pants. As he talked I studied the button and the thread still attached to it. Finally I heard him say,

"I know you don't believe me and this is a fucked up way to show it, but I do love you Casey!"

He stood up and began fumbling around with the zipper on his jeans and straightened his clothes. I stole a glance at him as he turned his back to me and instructed me to put my clothes on.

I got up cautiously from the bed and walked over to my closet by the door. The desire to run out of the room was strong but I knew I wouldn't get far, so continued to pray silently and ask God for strength.

"I'm fixin' to go, okay?" He said.

"Okay" I mumbled.

He walked past me but stopped at the door and turned around.

"I know about your little friend in the blue car."

"Blue Car, what blue car" I thought.

Then it hit me! *He was talking about Nahdia! She has a blue car"* I thought.

Now it was my turn to be shocked shitless!

"How does he know about her?" I wondered, hoping he wasn't about to attack me again.

Matt turned around and caught me looking at him.

"Yeah, that's right. I heard you were funny or some shit! I didn't want to believe it at first, but now I do."

I watched him silently, still clutching the comforter. As he spoke, his voice cracked revealing his pain,

"My thing is how do you know you're gay if you've never been with a man before?"

61

I was floored! Matt was outing me and I didn't know what to say nor did I have the courage to say it. His revelation was like pouring salt on a freshly inflicted wound. I quickly slipped on pair shorts and walked away from the closet, pulling a sweatshirt over my head. I sat down at my desk and reflected on his question.

"How do I know? Hell, how do you know! Where did you get this from?" I wondered.

I saw Matt studying me intently from across the room. I let out a deep sigh and dropped my shoulders as if a humongous bundle had just been lifted! I was exhausted. I sat down on my bed and glanced out the window. I didn't want to lie anymore, not to him or anyone. Deep down I knew he would never understand the feelings I had for Nahdia but I wanted this thing with him to be done. So, if he wanted a fight he was going to have to bring it on!

My body was already sore from our struggle earlier and I was tired as hell. I grew pissed that he could treat me this way just because I wanted out.

"Its not about sex Matt," I said as I kicked at the button lying on floor.

"Well what- is- it- about then?"

I took another deep breath and looked into his eyes,

"I really don't know myself"

When Love Aint Enough

Slowly he walked over to me and knelt down. He was calmer now and I knew it. He sat down on the floor in front of me like he used to do when we were on better terms. I wanted to reach out to him but I couldn't. I was still upset at what he had done. But our bond of over five years wouldn't allow me to hate him. I wanted him to know I cared but I didn't want to give him false hope. My body grew tense with his touch.

He gently laid his head in my lap. It always used to work on me when we'd argue and today was no different. Cautiously I rubbed my hand across his head tracing the line of his fresh haircut.

Matt was a beautiful man. And I knew he loved me even if he was a whore. I also knew he was right when he said that I had pushed him away. I had. Selfishly I had thought of no one other than myself. I knew no matter what, Matt would never understand why I was ending our relationship. I tried putting myself in his shoes and knew I would've felt the same way. But how could I make him understand that the person he knew was not actually the person I was or wanted to be? What part of his male ego could understand the love I'd found in Nahdia. It was something he as a man, could never give me no matter how hard he tried or how much I wished he could.

Being gay was no longer the choice I thought I'd been forced to make. My sexuality was a part of me and me of it. Though it was not the biggest part or the most important, it was something that I could no longer deny no matter how much I may have

63

wanted to in the past. Unknowingly I had come full circle. I was no longer afraid of living but afraid that I wouldn't be given the chance to live.

No longer was I willing to allow society or anyone else to tell me who I should love. Since I was a teen, society's ignorance of who I was had driven me into a hollow hole of self-hate and loathing.

As I looked down at him desperately trying to hold on, I realized he and I were a lot alike. We were both persistent for the things we wanted. And now, I desperately wanted to hold on to the life I'd realized was mine to live. And I wanted to love and be loved by the person of my choosing. But most of all I wanted normalcy. People didn't have to love it or even like, just allow it.

Matt reached up and placed his hand on top of mine.

"It makes no sense Casey?"

"I know…"

"Then why?" he asked

I thought for a moment,

"Because it feels right," I answered confidently.

Matt pulled his hand away and raised his head to look at me.

"So you admit it. You're a lesbian?!"

"Yeah, I guess I am. But it doesn't change who I am. I'm still the same person."

"But you have changed, can't you see it?" He insisted.

"No Matt I haven't. If you're talking about me sticking up for myself, then yeah, I've changed. But aside from that I am still the same person."

"But Casey it's a sin."

I looked away.

"How many times had I heard that my loving another woman was a sin?" I thought, *"Too many to count."* If it was a sin, it was no greater sin than any other sin.

"This is my life. I've got to do what will make me happy. I am an adult. Anything I do will be with another consenting adult! It will be our choice, not yours or anyone else's. But to hear you of all people sit here and tell me that my life is a sin is an insult. Did I tell you your child is a sin? No! Cause it's not right for me to judge you or anyone else. So please what ever you do don't try to judge me!"

Matt raised his head from my lap and stared at me as if he didn't know me. We had reached a stalemate. I wanted to be annoyed with him, push him off me and walk away. Because I was tired and didn't feel any justification of my life was needed. Lord knows I would probably have to try to justify it to my family. So instead, I exhaled. And with the all the bad I blew out I tried to suck in some good. Here was my chance to face it so I did,

"Matt you are a great guy and someday you are going to make someone a great husband. I'm just not that person."

"But I thought you loved me. You told me so hundreds of times!"

"I do but I have to love myself more. And to be with you would be to deny who I am and I just can't do it anymore." I sobbed

"Oh, so what, you gonna be out telling everybody you're gay now?"

"No, but I am going to live. I have that right just like anybody else in this world."

Matt lowered his head. We sat in silence both thinking about what the other one had said.

After some time, he left. I decided not to see Nahdia that night. I was tired as hell from fighting with Matt and for some inexplicable reason I felt guilty.

Nahdia was understanding and didn't question me. We decided to meet the next day.

I had made an important choice today. I had chosen myself. I wondered if it was truly the right one.

Nahdia had a friend from school named Deb. She was a junior and had been for the past two years. They'd met when she tried to get with Nahdia but upon realizing she wasn't getting anywhere, settled for her friendship. Deb was cool but she drank a lot and she tended to take pride in living off people, her lovers, to be exact. In fact she bragged on how she could meet a woman, screw her brains out then take up residency in the girl's house. Even in those days, with so few people to really look up to in the life, I knew she wasn't anyone I wanted to immulate.

Deb was a shell of a person. Aside from getting a fifth of some cheap liquor or maybe having her girlfriend buy her the latest Nike sneakers, she didn't have any goals. Her priority in life was to get through it as effortlessly as possible and to party her ass off every step of the way.

Saturday, Deb and her lover Tina, invited Nahdia and me to a barbecue. We arrived with a bottle of rum to make daiquiris, which was increasingly becoming a favorite past time of ours. Everybody appeared to be pretty laid back and the place had a nice mixture of couples and singles. I grabbed a spot at the spades table, thanks to Deb who needed a partner, and tried hard to blend in while Nahdy helped make daiquiris. Every once in a while she'd check to see if I was enjoying myself by coming over or blowing me a kiss from across the room. Deb noticed it and tried to jank me about it. But I didn't care. That was my baby and I loved the attention she gave me. When she'd finished with the drinks she came over and sat by me as Deb and I continued on our winning streak. Nahdy didn't play cards, so it was all greek to her. So I took it upon myself to teach her, as I played. Things were going good until a knock came at the door.

Tina answered it. It was a guy I had seen before at the club. I didn't know his name but I knew he hung with all the "In" people. I called them "In" because they were constantly in somebody's jail for writing bad checks or shoplifting. Tina invited him inside but he declined.

"Miss Thang, I got this crazy woman in the car tripping! And to keep down confusion, I decided to come on in here and ask if Deb could come outside to speak to her for a minute."
By this time people started to notice Tina still standing in the doorway talking with the guy so their attention shifted from the once rowdy card game to the conversation in the doorway.

Tina put her hands on her hips and turned around and called Deb. Deb put her cards down and went over to see what was going on. Tina repeated to Deb what ol boy had told her while Deb stared at the guy in disbelief. After a brief discussion, Deb and Tina followed the guy outside. About five minutes later, we heard yelling and cursing coming from the driveway.
Everybody stopped what they were doing and ran to the door to see what all the commotion was about.

Outside in front of Tina's duplex, a red Toyota MR2 was parked across the yard and the guy from the door was seated inside with both doors open. Lying on the ground in front of it was Tina, and a girl named Kim, one of Deb's ex girlfriends. Deb was pulling at Tina who sat straddled on top of Kim. Tina and Kim where pulling each other by the hair, both refusing to let go of the other as they kicked and screamed profanities.

Tina's blouse had been ripped in the front, exposing her red bra that was barely able hold her large golden breast. On the

68

other hand Kim wasn't that lucky. She'd been wearing halter top, was now bare-chested, with both chocolate breasts exposed and the halter top was lying ripped in pieces on the ground beside her. Deb was bleeding badly from a cut over her right eye after being slapped by Kim with a Chivas Regal bottle, which now lay broken in the driveway.

"Hold on now! Ya'll stop, ya'll stop it!" the guy yelled as he frantically searched through the car.

The neighbors were coming out of their house like ants to a picnic, shaking their heads in disapproval, to see what all the commotion was about.

"Lawd ham mercy! What in the world is going on over dare? exclaimed one of the ladies.

A male onlooker replied,

"It's dem bull-daggers acting a damn fool again!!"

Meanwhile, some girls from the party ran over to Deb and Tina to break up the fight. I elected to stay put and told Nahdia to do the same. Fearful the fight would get out of hand, I held on to Nahdia by the apartment door, amazed at what was transpiring before us. After quite a bit of struggling on the parts of all involved, it ended.

"You nothing ass bitch! You need to give me back my money!" screamed Kim towards Deb.

"Bitch get gone!" Deb yelled bucking as if she wanted to jump Kim.

Vivian M Kelly

"I wish you would," yelled Kim at Deb's advancement toward
her "I'd beat your bitch ass! You and yo dried up ass hoe!"
Another scuffle broke out when Tina broke away from the two
girls holding her and ran over to a surprised Kim, who was still
being held and clocked her in the head with her fist!
Kim stumbled backwards and let out a barrage of profanity that
would have made a sailor blush.

The guy in the car finally jumped out, waving a rag and
offered it to Deb, to wipe away the blood gushing from her
wound. She waived it away angrily and ordered him to get Kim
out of her yard.

"Bitch this aint you're damn house! Your broke ass don't
have a pot to piss in or a window to throw it out of!!!"
This brought about another cursing war between Deb and Kim
as party guest helped to usher Kim into the passenger seat of the
car. Kim, finally realizing her chest was naked, folded her arms
across her breasts to shield them from view as she continued to
curse Deb and Tina unmercifully.

As soon as Kim was safely in the car, the guy jumped in on
the driver's side and made his get away, driving like a bat out of
hell across the grass and back into the road. A badly bruised
Tina let out a short scream, threw up her hands and turned to
walk inside. As she walked past, Deb made a vain attempt to
put her hands around her waist to comfort her. Tina pushed
Deb's arm away and stormed into the house.   Deb followed
with her head down, shrugging her shoulders in disbelief.

70

Once back in the house Nahdia and I decided it was a good time to leave. We said our good-byes and quickly left. As we walked out to the car the neighbors were still outside discussing the fight. When one of the guys saw us he yelled out,

"See I told you ain't nothing but a bunch of dykes up in there"

Nahdia pulled at my arm as we continued on to the car. When I opened the door for Nahdia another one yelled out,

"Yeah a bunch of bulldaggers! He said in disgust.

Nahdia stood at the passenger doorway waiting for me to go around and get in. Somewhat apprehensive I walked to my side as yet another person yelled to us,

"What you need is good hard dick!"

I stopped and glared over in the direction from where the comment came to find a scrubby looking guy, grabbing his crotch in and exaggeratedly grotesque manner and grinning wildly. I let go of the car door and walked toward him. Nahdia raced around the car and grabbed me by my tee shirt.

"Baby no!!" She whispered. "He ain't worth it! Come on let's go."

I struggled toward him, with her pulling my shirt and holding my arm. I could feel my face growing hotter and as my body shook with anger. I continued to stare at him for what seemed like forever.

"Come on bitch you want to be a man! You think you can whoop my ass, come on!!"

71

Nahdia jumped in front of me and looked into my eyes, still pleading with me,

"Baby no!! Forget that fool, let's go"

I broke my stare with him and looked at her. Seeing the concern in her eyes, I slowly unclenched my fist. I loved Nahdia and I wasn't going to let anybody talk to either of us like that.

"You heard what that weak bitch said!" I yelled deliberately so he could hear me and know that I was by no means afraid of him.

"Yes baby and it doesn't matter. The only thing that matters is you, now come on lets go."

Still staring wildly into each other's eyes I saw the tears welling up. Reluctantly, I turned around and walked back to the car. She and I got in and drove off.

As I drove through the back streets and into the crowded Saturday traffic, neither of us said a word. The radio played and both of us appeared to be lost in our own worlds. After driving for miles we both began sputtering out our thoughts at the same time. Patiently, I stopped and waited for her to continue her sentence.

"I'm sorry," she began, "I apologize for putting you in that type of situation," she said, pressing her head up against the passenger window. "I knew Deb was trifling but I've never seen it lead up to anything like that."

"It's not your fault. She's the wanna be 'Playa'," I remarked sarcastically.

"The only person Deb is playing is herself. She's too-damn-old for all that childish drama!"

I nodded in agreement.

"Yep, hell, the so-called *"straight world"* already think we're sick-o's without morals or any kind of respect for ourselves. And there they go fighting like animals for the entire world to see. And for what, Deb?! What the hell could she be doing other than screwing the shit out of 'em. She can't do nothing else for 'em!" I said, still agitated.

"I know baby, it's really sad,"

"Yeah, it's fucking sad! I get so fucking tired of all this bullshit. And for that punk bitch that hollered about a hard dick, the only hard dick he's probably seen was the one going up his bitch ass! He is probably one of the biggest closet freaks you could ever meet. If he wasn't he wouldn't be so damn concerned about what other people do!"

I was fed up with it and everything else. Just yesterday I had admitted to my boyfriend of over five years that I was gay, now this shit! Nahdia didn't understand my mood. Still she was patient with me.

"He was ignorant, simple as that."

"People act like being gay is a choice. I damn sure didn't choose it!" I ranted.

73

Nahdia sat quietly listening. This was a conversation she and I had had many times.

"My thing is I try so hard to not let what others think get me down but in spite of it all,
I still find myself trying to prove to the world that I'm normal and not some kind of freak"

"I know baby."

"My sexuality is not the biggest part of me Nahdy and I don't feel I should have to use it to define who I am because that's not all I'm about. It's only a small aspect. Just like these so-called straight people. But then again in my opinion they make their sexuality the biggest part of them and they assume that we do too! When I meet a person I shouldn't have to tell them what I do in the privacy of my bedroom. Hell, I don't ask them what the fuck they do in theirs!!"

Nahdia reached over and rubbed my hand. By this time she realized that it was more than just the fiasco at Deb's place that was bothering me. She stared at me and asked if I was okay. I looked at her then kissed her hand.

"Deb scares me," I confessed. "When I see the life she's chosen, I don't want any part of it. Do you think that's judgmental of me to be embarrassed of her?"

"Deb should be embarrassed of herself. She's the one who uses people for a place to stay and money to live on. We all make choices baby, whether straight, gay, or crooked. It's up

the individual to make the right one. No, I don't think there is
anything wrong with the way you feel," she said

"I just wonder sometimes when they speak of gay pride
where's mine," I said reluctantly.

"Baby what we witnessed has nothing to do with gay it was
ignorance. It wasn't a gay or straight ignorance it was just
ignorance. Gay people aren't the only ones who fuss and fight.
People are people and they shouldn't be judged as a group."

I glanced at her

"Who are we to judge at all, that's God's job!"

"You're right."

She smiled and I smiled back. I was truly blessed to have
Nahdia in my life.

"Hey," I said.

"Have I told you that you're beautiful?"

She blushed.

"You are. Inside and out! Except for that barbecue sauce on
your chin," I kidded causing her to pull at the rearview to take a
look.

"I'm joking, but on the real, promise me we will always be
friends, no matter what happens.

Nahdia squeezed my hand, "I promise babe, but for the record, I
aint going no-where! You gonna have to leave-me!!"

"Well, I already knoooow that!" I joked. "After all you did
chase me down!"

75

"Girl I was tipsy, A-N-Y WAY! You loved every minute of it!" she teased back slapping me on the shoulder.

"Well to be honest I was more or less gonna "Mack" you but you were looking so innocent I decided to have mercy on you"

"Nawwww what happened was you got Macked and never knew it!!"

I shot her a look and we both laughed.

After driving around aimlessly we went back to the dorm. There we made love for the first time. It was an awakening.

I pulled her close to me hungry to feel her lips on mine. Her mouth was warm and her lips seemed to melt on mine as we kissed. We moved methodically, trembling slightly as we stood face to face undressing each other. I marveled at her beautiful curvaceous body. Her mini skirt hadn't done her justice. Timidly I touched her soft body exploring her tenderly.

Many times I had day dreamed of how it would all go down but never in my wildest dreams did I ever imagine I would feel as connected to a person as I did to her that day. As we lay with each other I could feel the beat of her heart beat out of step with mine. Our movements were mechanical and awkward at first but as the seconds turned into minutes and the minutes into hours we soon progressed to a level of sensuality neither of us ever knew existed. Soon our hearts beat together rhythmically as one.

When Love Aint Enough

If I had any doubts before of whether I truly loved this woman they were all dismissed that wonderful day as we made sweet passionate love. Yes, I loved her and now I was finally making love to her.

Over the summer she and I grew even closer, Lionel graduated from Melbourne and accepted a position teaching music at an area high school. Although we still hung out, Nahdia had most of my attention. Being the good friend that he was, he understood.

Nahdia and I dated for three beautifully, glorious years. Though we had our ups and downs like most couples, we seldom let the sun go down without settling it. She loved me unconditionally as did I her.

Two months before graduation she was accepted to Stanford University for grad school. After many late night debates we both agreed it was a chance in a lifetime for her and one she shouldn't pass up. Me, I still didn't know where or if I was going to go to Law School. I talked of taking a break from school. Though we would still date, her moving across country was a lot to deal with.

It was then that I decided to step out of the closet and introduce my mother to who I was. It was imperative if I were to be true to myself and my relationship with Nahdia.

It was a hot summer day and Nahdia was leaving in a month. My mom was outside hanging freshly washed clothes. At the time we had a washer but no dryer. My mom put a clothes line in the back yard to hang the laundry out to dry. While momma busily hung clothes I impetuously ran out to help her. I picked up the basket and passed her a piece of clothing then a couple of clothespins. As we worked our way down the line, I told her Nahdia would be leaving for school soon.

Not knowing what to say or how to begin, I nervously told her there was a rumor going around town that I was gay and wanted to know if she'd heard it. She stole a glance at me and held her hand out for another piece of laundry. I passed her a hand towel and waited for her response.

"Yeah I've heard it," she said and held her hand out for another pin. My heart raced as I reached into the bag to pull one out.

"Is it true?" she asked, stopping to look at me.

"Yes ma'am" I said

"I see," she said softly as she continued to hang the laundry items I was passing her from the almost empty basket. Though I had just dropped a bombshell I'd pledged to take to my grave, I felt remarkably calm. It was if my soul had dared to breathe for fear of dying and I had survived.

I went on to tell my mom how much I loved Nahdia and that she and I would someday have a family together. My mom was quiet. I couldn't quite pin point what she was thinking and stopped short of asking. I wanted to hug her and reassure her that I was normal and that this in no way changed me as a person. But despite the fact I hadn't been shot on the spot for such a revelation, I knew it might take time to get used to. Hell, it had taken me damn near half my life to accept it. Surely I could allow her the time she needed.

Turns out momma was shocked but never questioned me. Instead, as we talked about it years later, she questioned herself. She wondered if she'd done something wrong or if anyone she allowed to take care of me had done something to me.

In the end she realized my life was not a choice I'd made but one made by my creator. She became my strongest supporter. I was finally free. I attributed a lot of my strength that day to Nahdia because had it not been for her love and encouragement, I would have never accepted myself, as I needed to do in order to be accepted by others.

I learned and shared so much with Nahdia. In a sense we grew up together. I assured her a small thing like distance would never destroy the love I had for her. Often I would tell her whether we were lovers or not, I would always love her. The night before she left we got a hotel room and talked of our plans to meet after each semester. Our lovemaking was especially beautiful that night. We both cried and held on to each other for dear life.

Afterwards as we lay in bed, she asked me if I really thought she should go. I unselfishly told her yes. When she left for school we didn't know it but it was the last time we would see each other. Nahdia was killed four months after arriving in California in a car accident.

I was devastated. I had never known pain like the anguish I felt when I learned of her death. My world went into utterly and complete darkness. I blamed myself. I thought that if I had only asked her to stay she would still be alive.

Next I blamed God. Everything I'd ever believed in suddenly came into question. Fears of damnation were suddenly thrust back into my conscience like a splinter you can't seem to pull out. I felt betrayed by God. After all, hadn't he given me that beautiful creature to love and love me? Didn't he hear our prayers to be together forever and if that wasn't to be then why didn't he take away those feelings when I prayed not to be gay in the first place.

Yeah, I questioned his love for me and for Nahdia! Wasn't she a good person? Didn't she deserve to live?!!!!

I begged him to let Nahdia's death be some type of dream and if he did I promised never see her again. Just knowing she was alive somewhere would have been enough for me.

As reality set in, my heart turned into stone. I thought my own death was surely imminent because I was consumed with hers.

Soon, all I had were fading memories and regrets. Every woman I met paled in comparison to her. I was insulted by their offers of attention and wallowed in my own self pity. The realization that she was never coming back killed me softly daily.

When Love Aint Enough

The kids and house with the little picket fence we both so much desired, was now only a dream. We weren't going to grow old together. I would never feel her soft lips or see her beautiful smile again.

Again I was lost in the world and once again I secluded myself. I buried all the love I had to offer and swore not to give it to anyone ever again. The world could go fuck it self and take love right with it.

SHENA

After sitting out for a year, I decided to attend law school in Mississippi. It was an easy choice, it was home. And what I needed more than anything was the comfort only my family could provide.

When I graduated my favorite professor suggested I take a job at the Legal Aide office in Gulfport. He and the head attorney had served in the trenches together during the sixties. He thought it would be a great opportunity for me and give me the hands on experience I needed to decide which direction I wanted to take in my field.

I was partially interested for another reason, my best friend Lionel had recently moved back there after snagging a spot in the Gulf States Symphony. He offered me a room at his place but I graciously declined. Even though he and I adored each other, we couldn't dare live together. It would be like oil and vinegar.

Nahdia's love had changed me. I was no longer his little sidekick. Now I was reaching out for a sense of self. I still missed Nahdy terribly, but I had since met a young lady named Renee, who I found easy to talk to. And Lionel, well, he was still the same Lionel, loved to party and didn't let nothing slow him down. But I probably would have or if not that, aggravated the hell out of him with my mood swings.

In the end I took the job, convinced by both Lionel and Renee that the move would do me good. To help with the transition, Renée offered to go down and help me get settled in. That was the beginning of our relationship, because instead of leaving after the summer as planned, she stayed and we became roommates, then lovers.

I had been working at legal aide for about two years when I met Shena. She was a paralegal fresh out of school.

I never noticed her at first. In looking back, it's like one day she simply appeared out of nowhere. She was the kind of person who blended in well, like good office furniture. She was quite and very soft-spoken. Though she gave the impression of being bashful, I soon learned she was nowhere close to it.

One morning I bought donuts for some workers I'd worked on a case with. Since I was one of newest attorneys in the office, I thought it was a good opportunity to show my team spirit.

When I walked into the break room, Shena was there making a cup of hot chocolate. I walked by, said good morning and made my way to a nearby counter to get a tray for the donuts. As I searched the cabinets for napkins, a small voice asked,

"Mmm, are those donuts?"

"Yes," I replied without turning around.

"Can I have one?"

I paused and turned around. Shena, pulling the mug down from her lips, flashed me a sly smile. She wore a pink dress that hung softly on her body. She was around 5'2"inches tall and weighed about 115 lbs. She had jet black hair that brushed past her chin in a stylish chic wrap. She was a brown skinned sister with big beautiful brown eyes that could easily tease you.

I stood mesmerized by the aura she emitted. Her smile was pleasant yet seductive as hell! I shook my head trying to explain I'd only brought enough for my group. She looked at me in feigned surprised that I'd said no. I must admit, I was kind of surprised myself as I turned around to finish what I was doing. Moments later I heard her say "humph" as she walked out of the room.

When I'd finished, I walked out to my desk with the platter of donuts. As I walked to my little cubbyhole in the rear of the office, I noticed her at her desk. She looked at me and turned her head abruptly. Feeling a little awkward, I continued on to my desk and plopped down in my chair.

Eagerly I started the gruesome task of going through the mile high stack of papers in front of me and signed onto my computer. As I began the start of what was sure to be a busy day, the same little voice spoke to me again. This time I looked up.

"You mean to tell me you aint gonna give me one of them donuts?"

84

"It's not that," I said, again mesmerized by her eyes and the sensual way she looked at me. "Really, I only brought enough for the people in my group. Now that I think about it, I realize that was kind of messed up. But I still want to make sure they all get some before I start issuing them out to everyone else.

"Oh!!" she pouted. "Well, you could have said that at first, you didn't have to be so mean."

"Is she for real?" I thought.

"Well I'm sorry, I wasn't trying to be nasty. I really thought you were joking," I said apologetically.

"No, I really wasn't! I didn't get a chance to have breakfast this morning. But it's cool!"

"Ah man," I thought, *"She is serious."*

"Look, you can have mine," I said, motioning to it lying on a napkin on my desk.

"No, it's cool, really, I just couldn't believe you turned me down flat like that."

At that point it hit me. This little cat and mouse game wasn't about the donuts. She was flirting with me. The revelation was shocking considering I didn't think my business showed like that.

"I know I'm not the most feminine female up in here but I aint not dyke or no shit like that," I thought to myself.

For a moment I felt self-conscious, but it quickly dissipated into being flattered by her advances. I looked deep into her soft brown eyes and against my better judgment, played along.

"Well since you missed breakfast, would like to like to join me for lunch at the mall?"

"The mall, sure, I can do the mall with you. I need to look for some things anyway."

"Good, normally I go to lunch around one but since you're obviously starved we can go at whatever time is good for you".

She smiled softly and leaned her sexy body on the outward panel of my cubicle.

"Eleven is fine."

"Okay, cool with me. I'll see ya at eleven"

She stood up and slowly walked back to her desk. I watched inconspicuously as she walked away. Her walk was sexy and a tad bit exaggerated but it definitely kept a person's attention. She reminded me of a teenager who purposely tried to switch, capturing the attention of her intended victim.

My eyes followed her from the curves of her tiny shoulders all the way down to her honey brown feet. Her legs were slim and warmly inviting. She wore silver strapped heels that revealed her beautifully sculptured feet. When she arrived at her desk she casually turned and looked back in my direction. I quickly ducked back into my cubbyhole and studied my computer screen.

As I worked that morning I found the thought of having lunch with her very distracting. Try as I may, I couldn't concentrate on the tasks before me. I wanted eleven to come quickly so I could learn if my suspicions were correct.

Finally, it came, then went.

I continued to work at my computer while waiting for her to come get me. As the clock ticked on I wondered what was keeping her but

I refused to go over to her desk for fear of appearing anxious. Instead, I played it cool and continued to work on the brief I had been working on since I came into the office that morning. Around 11:20 she came sashaying over.

"Did you forget?"

"What time is it?"

"Almost 11:30"

"Girl I'm sorry I got caught up on this brief and lost track of time" I said, pretending to be busy.

"Do you still want to go?" she asked.

"Yeah, sure, give me a minute"

I continued to type then pulled my glasses down from tired eyes. Carefully I placed them back in their case, purposely not looking up for fear of betraying myself. I locked my computer, straightened some papers on my desk then stood up. The whole time she patiently waited. Then we left.

The Eastview Mall wasn't crowded that day. We went directly to the solarium and ordered salads. We grabbed a table in the corner and cozily ate our food and talked.

I usually did the lunch thing alone, if I did it at all, unfortunately I'd become introverted that way. So for me to share my private time with another person, let alone enjoy it, was refreshing and helped me to step out of the box, if only for a short time.

The company and conversation was surprisingly good. Even though she went "there" by asking me if I was married, I didn't cringe as I normally would have. Instead, I said no and left it at that. She on the other hand, had no problem telling me her life's story.

She told me she was in a long term relationship and had little boy, age four. She and the baby's father were planning on getting married but both, at one point or another, had gotten cold feet. Now they were at a standstill. And she was reevaluating their relationship. I got the impression that shit was rolling down hill fast!

When she told me so much of her business I felt guilty and told her a tad bit more about myself. My involvement with my roommate was touched on briefly. I didn't call names, allowing her to fill in the blanks. I used the old trusty "they" and "them" when I talked of Renee, a dead give away that you're referring to someone of the same sex.

I didn't think I owed her anymore than that. We'd have to know each other a hell of a lot better before I told her all of my damn business!

Still, she was nice and wildly sensual. As she talked I absorbed her every word wondering why I'd never noticed her before.

Before going back to the office we decided to do a little window shipping. As we walked past Victoria's Secret she stopped and went in to see if a teddy she'd seen earlier in the week was still there. I reluctantly walked in behind her and half heartedly fumbled around at some of the racks.

A sales rep came over and asked me if I needed help. I politely said no and pointed her in Shena's direction. They spoke then disappeared into the back part of the store. I took the opportunity to look over the goods to see if I could find something for my girlfriend.

Just as I was getting caught up in how Renee would look in one of the outfits, Shena came up from behind and tapped me on the shoulder.

"Turn around" she said casually.
I did, only to find her holding up a sheer violet teddy to her small frame. I blushed, hoping she hadn't noticed it, thinking if I had a Johnson it would be standing straight up!

"Do you think this is my color?" she asked, watching me out the corner of her eye as she squeezed by to look in the mirror behind me.

"Yeah it's nice"

"But do you like it?"

"Yeah, I like it. It's nice" I said, returning my attention to the rack of garments in front of me. I secretly hoped she would either buy it or put it back, either way, I wanted her to stop with the games. My patience was short and getting shorter by the minute.

She continued to look around and I continued to walk about oblivious of her, throwing my attention on the various racks of lingerie. I'd confirmed what I wanted to know, she was definitely flirting. Eventually she bought it and we left.

It had been a week since we'd done the lunch thing. And the flirting between us subtly lingered in the air like a cock roach everyone pretends not to see. The attention was flattering but I was dedicated to Renee' and my job. I knew it was way too risky to strike up anything more than a casual conversation with a woman as tempting as her.

One Friday, after everyone had left the office, I was still bogged down at my desk with work. My head was buried deep in a thick leather binder when Shena walked up.

"Hey girl,"

"Hey, what's up?"

"I was wondering if you wanted to grab a bite to eat. A client gave me some passes to Chatterley's and I thought maybe we could get something to eat and have a couple of drinks."

I looked up over the rim of my glasses and found she had her perched herself on the edge of my cubicle. It was casual day and she had on a pair of blue crop pants and a white-laced spaghetti strapped blouse that came just above her breast. Her hair was wrapped and pushed behind her ears. She stared intently, waiting for my answer. I started to say no but the look in her eyes swayed me. I thought for a second and then replied,

"What time?"

"Now if you're ready...."

I looked at my watch, it was six thirty. Consumed with work, I hadn't realized how late it was. I thought of Renée and wondered if she was home yet. Normally, on Fridays, she went out with her friends. At first, I felt left out, but she made the case that it was her opportunity to relax and have some Renée time.

And I could understand it because there were times when I needed space myself. But my own space was never that important that I wanted to exclude her. But that was one the differences between the two of us, so I tried to respect her feelings.

So, even though I figured she'd be out, I decided to call her just in case she'd had a change of plans. Meanwhile, Shena walked away to give me some privacy.

When I called her cell but there was no answer. Then I tried the apartment but still no answer. Finally I left a message on the machine and hung up.

As we gathered our things, I wondered where she was. Crazy thoughts tried to make their way into my brain but I quickly shook them off. Since Nahdia's death I'd become a chronic worrier. I constantly struggled with that. Tonight I decided to give it a rest. Renee was fine. If something jumped off she knew how to call me.

I grabbed my brief case and jacket then walked out into the breezy fall air with Shena.

Chatterley's was a new upscale restaurant nestled on the north end of the town. It was located on the already over crowded beachfront and traffic was always terrible. Since she and I lived on the same side of town we decided to take one car. Shena volunteered to ride with me. I was okay with it since I didn't trust anyone else's driving but my own.

So we jumped into my '89 Cutlass and took off. The radio was playing Brandy's new hit, "Have you ever loved somebody?" Shena said the song was the only one she'd ever liked by Brandy. This stirred up a hot debate which led to other topics. We laughed and talked as we rode up the highway. There was a sense of familiarity we seemed to share from the beginning.

The traffic was heavy, as expected. After all it was a Friday night in Gulfport, MS. Some parts of I-10 traffic was backed up for miles. In the past five years the coast had really began to boom into one of Mississippi's largest tourist attractions. So much so that we wondered how the new restaurant would fare among its competition once the newness wore off.

We arrived there around seven thirty and it was already packed. We were surprised at the number people waiting outside to get in. Shena jumped out to grab a place in line while I parked the car. I joined her shortly and learned it would be an hour and half wait for the first available table.

I cringed at the thought of having to wait so long in the cold or stand in the foyer. Shena was excited but left the decision up to me. She said we could make it fun and asked one of the hostesses passing by if there was any room inside, at the bar. The hostess went inside to check and returned informing us it was pretty much standing room only. We decided to do the bar thing instead of stand outside. I followed closely as she led the way through the sea of people standing near the crammed bar area.

The atmosphere was light and cheerful. A local jazz band was playing on stage. They were loud for a lack of being talented but it seemed to appease the patrons who were grooving to the tunes they were spitting out. Loving Jazz like I do, I was determined to get my groove on as well.

As we struggled to place a drink order, I looked around for familiar faces and found one. It was a guy named John. He was a paralegal from the office. Though I had seen him around I had

93

never held a conversation with him. He worked for one of the senior attorneys so our paths rarely crossed. His presence, however, reminded me of the nagging sense of propriety in my subconscious that said I was fraternizing with a subordinate.

I tried to dismiss my anxieties by reasoning since she didn't report to me and I wasn't doing anything wrong. Plus, it was hard for me to feel like anyone's superior in the office since I was relatively new there myself. Still I realized things could get complicated as far as another subordinate accusing me of favoritism but I prided myself on being fair and above board. So I dismissed the thought and pointed John out to Shena, who looked casually in his direction.

Curiously, I thought we made eye contact but noticeably no one bothered to wave. He was seated with a group of guys that neither of us knew. I commented on the great table he'd managed to get. And Shena said,

"Yeah, you'd have to have left the office around two to get a spot like that in this crowded joint!"

She turned abruptly and continued trying to get a bartender's attention. Finally a handsome young man came to her rescue. With a big smile he welcomed us to Chatterley's and took our order. Shena ordered a rum and coke and I got my usual, a Long Island Ice Tea." I returned my attention to all the patrons who graced the room. The crowd was a mixture of ages and socio

94

classes. People with money and some broke as a joke. Still I was impressed.

Our drinks came not a minute too soon. We sipped and listened to the music while the crowd swelled by the minute, pushing us together like sardines. Shena joked about it and held on to my jacket so as not to float way.

The band was playing its rendition of a Kenny G song. It was okay but not the greatest I had ever heard. I found myself critiquing every note. But after our third round of cocktails I was feeling no pain. I loosened up and actually begun to think the band was doing a damn good job!

I had always been able to hold my liquor but tonight it was having a devastating affect on me. The liquor was running through me like water and I found myself constantly running back and forth to the bathroom. The last time, as I clumsily made my way back, I could barley see the top of Shena's head through all the people. As I approached I noticed her talking with someone. It was a guy and he had his back turned to me. As I grew nearer I saw it was John.

When I reached them, he and I exchanged pleasantries and he returned to his conversation with Shena. She was doing a lot of smiling, as was John. I attempted to ignore both of them and pick up where I'd left off, enjoying the band. After a couple of minutes John returned to the group of guys he had left at his table. Shena asked me if I wanted anything else to drink and I replied no. I had reached my limit. I realized it in the bathroom when I saw the stupid grin plastered all over my face. Shena claimed she was tight too, so we chilled and enjoyed the music.

Another fifteen minutes went by and I asked if she wanted to continue to wait for a table. She replied that it was up to me.

"John asked if we wanted to join him but I told him no," she remarked casually.

"Why not, he seems cool," I said.

"He's alright."

"Then why'd you say no?"

"I don't know. I didn't feel like being bothered I guess."

"Oh he must be trying to holla or something?"

"Girl that's a long story, I just ain't trying to do that tonight"

As we talked, the pager, the hostess had given her, went off. She reached into her pocket and pulled out the flashing red disc. We quickly made our way to the hostess stand and were led to a table not far from the one John and his friends were seated at. I sank into the overstuffed booth and checked my watch for the time. It was nine forty-five. I took out my cell phone and called home. There was still no answer. The band was winding down for an intermission so the club had grown noisier with the chatter of conversations around us.

I was facing the table where John was seated and noticed him staring in our direction. When I mentioned this to Shena she responded,

"Ignore him"

"What?"

"Ignore him, he's silly like that"

At one point, his constant glaring became so uncomfortable that I asked if she wanted to change seats with me because his staring was getting kind of spooky. Again she told me to dismiss it.

"He's trips like that"

I thought it was silly as hell and tried to relax like she suggested even though I was becoming aggravated the hell out of me because he was blowing my high.

"He act like he's slow or something"

"No, he likes attention"

The wait was well worth it, we topped the evening off with a splendidly cooked seafood meal. I chose the lobster and steak and Shena ordered a pail of crab legs and scampi. We must have been hungry as hell because when the food came all conversation stopped. I ordered another Long Island Iced Tea and it was on!

Later as I drove Shena to her car, we laughed our butts off at how we'd killed our meal. Outside a storm was brewing. It was past 11pm now and the last time I checked there was still no answer at my house.

I waited while Shena got into her car and drove off, then I went home.

When I arrived at my apartment Renée was lying on the sofa asleep. I shook her lightly telling her to come to bed. I asked where she'd been all night and she replied,

"Here"

I looked at her suspiciously, not wanting to argue the issue and walked into the bedroom.

The next day was Saturday. I lived for it and the ability to do what I craved to do at the end of each week, sleep late. I turned over in the bed feeling for Renée who wasn't there. I lay there with my eyes closed listening to faint whispers of someone talking in the bathroom. I tried to ignore it for a while but became fully awake when I heard the sound of the exercise bike cranking up as Renée rode it in the den. I threw the covers over my head and attempted to lull myself back into a deep slumber.

But it was to no use. So I got up and stumbled into the bathroom. Grudgingly I looked in the mirror. The person looking back looked a hot mess. My scarf had turned sideways on my head with more hair sticking out than was being covered up. I splashed some cold water on my face and rubbed my eyes. I grabbed my toothbrush and opened my mouth to see my tongue.

"Ugh" I thought. "I can't taste anything but liquor!"

After showering, I sauntered into the kitchen for a cup of coffee.

When Love Aint Enough

Renée was seated at the bar eating a bowl of fruit and reading the paper. She and I had been living together for the past two years. The way we met was a trip.

I had just left the gym and was driving up the freeway when a car pulled along side me to past by. But instead of passing, one of the girls waived. It was Renée with two of her girl friends. She motioned for me to follow them.

Intrigued by this overt come-on I did as she instructed. I followed her to a parking lot where she immediately got out and walked over to my car where I was still seated. She was a short blond haired sista with a short-cropped Afro looking sexy as hell. She flashed a big grin showing off a beautiful smile. I smiled back and we introduced ourselves.

I hadn't dated anyone since Nahdia and hadn't planned on it then but something about this girl's attitude that took me by storm. We exchanged numbers and continued to talk over phone for the next couple of months. Initially she accused me of only liking her because she was a great conversationalist. Though I never admitted it to her, I did miss the stimulating conversation of a sexy woman.

But at that point in my life, a woman didn't stand a chance with me. For me she would have to walk on water. I soon thought Renée did. After a year I was deeply smitten with her. At first I had a problem acknowledging I loved her but at the risk of losing her on several occasions, I gave in. I had found love again or something close to it. After a year of knowing each other we moved to the coast as roommates. Soon we were inseparable. It was cool. We complimented each other. For me she brought life back into my existence and to her I gave unconditional love. It was great for a while.

"Good morning" I said as I walked up behind her and slid my arms around her waist kissing her softly on the back of her neck"

"Good morning yourself" She said looking at me suspiciously from head to toe.

I walked over to the refrigerator and opened the door wide to get good look of its contents. I grabbed the milk and closed the door. Lazily I poured a bowl of cereal and joined Renée at the bar.

"So what did you do last night" I asked with my mouth full corn flakes.

"Nothing" she replied.

I looked up at her then continued to eat my cereal. As I ate I tried it again.

"I left you a couple of messages, did you get them?

"Obviously not. What's up with the third degree?" she said visibly agitated

"It's not the third degree" I snapped back.

"I just find it hard to believe that you were here last night but you didn't answer the phone and didn't return any of my calls. It doesn't make sense!"

"Well I was. I was studying for a test and I turned the ringer off! Damn!"

I glared at her and then got up from the stool.

"Well why you didn't just say that then instead of trying to make it seem like it's some big mystery or something!"

"Whatever Casey!" She snapped as she got up from her chair and walked into the living room. I took my bowl to the sink and put it down. As I reached for the dishtowel I saw two wineglasses sitting on the counter. I noticed both glasses had lipstick on them. I shook my head,

"Studying for a test my ass!" I thought.

Sunday night, Renée and I went to a gospel play in Biloxi. I normally didn't attend them but Renée was on her kick about spending some quality time, so I went. Afterwards we grabbed a bite to eat at the restaurant across from the theater. The place was packed with people who'd attended the play. For the first time in a minute we sat eating and talking like we were happy to be together.

As we were leaving we bumped into some of Renee's friends from school. As they chatted, I stood awkwardly waiting to be introduced. I never was. When we got into the car I asked her about it and she shrugged me off.

"No, really, why didn't you introduce me to your friends, you know all of mine," I said.

"Casey, its no big deal"

"No, it's not a big deal but I felt a little stupid standing there while y'all talked for over ten minutes."

101

"See that's my problem with you. You make something out of everything. I didn't think to introduce you, is that okay with you?!"

I glanced at her then started up the car. I turned the radio off and we drove home in complete silence, with each of us staring out into darkness.

Things had been very strained since she quit her job to attend nursing school fulltime. I wasn't making very much at Legal Aide and Renée wasn't a cheap woman to have around. She was definitely high maintenance. Though I supported her efforts to get a degree, I was getting damn tired of her shitty attitude while I was out busting my butt for the both of us.

Lately I was getting vibes from her that she was keeping something from me. Though I couldn't quite put my finger on, it I felt there was a lot more going on than she wanted me to know about. Being me. I'd confronted her several times asking if her if she was happy with our relationship and each time she said yes.

So I chilled and tried not to stress her for fear that she would accused me of not trusting her or worse yet of being a nag. I decided to ride it out and let the chips fall where they may. Cause like my mom always said,

"What's done in the dark will come to the light."

Monday morning I stopped by the local donut shop. This time I bought enough for everyone. When I arrived at Legal

Aide I walked through the room announcing the arrival of breakfast and proceeded to the break room to put them out for everyone. I was startled when I walked in on Shena and John huddled together. When Shena saw me enter she moved away from John. John turned around.

"Hey, what's up?" he said

"Yeah, what's" I replied.

Shena, with folded arms, looked down at the box and back up at me. I moved over to the counter and sat the donuts down. Shena laughed.

"Can I get one of those donuts?"

"Sure, I brought enough for everybody this time!" I said pointing to the box.

I grabbed a cup from the cabinets and walked over to the coffee pot. John watched Shena inspect the donuts then whispered in her ear. She nodded her head and said,

"Okay"

Then he left. I looked for a stirrer and continued to fix my coffee.

"How was your weekend" she asked

"It was nice"

I returned the question and she told me of her trip with her ex-boyfriend to Bourbon Street.

"Man I aint been to New Orleans in years."

Then we walked out onto the floor together. As we approached her desk I noticed John standing at his looking in our direction.

103

I looked away and back at Shena. She sat down and I stood beside her cubicle chatting for a minute before going to start my day.

The following weeks I noticed John and Shena in deep conversation in and around the office. They looked fuck-buddy chummy and Shena was definitely enjoying it. John, as silly as ever, would shoot me little looks every once in a while. I finally realized the boy evidently viewed me as competition. At first I was shocked, then I felt sorry for him. I figured it was his way of pissing on his territory and warning me to stay away. I decided that Shena obviously wasn't telling me the whole story, so I slacked off my conversations with her.

One day, in the bathroom she approached me about it.

"I didn't sleep with you last night," she kidded, "You ain't gonna speak?"

"Hey chic, my mind was elsewhere. I've got a meeting with the bosses,   what's up?" I asked.

"Same o same o," she responded.

"Yeah bet" I said unable to hide my sarcasm.

"Well that was nasty!" she said pretending to pout.

"It wasn't meant to be," I lied.

"Well it was," she said. I don't think I am going to talk to you anymore, you're fired.

"Fired?" I laughed. "You can't fire me because I was never hired. Now maybe you can fire old John over there because he looks like he's been working for you for a minute now."

Shena rolled her eyes and whispered.

"Aint nothing to that."

"Yeah right" I said and turned to walk off.

"No really, I know what it looks like but he does that on purpose to cock block."

"Who's he trying to cock block"

"Everybody"

"Yeah and you let him!"

"No, I really don't! He has been jocking me since I went out with him"

"See, that's what I'm talking about!!" I whispered to her.

"No it wasn't anything. I only went out with him trying to get over my ex," she explained still whispering and looking back to make sure no one coming in would over hear our conversation.

"Oh, okay I got you." I smirked and turned to walk away.

"I am telling you the truth Casey. Since then he's been bugging me to go out again. Since he couldn't get it up he feels he has something to prove"

I looked at her incredulously.

"You slept with him!"

"It wasn't anything I'm telling you! I told you he couldn't get it up!"

"Well that's y'all's business please leave me out of it! And tell his silly ass to stop staring at me, I aint impressed!"

I turned and walked out of the bathroom. As I walked back to my desk I realized that I was mad as hell. This girl was turning

out to be one big surprise and I didn't like surprises. I went to
my meeting and later left the office without bothering to look in
her direction.

The next couple of weeks were very strained. I had been
assigned the case of an elderly woman who was being evicted
from her home of thirty years. Her mortgage loan officers had
accelerated her payments and her loan was now in default.
Shena was assigned to assist me in preparation for the case.
This meant she and I had to spend many evenings pulling late
hours in the office. It was a bit strained at first but I had more
important things to concentrate on besides a chic that seemed to
enjoy the attention of so many. So I restricted my conversations
to business and encouraged her to do the same.

I wasn't surprised to see John hanging out at her desk most of
the time. The guy obviously had a serious hard on for her, or so
he wished. One evening around seven she and I were in the
office when John came in. He had already left for the day, as
had everyone else in the office. But for some reason he was
back again and perched on top of her desk.

On top of that, I had memos that needed typing before I could
leave, thinking his visit would be brief I decided to wait until he
left before I approached her. That was mistake #1 on my part.
Because then I grew aggravated and resented waiting for him to
finish his conversation before I could complete my business for

the day. Still, I sat at my desk working on other things trying not to intrude.

Around eight fifteen he was still there. Now he was sitting at the desk with her, facing her, in deep conversation. I found it highly unlikely that they were discussing business and I still hadn't told her about the memos I needed typed for the next day. The whole thing reeked for me.

I called her extension and asked her to come over. She came bouncing over without hesitation and asked me what was up. I had hoped my aggravation would not show as I explained what I needed. She took the notes from me and assured me she could have them to me in thirty minutes. Knowing she was more than capable of doing so I said okay.

Still I was bothered by the lack of professionalism she exhibited by allowing someone to come to her place of work and take up so much of her time while we tried to tie things up. I felt she should tell him to leave or help out.

As we talked I avoided looking at her. I was pissed and like it or not, it showed. Something had come over me, I was jealous and her pretentious attitude only assisted in pissing me off more. So in the midst of my speech on how important the case was she stopped me.

"Is there something wrong?"

Never having been good at hiding my feelings I answered,

"Yeah, something is wrong."

"What is it?" She asked innocently.

107

I looked at her incredulous and thought to myself,

"She obviously isn't the professional I'd assumed if she doesn't know how inappropriate it was for him to be there while we worked to meet a timeline."

Steaming with frustration, I stared at her.

"What is it!" she demanded.

"It's this! What is all that at your desk?"

"What about my desk" she asked placing her hand on her hip and looking down toward her desk and back at me.

"Well since you pretend or obviously don't know, this is an office. We have a case with a deadline fast approaching. This evidently doesn't matter to you since you're able to find time to entertain on company time!"

"Entertain!"

"Yes entertain!"

"For your information John works here too so I can't just tell him to leave. Plus what harm is it doing to you!"

"In case you didn't realize he has been her since 7pm and I have been here since eight this morning and don't plan on staying here all night just because you and he are trying to get your groove on. This is an office, in case you forgot, not a night club!"

Shena and I glared at each other. I stole a glance at John, who was at us. I looked back at Shena.

"If he isn't here on business you need to tell your company that you're busy."

I returned my attention to the computer screen. I felt her icy stare on the side of my head but I refused to look up. I'd said what I had to say and I was through with it.

"Well since I am just a paralegal around here and it's all about "the business" with you, you can tell him yourself!"

I gave her a look that should have knocked her out cold!

"Are you refusing to do as I asked?!"

"It don't make no sense man"

"It makes a lot of sense MAN!"

Angrily I got up and hurriedly walked over to Shena's desk where John was seated.

"John," I said with all the calmness I could muster. "Shena and I have a deadline to meet and neither of us wants to be here all night, so unless you are here to assist us with this project I am going to have to ask you to leave"

John looked at me then at Shena. I held fast to my position and waited for him to get up.

"Oh, so you're putting me out" he said jokingly.

"What ever you want to call it," I said. "We are trying to work and I think your presence is a distraction."

"Distraction?" John raised his hand and beckoning for Shena. Shena promptly walked back to her desk.

"Am I distracting you?"

I didn't bother to turn to see Shena's response but continued looking at John.

"Well am I?" he repeated.

109

"This isn't Shena's call. It's mine. So like I said, if you're not here to help then I would appreciate your leaving, ok." John turned his attention back to me and mumbled,

"Humph!"

I restrained my natural urge to ask if there was a problem and waited patiently for him to leave. After he had left Shena brushed past me. I ignored her and went back to my desk. For the rest of the evening we only spoke to each other when it was absolutely necessary. Around ten thirty Shena left and I followed shortly thereafter.

When I got into my car to go home that night, I was pissed. I didn't appreciate Shena's putting me in a situation where I had to be the bad guy. And I damn sure didn't appreciate John thinking he could use my time to rendezvous with Shena. The entire situation was fucked up and made me uncomfortable as hell.

"How *in the hell are they gonna try to challenge my authority*"

I made a mental note to speak with Senior Attorney Richards about what had happened.

"Attorney Richards wouldn't have had to say anything," I thought. *"Hell he wouldn't have even tried that shit if he'd been there, let alone sit down and talk for over an hour and a half.*

"Trifling bitches!"

By the time I pulled up to my apartment I had calmed down and had decided to let the incident slide. Tired as hell, I jumped out of my car and walked up to my door. As I approached I noticed the lights were still on. That wasn't surprising. But the silhouette of more than one person was! I wondered what was up since Renée normally went to bed at nine like clockwork when she had class the next day.

As I reached the front door a feeling of trepidation consumed me. I took a deep breath and then put my key in the hole. Slowly I opened it expecting to see two people in the front room as I had observed from outside. But the room was empty. I walked quietly into the apartment and sat my briefcase on the floor beside the sofa. I started to call Renee's name but instead decided to walk through the house to see where she was.

As I walked through the halls, the same feeling of trepidation hit me again, only this time, it was stronger and made my heart quicken. Quietly I walked to the bathroom and peeped in but no one was there. I continued down the hall to our bedroom with my feet becoming heavier with every step. The bedroom door it was slightly ajar and I heard voices coming from the room. It was Renee's and a man. I flung the door open to find a man sitting on the edge of the bed while Renée talked to him from inside the walk-in closet. The guy stopped in mid sentence when I entered the room.

111

Wifey

I was shocked, to say the least, at finding someone other than Renée in our bedroom at that time of night.

She was still talking to him when she walked out of the closet and saw me standing in the doorway. The guy, who had been sitting on the edge of our bed, was standing now.

He was around six feet tall with a dark brown complexion and an athletic build. I quickly appraised him and the shinny dark blue jogging suit he was wearing. He looked like something out of a Village People Magazine. Renée, sensing my apprehension, bounced over and grabbed my arm, pulling me into the room toward the guy.

"Hey ba-be, I didn't hear you come in"

Still shocked by the scene, I quietly stared back at the guy who was also staring at me.

"This is my cousin Chuck. He just got in from Atlanta."

"Cousin?" I repeated.

"Yeah, he got in this morning and came by the school to find me, wasn't that sweet" she laughed. "I almost didn't know who he was. He's has gotten so big and everything" Renée kidded.

"Gone with dat," said Chuck, smiling back at Renée but still sizing me up as I had him.

I stepped toward him and extended my hand. He grabbed it and shook it like he was trying to shake lint off a towel.

"Chuck, this my baby Casey I told you about," she said with pride.

I looked at her, then him and forced out a smile. Already tired as hell from work and my disagreement with Sheena, I wasn't in the mood for company. But for Renee's sake I tried to make small talk.

Chuck told me he was in the process of moving from Atlanta back to Mississippi. As he talked and reminisced, Renee kept interrupting, finishing his sentences for him. I sat on the chaise, beside the bed, observing and trying to look interested.

After about ten minutes of the bullshit, Renée again interrupted Chuck, who was telling me about his job, this time to tell me he was on his way to New Orleans.

"He asked if I'd ride down with him" she blurted out anxiously.

I was blown away and my face showed it. After all, she has classes tomorrow and she never missed class, never.

Cousin Chuck sensed my skepticism and added that it was business trip.

"But since Renée wants to go I'm gonna make a weekend of it and drop in on some of my college buddies down there."

113

I looked at Renée who was looking at me, weighing my reaction. Sensing an argument, she ushered Chuck into the living room and closed the bedroom door.

Before I could get a word out she was pleading her case.

"Babe I am burnt out! School is stressing the shit out me. I figured since I'm starting clinical in two weeks and its slow, now is the best time to get my head together. It's only for the weekend."

I rubbed my hand wearily over my face and looked at her. I wasn't prepared to deal with this shit, not tonight. I could think of a thousand reasons why she shouldn't go but I could tell from her tone that her mind was made up. Still, I gave it a shot.

"I know ya tired but why not wait until tomorrow after class. Besides, what am I supposed to do while you're gone?"

"This aint about you, it's about me!"

"I'm not saying it is, you're the one always stressing quality time and saying we don't spend any time together"

"That's because all you do is work! Now as for school, I got it covered" she stated matter of factly, and walked over to the dresser and began pulling out clothes to take on the trip.

I could feel my face getting hot. I didn't want to over react but the conversation was becoming annoying since I was still more than a little miss trusting of this so called cousin.

"So now you have a problem with my job?

114

"No I don't have a problem with your job! It's just that you expect me to sit at this house and wait for you to get home heaven knows when, day in and day out"

"I didn't know it bothered you so much to be here."

"Naw, it's not that Casey, don't be petty! But sometimes I do want to get out and do things. But every time I try you always try to make me feel guilty because you can't come."

I stood up and walked over to her.

"Look if it's that important to you, I'll take the day off tomorrow and you and I can drive down there together"

"What? And miss the 'big deadline' you been hollering about for weeks?" She said sarcastically shaking her head. "Naw, you aint gonna put that one on me"

"I can work on it while I'm there," I suggested knowing deep down that would be next to impossible but at least I wouldn't be left at home alone.

Renee stopped packing and stared at me.

"What kind of fun is that Casey? You'll still be working"

Desperately I tried to figure out how I could fit this spur of the moment trip into my schedule.

"Just stay here"

"Well maybe I can meet ya'll Saturday evening or something," I said trying to be more realistic and less frantic about her leaving.

Renee, sensing my frustration, walked up and put her arms around my neck. Then tried coming at me another way,

"Baby look, I am not trying to get away from you or anything it's just that my cousin is here and I haven't seen him in ages. I want to kick it with him and chill a little bit." She said kissing me softly on the lips and looking deep into my tired eyes. Is that too much to ask?" she pouted.

"No, I guess not," I said trying not to let my disappointment show. "I just thought we could hang too"

"We can. When I get back" said Renée as she let go of me and walked back over to her luggage and continued to pack.

I picked up her bra that was lying on my side of the bed and tossed it to the other side.

"Yeah, when you get back" I mumbled."

I sat down on the bed and fell back on the pillows and watched her pack.

"Now what the hell am I going to do all weekend?"

Friday was casual day and a good thing too since I'd tossed and turned all night from not having Renee there beside me, then overslept! I took a quick hoe bath and slipped on a pair of button fly jeans, a Gap sweatshirt and a pair Cole Haan loafers. Already late, I pulled my hair back in a ponytail and rolled out.

When I got to the office it was buzzing as usual. Like they say the eagle flies on Friday, but for me it had landed on top my head that ached from lack of sleep. So, after flashing a couple of good morning smiles to my co workers, I slipped into the break room to grab a cup of black coffee.

When I got to my desk a manila folder was lying in the chair with the memos I'd asked Shena to type the night before. I looked over the material and set it aside to be assimilated later with the rest of my briefs.

Soon after sitting down my phone rang and on the other end was Attorney Richards asking me to come by his office at my convenience. Since I wasn't busy, I told him I'd come then. Attorney Richards, a man in his late 50's was a product of the old school. He'd made his mark early in life during the civil rights era and was very much a libertarian. He was about 6 feet 2 with sprigs of gray around his temples. He was the color of bark and had pearly white teeth that looked like they could tear a witness in half if he wanted to. Most of the women considered him to be a very distinguished looking gentleman. I on the other hand respected him for his diversity. He was cool as hell if you weren't stupid enough to get on his bad side.

When I reached his office I politely knocked on the door. A thunderous voice from inside instructed me to come in and I did, cautiously.

The room was big but not grand by any means for a man of his stature. He was seated at his oversized mahogany desk surrounded by pillars of shelves stuffed with books. A small

117

radio on the desk played softly almost allowing me to relax for a minute. Papers and files were everywhere. But his filing system must have fit his needs because he always seemed to know where everything was in spite of the constant clutter of papers lying about. As I approached he motioned to me to sit in the chair to the left of his desk.

"How are you this morning?" I asked, positioning myself neatly in the uncomfortable chair.

"Fine, fine" he replied. "How's the Vickers case going?" He asked.

"Good sir, we're meeting our deadlines. I have a phone interview scheduled with two of the neighbors later today."

"Good, good" he said, watching me suspiciously from behind his horn rimmed glasses.

"Listen Casey, I called you in here to talk with you about John."

"John sir?" I repeated.

"Yes, he called me last night very upset saying you had ordered him out of the building."

I listened quietly to what was to come next. Attorney Richards cleared his throat and continued,

"He says he came by to speak with your assistant regarding an issue that had arisen earlier that day and after talking with her for about 15 minutes you came over and abruptly told him to leave."

I was stunned. I couldn't believe what I was hearing. The boy had flat out lied on me! Damn! And after I'd decided to drop the whole thang!

"Aint this- some shit!" I thought.

As he continued talking, I grew increasingly uncomfortable with the whole subject. I sat attentive in my chair and waited for my turn to talk.

"Of course you know," he continued, "John's been with us for a while now and we all try to get along here. We're a small group and we all have to work together, you know what I mean, get along so to speak."

"Yes sir, I understand."

"I told him I would speak with you and get your side of the story" he paused.

"Well I'd actually thought of speaking to you about the issue myself but after some thought I had decided to dismiss it. But since you brought it up here's what actually happened," I said. I then went in chronological order telling him exactly what had happened, being careful not to say anything that would have made him think the actions I had chosen were anything other than business. When I'd finished Attorney Richards looked away thoughtfully. I held my breath for his response.

"I see" he said tapping his fingers together, holding them up in a prayer like fashion.

119

"Well as I told John, I wanted to speak with you to get your side of the story. I will be speaking with him later and I will definitely uphold your actions."

"Thank you sir."

"Shena, is she here today?"

I told him I wasn't sure but I'd be happy to check. He asked me not to bother and said he would handle it. We continued to discuss some of the facts of my case and I was dismissed to return to my desk. As I walked out of his office, I noticed John standing at his desk, looking in my direction grinning. I looked at him and shook my head in disbelief as I continued on to my desk.

The rest of the day compared to that was pretty uneventful. I conducted my phone interviews and gave some memos to Shena for typing. She was noticeably quite but I didn't care. I assumed she was still upset over the night before and I didn't give a damn. Hell, I was pissed too! But I refused to let her know it!

At the end of the day while everyone was leaving Shena came over to my desk. Sensing her presence I didn't bother to look up as she provocatively walked up to me and placed a note on my desk. Against my better judgment I picked it up and read aloud the number that was scribbled on it.

"What's this? I asked still looking at the paper.

"My telephone number," she said casually.

"What's it for"

"For you to call me"

"Why?"

"I thought maybe we could work on the case. But it's up to you. I'm bout it - bout it!"

"Bout it - bout it?" I asked, unclear as to what she meant.

"Yeah bout it bout it," she repeated and walked off.

I sat there with the number in my hand wondering what kind of childish game she was playing now. I balled up the paper and tossed it in the garbage can beside my desk and left.

When I got home that evening I was exhausted. I walked over to the stereo and put in my favorite Luther Vandross CD and made my way to the shower. As the hot water beat down on my tired body, my mind replayed the events of the day.

"What the hell was that all about?" I said aloud. First her boyfriend tries to get me in trouble with the boss and she doesn't say shit to me all day. Then she gives me her phone number?!" *"Uhn huh, sabotage!"* I thought.

"It's got to be a set up." I said aloud, proud of myself for recognizing the bullshit. "Hump, like I'm really going to stick a quarter up my ass and play myself. Yeah right!! Wait on it motherfuckers!" I yelled out in the quiet empty apartment.

When Renée got back from New Orleans she seemed different. I asked her how her trip had gone and she was pretty much non-responsive. After she saw I wasn't going to let it rest she told me her cousin was in meetings most of time leaving her to find things to do on her own. Secretly I was glad but a little pissed. If that was the case, then I could have gone and did the same thing! My attempts to get any affection from her fell on deaf ears which only made me speculate wildly as to what was really going on with her. Her defense was that school was stressing her and she had a lot on her mind.

Meanwhile, at work, things were becoming a bit stressful for me as well. My case had come and gone and the client had won. But that victory was overshadowed by rumors that I was cock blocking on John and Shena! Fed up with both of them, I confronted Shena. She of course denied any knowledge of the rumor and because it wasn't directly affecting her, ignored it. I accused John of starting the rumors but she quickly came to his defense. In Shena's eyes John could do no wrong and portrayed him as a good friend who cared for her and wouldn't do anything that childish. But I knew better. I had seen his kind before. The all "Too-secure male" who really wasn't secure at all! The kind that's threatened by anyone he thinks can satisfy a woman better than he could. And in his case it didn't take much. Still, that was his problem, not mine and I was sick of his childish behavior and bullshit. Unlike him, I didn't dislike him because of Shena, I disliked him because he was foolish as hell and got on my last fucking nerves.

When Love Aint Enough

Whenever she and I talked, he watched us like a buzzard watching his prey. At times I even found myself stooping to his level.

Though she and I weren't romantically involved there was definitely something there. But it wasn't just with me. She was the same way with him. I naively thought she was trying to make me jealous to make me step up to the plate.

At home things were deteriorating fast. Renee's soap box had fast become keeping up with the Jones. There was a Lesbian group she'd been a member of for sometime but because of her studies she had backed off. Now she was back in full force, attending meetings, entertaining them at the house and going to parties. I, of course, clashed with all of them, even their lovers. They were pretentious and overbearing in their ideas of what a true lesbian should be. But Renée was my wife. So whenever they threw a party or had one of their little modeling shows, I was obliged to show my face.

This was yet another topic to argue about. In the midst of all the arguing our relationship was taking a beating. In the beginning we made love like rabbits, morning, noon and night. Now making love became a rarity at our place. And when it did happen it was more out of a sense of obligation than any real feeling or emotion. We became like robots that were programmed to talk a certain way, act a certain way and fuck a certain way.

123

One Sunday morning while doing the laundry I found a key in the dryer. The key had the name of a Biloxi hotel on it. When I asked Renée about it she shrugged me off saying it wasn't hers. Well I was pretty damn sure it wasn't mine so we argued! Renée accused me of being a control freak. After about 45 minutes of heated arguing she locked herself in the guest room and I left. I drove down to the beach to grab a beer to get my head together.

I didn't want to believe she was cheating on me but where else could the key have come from and why else would she have it. Her behavior for the past few months had been suspicious, to say the least. And lately if I walked into a room and she was on the phone she would either walk out or end the conversation abruptly. People had even begun calling the house and hanging up whenever I answered the phone. Any attempts to talk to her about it only started an argument that led to one of us isolating ourselves from the other.

When I first realized I was attracted to Shena I tried to dismiss the idea. Though Shena was beautiful, I was in love with Renee. I felt she and I had a future together and I couldn't imagine giving that up for a cheap affair.

Renée had brought me out of the darkness I'd surrounded myself in after losing Nahdy. She'd made me want to live again. But now she was pushing me away and I didn't know why. I wanted desperately to get back what we once shared. But we'd become strangers to one another.

As I drove up the beach my office pager went off. I had a voicemail. Deep down I hoped it was Renee calling. But when I checked it I found it was from Shena. In a hurry to get out of the house, I'd left my cell phone so I stopped at the first pay phone I saw.

Shena needed a favor and asked me to call her. I did. She and her boyfriend had been fighting. She said she wouldn't be in because she had a black eye and bruises. The dog in me wanted to run to her rescue but common sense prevailed. Instead I told her I'd cover for her. She thanked me and we hung up.

Later that week, she came in looking like the same ol' Shena. She and John resumed their ritual of flirting from morning till evening and I quickly dismissed my earlier thoughts of getting payback on Renee by trying to get in her panties. Her behavior constantly appalled me and I couldn't for the life of me understand why I felt such a strong attraction for someone who was so damn fickle.

Yet again I tried to step aside and get out of the triangle. After all, I had enough drama at home! To entertain more at work might make me snap.

At some point during the day, she realized I wasn't playing her little game, she came to my desk. She was wearing stonewashed jeans and snug fitting crème Cashmere sweater. As

125

I watched her approach I was more resolved than ever to end the game. After all,

"*Enough is enough*" I thought. *This broad just wants attention and she don't care who from. She aint said shit to me all day so now what? She can miss me"*

When she arrived I looked up casually then returned my attention to the documents on my desk."

"I appreciate you covering for me Casey"

"Its cool" I said trying not show my agitation with her.

She took it as a welcome sign and perched herself on the corner of my desk and started talking. I must admit, the girl had a way of disarming a person because before I knew it, I was engrossed in her conversation and genuinely enjoying her presence. But reality soon crept back in as I glimpsed the "nut" out of the corner of my eye, staring in our direction. I could have kicked myself in the butt for falling for the okey doke again. Shena, noticing my sudden edginess tried to save the declining conversation by inviting me out for cocktails after work. Though the idea was tempting I was now thinking with the right head again and new it would only pull me deeper into the madness, so I declined politely. Unbeknownst to me, Shena wasn't about to accept no for an answer. She grew insistent, claiming it would do me good.

"I don't see why not, you look like you could use one."

She was right on point with her assertion but I wasn't about to admit it. So again, I declined and asked for a rain check. But as I did, John walked past us and our eyes met. The smug look on his face made me want to "bitch slap him." Sensing his presence had served its purpose he smiled, and imitating me, shook his head. I watched him as he walked over to Shena's desk and took a seat. And there he sat perched like the buzzard he was with his long gangly legs spread wide apart slouched down in the chair as if he was at the club waiting on a lap.

His whole appearance reeked of fake masculinity. I figured anybody that tried that hard must have a lot of sexual identity issues. Years later I learned I'd hit the nail on the proverbial head! But for today, pride kicked in and I felt it my duty to show the bitch that he was just that, a bitch. And if he really wanted to fuck with someone he had chosen the right one!

So I stroked the devils dick and accepted Shena's invitation. She was more surprised than I was to hear me say yes.

She smiled seductively and glanced toward her desk. She quickly looked back at me but didn't dare say a word. I didn't bother to either. Shena excused herself then walked down the isle. About fifteen minutes later she called my extension.

"This is Casey" I answered casually

"What time do you want to leave?"

Surprised that she still wanted to go after talking to big boy, I said,

"I'm ready when you are"

"Ok, I'll be through in ten minutes"

"Am I following you or what?" I asked already knowing the answer.

"You know I don't like driving"

"Ok cool".

The devil had bit me on the ass again and I was back in the game once more.

Since we'd found Chatterley's to be so much fun we decided to go again. It wasn't as full as the first time we'd went but the crowd was still nice for a weekday.

We were seated almost immediately. After a couple of drinks we ordered appetizers. For the first time in weeks I was actually enjoying myself. It was a great stress reliever being able to get out and forget about the chaos that surrounded me and Renee. Still out of a sense of loyalty I called her and told her of my plans before leaving the office. To my surprise she was cool with it and told me to have fun. Before hanging up she asked me to call her when I left so we could meet me at the apartment. I happily said ok.

As Shena and I talked I tried hard not to bring up the subject of the idiot , but it came up anyway. Shena laughed.

"Why are you laughing?"

"Cause all that boy wants to do is eat my pussy!"

"I don't believe that!"

"For real, I've gone to his place a couple of times and each time he begs to do it.

"Girl please, ain't no real man gonna stop at eating your pussy!

She laughed.

"Its like I told you before, he can't get it up."

"So when was the last time you let him do that."

"It's been about a month."

I calculated the time in my head and flashed back at her,

"That's around the time you and I were working on the case together, right."

"Yeah…"

"But you told me then y'all were just friends."

"We were and still are. That didn't mean anything to me" she insisted. He likes me and I know it so I'm not going to hurt his feelings, he's nice."

"That messed up. But it explains why he's been acting so damn crazy with me"

"Yeah but I ain't into him. He's not my type and for the last time the boy can't get his dick up!"

"Girl please, the boy is eating you out daily and can't get it up and then there's me. I think you know you're driving the nigga crazy with jealousy and trying to do the same to me. But if I haven't said it before, I will say it now, as far as I'm concerned, I wouldn't mind hitting that but I don't have no plans to leave my wife."

Shena looked up from the straw she was sucking on and laughed.

129

"What makes you think I would let you hit it?"

"Oh you'd let me."

"Naw baby, it ain't that easy, because if I'd wanted you to have it you would have had it by now. I'm not gay!"

"I didn't say you were. I'm just letting you know the rules."

"Well we'd better go because you are talking crazy, because this ain't even free!"

"You've been letting him lap on it like it was."

"Fuck you! You don't know me."

"You're right I don't and you don't know me."

Shena glared at me and I smiled back and continued to sip on my cocktail. We left thirty minutes later.

When I arrived home the apartment was dark. Then I remembered what Renée had said about calling her. I took out my phone but decided not to. It was no since interrupting her just because my night ended abruptly.

I opened the door without turning on the lights and made my way to the bedroom. As I walked up to the door and reached for the knob I heard the faint sound of moaning coming from inside. My heart began to quicken as I leaned in to peep through the cracked door. The only light in the room came from the bathroom. Still I was able to make out the upper part of Renee's unclothed body. The covers had been pushed aside and her head was turned toward the opposite wall, as she moaned and ran her hands slowly across her breast and stomach. Nervously I nudged at the door to see more of what was going on inside.

Then I did, another female kneeling on the floor at the foot of bed carrying the weight of Renée's short legs on her shoulders and eating her out like 'ninety going north'!

The blood rushed through my veins and into my face sending me flying into the room, kicking the door wide open and throwing on the lights. The women, both butt naked were jumping about like rats as they searched frantically for clothes. Renée, clutching a sheet she'd grabbed off the floor made a step toward me but thought better of it and stopped dead in her tracks. She stared at me in disbelief while the other chic hid behind her.

"What the fuck...." I yelled as I walked toward both of them, throwing my brief case to the floor.

The girl, still hiding behind Renée, seized the opportunity to run into the closet and closed the door. As I walked over to the dresser, Renee stopped me by pulling at my arm. Tearfully she tried to reason with me. I pushed her aside and rambled through the drawers tossing socks and panties out as I searched for my gun. Renée's face grew white as the sheet she was holding when she realized what I was looking for. Out of the blue she lunged at me pushing me up against the dresser and catching my hand in the drawer.

"Get the fuck off me Renee" I yelled, pulling my bruised hand from the drawer and knocking her to the floor with the other one. Not about to let me get my hands on the gun, she struggled to her feet and charged me again. This time she

131

grabbed a fist full of my hair. I froze me in my tracks and tried to pry her hands loose.

"Let my hair go!"

"Stop then!" she commanded

Since she wouldn't let go I decided to choke her! We struggled violently each demanding that the other let go first. In the midst of the fight I pinned her to the wall. It was a draw. We stood face to face, looking fiercely into each others eyes. I was prepared to choke the shit out of her while she held on to my hair for dear life. Tears rolled down my face as I searched her eyes for something of the person I had once adored and who I thought adored me. But the look she gave back told me I didn't know her at all.

She was no longer the person who'd brought me out of the darkness. No, this person standing before me was something else. A person I didn't know nor did I want to know. My tears were coming faster now. Slowly I let go of her. She looked at me with blank surprise then cautiously let go of my hair as well and tried to explain. I shook my head violently not wanting to hear a damn thing she had to say. Calmly I walked over to the closet and flung it open.

"Get the fuck out of my house bitch before I kill you!" I yelled at the still nude woman, hiding inside. That was all she needed to hear. She tried to run past me but she wasn't quick enough to escape my foot that connected with the crack of her butt as when she went by me. She let out a low whimper as she scurried out of my kicking range.

I stormed into the closet and grabbed a bag from the shelf and started throwing clothes in it. In a trance like state I pulled clothes from the racks three and four items at a time, stuffing them inside it.

After the bag was full I began throwing the clothes on the floor beside it. Renée rushed in begging me not to leave but to listen to what she had to say. I stopped.

"Bitch I ain't going nowhere! You are!"

"What!! Baby please listen to me, calm down!" she screamed. The word *baby* was a slap me in the face after what I'd just witnessed!

"Calm down! I walk in here and find your ass fucking someone in my bed and you want me to calm down! Have you've lost your fucking mind!"
She stopped in mid syllable upon realizing her words only added fuel to the fire.

"For months you've been walking around here like I don't exist. And like a fool I let you because I didn't want to be a 'nag' about it. Now you go and do this to me!! You brought a bitch in our home and fucked her in our bed!!

"That's not true!" she screamed with out stretched hands.

"It is true! Do you hate me that much Renée? Huh!!" I cried as tears rolled down my face onto my white linen blouse.

"Well do you?! Do you hate me that much?!!" I screamed at her again.

Renée was crying now and holding her hands up to her face.

"I'm the motherfucker who takes care of you Renee! I'm that motherfucker!" I said, walking past her and back into the bedroom, pushing aside the vanity she used to sit at doing her makeup while I watched adoringly.

"And this is how you repay me!!! BITCH GET YOUR SHIT AND GET OUT!"

"Baby please…"

"Please my ass! Renee get out of here before I do something we'll both regret!

"I'm not going no where until you calm down and talk to me," she begged.

Her words incited me to run up to her and push her violently against the wall.

"What?!...oh yeah you're going bitch! You're going if I have to pick your ass up and throw you out!"

I grabbed her by the arm and she swung her fist, hitting me just above my left eyebrow. And the fight was on! As I struggled to subdue her, I wiped at the sweat pouring down my face. I rubbed the sweat on my blouse and noticed it was red. I wasn't sweating at all, I was bleeding like a pig!

I ran into the bathroom to look in the mirror. My forehead and face was covered with blood. Renée had stabbed me with the keys she held in her hands. I thought I'd pass out as the

134

blood gushed from the head, down my face and onto my clothes. I staggered out past Renee and over to the dresser. This time I found my gun and pulled it out.

Though I always kept it unloaded Renee didn't know it. She was terribly afraid of guns, so the minute she saw me pull it from the drawer she started running. I walked calmly behind her to make sure she was leaving. The sheet she'd been holding got caught on the door knob as she ran butt naked out into the still night and jumped into her car. When she was tucked away safely in the car she sat looking at me as I stood in the doorway. I pointed the gun at her and she quickly started up the car and sped out of the parking lot. I went back inside locking the door behind me.

I cleaned myself up and drove to the nearest emergency room. The doctor told me that if the puncture had gone a fraction of an inch deeper I could have sustained a serious injury. As it was, the wound required stitches, eight of them.

To my dismay he continuously asked me how it happened. I held on to the lie that I'd fallen on my keys and stabbed myself. While being stitched up, my mind constantly replayed the night's events. It was like a bad dream. I couldn't believe Renée had betrayed me like that. I felt stupid for all the bragging I had done earlier about her to Shena. I soon grew too tired to think about it any more. And I grew numb.

135

I got home around three am and walked into an empty apartment. It was in shambles. Renée had come back while I was out and gotten some of her things. That was fine. I didn't want to see or hear from her. I made a mental note to have the locks changed and go from there. Exhausted, I showered and went into guestroom to sleep. When I finally fell asleep all I dreamed about was her.

The phone rang waking me up around 10 the next morning. It was Lionel, Renee had called him to tell him about the fight and asked him to talk to me.

"Hey Girl"

"Hey what's up?"

"Are you alright? Ms. Renée called me late last night…" he started.

"Oh really,"

"She said ya'll got into it and you pulled a pistol on her."

"A pistol?! Naw I pulled a gun on that bitch!" I announced. Lionel laughed.

"What in the hell happened? That don't even sound like something you'd do!"

"I came home last night and caught her nasty ass in my bed with some chic between her legs!"

"Whaaa-t?!"

"Yeah, I caught her fucking some girl in my bed!"

"You got to be kidding. No Miss Thang didn't get caught doing the do and then called me with a sob ass story saying you'd went crazy!!" Lionel announced surprised.

"Naw I aint lost my mind by a long damn shot. What I should have lost was my foot up in her narrow ass!!"

"No you have to much to loose to be fighting? But you're right that was some trifling shit she did!"

"Yep very trifling!"

"Well, are you okay? She said your head started bleeding while y'all were tussling."

"She stabbed me with a key!"

"Girl now you got to be joking. Renée stabbed you with a key?"

"Yeah"

"Casey you're lucky you ain't dead or somethin"

"I know it. And to think I've been practically running from pussy on her behalf."

"Well you the fool! The only running I'm going to do is to get to some not from some, love or no love!"

"I know! I am a fool. But mark my word, o'l girl at work is going to get some of this and that's for sure."

"What's her name? Have I met her?"

"Naw man, her name is Shena and she's fine as hell too! I just didn't want to do it like that but you see what I get for trying to do the right thing, fucked!"

137

"Well all I know is you deserve better than that shit" Miss Renee was wrong, dead wrong!"

"Yeah" I said quietly not knowing if I did or not. Either way, I told Lionel all about Shena. I even told him about the docu-drama I'd been going through on her behalf with John. Lionel didn't believe in straddling the fence sexually. With him either you gay or straight, yet he was sympathetic to my situation and cautioned me to watch where I stepped when it came to her.

Lionel and I continued to talking about the fight and what was to come next. That was the big question, what next? I loved Renée but after last night I didn't see any way for us to possibly get past this? It was the first time we'd ever fought. My heart ached at the thought of what she'd done. I knew we had problems but disrespect on that level was inconceivable.

Before hanging up we made plans to meet for lunch at the Café. It was located in downtown Gulfport on the beach. It was an area where tourist went to shop and party called The Bordeaux. The streets were lined with restaurant taverns and novelty stores. The Café had an outdoor deck for those who wanted to enjoy the beach front view. I liked to sit out there to watch the tourist at play.

It was around three pm when I finished cleaning up. I met Lionel at the Café around five. He was already seated on the veranda with a cocktail in tow.

As I walked up, he stood to greet me with a hug. It had been a minute since we'd hung out due to our busy schedules. If he wasn't on the road with the symphony I busy trying to meet some timeline. Our lives had become quite complex since college.

We sat on the veranda sipping our cocktails, watching the passers by and playing catch up. Lionel wasn't the type to pry so he waited for me to bring up the fight. But I didn't. I was tired of thinking about it and chose not to bore him with my problems.

Aside from being concerned about what was going on with me, things with Lionel was looking really good. The symphony was about to take their annual European tour and he was ecstatic. It would be his first trip.

"Girl can you see me in gay Pa'ris?"

I thought on it for a moment.

"Yep" I said as we both burst into laughter.

"Baby girl I worry about you. Like now you look like you're a million miles away"

"I'm good. I'm sore as hell, but I'm good"

"You need to get out more Casey, I've told you that. You aint gonna solve nothing by hiding in your shell every time there's a crisis."

"I know Lionel. I'm just so tired. I'm tired of this man!"

"Tired of what, life?"

"Is this life. I mean, you work hard, you devote yourself to another person and all for what. Everything is subject to chance. I'm tired of living my life like this. I want to be settled"

"Shit as long as I've known you that's all you've ever wanted to be! I aint never met nobody who wanted to settle down as much as you do!"

"What's wrong with that?"

"Nothing, but it's like you want everything to be perfect all the time and life's not like that."

"No, I don't want everything to be perfect but it would be nice if I could at least have some peace every once in a while and not have to go through this shit. Cause see, Renee didn't have to do it like that. I didn't put a gun to her head make her stay there."

"Well girl you did pull a pistol" Lionel said joking trying to make me lighten up.

"Look bitch, I'm for real and I told you, that wasn't a pistol it was nine millimeter and I would have used it too if she hadn't broke up out of there!"

"Girl you wasn't gonna do shit! You aint nothing but a big baby and if Renee's whorish ass had any sense she'd get her act together cause she aint gonna find another Casey"

"You really think so man?"

"Casey, baby, you're hot, you know that! You're independent and you have a good heart what else could a person want?"

"Sometimes I think this gay shit is all a waste of time. Hell if I'd been straight I know I would have been married by now and have at least 2.5 kids. I'd have a family."

"Yeah you would but would you be happy living a lie"

"But it wouldn't be a lie, I would be straight"

"Then it wouldn't be you"

I looked off into the crowded sidewalks.

"But it just seems like it never lasts" I said thinking about both Nahdia and Renee.

"It will when you meet the right one"

"But I did, Nahdia…"

"Baby, I know but that was different, now you've got to go on and you can't let these people pull you down like that, you're better than that, a hell of a lot better.

"Thanks Lionel"

"You're welcome, just watch your gonna meet miss right when you least expect it and live happily ever after!"

.

It had been two weeks since Renée and I'd fought. She was staying with some friends, or so she said and I was at the apartment alone. In her vain attempts toward forgiveness she sent me a dozen roses with a card begging me to take her back. I trashed both the card and the flowers.

Daily I immersed myself into my work to preoccupy my wandering mind from the thoughts that were constantly flooding my head. Most times I found myself questioning whether it was something I'd done to drive her to someone else. It was a hard pill to swallow, admitting your lover needed or wanted someone other you.

One evening I decided to take my work home with me instead of staying late in the office. Shena, sensing my agitation offered to come along to help me. I thought it was a good idea and invited her over.

After completing most of our action items we decided to get some take out from a nearby Chinese restaurant. As we walked back in the door the phone rang. I checked the Caller ID then laid it back down. Shena watched me curiously as I walked off into the kitchen to get something to drink. I grabbed a bottle of wine from the racks and two glasses. I walked back, plopped down on the sofa with Shena. As I began eating my food, the phone started ringing again. This time I picked it up and turned the ringer off.

"Renee could go fuck herself!" I thought angrily.

Then it hit me! If it was good enough for Renée, it was good enough for me. Shena was immersed in the wrestling match as I coyly reached over and placed my hand around her shoulder. She jumped, kicking over her wine glass that sat at her feet and spilling what was left to be eaten of her food on the sofa. Surprised by her reaction, I jumped back to my side of the sofa.

"What's up with that?" She asked nervously using her napkin to clean up the mess she'd made.

"What's up with what?" I repeated wishing like hell I could disappear.

"You're not crazy! What's up with the arm and everything?" Sensing I was under attack I went on the defensive

"You have been giving me the come on for months, what's up with you?" I asked genuinely confused at her reaction.

"Oh and that gives you a right to feel me up like that?"

"Feel you up! Hell you're the one that said you were bout it bout it"

"Naw slick you got me wrong. I like to flirt but I aint gay, I told you that!"

My face grew hot. This was more of the same shit and I was not amused.

"Well guess what…you can find someone else to flirt and play your childish games with because I'm not amused"

"I'm aint been playing no games. I aint never done nothing like that before Casey!"

"Like what?"

"I've never been with a woman before" she said softly, sensing I was pissed and it was probably her fault.

"Well you sure fooled the hell out of me!"

Now I was pissed for real. I looked at her then looked away.

"Why was it always so easy for everybody else but when I wanted to step out there was always a problem, damn" I thought.

143

The thought of trying to convince someone, anyone, to be with me was an insult. Shit, as far as I was concerned I could do without it! I really hated Renee now! It had been so easy for her to cheat on me but now, when I tried to return the favor with a person who's been practically throwing the pussy at me for months, I had to hear this!

"Fuck it!" I thought.

I got up from the sofa and stalked off into the kitchen to get something stronger to drink. All I had was beer in the fridge. I popped the top off and took a long swig. Shena was still standing when I returned. I walked over to the bay window and sat down.

"Oh so now you're mad?"

"Naw I aint mad" I said half pouting half wanting to put her the fuck out of my house.

Shena walked over to me and stood watching me. She ran her hand through my hair and smiled.

"I'm sorry if I made you think I was gay. And I'm not trying to get turned out either"

I laughed slightly.

"That's it. Now I'm recruiting members. Shit it don't get no better than this," I thought angrily.

"Well I don't think I have the powers to make you gay if you're not," I said sarcastically.

"But you do have the power to take me too fast"

I took another long gulp of my beer and looked out the window. The expression on her face was unnerving. She was a hard person to read and I was tired of trying to figure anything out. I got up from my seat and walked back into the kitchen with my empty beer bottle. I sat it on the counter and grabbed another one.

"What about your wife?" she yelled to me

"What about her?"

"The other night you were saying how much you loved her now today you want to fuck me!"

I stood in the kitchen until I'd finished my beer then walked over to her and stared deep into her big brown eyes.

"No you're wrong! I didn't want to fuck you! I wanted to make love to you. Can you handle that?"

Shena pondered the question for a moment then answered,

"Maybe"

I looked at her suspiciously. Timidly I held out my hand.

"Then let's do this"

She took it but whispered softly,

"But I'm not ready yet Casey"

"Ah man come on this is crazy," I said dropping her hand and walking back to the window.

"Shena, I want you, you know that. I guess I've always wanted you but I was with Renee. Now she's gone and there's only you and I left. And for some stupid reason I actually allowed myself to believe that you wanted me too"

"Maybe I do" she admitted. "But not as some rebound case. Why do you have to go so fast! You can't expect me to do it like that. It's not fair!"

I hung my head down, shaking it frustration.
Deep down I knew she was right but I was tired of trying to play fair. No one had bothered to play fair with me. Not Renee, not God for taking Nahdy and not even her. But if she didn't want to do what I wanted to do I refused to try to convince her. Either she was game or she wasn't. It was as simple as that! I stood firm in my convictions not to beg and continued to stare out the window.

Moments later the vibration of her footsteps on the carpet sent chills up my spine as she walked up behind me and put her arms around my neck. Her body pressed up against mine awakening the butterflies and weakening my knees. My tired soul ached for her. It took everything I had in me not to spin around and sweep her up into my arms and get lost in her love. But instead I chilled and waited on her to make the first move. I had made one too many already and none had panned out. The ball was in her court.

She pressed her lips to my ear and whispered softly,
"Kiss me"
My palms grew sweaty and my head spun lightly from a combination of excitement and the two St Pauli's Girls I had drank.

I allowed her to turn me around as she slipped her arms around my waist. Clumsily I leaned in to kiss her only to be stopped by her hand.

"Softly" she cautioned.

I slipped my arms under hers, directing them up to my stiffening shoulders and pulled her close to me. Gently I etched my face toward hers then gently pressed my full lips on her tiny mouth. My head began to lighten as she sucked and nibbled at my lips until I thought I would pass out from the butterflies stirring around in my pelvis.

Kissing her felt familiar, as familiar as drinking a glass of cold water on a hot a summers day. Anxiously we made our way to the floor as I pushed back the stack of papers with my foot. Gently I lay on top of her and unbuttoned her clothes with one hand and softly squeezed her treasure chest with the other.

I pulled up her skirt and pushed aside the black lace panties that sheltered her spot. A warm stream of air escaped from it as though imprisoned, brushing against my trembling fingers as I pushed them inside her. Had my fingers been a thermometer the heat would have made the mercury come to a boil.

Reluctantly I pulled my lips from the tender clutches of her teeth and did some biting of my own running mine across the print, her hard nipples made in her blouse. They grew rock hard as I blew on their imprint and sucked them softly through her blouse. Shena moaned as I unbuttoned her blouse with my

147

mouth, freeing her breast from bondage. I held them firmly and sucked each one deep into my warm mouth.

She moved rhythmically beneath me pushing her pelvis up into mine as I positioned myself on top her pressing my aching clitoris strategically where I knew hers to be and grinding sensually into her spot as if I was trying to make a baby. Her lips parted slightly to whisper my name as her eyes rolled back in her head from the sensation, but nothing came out. Gently I brushed her hair way from her face and kissed her passionately as we continued to grind in anticipation of a good fucking.

Abruptly I stopped and got up from the floor and ran into the bedroom. My heart raced wildly as I searched about the bedroom closet. My spot ached terribly longing for the grinding movements of her body on mine again. Eagerly I slipped on Charlie, which seemed to pacify my spot for a moment and put on a pair of silk boxers. When I returned Shena was lying in the fetal position with her eyes closed.

I got back down on the floor and spooned her from behind allowing Charlie to race up her butt making his presence known. She turned around, and pulled me closer as I pumped slowly into her backside. Her ass seemed to welcome me as she scooted and pushed her butt into me twisting and turning, teasing me ever so slightly, letting me know that her pussy was at my beck and call.

I'd never been known to deny a lady so I rolled her onto her back and watched intently as she squirmed around on the carpet moving seductively, beckoning me feverishly to take her. I let

148

my lips do the talking as I began kissing every inch of her body while she clawed at my hair, pulling it, rubbing it, caressing it. Soon the sweet musky smell of a fresh pussy drew me to her bush. A girl almost couldn't see the forest for the trees. Her spot was immersed in a dense forest of black curly hair. As I tongued my way through it, my excitement grew in anticipation of finally hitting the mother load. When I reached my intended target I gently pushed the lips apart with my nose and slowly slid my tongue up and down her spot licking it as if it were my favorite ice cream.

She tasted wonderful. The aroma from her mound made me want to push Charlie deep inside her but I resisted. Instead, I tongued her ferociously as she moaned and pulled my mangled hair. Suddenly, out of nowhere a gush of fluid squirted out at me. I was more than a little surprised. She'd climaxed! But still, I had never seen it happen so soon before or so forcefully.

Now I wanted her more than ever. Gently I pulled her up to me and positioned her on her hands and knees. Slowly I licked her spot and traced the edged of her butt with my tongue. I took my love in my hand and pushed it inside her spot. Shena reeled back as though struck by lightening. I massaged her back assuring her it would be okay and continued to force my love in and out of her tight hole. We made love for what seemed an eternity. The more I pumped inside her the more I wanted to.

Finally, Shena fell to the floor and rolled over trembling. I crawled on top of her and slipped my love back into her bush.

149

We lay there not moving with me inside her. Slowly we began to grind into each other. Shena was screaming. I tried to quiet her by sticking my tongue in her mouth but it did no good. She would only twist away and scream louder.

Her movements were so wild that she threw me off of her. I grabbed her spot with my hand and stuck my fingers inside her rotating them vigorously. After regaining control of her, I eased back down between her legs started eating her as if I'd lost my mind. Shena began to cry as the joys of her climax took over her trembling body. I laid my head on top of her mound and rested.

A week, later Renee and I decided to meet at the Café for drinks. Though I was still furious with her, something in me missed her terribly. I wanted to believe her explanation about her affair with ol girl. She told me it was a one-time thing that meant nothing to her.

She knew all the right things to say to tug at my heart, reminding me of how much we'd shared, our dreams and that we once loved each other. Still, the betrayal I felt was consuming me. The conversation grew heated and we argued causing the other patrons to stare at times.

We continued to talk on and off for another week before I decided to give our relationship another try.

We needed to reacquaint ourselves with each other because we'd both changed. So she moved back in and we started over.

Now I was faced with the task if telling Shena.

But for the most part, things were okay with Shena and me. The second time we made love I gave her a gold antique bracelet, then I told her about Renée moving back in. She cried telling me that meant we wouldn't be giving us a real try. And though I was crazy about her, the John issue weighed heavily in my decision to try to work things out with Renée. I asked her for time to sort things out. She grudgingly said she would. And that made it official.

Though we were dating, she and John were still very close. She constantly tried to reassure me the relationship was purely platonic but I still didn't like it. So I gave her an ultimatum to stop dealing with him. But she used my decision to stay with Renee as her rational for "having friends" as she called it.

Meanwhile he continuously tried to manipulate situations into seeming I was harassing him. I eventually found myself in a tangled web of love and lust with Shena and a wife who was becoming increasingly suspicious. Deep down I wanted to end it with both women and just start over. But I couldn't. My fear of being alone again far out weighed my desire for peace of mind. So I stayed in the relationships even though anyone could plainly see that my life was spinning wildly out of control.

Shena and I continued to date for the next two years. And so did Renée and me. It was a hard juggling act because Renée had become increasingly suspicious and questioned damn near every move I made.

One summer's day, as Shena and I were riding down I-10 East, Renee drove up behind us. Shena was pouting because I had to go home. Trying to lighten her mood I leaned over to steal a kiss. As I returned to an upright position, a car, looking strikingly familiar, pulled up beside me. It was Renée and I was cold busted! Her face was visibly flushed and she was pointing wildly demanding that I pull over. Shocked shitless, I didn't know what to do! But I did know what not to do! I knew if I pulled over I was gonna have to fight and it was not going to be pretty, so I kept going hoping she would do the same.

But she didn't, instead she rammed her car into mine instantly driving my car off the road and across the median into the on coming highway traffic for I-10 west. The opposite fucking direction!

People say when you have a near death experience, your life passes before your eyes... mine didn't! Instead all I saw was Shena grabbing for the wheel and yelling like a crazy woman as we went from the grass to the street and then back into the grass!

When the car came to a halt I found myself reaching for the door to get out and check the damage to my car. But the thought was short lived as I glimpsed Renee's car trying to drive across the median still in hot pursuit. I scrambled back inside to a hysterically Shena screaming.

"Take me home!!" Sweat the size of golf balls, ran down my face as I yelled to her to be quite!

The front wheels were wobbling making the car difficult to control. I was forced to drive around 35 miles per hour as I made my getaway. And I was damned determined not to stop until I reached safety or found a police officer!

Renée had moved out when I got home. But before she did she left me something's to remember her by. Unable to get her hands on me she went through the house on a vindictive spree. She put my clothes in the fireplace and set them on fire. My shoes she carved into sandals with a razor and placed them back neatly in their assigned shoe box. Not one appliance escaped her wrath, with them she either cut off the cord or demolished it with a hammer. But the most impressive thing she did was to mix raw egg and cocoa and paint the underside of the white sofa cushions! I didn't learn of it until weeks later when it was too late to salvage the furniture. That bitch went off!! It was a fucking mess which can only be described as a woman scorned and gone fucking crazy!!

After leaving the police station I'd gone to Lionel's place. He convinced me to stay over night. When I found the mess she'd left for me , I thanked God for sparing me because I knew

if I'd I returned home that night one of us would not have lived
another day. Weeks later, she called trying to talk but by that
time I was scared to death of her!   So, when she threw out her
teary eyed plea for me to drop Shena I didn't. When I think
back on it now it wasn't so much that I loved Shena it was more
so that I no longer wanted Renee. Her cheating had killed all the
love I once thought was irrevocable.

"No, it's over Renee, I'm sorry."

I had taken a bold step by leaving one person for another one
and deep down I knew it. Because like my mom always said,

"Two wrongs don't make a right!"
And man was she ever right. Yep, I had been whooped by
Shena. Pussy whooped! And it was evident to everybody in the
world except my naïve ass. Instead I miss took it for love and I
was determined to hold on to her even if it killed me. And I
damn near got my wish!

I soon learned that not only did Shena not love me but I was
no longer the flavor of the week.
Our relationship came to an abrupt end after months of deceit.
The tables had turned on me when Renee was out of the picture
and it was only she and I. Shena dropped me like I was
yesterday's fashions.

Whenever she'd hear I was dating, she would comeback
with the same ol shit professing her love for me. And most

times I would foolishly take her back. Then she was off again doing whatever and whomever she wanted to do. I found myself doing a "Renee" hiding in bushes, (not literally) and combing the streets trying to find evidence of her infidelity.

At one stupid point in my life I had the nerve to blame myself for her cheating. She accused me of driving her crazy with my jealousy. And I bought it hook line and sinker until I caught her coming out of his apartment one night around three am. Yep, three in the morning! My dumb ass had been on stake out all night trying to get the goods on her. Her response to being caught was she needed someone to talk to. And even then I didn't leave her ass alone! I just hollered like the bitch I'd become and tried to make her jealous. But one thing I learned was you can't make a person jealous who don't give a damn!

I realized my problem was rejection. I couldn't imagine her rejecting me for him. And even though I no longer respected or desired her love I couldn't handle the word 'no'.

In the process of trying to keep the one- sided relationship alive, I'd done irreparable damage to my credibility. I made of fool of myself in front of my peers. It was if I forgot who I was or what I was. I'd fell off and it was time to get own with my life.

I applied for a position with a firm in Norfolk, VA and got it. An old friend, Kris Fuqua, lived there. She helped me plan the move. And I was excited about the change.

Kris and I had been friends since Law School. We'd met one night after a game between Melbourne and Southern University. James had tricked me into going. After the game everyone went to the Bar for the after party. That's where we met.

She was about six feet tall and had a slightly boyish build. She was slim with a pecan tan complexion. Her hair was dreaded and spoke with a thick Caribbean accent.

She and I were competing for a bartender's attention. She saw my Melbourne sweatshirt and started talking shit! We struck up a conversation and the rest was history. We exchanged numbers and stayed in contact.

When I arrived in Norfolk, Kris took me around, introducing me to everyone she knew. On those nights when I was feeling especially melancholy, she baby-sat me at her restaurant, Claude's. It was like old times.

Jade

Jade and I had our ups and down like most couples. Lately we had more downs than ups because of her closeted behavior. She was truly the girl of my dreams. I think I loved her from the first moment I set eyes on her in Claude's, Kris's Caribbean Restaurant on the Seaboard. That was over two years ago. But after years of trying to convince her that it was okay to love me openly she was still no closer to commitment than she'd been since we first got together.

I'd been in Norfolk for over four years when I met her. She and Kris were friends. But our getting together wasn't a set up, in fact Kris warned me against pursuing her, saying she was straight. But I was hard headed. I saw something I wanted and went after it. According to Kris I didn't have a snow ball's chance in hell of getting with her.

On this particular night, I was feeling good and I looked even better. As I made my way through the foyer I caught a glimpse of her and Kris standing near the bar. When I saw her something inside me told me to go for it. So I did. I walked over and said hello. Kris smiled and introduced us. We exchanged pleasantries and sized each other up. A couple of minutes later, I excused myself to go sit at the bar. She smiled

157

and my heart was hers. It was a brief smile but I felt
encouraged. I walked away confident she was watching me as I
did so. When I got to the bar I chose a seat that would give me
an indirect view of her.

    I sat sipping margaritas and stealing peeks at Jade. Once I
caught her stealing one back. I casually looked past her
pretending I was wildly interested in something else. I must
have been convincing because she turned slightly to look also.
When she did, I quickly returned my attention to my menu and
continued sipping on my drink.

    "What's up man?"
  I looked up to see Kris with a big grin on her face. I
instinctively looked over in Jade's direction but saw she'd
disappeared into the crowd. I looked back at Kris.
    "Nothing man, trying to get some of this fine cuisine."
    "You talking about the menu or Jade"
    "The menu smart ass," I grinned.
  Kris sat down on the stool beside me and called the bartender
over to us.
    "Hey, this is my best friend, whatever she wants is on the
house" Kris instructed.
The young man looked at me again, this time with a familiar
look.

"Damn!" I thought. *"Is it me or does every person in this world see two gay women together and assume they're having each other."*

After he'd walked away I looked at Kris and elbowed her.

"There you go trying to bitch me out again. He probably thinks I'm another one of your little women trying to get a freebie."

"What ever he thinks he better keep it to himself because I run this"

We looked at each other and burst out laughing.

"Any-way, what's the verdict? Did she say anything after I left?

"She was cool, I don't think she knew you were coming on to her though," said Kris looking at me with the silly grin still plastered on her face, waiting for me to beg for more information.

"So she didn't say anything huh?"

Kris shook her head.

"That's cool, I didn't expect her to throw me her panties and fall at my feet" I said surprised she hadn't said anything.

"Calm down, she did say she likes your hair."

"My hair, really?" I blushed.

"Yeah, really," said Kris.

I laughed to myself,

"Gottcha"

Kris and I talked for a while then she left to mingle and check on her staff.

Kris was one cool pimp! I watched her as she walked around her restaurant meeting and greeting everyone. They all seemed to like her, men and women both. And she seemed genuinely pleased to see each of them. Though she towered over most of the females and some of the males, her presence was soft and inviting. I was truly happy for her success. She'd worked hard to get where she was today. It wasn't easy for an openly gay woman to enter into the trenches of the culinary world, exceed expectations and beat the odds.

Claude's was a testimony to her success. It was highly acclaimed for its food and rich authentic atmosphere. People came from all over to enjoy the Claude's experience.

After polishing off a healthy serving of buttery lobster ettufee' and black bread, I tipped the barkeep and waived goodbye to Kris.

On Labor Day weekend Kris hosted her annual invitation only, Caribbean barbecue at the restaurant. I arrived early to get a good table. When I got there I realized half the guest list must have had the same idea.

I parked my Mercedes M 500 and jumped out to wade through the sea of people standing around in the parking lot. The deck was lined with tiki torches seductively inviting the patrons in. The band had just finished setting up and was churning out music already. Bartenders, dressed in khaki shorts and black tees were busy serving up drinks.

When I stepped unto the deck and saw all the couples I felt a bit awkward. I immediately decided I wasn't going to stay long.

"I'll show my face, then I'm dipping!"

I walked directly to the bar and ordered a bucket of Coronas and a margarita. Then I luckily snagged a table near the band and the exit steps.

Kris had outdone herself. And by the look of things it was going to be pretty nice. Despite my earlier misgivings, I relaxed and tried to enjoy myself.

It was a beautiful day for a barbeque as the sun hung high in the sky pouring down warmth through the broken clouds. The ocean, 20 feet below the restaurant, rolled gently onto the beach as a flurry of seagulls darted in and out of the water plucking their holiday meal from its clutches.

I'd been sitting there for about hour sipping cocktails and enjoying the band when someone tapped me on the shoulder. I turned around to see Jade's smiling face.

She was wearing blue jean skorts and a pink tank top that cutoff at midriff exposing her caramel colored abs. Her shoulder length, sandy brown hair blew gently with each lazy breeze from the ocean. Every muscle in my body grew tense as I smiled back nervously.

161

"You must have got here early to get such a good spot," she kidded.

"Yeah kind of," I laughed.

"We thought we were doing something by coming 30 minutes early but the parking lot was packed when we got here!" She said looking around the deck at all the people.

"It was kind of full when I got here an hour ago," I said awkwardly.

There was a brief silence as we both looked around at all the people.

"Are you here alone?"

"No I'm with some friends," she said turning to point at two other gorgeous women standing in the line at the bar waiting to be served.

"Cool…"

"Are you here with anyone?" She asked to my surprise.

"No, No, I just came by to show face so Kris wouldn't call me a bum for not showing up," I kidded.

She laughed though I knew my joke wasn't that funny.

"Do y'all have a table yet?"

"Nope not yet' she responded looking around to find one.

"Well nobody's sitting with me, do y'all want to sit down?"
Jade looked at the seats and glanced back at her friends who were making little head way in placing a drink order."

"What the hell! There doesn't seem to be anywhere else to sit and these heels are killing me."

When Love Aint Enough

I looked down at her feet as she slid into the chair beside me. We laughed as she peeled off the three inch heels. Ten minutes later her friends joined us. Jade introduced us and we all sat there chilling and enjoying the gentle breezes and sweet Caribbean music.

That night Jade and I exchanged numbers. She told me she needed some legal advice and I anxiously gave her my card. About a week later she called and we made plans to meet for lunch at Griffins Steak House on 34th and Main.

It was around three pm in the afternoon and I hadn't eaten anything since breakfast waiting for our luncheon date. I was starving by the time we were seated at our table. We both ordered water with lemon and gave the waiter our order. I sat coolly in my chair wondering how the scene would play out. I suspected whatever Jade had on her mind was less about business than she professed. About 15 minutes into some casual chit chat I finally I went for it,

"So what's up with this legal issue you have?"
Jade looked at me suspiciously and leaned back into the contours of the plush wingback chair. She picked up the cloth napkin from the mahogany table and dabbed daintily at the corners of her mouth, then laid it down again. She flashed a sly grin and looked me squarely in the eyes.

"I lied."

"What?"

163

"I lied, I confess. We were having such a good time I wanted to spend more time with you and that was the only excuse I could think of without giving myself away in front of everybody. I can't believe a player such as yourself didn't pick up on a little thing like that!"

By calling me a player she was either playing me or giving more credit than I deserved. But she was right, game recognizes game.

From the beginning, I under estimated her. Something I continued to do during the entirety of our relationship

"Well that's interesting! Unfortunately I can't say I'm disappointed."

"No?" she asked, watching me as she took a sip of her water.

"No, definitely not,"

"Good"

I made myself comfortable and ingested everything she wanted to talk about. Her mere presence captivated me. She was everything that I had ever loved about women. Her features were soft and seductive. Her hazel eyes twinkled as she talked about growing up in the south and her love for her family and 6 year old daughter Jasmene.

She was a corporate executive at one of the local TV stations and had actually been engaged to marry a guy who had played semi professional ball over in Europe who was about to go pro. But her plans to wed had fallen through after catching him cheating on her on more than one occasion. Jade claimed his ego had gone through the roof after being signed by the NBA. After that, he treated her more like a possession than a lover.

Knowing the hell I'd gone through in recent years, I was impressed by her honesty. I knew all too well the self degradation a person could endure before accepting the truth about a doomed relationship. We found we had that in common.

Still I hoped I was meeting the true person and not her representative. After a two hour lunch we decided to go back to my place.

Well much to my surprise, we didn't end up in the sack. That came about two months later. And it was well worth the wait. I was more than impressed with her sensuality and the way she responded to my touch than the actual act. Afterwards she asked me if our making love had made her gay. I genuinely believed she thought that and tried to comfort her by saying no. That night I wanted to hold her in my arms forever, never letting her go but she eventually left with a promise to spend the night soon. Though I cautioned myself to take it slow, it was back in the game.

After Jade and I had been dating for about six months I learned that she was seeing someone else. A friend as she called him.

One night we made plans to spend the weekend together. Well when the weekend came, Jade disappeared. Not only did she not show up but she was nowhere to be found. All kinds of thoughts went through my head as I worried the hell out of myself thinking the worst.

The following Tuesday she called me. I didn't know whether to be relieved or curse her fuck out! But her explanation was more startling than her disappearing act!

Baby girl spun a tale so unbelievable I almost just called the whole damn thing off! I sat at my desk listening incredulously as she told me of how stressed she'd suddenly become and as a result was hospitalized for the weekend and surrounded by her family.

Now by no means am I slow. Although I admit I can play awful dumb when the time warrants. But miss girl must have thought I had suffered brain damage from lack of oxygen after burying my face so deep between her legs. And as a result I would believe any damn thing!

I held the phone out from my ear and looked at it.

"What?"

My response must have fueled her tale because she continued with the lie, telling me she never had a moment alone to even call me, being surrounded like she was, day and night.

"That's it," I thought, *"She's killed the illusion. O'l girl is a liar and a bad one at that!"* I thought as she continued on with her sob ass tale. At some point during her lie I got pissed and told her so. The words began to fly and neither she nor I was willing to back down.

When Love Aint Enough

"Who are you calling a liar? I don't have to lie to you, who are you"

"I should hope not since I haven't lied to you. But this sounds crazy. Am I supposed to believe you've been hemmed up all weekend at the hospital and you couldn't tell me anything?

That was our first fight. It lasted all of thirty minutes before I hung up in the midst of her cursing. Not to be out done, she called back to finish the verbal attack that I had disrupted by hanging up on her ass the first time. But she only got more of the same treatment. I hung up again and instructed Ronni to screen my calls.

After days of not speaking to one another Jade surprised me by coming to my house one evening. I'd missed her so much during our little separation that I gladly welcomed her inside. That's the night she told me about him. She claimed that it was more a relationship of convenience than that of love. She said he escorted her to various functions and was there for her daughter who very much needed a father figure after the baby's daddy had died. As she passionately explained that she no longer enjoyed making love with him but instead wanted what we had, red flags sprang up all around me.

The thought of my having gone behind someone else when we made love, made me mad as hell. I wanted to end it but was foolishly talked out of it by the pleading and begging of a beautiful woman telling me she cared and needed time. In her attempts to justify her relationship with him she went so far as to say it would be okay if I saw other people since she was involved with someone. I rejected the idea and questioned whether she had any real feelings for me if she was willing to share me.

To a person with any common sense this should have been the straw that not only broke the camel's back but severely handicapped him for the rest of his life. But naw, not for me! At that point, common sense eluded me, again. My second and more persuasive head started doing all the thinking.

I started viewing it as a game I could easily win! My melancholy nature reminded me of my own feelings of apprehension when faced with my own sexuality. I told myself that if time was what she needed, then time was what I'd give her. I was determined to be to her what Nahdia was for me, her saving grace. Besides, she was my dream girl. And I wasn't gonna let her slip away that easily.

So, I waited and waited and waited. And when I got tired of waiting she would beg me to patient and I would wait some more. I was falling hard for her and the more time we spent together, the harder I fell.

JINGLE BELL BABY

Soon the holiday season was upon us. And the city of
Norfolk was buzzing. The snow came pouring down daily
clothing the city like a wool blanket. In Norfolk, traffic was
always hectic. But this time of the year always added more to
the calamity. Being from the Deep South, the worst weather we
ever had to contend with was an ice storm every five years and
when that happened I never had to worry about driving in it
because the whole state would shut down. Thus, problem
solved!

Anyway, it was December and I hadn't done any Christmas
shopping so I decided to bite the bullet and take the plunge. As I
drove up the coast into the city a feeling of excitement came
over me. I wasn't big on the malls but I had a flair for buying
the right thing for the right person. Besides Christmas time
always brought me joy. I was like a little kid all over again.
And now, for the first time in years I had someone special to
share it with. I was overjoyed as I jumped out of my truck and
raced into the mall with my shopping list tucked neatly in my
corduroy jacket.

I went from store to store wreaking havoc with my credit
cards. First I picked up my mom's gift, a pair of teardrop

diamond earrings and a matching necklace. As I paid for them I
could hear her saying,

"Babe you shouldn't spend that kind of money on me,
Christmas aint about that expensive stuff!"
I laughed to myself as I handed the sales girl my card.

Of course I knew that but with her being my favorite girl I
wasn't trying to hear it.
"You'll just have to be mad"

Next I went to my sister's favorite store and got her favorite
perfume. While I was there I picked up some for myself too.
Then it was off to the toy store. I couldn't forget about my
babies, Jasmene and my brand new niece Endi

As I went through the isles I was reminded of my childhood.
We weren't the wealthiest family on the blocked but we were
blessed. Each year my mom would get us what we'd asked
Santa for and then some. I longed to be a little child's Santa. I
wanted to fulfill their wildest dreams and see their beaming
faces on Christmas morning as they realized Santa had been
there.

My eyes glistened as I tested out all the latest toys and tried
to pick out what I thought they would like. When I finished the
clerk gave me a total of $973. 89

"Damn! I thought.

Reluctantly I decided to make my way back to the truck to
pack everything in. Graciously, one of the store clerks offered
to assist me and I gladly accepted. As we fought our way

through the sea of people back to the parking garage, my phone rang.

I ignored it at first but the constant ringing got the best of me so I asked him if we could stop for a minute. He smiled and nodded his head. I put down my bags and answered it. It was my mother.

"Hey girl" she beamed through the phone.

"Hey mom," I shrilled back.

"What cha doing?"

"Oh just trying to get a little of my Christmas outta the way"

"Yeah, me too."

"I guess great minds think a like huh?" I joked.

"Yeah they do" she laughed "Well I wont hold you up I just wanted to let you know that Lionel came by and asked for your number and I gave it to him"

"I didn't know he was back in Mississippi."

"He came home for the holidays. He says he'll be here until New Years."

"Well that's fine. I haven't talked to him in years." I said remembering the young man still holding most of my packages.

"Ah, mom, I'll call you later I have someone helping me carry my bags and he looks like he's about to fall out" I kidded flashing a smile to the young man as he patiently waited for me to get off the phone.

"Okay baby, well look don't spend a lot of money on me…"

171

"Momma, don't even start. You deserve more than I could ever buy" I interrupted

Mom was quiet.

"I love you. I'll call you later okay?"

"Okay. I love you too!" she said

"Okay, bye"

"Hey mom" I called out as I glanced over at the young guy who was leaning on the wall watching the passerby's,

"Where is Endi?"

"Child she's with her mama. That girl is something!" she laughed.

"I bet. Look, I'll call you tonight. Love you - bye."

I tucked the phone back into my down jacket told the guy I was ready.

When we finally made it to my truck I could barely get out instructions where I wanted everything to go for the shrills and cat calls the young man was making at the sight of my truck. "Ah snap! This is sweet!" he exclaimed as we arranged the packages inside.

I keyed the remote and patiently allowed him to sit in the driver's seat check out the sound system and other gadgets, which seemed to make his day more than the fifty buck tip I gave him for helping me. After he'd finished his inventory of the truck, he went on his merry way and I returned to the stores to finish my shopping.

When Love Aint Enough

After finding my last gift, I decided to celebrate by going to the movies. There were was one in particular that Jade had been talking about for weeks. So I called to see if she wanted to go. In the back of my mind I knew it was a long shot since we hadn't gone out together since we started dating.

She rationalized her high profile position made it impossible to do so. I disagreed but it was to no avail because she didn't budge on the subject.

Secretly I missed the intimacy of going out with my lady. Although those things didn't make a relationship it damn sure added to it. But I was like a puppet when it came to her. I couldn't discount the fact that a lot of people didn't understand our lifestyle. So when she started on that band wagon, most times I understood and didn't push the issue.

Even so, I wasn't totally convinced she wasn't ashamed of us, ashamed of me. When I questioned her it was always the same thing,

"I not ashamed of you baby, it's me, I'm ashamed of myself what I'm doing. I'm not gay Casey"

But today was different, it was the holidays. So I called her.

"Hey girl"

"Hey baby" she replied.

"What's up with you?"

"Nothing I just left my mom's house. I helped her put up Christmas decorations"

"So you're in the spirit too I see."

173

Jade laughingly admitted she was.

"Look, I was wondering if you wanted to catch a movie and chill with your baby for a minute."

"What movie are you going to see?"

"It doesn't matter to me. Maybe we can catch the one you were talking about a couple of days ago"

There was a brief silence.

"What theater are you going to?" she asked guardedly.

"I don't know. I guess maybe the one here at the mall. That's where I'm at now"

"Naw, that's too many people. I might run into somebody I know or someone who knows me. That's too close for comfort baby, where else"

"Well..." I began.

"And why would you ask me something like that anyway?" she snapped all of a sudden throwing me for a loop.

"I didn't think it was a big deal. All we'd be doing is going to the movies"

"You're not crazy. You know how people are"

"I do but then again what does it matter. Do you think people are going to automatically know we're dating just because they see us at a movie? Stop tripping!"

"See that's what I'm talking about. I'm not out like you Casey and I wished you'd stopped trying to bring me out!"

"Now you're really tripping, what do you mean, "bring you out? Hell, I just thought it'd be nice to….."

"It doesn't matter I can't anyway. I just picked up Jas from my mom's house. She spent the night there last night"

"Why did she do that, where were you"

"I was at home! What's with the third degree?"

"It's no third degree! I was just wondering because I didn't see or talk to you and you evidently had some free time on your hands, but whatever"

"Yeah right, what-ever"

"I guess I can take that to mean…"

"Whatever!" she snapped.

Then I grew silent. I knew if I kept going where the conversation would lead and I was in too good of a mood to let anyone spoil it. Jade sensed my reluctance to argue and tried as usual to pacify me.

"What if I came by your place tonight?" she asked on a calmer note.

"Oh really…" I said half heartedly sulking from her last remark.

"Yes really. I can pick up a couple of movies and a bottle of wine. I'll even cook for you" she offered, realizing her attitude had been a little over the top earlier.

"What are you gonna cook?" I asked trying to dismiss the rejection I was feeling.

"What about catfish? That's your favorite isn't it?"

"The girl could burn. Maybe staying at home with her wasn't such a cop out," I thought

"Ok that sounds good."

"Alright baby I have to get a baby sitter for Jasmene then I'll be over there"

"Do want me to pick up anything?"

"If it's not too much trouble you could go by the market and get some fish and anything else you want to go with it. That will save me time so I can come right over after I get a sitter."

"Okay"

"See you in a little bit" she said.

"Bye"

I hung up the phone and headed back to my truck.

I got home about an hour later, after picking up the groceries. I grabbed the remote and turned on the fireplace and started cleaning. As I walked through the house picking up after myself, the phone rang. I glanced at the Caller ID before answering and saw it was Jade.

"Hello"

"Hey"

"What's up, what time are you coming?"

"I'm not gonna be able to make it" she blurted out.

"Why, what's wrong?" I asked.

"Jasmene reminded me of the Christmas play at her school tonight"

"Well it sounds like fun. I could meet my two favorite girls there?"

"Come on Casey you know better" she said annoyed.

"What's wrong with that?"

"Nothing's wrong with it but how would I explain it?"

"What's to explain? I'm sure I don't know any of those people and I'm even more positive they don't know me," I reasoned.

"Probably not but, it would be awkward. Plus….," she paused.

"Plus what?" I asked

"Richard's coming"

"Why?"

"Because Jasmene asked him too. He always attends her school functions."

"No shit! So I guess you're gonna be playing family tonight!" I snapped.

"See that's the shit I don't need to hear!" She said agitated. "I'm going to a play with my daughter, what's the big deal"

"Don't forget about Richard!"

"And your point is?!"

"You just don't get it do you?!"

"No but I'm sure you're going to tell me!" she said sarcastically

"Aint this a bitch!"

"You're blowing the whole thing out of proportion, what is your problem?!" she tried to reason.

"It's him damn it! I'm sick of him. He sees you when I can't! Hell for all I know there might not even be a damn play at Jas's school!" I blurted out. "This is crazy! Every time we make plans something conveniently comes up. The shit gets old you know?!"

"You act as if I planned it Casey! I wanted to see you just as much as you want to see me. I can't very well tell Jas I can't go and come lay up with you now can I?" she yelled.

"I don't expect you to!" I yelled back.

"Well then what's the problem?"

"It's always something! Damn I hardly see you as it is! Do you ever think about my needs? And maybe, just maybe, I would like to do the family thang sometime with ya'll my damn self!"

"What do you want me to do Casey?"

"I guess there's nothing you can do! Jas wants to go the play with you and Richard" I snapped sarcastically.

"I don't have to lie Casey! And you're right, it is getting old. You knew my situation from the start!"

"That's a damn lie! You didn't bother to tell me about your man until months later! And you didn't tell me then! I had to figure the shit out!" I yelled.

Jade was quite. We'd had this conversation hundreds of time before and it always ended the same way, with both of us mad as hell!

"The whole thing is bullshit!" I continued. "And besides, even if I did know about him things change!" I declared.

"Like I said you knew my situation. Now I have to get dressed so you let me know if you want to meet tomorrow or not!" she yelled.

"Not!"

"Bye!" She yelled as she hung up the phone.

I stood holding the receiver as steam poured from nostrils. I was sick and tired of being sick and tired! Jade needed to make a fucking choice as to who she wanted to be with and this time I meant it!

I grabbed a cocktail and made my way to the sofa. Hours later the phone rang. I reached down from where I lay and picked it up.

"Hello" I said heavily.

"Hey babe!!" exclaimed the man's voice on the other end.

"Who is this?" I said groggily.

"Oh bitch now you done went and hurt my feelings! Its Lionel, Blanche!" he said playfully.

I sat straight up on the sofa.

"Lionel!" What the hell?" I screamed happily into the phone.

"Now that's more like it girl, show a sissy some love! "How the hell are ya?"

179

"I'm fine, I'm fine. Momma told me she gave you my number but I didn't think your ass would really call me!' I said, still shocked to hear his voice.

"Girl now you knew there was no way you were going to get out of talking to me. Shit how long has it been?" he asked laughing.

"Too damn long!"

"I know that's real!"

"How've you been?"

"Girl you know me, I been parlaying here and there."

"Well you sound great!"

"You too. Although at first I thought I'd caught you doing the do or something. You had that old sexy husk in your voice" he kidded.

"Naw it ain't like that. I was asleep on the sofa"

"Alone?!"

"Yes bitch alone." I replied.

"Well I can see you've changed because that ain't like you at all"

I ignored his remark and went on to ask him a thousand questions. Lionel told me of his life in Spain. He lived in Rota, a city he says he fell in love with the moment he first stepped off the plane some five years ago. Lionel had always been a confirmed bachelor but now he reported he was married.

"You lying?!" I exclaimed.

"Yep prince charming swept me off my feet and made an honest man out of me!"

He and I laughed at the idea of him being married.

"That's great Lionel. I'm so happy for you!"

"Girl my hubby is a photographer. He's jealous as hell, but he's mine all mine!" He smirked.

"Did he come home with you?"

"Naw he has business to tend to so I came alone, thank God! He would have a fit if he met any of my ol pieces of trade." I laughed violently. Lionel wasn't exaggerating! He'd definitely been through some 'boys' as he so passionately referred to them. For a moment I was envious. He sounded deliriously happy. Suddenly my mind drifted to Jade. I wondered where she was that very moment. A bitterness filled me as I remembered she was with Richard.

"You hoo..." interrupted Lionel.

"Oh I'm sorry babe," I said apologetically.

"What's going on with you Casey? Do you have that wife and the 2.5 kids you always said you wanted?

"No, not quite" I answered somberly as I revisited my dreams of days gone by.

"Well do tell dear heart, who's the lucky woman in your life now?"

"Her name's Jade" I said reluctantly.

Lionel detected my reluctance to talk about her and didn't bother to pursue it. Instead he told me about his villa in Rota. I listened intently picturing myself there wishing I was able to boast of a beautifully peaceful life with Jade. I'd never envied anyone as much as I envied Lionel at that very moment as he talked of his lover and their life together.

He talked about everything from the people he'd met to the spectacular view he had from his flower encased balcony that over looked the Mediterranean Sea. I was entranced as he described his home and his lover Papua.

"Honey hold on a sec" he said as he placed me on hold to answer another call.

I waited patiently for him to return.

After a couple of minutes he came back.

"Babe I need to call you back? Are you going to be up for a while? He asked in a giddy voice.

"Must be some trade?" I quizzed.

"I's married now but I ain't dead!"

I laughed and told him I'd wait for his call.

I hung up the phone and got up from the sofa and went to the bar to get a glass of water. Then I returned to the sofa to wait for Lionel's call.

Over two hours had gone by and still no call from Lionel. Lazily I got up from the sofa and began to close down the house for the night when the doorbell rang. I walked over and looked out the peephole. No one was there. I turned the knob and snatched it open.

To my amazement there stood a much more matured looking Lionel than I remembered.

"Ahhhh what the hell?!" I screamed in joy.

Lionel stood there with a big grin on his face donning a posh full-length leather British tan trench coat and a Burberry scarf draped around his neck. With both arms out stretched, holding a liter of XO in one, he screamed,

"Can a bitch get a glass!"

Lionel and I ran into each other's arms and held on for dear life. I led him inside as he awed and gasp at the décor of my home.

"I can't believe you! No you didn't!" I said still shocked to see him.

Lionel was filled with giggles.

"How'd you get here? What the fuck!" I exclaimed.

"Your momma gave me the address. Your ass was sounding so pitiful on the phone I had to come!" he explained still smiling broadly.

"You didn't mention anything to her did you" I said momentarily alarmed at the thought of making her worry.

"Of course not Ms Thang, I made it seem like I wanted to send you a Christmas gift. She loves me so she didn't give it a second thought" he smiled warmly.

183

I smiled back warmly still holding his hand and looking at him in disbelief that he was actually standing in front of me.

Lionel said that he'd flown from Spain in his hubby's private jet. So after hearing how down I sounded, he'd called the airport and told them to fuel up because he was going out!

"I am sooo glad you came!" I exclaimed fighting back the tears that choked painfully in my throat.

Lionel insisted I give him a tour of the house. And I happily obliged. First we walked down into the living room with its twelve feet high bay windows and a movie screen that descended from the twenty foot ceiling. The color décor for the room was crème, bronze and silver. A large contemporary crème leather sofa with wooden bowlegs graced the middle of the room with a crème colored Italian marble coffee table sitting in front of it. On top of the table sat a two feet tall Waterford crystal vase filled with freshly cut tulips. Over in the corner by the patio doors was a cream double chaise lounger decorated with a leopard print and golden pillows. A mustard cashmere throw was draped across its side casually.

On each side of stood a towering silver and bronze touchier for those nights when all I wanted to do was relax with a good book. But by far my favorite spot in the entire room was my trusty overstuffed bronze leather recliner that was strategically placed to avoid any and all glare to the television when I was deeply immersed in my football games or a good movie. Beside my chair was a console that controlled everything electronically in the house from the TV to the locks on the doors. My collection of authentic African art was encased in locked stainless steel curio that covered over half of the wall to the left of the patio doors.

Next we walked up the spiraling staircase and through the hallway to the master bedroom, or my Sahara, as I liked to call it. It was rich in Asiatic themes, complete with a California king Mahogany Malaysian sleigh bed adorned with bronze and crème burnt Egyptian linen. The walls were decorated with Malaysian tapestries encased in Mahogany frames. A skylight hovered above over the bed allowing the sun and the moon to pour in at all times through the sheer canopy sheet. On the wall hung my prized possession of the room, a sixty-inch Plasma TV. Tucked away in the corner was an electric fireplace that was glistening from my earlier expectations of Jade coming over. I quickly grabbed the remote and turned it off, annoyed with the thought that I had even went through the trouble of turning it on for someone so obviously undeserving as she was at that moment.

Lionel claimed the house was the epitome of the Casey he remembered, a gadget guru. He fell in love with the private balcony outside my bedroom, adorned with a loveseat chase, stone table and candle touchier that adorned the small space built for two. A canopy protected it from the elements and also provided a bit of privacy when I wanted to get romantic. We looked at each other mischievously, knowing exactly what that space was mostly used for. He laughed and told me I was still a nut.

After showing him the other two bedrooms and taking a tour of the Greek styled kitchen we retired to the balcony outside the living room to talk. It was around forty degrees outside but after firing up the Chimenea and a couple sips of the XO, the cold was not a factor. We had a lot to catch up on.

Curiosity soon got the best of him and he asked me to tell him about Jade. So I did. It was a complex tale so I took my time. I grew embarrassed as I told him how I felt compelled to wait it out. It was no big surprise to him when I admitted how much I loved her and believed with all my heart that she would eventually realize what other people thought didn't matter when it came to being with the person you loved.

Occasionally sipping my drink and watching him, I continued on with my story. Lionel listened intently, offering a few 'Un huh's' here and there, careful not to interrupt. When I'd finished, he just sat there with his legs crossed.

"What's that look for?" I asked uneasily.

"Are you happy?" he asked earnestly.

"That's a hard question," I said pondering whether I was or not.

"No that's an easy question." Said Lionel in his matter of factly sort of way. "The hard question is can you accept it if she never comes to your way of thinking?

I looked at Lionel and then looked out into the still blackness.

"I love her man! We have our ups and downs but then there are times when were deliriously happy"

"And that's understandable. Everybody goes through something. My thing is this, is what you're going through worth it? Is it healthy?"

"Well let me say...." I began uneasily but was abruptly interrupted by Lionel waving his out stretched hand signaling me to stop.

"Because, if I'm correct in what I'm hearing, sounds like you're riding an emotional rollercoaster and the ride is giving you hell! Shit you look good now but give her a couple more months of this and your gonna start to age baby. And babe aint nothing worth that!

I anxiously threw up my hand to interject into the conversation. I needed to defend myself, defend Jade. Lionel acknowledged me and was quiet as I spoke.

"Man you know me and I know how all this must look. Hell I ask myself all the time if I've lost my "rabbit ass" mind by getting involved with another bisexual woman. And to top it off, share her with a married man! Of course I don't want to share the woman I love with anyone, male or female. And I'll be the first to admit the shit gets crazy sometimes and I'm tempted to say to hell with it! But I can't quit! I love her and I know she loves me too. I've got see this through and know I gave it my one hundred percent. Or else I'll have regrets for giving up on us.

"But sweetie don't you think this is a repeat of the Shena fiasco? You know I warned you about that bitch, but naw you wouldn't listen to me?"

"No, no this is different. Shena was tripping. Jade aint putting nothing in my face like Shena did!"

"But Jade's got a man"

"Yeah, but it's different. Hell, I told you the shit was crazy!"

"So you admit it, you're not happy"

"I'll say I'm not satisfied. But I love her so damn much. So, when she asks me to patient and give her time, I can't help but do so."

"But how much time does Ms. Thing need to know if you're the person she wants to be with? How long y'all been seeing each other?"

"Almost two years now"

"That's a long time to call your self confused!" Lionel said in his exaggerated tone

"I know. But every time we start making a progressive step forward something happens to push us two steps back"

"Like what?"

"Like tonight. Do you want to know where she is right now? Lionel was quiet.

"She's with him and my daughter at her school's Christmas play"

188

"Girl please"

"Exactly" I said

"Why aren't you there?"

"Because she thinks being seen together will out her! Man its shit like that that makes me feel like she's ashamed of me. And that's the two steps back part!"

"Well I know what you're saying about the ashamed part but maybe she's ashamed of herself. It might not be you," he said trying to comfort my wounded pride.

"And that what she says too. But it doesn't matter. I want to be there and I should be but I know I'm not welcome and it kills me. But I love her so I stay in this and I wait for the day when it will be okay"

"Casey baby….." Lionel began.

"No, stop, you've been here all of forty-five minutes and you're already judging me" I said sadly.

"No babe I'm not judging you" Lionel said moving to the edge of his seat and looking intently in my direction.

"I know you Casey. I know you better than I think you know yourself. You're a good one! A damn good one! And I know you probably love this woman but what I'm wondering is can you love her and love yourself too!'

"What do you mean by that?"

"Jade is probably gorgeous right? Cause we both know your dick want get up with a chick that aint drop dead gorgeous!" he said flamboyantly.

"Yeah she looks nice"

"For as long as I've known you and that's been what, uh-h 15 years, your need for love and acceptance has been your down fall! I think it started with Nahdia. God knows you loved that woman. And I know losing her was like losing a part of yourself. And now it's like you'll do anything to recapture what you had with her."

I took a long sip of my cocktail and looked away. Not a day went by that I didn't think of her.

"So I what's wrong with that?" I mumbled.

"Nothing is wrong with it. But when you live for others and not yourself you aint living baby you simply exist. You've got to live for you baby. Life's too short to do anything but that."

"But that's not completely true though," I argued staring at him defiantly.

"Ms Thing I know your ass! And I'm sure Ms Jade does too and that's why your ass is stuck like Chuck!"

"Is this read Casey night or what?!" I asked irritated with Lionel's two minute of analogy of my person and more than a little bit intoxicated from XO.

"Now don't beat a girl for telling the truth!" He kidded trying to lighten my increasingly intense mood. "All I'm trying to say

190

is look out for you. If she comes around great but if not then be okay enough with yourself to go on and be strong!"

"I will," I said trying to convince him and myself that I was well prepared for any outcome.

"I got this babe. I got this!" I said wondering deep down if I had it or it had me.

Lionel looked at me and smiled.

"Girl you're a beautiful, loving person and you deserve love. And I see you're still running around trying to find it when it's right in your face. You've got to love you and the rest will come.

"But I do love myself, I know I look good"

"I'm not talking about arrogance, yeah you're that! You're arrogant as hell but more so because you're so damn smart. But when it comes to love things get hazy for you. It's like you don't believe you're worthy of love, but you are."

My mind was spinning. I didn't know if it was the liquor or his words but something was taking hold of me. Lionel leaned over and touched my knee and smiled at me reassuringly.

"I've told ya you'd be the perfect man for me because you know how to treat a gur-l! Hell I know how to cook a big breakfast with grits and eggs and stuff!" He shrilled. "Awe baby, when I get through loving you, you can adorn me with all the trinkets you like. Baby I'll take em. And I'll give you those two point five kids you want. Shit I can even do the picket fence

191

and live in Mayberry. I'll make you feel like the gorgeous magnificent wo-man your really are!"

I blushed shaking with laughter.

"Man you still crazy!"

Lionel sat back in his chair, crossed his legs and raised his glass.

"To love, may we all have it!" he yelled out.

"Damn right" I said thinking wishfully of Jade.

Lionel and I stayed up the entire night reminiscing about old times. It was wonderfully rejuvenating. Though our bottle was empty, we were full.

Lionel left later that day. As I drove him to the airport we made plans to visit each other and do a better job of keeping in touch. Before walking inside the terminal, he turned to me and pushed something soft into my hand.

To my surprise it was a gigantic marijuana cigarette.

"What the hell?" I blurted out.

"Ah girl don't act like you don't desperately need one!" answered Lionel smiling broadly

"Baby it's been so long since I did something like this I'd probably have a heart attack!"

"Baby you getting old" he kidded

"Done got old baby! Done got old!" I said slipping the joint deep into my jean pocket.

"Give me a hug sweetie" he said extending his arms out.

I gladly obliged as I fought back my tears. I realized then how very much both our lives had changed, me with my career and him and his hubby living the fabu-life in Europe. It tore at my heart to see him go. His visit had done wonders for me.

After our goodbyes I drove home in silence thinking of all the things he and I had talked about. He was right. I did need to be prepared in the unlikely event things didn't work out with Jade and me. And though I couldn't imagine not having her in my life I wasn't oblivious to the possibility that she might not be there in the long run. The thought began to depress me so I dismissed it and rubbed at the joint Lionel had given me that was tucked away in my pocket.

Everything is Everything!

For the next six months things were good with Jade and me. I attributed it to my new outlook and the possibility that our last argument had somehow made an impact on her. Jades birthday was fast approaching, July 4th. She was turning the big three zero. As the day fast approached we discussed how she should celebrate it. Jade's take on it was it was a day, like any other day. She told me she never really celebrated her birthdays. I was shocked because I celebrated mine the entire month. Jade thought it was silly but I didn't. I was celebrating life. And life for me at that point was good.

Though I traveled all the time on business, Jade and I had never taken a trip together. So I propositioned her with the idea of going out of town for her birthday. I convinced her it would be a great opportunity to go some place where no one knew either of us. A place where we could spend quality time together doing all of the things she was so afraid to do in Norfolk. After a bit of coaxing she agreed it was a great idea.

I was like a kid waiting on Christmas. I immediately began making plans. My goal was to go some place we could let our hair down without the fear of being noticed. A place where we would blend into the crowd. And I knew just the spot, my old stomping grounds, New Orleans, Louisiana. It was perfect. People down there live by the slogan, "Let the Good times roll!" What made it even better was Jade had never been there.

When I ran it by her she was more than pleased. Taking that as a go ahead, I proceeded to plan the perfect trip. I reserved a suite with a balcony at the 'Bourbon Orleans' overlooking Bourbon Street. I figured if she got cold feet about going out to party, we could always enjoy the panoramic view from our balcony.

Next, I reserved a private dining room at Olivia's. The final touch was the limousine. The chauffeur would be at our disposal from the moment we landed in New Orleans until we were back at my place.

It had been years since I'd visited New Orleans and I think in many ways, I was more excited than Jade could ever be. For days I anxiously walked around singing in anticipation of our trip. When Jade arranged for Jas to stay with her mother, I finally exhaled and dared to believe that the trip was actually going to happen. Everything was all a go!

However, there was a close call a week before our trip. Jade called. Her tone was strained. When the subject of the trip came up she grew quite. When I asked if she was having second thoughts about going, she became agitated and accused me of being paranoid. I admit the thought of her canceling out at the last minute had crept into my mind several times but I dismissed

195

it. I truly hoped she thought more of me than to play those kinds of games.

Still, she seemed to grow more agitated as I talked of all the things I wanted to do when we got there. Our conversation was cut short when she got another call. She told me she would call me back, but didn't.

I didn't trip on it and figured we'd talk the next day if her mood had improved. I knew birthdays could make a person melancholy. Thirty had been a hurdle for me and I figured maybe that was part of her problem.

When the big day finally came I didn't go into the office. I was too excited and I knew my whole thoughts would be of nothing but our impending getaway and I'd barely slept the night before in anticipation. I'd asked Jade to spend the night so we could leave from the house but she had some last minute packing to do.

The next morning I made a big breakfast of grits, eggs and bacon, put on pot of coffee then called Jade. She didn't answer so I left a good morning message. After breakfast, I went upstairs to finish packing. Around noon the phone rang. It was Jade. She sounded anxious. She told me her office was in chaos and she'd gone in early to defuse a problem with one of the producers. My heart fell as I listened anxiously to her explain how it would probably be an all day thing.

She wanted to meet me New Orleans instead of flying out together. I tried to calm the little voice in the back of my mind that told me this was a diversion from what was really happening. I reasoned she wouldn't dare let me go on before her and then not show up.

"I aint no killer but hell don't push me," I thought, at the mere possibility of her standing my black ass up all the way down there.

"I don't know..." I said cautiously. "We could always take a later flight, I hate flying alone" I lied, trying to ignore the feeling welling up in the pit of my stomach.

"No baby, I know how excited you are about getting down there so when I finish up here I'll take the first flight out to meet you. Where are we staying?" she asked.

"The Bourbon ...but look I don't mind waiting for you babe" I insisted.

"It will be fine Casey. Plus I don't know how long I'll be here today and I'd feel better if you went on ahead" she insisted.

"Jade…"

"Babe I know what you're thinking but I promise, I'll be there, you trust me don't you?"

"Of course I do but it's going to throw everything off. I have a limo reserved and everything…"

"Ahhhh, that's so sweet baby. You really did the damn thing didn't you!" she squealed.

197

Her excitement somehow helped to reassure me that she wasn't doing the bunny rabbit dance on my ass and this wasn't some last minute ploy to get out of going. So I replied,

"Of course!"

"Okay then you go ahead and I'll meet you there"

"Okay, but I'll have the limo at the airport waiting for you to arrive." I said reluctantly.

"Great, now I've got to get back to work. I feel like I've been putting out fires all morning around this place"

"Well don't work too hard you're going to need your energy when you get there"

"I'm never too tired for that baby! Love you," she said sending me kisses through the phone.

"I love you too. Call me when you're ready to come so I can make sure the driver is at the airport to pick you up."

"Okay baby, I will"

I hung up the phone and ran my hands through my hair. My mom always said I worried to much but this time I thought it was definitely justified. Slowly I walked into the kitchen, numb from the conversation. I grabbed a Heineken from the fridge and took the whole damn thing down. Then a grabbed another one and walked out of the kitchen.

"Jade knew how important this trip was for both of us" I thought

Silently I walked back into the living room and glared out of the patio doors trying to dismiss the negative thoughts that were going through my mind. I knew she was dedicated to her job but still there was feeling in the pit of my stomach I couldn't shake.

After finishing my beer I walked up stairs to continue packing. When I finished, I called a cab and left for the airport.

The flight was nice but it would have been much better if we had taken it together. As planned, our driver was standing in airport with a sign reading, 'Jade Montgomery.' I walked over and identified myself. He took my luggage and whisked me off to the hotel.

After checking into our room I called Jade's office. Her receptionist answered and told me she had left for the day. I was elated. I figured I could probably catch her at home packing. I anxiously called her there. The phone rang several times before her answering machine came on. I left a message asking her to call me and gave her the number to our room. I hung up the phone and told myself she was either in route to the house or the airport.

About fifteen minutes later I called her cell phone, she didn't answer. In fact it was turned off. Again my reasoning kicked in. This time telling me she was probably on the plane. And everyone knows, you have to turn cell phones off before boarding a plane. I told myself not to think about it any more. So I busied myself by unpacking my luggage and leaving ample room for all the stuff I guessed Jade would bring.

Our room was beautiful. The sitting area was adorned with large patio doors that led outside to an oval wrought iron balcony overlooking Bourbon Street. I flung open the doors and walked outside. People were already walking around with cocktails. I inhaled the salty air and walked inside. The fragrance from the exotic wild flowers filled my nostrils. I looked about the room and was quite pleased. A crystal chandelier hung from the vaulted ceilings, casting an array of light on the Victorian furnishing giving the place a homey feeling. Anxiously I inventoried the suite to ensure everything was as I had specified.

I walked into the bedroom and pulled the covers back slightly to reveal soft rose petals sprinkled about the white silk sheets. It looked better than I'd imagined. I recovered the bed and sauntered happily back into the living room to call the front desk to order champagne and fruit delivered in an hour.

An hour passed and still no sign of Jade. Again I called both her home and cell phone, still no answer. I started to worry. It was seven thirty N O time and eight thirty at the house. Then doorbell rang!

I jumped from my chair and skipped over to answer it.

"Girl you had me ...," I stopped abruptly when I saw the surprised busboy standing behind his white table clothed cart adorned with crystal goblets and two bottles of Dom Perignon and a assortment of fresh fruit. My racing heart sank to the floor. I looked past him still hoping she was out there trying to

200

surprise me. But there was only him, watching me curiously, waiting to get into the room. Disappointed and more than a little embarrassed I moved aside and showed him in.

When he'd finished setting up, I gave him a ten and walked him to the door. As soon as the door closed total apprehension took me over.

The more I tried to relax as the time ticked loudly by without word from her, the more my worry turned to anger. Unable to stand the confines of the suite any longer, I decided to go downstairs to the cocktail lounge. I grabbed my keys and angrily walked out of the room slamming the door behind me.

The hotel bar was empty except for a few couples huddled in the rear and a female sitting at the bar. There was an oyster and shrimp buffet fountain located in the middle of the room. Though I love shrimp I was too weak to eat. Instead, I walked by it stiffly, heading to the bar to get a drink. The lights were dim and the loudspeakers were softly playing Zydeco music as the house band set up. I plopped down on the closest barstool and ordered a Long Island Iced Tea with a shot of rum, neat, and settled in for some serious drinking.

In between drinks I continued to call Jade but still there was no answer. Now I was mad as hell. I had been sitting at the bar for about an hour when lady came in and sat down beside me. Innocently she tried to strike up a conversation but it was to no use. I wasn't having it! I quickly appraised her slim body and

201

cute Carmel face and my words were like acid, short, quick and nothing to play with.

After my fifth Tea, I looked around at the sweltering crowd and jumped off my stool to stager back to my room. It was past midnight and I had exhausted every possible reason why Jade was missing in action.

"She'd better have a damn good reason for this shit" I said aloud as I fumbled through my pockets for the card to the room.

When I got back to the room I slowly made my way inside dreading the loneliness of its spacious walls. I slammed the door behind me and stumbled over to the sofa. I kicked off my shoes, closed my eyes and lay down to get some overdue rest.

Then a voice called out to me!

Too drunk to open both eyes I decided to peep out of only one. And there she was, Jade, standing in front of me wearing the short black negligee I had given her for Valentines Day. I struggled to my feet and grabbed her by her arms.

"Where in the hell have you been?! I've been worried sick about you!"
Jade smiled nervously as she wiggled from my tight grasp and placed her arms loosely around my neck.

"I got here over an hour ago. I've been waiting for you. Where were you?" she asked calmly.

"Oh no, don't even try it! I've been downstairs in the lounge trying to reach you! I snapped pulling her arms from around my neck.

"Then why was your phone off?" She asked, placing her hands on her hips pretending to be annoyed.

I grabbed my phone out of my pocket to check it. I had three new messages!

"So she called! So what! It still didn't explain where she'd been all damn day!" I thought angrily.

"Where have you been? I've been calling you all night!" I barked at her.

Jade reached up again and slipped her arms around my neck.

"I got tied up, that's all silly but- I'm- here- now," she whispered giving me light kisses between each word she spoke.

"But I've been calling ..." I began but was quickly quieted as she gently kissed me again and again, preventing me from saying what I so desperately wanted to say.

"Babe I know you're pissed and I'm sorry I was late but I'm here now, that's all that really matters. I'm here." She whispered then kissed me again. "Okay?" she said looking up into my eyes seductively.

Deep down fighting was the last thing I wanted to do. My soul was happy. She was with me, so she was hours late getting there, so what! She was here now and all I wanted to do was

203

hold on to her and never let go. Jade sensed she was winning the battle and seductively pushed her body into mind and held me like she had never held me before.

I was done! I didn't have to say another word. She knew my heart.

Quietly she took my hand and led me into the bedroom. I followed willingly.

Once inside, she slowly undressed me, kissing and caressing my body, throwing my clothing to the floor.

Stripped naked of our clothing we slipped under the covers and made passionate love holding each other so tight I felt I would pass out from the sheer excitement of it all.

The next morning the sun beams spilled through the sheer curtains sending light fairies to dance around the room. Lazily I rolled over and looked down at Jade curled up in my arms. I brushed her hair back to see her beautiful face and kissed her softly on the forehead. As I watched her sleep she began to move about finally awakening to find me looking at her adoringly.

"Good morning birthday girl" I whispered, kissing her, this time on the lips. She threw her arm around me and whispered back,

"Good morning babe"

To see her in this light fueled my passion for her all over again. Gently I pulled her on top of me and held her tight as I softly slid my tongue into her mouth and kissed her deeply. Her body trembled as I pushed aside the panties she'd slipped on before going to sleep and slipped my love deep inside her. We moaned as our skin touched causing us to move rhythmically to our passions for each other.

Making love to her so early in the morning brought out the animal in me as I clawed her butt pulling it down hard on my love and pumped deep inside her, searching for her hidden spot. Her breath became shallow and my body grew rigid from the pleasure of my entering her forcefully while she nibbled on my neck biting and kissing it as though it were her favorite candy. Quietly we rolled from side to side in the bed fucking and sucking each other as though it were our first time beholding the pleasure of such love. My wood was so deep in her now I could taste her. My mouth craved to sample her juices as a baby craves milk. Gently I pulled out of her and pulled her on top of my face as I lay on my back thrusting my tongue in and out of her love spot savoring its juices and filling my mouth with her pussy.

She moved up and down slowly, sensually grinding causing my tongue to explore the deepest depths of her spot. Slowly I licked and caressed her pussy as she moaned sensually bouncing her round ass on my chest. Not wanting her to come too fast I ran my tongue from her spot to her button, then up to her navel, then back again, repeatedly. The sensation was driving her wild, making her jump each time my tongue went across her button.

Softly I slipped my fingers inside her while French kissing her
button, biting and sucking it causing her to lose her breath and
shudder uncontrollably.

"Oh ba-by you gonna make me cu-m" she purred
I knew how she felt, I was almost there myself! Abruptly I
stopped and pushed her back down on my dick and rolled on top
of her. I pushed her legs high above my shoulders and pumped
into her like I was going crazy. My hard dick met with her
pulsating spot like thunder. Furiously I pumped into her forcing
her to bite into my flesh and claw my back wonderfully. My
body grew rigid as I slowly and deliberately tried to drill my
way into her soul pulling her ass up to meet every stroke until I
was too weak to pump into her awaiting pussy and it juices
running callously down her leg.

"Ooh baby yes-s-s-s fuck me! Fuck Me Casey!" She screamed
deliriously.

Obliged to fulfill her demand, I rolled her over on her hands
and knees then came up behind her to lick her aching spot. She
looked back at me still purring like a kitten. I kissed her deeply
allowing her to taste herself. Then I gently pushed inside her
once again, pumping deep and slow as she clawed at the sheets.
My legs grew weak as I forced the shaft deeper and deeper
inside her quivering body. Jade screamed out my name as her
love juices drizzled down its shaft and down her hips. Her body
grew stiff and trembled from the pounding I was putting on it.
Soon she was screaming as multiple organisms took over her

body and she fell limp in the bed. Exhausted, I lay down beside her. Pulling her close, I wiped the perspiration from her forehead and whispered, again,

"Happy birthday babe"

After a well deserved nap, we showered and prepared to hit the streets of New Orleans. Our first stop was the mall, all of them. Jade took shopping as serious as she did her job. I knew I was in trouble but I'd promised to be patient, it was her day. So, patiently, yet exhausted, I trudged behind her as she went into ever store, some of them twice.

When she'd finished giving my credit card hell we went to lunch at Ralph and KaKoos on Toulouse St. The waiting line was half a block long. But it was the best place to get Blackened Shrimp Ettufee, Jades favorite.

The food was spectacular just like I'd remembered. Jade appeared relaxed and comfortable as we laugh and talked over lunch. It was good to finally see her let her hair down with me in public. She was happy and I was elated! She was finally validating our relationship after almost two years by stepping out of the closet, if only for a short while.

After lunch the limo driver drove us through the busy streets to the flea market on Decatur Street. As we neared the Café Du Monde, I told him to let us out and told him we'd call when we were ready for him.

207

Vivian M Kelly

The streets were packed as usual. People from all walks of life had converged on the city. Musicians and Mimes eagerly performed on the sidewalks entertaining crowds while little boys in baggy pants and sneakers with taps on the bottom, danced their hearts out to earn a tip from the passerby's. Jade was taken with the tap dancers, especially the younger ones and insisted on giving them dollars. Well as you might expect news of her generosity began spreading like wild fire up the sidewalks and at one point we had about 10 little boys gathered around us tapping their butts off for more money.

Jade quickly became overwhelmed with all of the attention. She was surprised that her generosity had generated that kind of a reaction.

"What did you expect when you took your money roll out like that. Now everybody wants to get in on the action, can you blame 'em? Hell, I'll do a jig for you if you give me some," I joked much to her dismay.

Seeing the look on her face, I knew she wouldn't last much longer. So I gave forty dollars and sent them on their way to divided it as they wanted. Jade breathed a sigh of relief and we continued our journey through the crowds.

When we neared the food market my mouth began to water. The French Market consisted of a collage of vendors who sold everything from Alligator heads to Voodoo elixirs. If they sold it in New Orleans you could probably find it in the flea market for the low-low. The isles were lined with hundreds of spices and a variety of Cajun delicacies. Some like it hot, but I want it to burn. So I immediately started loading up on hot sauce digging the variety available with colorful names like Screamin' Demon and Ass in the Tub was exhilarating. I grabbed a basket and eagerly filled it with loot to take home.

As we continued through the market we arrived at one of my favorite stores, the French Quarter Seafood Market. The smell of roasted alligator sausage as it spun in the rotisserie was calling my name. The store served it on a stick. My mouth watered as the clerk passed me two of 'em along with some homemade hot sauce, while Jade inspected the gigantic prawn in a corner foot-tub.

When she came over she asked me what I'd bought, before I could say anything she'd leaned in and took a bit off one.

"Umm, that's good. Is one of those for me?

.

"Sure" I said knowing that if she knew it was alligator she'd would have tried to vomit on the spot.
Jade happily took it and bit it again. I smiled and looked off.

"What's the red stuff?" she said pointing at the paper cup I was holding.

"Homemade hot sauce, something you can't handle it, trust me," I warned.

"Oh really, I love hot sauce" she said with a mischievous smile. "See there you go underestimating me again" she said sticking her alligator deep into the cup and twirling it around. .

Jade took a small bit and her eyes grew big as quarters, instantly filling with water. At first I was shocked then it was just funny as hell as her mouth dropped open and she scrambled around for something to stop the burn. All the time, still holding on to the alligator.

A vendor, who was watching, came to her rescue by passing her a bottle of water. She damned near drank the whole thing in one gulp. Water was running down both sides of her mouth as she tried to consume it. When she finally caught her breath, she glared at me. Her eyes were as red as a pepper pudding! I laughed so hard water started coming from my eyes.

She punched me on my shoulder and exclaimed,

"You dirty dog!"

"May-be, but you lost so many cool points with that one, its pathetic, I was shame for ya!" I joked, dabbing at the water dribbling off her chin while she continued to hit at me.

After her second bottle of water and the piece of ice that she taken from the bin, we continued our journey through the market visiting all the tables and nibbling on alligator. It wasn't until after she'd finished it that I told her what it was!

"Ooh you're an asshole" she joked. "What's next barbeque snake?!" she said sarcastically.

"You nasty, you know that!" I joked

She swung at me again, this time landing a punch on my shoulder, much to my surprise.

After leaving the French Market, I took her on a tour of the back streets. Jade loved the themed shopping stores and I soon realized I'd made a mistake. Because she soon had me going in and out of every store, again! When I couldn't walk another step I called the driver. I plopped down in the car and pushed off my shoes. My feet were burning and throbbing from the miles of pavement we'd walked. For me another nap was definitely in order if we were going to do the club later that night.

Exhausted, I stripped and jumped in the shower. Jade, still frisky from the morning decided to join me. Though the water pressure was low it did nothing to reduce the steam flowing from the standing room only shower. To my surprise Jade wanted to do a bit of experimenting. Though we had talked about it many times before, she'd sworn that she could never satisfy me the way I satisfied her. In her eyes it would mean that she was gay and after all she was definitely not that!

As baby girl bent down on her knees in the shower I smiled to myself thinking of all the times she had declared she wouldn't do it. I imagined the intoxicating atmosphere of the city had made its way into her "prim and proper" veins driving her to venture outside the box, so to speak. I simply waited to see what she would do.

Jade began by kissing my stomach and tonguing my navel. I brushed back her hair as she continued to make her way down further. I prided myself in being able to maintain control, but the touch of her lips on my skin made me tremble. I held on to the shower railing to balance myself as she timidly kissed away at my spot. She teased me lovingly slipping her tongue in and out seductively. She stopped only to look up and ask,

"Am I doing it right?"

Catching me totally off guard and totally caught up in the way she was making me feel I whispered awkwardly,

"Yeah you're doing it right" I whispered, rubbing my hands through her hair.

Jade returned her attention to it, licking and sucking my button softly, running her hands across my butt, pulling me closer to her. Water dripped from the shower onto her head as she pushed her face deeper and deeper between my legs. I arched back, allowing her room to move around as she continued to lick and suck away at my private spot. Her hands traveled up my body, squeezing and caressing me into a frenzy until I thought I'd explode. Slowly, I moved to her labor of love. My feeling of domination and conquest was quickly replaced by those of adoration. My woman had taken this moment to show me what I meant to her. She had given to me what I was forever giving to her. I was touched but more than that I was coming. And it felt so right for so long.

I'd made special plans for the birthday girl. After resting from our torridly busy day, we went out to dinner at Olivia's. I'd reserved a private dining room equipped with our own serving staff and a saxophonist who played during the entire meal. Jades eyes grew wild with excitement when she realized all of this was for her. Over the candlelit table she mouthed to me,

"I love you"

And I smiled. I didn't have to tell her how much I loved her because it showed all over my face. Things were going well and my lady was happy and that's all that mattered to me at that moment. It was like falling in love all over again. I felt like a kid tasting the passion fruit of love for the first time. We ate our meal and even danced a slow dance while the saxophonist played "My Girl" in the background.

Our desert was the coupe de la gras. The chief prepared a special soufflé dripping in Bohemian chocolate, garnished with a slice of strawberry. Tears rolled down her cheek as the waiter placed it in front of her and the staff sang happy birthday. I gave her a sly wink and blew her a kiss from across the table. The sight of her happiness made me want to cry. I had done my very best to show her a glimpse of what she meant to me. By the look in her eyes I knew I had succeeded.

After dinner our next stop was a member's only Lesbian club called 'The Well', located in a posh antebellum home in the Garden District. As we got our boogey on through out the night I couldn't help but wish time would stand still and the moment could last forever. Jade was having a great time and I was in heaven.

When we stepped outside to leave the club, the horse drawn carriage I'd reserved was waiting on us. He navigated us through the garden district and back to the quarter. It was late and the streets were dreary from a brief rain earlier. Steam poured lazily out of the sewer cracks giving the illusion of a European setting.

As we strolled through the quarter Jade was surprised to find that Bourbon Street was still going strong. And even though at times, our carriage was surrounded by partygoers, she didn't allow it shake her mood. She kissed me openly and looked loving in my eyes as we talked of our night on the town together. As we rode, I spotted a rose peddler I allowed the driver to pass him. Then I asked him to pull over at the next corner. I jumped out, pretending to go to the bathroom and ran back to buy a rose for Jade. As I walked back to the carriage, hiding the rose behind my back, I gently presented it to her as I climbed back into my seat. She smiled broadly and said,

"This is the best birthday I've ever had. I love you Casey"

When Love Aint Enough

"I love you too beautiful," I whispered in her ear as I kissed her neck. After our tour, the horseman drove us back to our hotel. Outside our room, I picked Jade up in my arms and carried her over the threshold, just as I'd planned to do if we'd arrived together. Gently I placed her on the bed and lay down on top of her. I had to get that one more time. And she gladly obliged me.

The next morning was just like the morning before it, Jade and I made love until we could make love no more. Against my will I was forced out of bed by Jade, literally, she pushed me out because I could have stayed in it forever. But it was getting late and we had a plane to catch so I volunteered to shower first, knowing how long it took her to shower and dress.

After showering, I slipped on my clothes and began the tedious job of packing. As I walked around the suite picking up our belongings a card fell out of Jades jacket. I picked it up and was about to put it on the dresser but the words on it jumped out at me and making the hair on the back of neck stand up. It read:

'Sweetheart, you are so-o very good at the things you do! I almost felt like it was my birthday. I'll tell you when you get home just how good you really are.

All my Love,

Richard'

My palms grew sweaty and I began to tremble. Nervously I paced the room with the note gripped tight in my sweaty palm.

215

Painfully I read it over and over hoping I'd been mistaken in what I'd read the time before. My heart raced wildly as each word cut through me. A sickening feeling overwhelmed me making me light headed and anxious. I wanted to storm into the bathroom and confront her with what I'd found. But I couldn't. Instead I felt embarrassed, humiliated and most of all devastated by what I had read.

"So this is why she was late getting here," I thought, as I continued to pace the floor. *"She was fucking him while I sat here like a fool waiting on her!"*

The thought of the two of them together drove me wild.

Then the water stopped. I anxiously walked over to the door and waited for her to come out. After an eternity, she sauntered out wearing nothing but a towel, wrapped around her head and smiling. My presence by the door caught her off guard and she stopped abruptly. Slowly I handed her the card. Recognizing it immediately, she balled it up and searched my face for a sign. I didn't bother to give her one. Instead, I walked into the living room and sat down at the dinning room table. Jade followed closely.

"Baby let me explain…." she began nervously.

"What's to explain? It's evident you are good at the things you do to him, I can only venture to guess what those things are," I said painfully.

"Where did you get this Casey?"

"Why? What does it matter! It's your aint it?!" I asked foolishly, hoping there was a believable explanation for the note. And that it didn't mean what I thought it did.

"Yes its mine" she said softly reaching across the table to touch my hand.

"That's what I figured," I said as my heart plummeted deep inside my chest.

"Casey you know I'm dating him so why do you always act surprised when his name comes up? She asked softly.

I looked at her as though I was seeing her for the first time. "Damn it Jade the man just said you're good at the things you do! Now he can only be referring to you're either sucking his dick or fucking him?! So you tell me how in the hell am I suppose to react to that?!"

"Casey please, it's been a beautiful trip let's not spoil it by arguing" Jade begged.

I looked at her in amazement. She didn't have a clue how this was affecting me. As far as she was concerned I should just accept it and go on. Well that's not what I felt and I refused to pretend I didn't give a damn anymore because I did. I very much gave a damn and the idea of someone other than me making love to her was killing me!

I was at a loss for words. I looked in her eyes but couldn't say anything, so I looked away. I didn't want to show my pain and I damn sure didn't want her to see me cry. I felt defeated.

The trip never had chance of being a success when it came down to the nigga in her life.

After all, *"Didn't she put me on hold to fuck him before joining me?"* I thought.

I was devastated but I kept telling myself to keep it together. I knew I had to, for my own sake. I was alone. No one gave a damn about how I was feeling or if I felt anything at all. All of a sudden the world grew vicious in my eyes and I was afraid. Afraid of being found out as the naïve fool I'd obviously been taken for. I was ashamed at having lavished so much attention on a person who could hurt me so deeply and disregard my feelings at will. I wanted to shrivel up into a ball and roll off into a corner or better yet give away my heart so it wouldn't hurt as much as it did. The pain was unbearable. It choked in my throat like a lump and made me want to gasp for air.

Jade stood up and walked over to me. She held out her hand for me to take it. But I couldn't. It was too much. I sat silently staring into oblivion. Dismayed with my attitude she returned to the bedroom. I could hear her crying, but I didn't care how she was feeling. Hell she hadn't cared how I was feeling when she was with him!

"Fuck her," I screamed to myself.

The flight home was quiet. A limo driver was waiting for us when we arrived in Norfolk, as I'd plan. I had him to take Jade home first. We rode in silence. I focused all of my attention on the other cars traveling on the freeway. When we arrived at

Jade's place, the driver carried her luggage into the lobby leaving me and her alone for the first time since leaving the hotel.

"The trip was wonderful Casey. Thank you." She said solemnly.

"You're welcome" I said coldly.

"Will you call me when you get home?" she asked

"Sure"

"Bye" she said as she leaned over to kiss me.

A picture of her sucking Richard's dick flashed through my head and I turned my cheek to catch her kiss. She sat up abruptly. I could feel her staring at me. So, I looked off into space hoping she'd leave before tears started rolling down my face.

"I understand," she said.

She got out and walked into her building.

In time, I was able to forgive Jade but I didn't forget it. Hardly a day went by that we didn't argue about something. I grew insanely jealous of her and Richard. When she wasn't with me I assumed she was with him and the thought tormented the hell out of me. Our relationship was falling apart fast and we were soon at our breaking points. One morning, after not being able to locate her all damn night, I called her. It was the usual with us, I told her she was selfish and not to be trusted. And she told me to grow up and accept life for what it was. We argued. I cursed. She cursed.

219

"You're stressing me the fuck out!" She exclaimed. I need some space from this, from you!

Enough said, so I gave it to her!

BOOTY CALL

It was around nine pm and I was still at the office. As I sat at my desk I realized I didn't want to go home to an empty house.

 Since Jade and I broke up, all I did was sit and wait for her to come back. I wasn't going to do it tonight.

 "Who knows what she's doing?" I thought. *"She's probably with him doing the things she's so good at doing!"*

 I picked up the phone to call her but quickly decided not to. What I needed was a fine cutie, butt naked in my bed with her legs wide open, telling me to make love to her.

 "Damn, I've waited long enough. Jade ain't coming back and if she does it will be too late. I am tired of going to an empty house, night after night, while she's out doing her thang. I picked up the receiver again. This time I dialed the number and waited for an answer. And she did.

 "Hello"

 "What's up? I said, surprised she'd answered so quickly.

 "You"

I smiled.

 "What are you doing tonight?" I asked, hoping she would say me.

221

"I'm listening to music and having a glass of wine."

Without hesitation I asked,

"Would you like some company?"

"Sure,"

I smiled to myself.

"Well, I'll be leaving the office in about 15 minutes. How about I pick you up and we go to my house for drinks and a movie?"

"Sounds good to me"

After giving me directions to her house we hung up. I contemplated whether I was really going to go through with it.

Karen was a clerk in our Accounting Department. I'd met her months ago in the Grill, one of the restaurants in the building. It turned out to be her favorite hangout. She and I only talked briefly but the vibes were definitely there. And we both knew it. On the sly she'd given me her number and invited me out a couple of times but I declined always thinking I'd somehow be betraying Jade. Failing to realize, you can't cheat on somebody who's got somebody else! Dah!

But now things were different. Jade was out of the picture and from the vibes I got from Karen she was definitely interested in more than just conversation. She seemed like the type of woman who was ready, willing and able to please a nigga. And right now a nigga needed to be pleased!

"Hell, I have needs just like Jade. And if she wants to play, hide and go seek then that's on her."

But like my grandmamma used to say,

  "She needs to shit or get off the pot"

I needed someone who wanted to do what I wanted to do when I wanted to do it!

My thoughts were interrupted as the elevator came to a halt. As I walked toward my truck I clicked the remote and took off my jacket.

"To hell with this, I'm fucking somebody's daughter tonight!" I mumbled raising the engine in affirmation of my decision.

I settled back in my truck and continued to reassure myself that I was doing the right thing. As I turned into Karen's neighborhood my conscience kicked in again. *Karen seemed* cool *and she was definitely beautiful but was sleeping with her going to solve anything? She was attentive, funny and most of all she didn't act as if she was ashamed of me. Jade and her closeted ass had begun to make me doubt my own self! And that, right there, was dangerous ground. Hell I knew who I was and what I wanted! She was the one confused, not me*!

The thought of her betrayal in New Orleans, combined with her refusal to validate me in her life, fueled inside me like a wild fire. *Fuck it! I'm doing it. Stop analyzing the shit! What ever happens, happens! At least I won't be alone again tonight wondering what the hell she's doing or who she's doing it with,"*
I thought.

223

Dubarkis Street.

The street sign jumped out at me like a deer caught in headlights. Slowly I searched for her house.

It was a contemporary crème colored stucco house with green shutters. Her driveway went all the way to the back but I parked in the front. Calmly I got out and climbed the stairs to the front door. I knocked awkwardly, hoping to be heard over the sounds of Anita Baker pulsating through the walls. Karen opened the door almost immediately, looking sexier than I'd ever seen her.

"Hey you!" she said smiling broadly.

Her smile was warm and inviting helping me to relax and dismiss the doubts I'd had on the drive over.

"Hey, you ready?" I asked smiling back.

"Yeah, come in while I get my purse."

The sweet smell of perfume lingered in the air as I walked through the entrance and into the foyer. A huge mirror was hanging on the wall directly in front of me. I quickly checked myself out. I almost didn't recognize the person smiling back at me. For the first time in weeks I dared to be smiling and it felt good.

I followed Karen into her den. It was a cozy spacious room, with large over stuffed furniture and tall plants placed neatly around. She walked over to me and slipped her arms around my neck to give me a big hug. Surprised by her boldness, I responded likewise, hugging her and holding her a little bit longer than called for, while inhaling her DNKY perfume. She

leaned back in my arms and looked at me. Softly she brushed
aside my hair and searched my eyes. Her stare was intent but
not invasive. She gave me a big smile then grabbed her purse.
A picture of a small boy, looking striking like her, hung on the
wall. He was a handsome little fellow with a sheepish grin on
his face. I'd never heard her mention any kids so I asked who he
was. She said it was her baby. Then she added,

"He lives with my mother"

"Damn, strike one!" I thought.

As we drove down the coastline listening to a new Maxwell
CD I tried to dismiss all thoughts of Jade. The music must have
had a similar soothing effect on Karen as well because after
some casual conversation she began rubbing her hand up and
down my leg. I grew a bit tense as butterflies welled up inside
me. The woman was turning me on like crazy! I could feel my
button tingling. I readjusted myself in my seat giving me a little
relief from the stimulation. I glanced at her and rubbed my
crotch to show her I was definitely hot and bothered. She smiled
seductively and unsnapped her seatbelt. Then she leaned over
and laid her head on my shoulder.

When we exited the highway to Kelp's Cove I was even more
relaxed with my decision. As I approached my house I reached
up and opened the garage door. It was a two Tudor styled home
overlooking the Chesapeake Bay. I had been there for about two
years. I had it custom built after receiving a substantial bonus

225

and my new promotion. We walked into the house holding hands like kids.

The first thing to catch Karen's eye was the remarkable crystal chandelier that hovered in the foyer as we walked through into the sunken living room. She was quite impressed as she walked about the room admiring the décor and running her hand across the Cashmere throw that lay on the chaise. A sparkle shown in her eyes as she looked into the steel case filled of authentic African Art. I didn't know it then but her mind was working over time.

I walked up behind her and ran my hands up and down her arms sniffing at her perfumed neck as she questioned me about several of the pieces. She leaned back into my kisses tilting her head slightly and pulled her hair back. My button throbbed wildly as I pulled her into me and nibbled on her soft skin allowing my tongue to give her neck a preview of what her pussy was going to get. Suddenly Karen spun around and threw her arms around my neck kissing me passionately. I allowed my hands to travel to her plump butt then around to her tight spot and squeezed it adoringly. She grind her pussy into my hand moaning deeply as I worked at pulling up her skirt to get to it. Almost as sudden as she had kissed me she stopped and pulled back. She looked at me almost wickedly and whispered,

"Your home is beautiful but it could stand a woman's touch to brighten it up a bit"

I pulled her close and whispered back,

"Well, ain't I a woman?"

She smiled and grabbed my hand leading me seductively to the sofa. I followed dutifully watching her beautifully sculptured ass as I went.

"Strike Two" I noted to myself.

As Karen made herself comfortable on the sofa I worked the remote taking things up a notch. I pointed it towards the fireplace and an instant fire began raging. I adjusted the temperature to what felt comfortable and then turned my attention to the patio. I loved to see the moon dripping over the bay in the middle of the night. The view from my house was flawless. Casually I parted the blinds with the remote and dimmed the lights. Karen moaned blissfully as the moon beamed in off the water into the room. Then I lowered the 72-inch screen, simultaneously turning it on.

Karen whirled around fascinated as I worked my magic. Though she didn't want to me to know it, I could tell by the expression on her face, she was damned impressed. I walked over and handed her the remote. I sat down on the sofa beside her to give her a brief lesson on how to work it. I didn't know it, but Karen was bound and determined to show me how to work something too that night.

After the tutorial I went over to the bar to mix our drinks. I poured two healthy glasses of Cognac with a shot of lime and sprite.

We exchanged some small talk and searched the menus for something to watch. Finally we decided on a Law and Order rerun. We lay back on the sofa laughing and talking trying to guess who the guilty party was as we sipped our cocktails. Soon the momentum of the conversation changed.

We started talking about significant others. Karen, giddy from her drink, explained that she lived alone due to her financial situation. She was recently divorced and going through a restructuring period. She had two kids, a son and daughter and they both lived with her mother in Portsmouth. As she talked of her home life, I wondered how much of what's going on with me was safe to tell.

I was having a good time for the first time in weeks and I didn't want to jeopardize it by tipping my hand. But I didn't want to mislead her either. So I decided to be a woman about it and tell the truth. I told her of my relationship with Jade but was quick to add we were separated. Karen's body language began to change as I described the up and down relationship. I knew I'd talked too much when she avoided eye contact with me and stared at the television. I let out a sigh and repositioned myself in my little area of the sofa.

I understood how she felt. I'd felt the same way only I didn't get the privilege of deciding until after the sex act.

"But what could I do?"

She deserved the truth. And I didn't have anything to hide. As the silence persisted reservations crept into my mind,

228

"Hell, I hope I haven't talked myself out of some good loving!" I thought, grabbing the remote to do some damage control. Karen got up from her seat and asked if she could use the bathroom. While she was gone I took the opportunity to freshen up our drinks. When she came out I was already seated with fresh cocktails waiting for her. She walked over still avoiding eye contact and sat down neatly on the opposite end of the sofa. I leaned over and offered her the drink. She thanked me and quietly sipped it.

In an effort to get things back on track I remembered the joint Lionel had given me months ago. I asked if she smoked. Checking me out suspiciously she remarked,

"Sometimes"

I smiled.

"Don't worry I'm not a druggy or anything I just happen to have one a friend gave to me. I've been saving it for a special occasion. Want to try it?" I asked

Karen seemed hesitant.

"Its cool if you don't" I offered

"Sure"

I went upstairs to the bedroom. The joint was tucked away in a wooden box in the bathroom. Holding it triumphantly, I jogged down the staircase and walked calmly in to the living room.

"Here we go, I hope it doesn't knock us out." I said passing it to her like it was the sacred torch or some shit, meanwhile taking the opportunity move closer.

"Fire it up!"

Karen put it up to her lips and I lit it. She inhaled, held it, and then blew the smoke out evenly.

"How long have you had this?" she said letting out a slight cough.

"It's been a minute. A friend gave it to me around Christmas"

She took a couple more pulls and handed it to me. Then lay back on the sofa. I took a deep breath, thumped the ashes into the crystal ashtray and took a long pull. The harshness of the smoke immediately burned the back of my throat as I inhaled. A couple pulls later, I was coughing uncontrollably.

Karen rose up to look at me. When I couldn't stop coughing she gently pat me on the back and looked into my eyes to see if I was okay. I wasn't but I was too embarrassed to tell her. She motherly wiped away the perspiration that had collected on my forehead. Then I took the joint. I took a big gulp of my drink and lay back on the sofa. I didn't have to wait long to feel the side affects of the weed.

My head grew light and my tongue heavy. The sounds around me grew into a sea of blah-blah blahs. I couldn't make out shit that was being said. I almost freaked out until I looked at Karen who was busy inhaling the remnants of the joint like a professional. She held it precisely between her fingers and smoked it until it was barely visible.

"Damn! She's a pro!" I thought and started laughing my ass off.

Ignoring me, Karen, savored the smoke, holding her breath, while gesturing to me to take it. I threw up my hands to decline. Karen continued to smoke and inhale on the roach until it turned to ash. Her eyes rolled in the back of her head as she digested the smoke. When she could hold it no longer a big ball of smoke escaped and she started coughing. Soon we were both laughing uncontrollably.

"Damn this is some good shit!" she said in between the laughter.

"It's Italian!" I hollered, falling out laughing.

Now, everything was funny as hell. I tried to compose myself but couldn't. I looked at Karen and she was fucked up too. It had achieved its goal. Karen was smiling again. She laid back on the sofa and I stretched out, laying my head in her lap.

Karen was talking nonstop. First on her agenda was the office. I was high but not that high. I didn't like discussing the job after leaving it and told her so. She on the other hand seemed to enjoy it immensely as she talked of her boss, Jason Andrews. He was constantly asking her out despite her rejection of him. I figured she wasn't exaggerating because I'd heard about him.

Vivian M Kelly

Jason was known for his attraction for the ladies. In fact he was notorious for it. The only thing that saved his ass was the fact he was married to the daughter of one of the senior partners, who happened to be a whore himself. He was a swanky want to be Yuppie who'd married into money but his actions showed his morals were dirt cheap.

After telling me her business, she tried to get into mine by asking me about the partners. I lied saying I didn't know them personally.

"I think I get along pretty good with everyone. But you can never tell, people are fickle and will surprise you." I added, thinking about Jade, for the first time since I got home.

"You're right" she agreed

"Anyway that's enough shop talk,"

I looked at my watch. It was 2:00am.

"Baby, its late, what do you want to do?"

She pretended to think about the question for a minute, then stood up and stretched out her arms toward me.

"You haven't showed me your bedroom"

Without hesitation I stood up and lead her upstairs.

While she showered, I eagerly got ready for her, dimming the lights and putting away the big picture of Jade I kept beside the bed.

Karen walked out of the bathroom wearing nothing but a smile as I was slipping between the cool cotton sheets. Her curvaceous silhouette danced off the flickering candles teasing all that were blessed to see it. Her silky black hair lay limp on her neck, damp from the steam, added to her seductiveness. She looked delicious as she walked up to me. My head spun slightly when I rose up on my elbow to get a better view of her golden 5ft frame. She was perfect from head to toe.

The tips of her nipples rubbed across my mouth as she crawled over me to get in bed. Once snug under the covers, she nestled under me, laying her head on my shoulder and simultaneously running her hand across my abdomen and over my breasts. The smell of DKNY was still on her skin. She rose up and looked into my eyes. She looked at me thoughtfully for a moment then leaned down and pressed her lips to mine. Tenderly she moaned as she pushed her tongue inside my mouth.

Her kisses were hungry. I could sense from her kisses that she was in desperate need of someone to make love to her. The butterflies in my stomach were doing cartwheels causing my flesh to tingle with the slightest touch. Seductively she climbed on top me, moaning and grinding her pelvis into mine. I reached down and grabbed her butt, squeezing it and pulling it closer. Slowly I rolled her over in the bed until I was on top of her. Once on top, I began to kiss her neck and pinch her breast with my fingertips. Her nipples grew hard and her small breast stood at attention from my touch.

"Oh baby," I whispered. "I need you so much"

She began to move more beneath me. I slowly made my way down her body, kissing and licking her soft damp skin.

"Oh Casey," she moaned.

The sound of her wispy voice made me want to fill her nest with something extra but I chilled and I took my time. When I arrived at her hairless mound I ran my tongue inside it as though I was tonguing her mouth. My tongue slide deep inside and my mouth encased her spot like a tight fitting glove. Karen pushed her pelvis up, forcing my tongue even deeper inside her.

My hands traveled her soft body massaging and teasing her breast. I opened my eyes and watched her squirm with delight from my hungry fervor. The sight energized me as I raised her torso and pushed my fingers deep inside her ticking her insides. She arched her body up and let out a deep moan. I continued to move my fingers around inside as I kissed her stomach softly and tongued her navel. The passion inside me was growing like a wildfire. My button was aching like crazy desiring some relief. I grabbed my crotch and rubbed it hard telling myself to hold on while I pleased this beautiful creature.

Meanwhile Karen was going nuts in anticipation. I could hardly contain her wild movements to the bed as she tossed and jumped around desiring more of what I was giving her. Her face was contorted as she tried to endure the sensations that made her body want to explode. Trying to desperately not to release her pleasure too soon, she ran her fingers vigorously through my hair. I made my way back to her breast and was sucking so hard I thought I'd draw milk!

Slowly I pulled my fingers out of her and rubbed the remnants of her fluids across her lips to give her a taste of her own sweet pussy. Her moist body trembled in anticipation of what was to happen next. Karen licked and sucked my fingers removing all traces of her off my fingertips. I slid back down to her crotch and blew warm air on her clitoris and traced it with the tip of my tongue. Her body grew stiff and her breathing heavier, as I alternated back and forth from the tip of her clitoris to the inside of her vagina. I could sense my teasing was getting the best of her so I concentrated all of my attention on her protruding clit, licking and sucking feverishly as though it was ice cream. Karen moved about the bed wildly calling my name and burying my head firmly into her pussy with her tiny hands.

Suddenly she arched her back and threw her body into the air. She was coming, but it was too fast. Abruptly I stopped and climbed on top of her. I kissed her cold lips and put my hands into my boxers. As I pushed her legs apart with mine I gently pushed Charlie deep inside her. Karen, whose eyes were half closed opened them wide and stared at me. Her gaze was intense as I continued to push my dick deeper and pump into her spot ferociously. I enjoyed the look of surprise on her face and wrapped my lips around breast sucking them deep into my mouth. Karen clawed at my back trusting her body upward grinding on my dick as if it were the last game in town.

I was content to fuck her until the cows came home but her body grew rigid with spasmodic jerking and she let out a blood curdling scream into the quite house.

I rolled over onto the damp sheets to allow her rest for a moment. But it was only a moment, because before I knew it, Karen had jumped on top of me and was riding my dick like Roy rode Trigger.

The girl was perched in a squat, deep throating my dick with her pussy like a damn professional. It was all I could do to hold on and enjoy the ride. Happily I continued to fuck her demanding that she scream my name as I pounded upward into her hole and slapped her hard on her round juicy ass. After several hours of serious fucking we lay in each other's arms. She fell asleep but I was wide awake!

I looked at Karen sleeping peacefully and carefully moved my arm from underneath her head. I peeped over at the clock on the nearby nightstand. It was 4:37 am. I turned over carefully so as not to wake her, to get some sleep.

From the skylight above I could hear the pitter patter of rain outside.

"Good, it'll help me sleep" I thought to myself as I snuggled under the down comforter and into my goose pillow.

It was seven thirty and the aroma of bacon ran swiftly through my bedroom slowly awakening all my senses.

"Wake up sleepy head," she whispered in my ear, kissing me on the back of my neck. I rolled over and smiled, dreaming it was Jade. As I opened my eyes I saw Karen looking down at me wearing a pair of my boxers and a tee shirt. She sat on the edge of the bed smiling and began running her fingers through my hair. And just like that I knew I had fucked up!

"Damn she's still here!" I thought, alarmed. I closed my eyes tight and then opened them again to find her still sitting there.

"Of course she's still here! You got fucked up, fucked her and fucking went to sleep you damn dummy!" I remembered in disbelief.

I rose up slowly and leaned on the headboard, trying to think of something to say to her. She was smiling her butt off
I smiled back.

"Hey beautiful did you sleep okay?" I whispered

"Of course," she said leaning over to give me a kiss. "I hope you don't mind, but I was hungry, so I made some breakfast"

"That was sweet, thank you"

"I hope you like it" she purred at me.

"I'm sure I will" I smiled back.

"Then get showered and I'll have it ready for you when you come down" She said, standing up to go down to the kitchen.

"I'll be there in fifteen minutes" I said as she walked out of the room.

I threw my legs over the side of the bed and sat on the edge to compose myself before standing. Slowly I got up and walked into the bathroom. I avoided looking into the mirror as I passed by it.

The smell of bacon filled the air prompting me to put a rush on my morning routine and leaving little time for me to think about anything else.

"Pull yourself together" I mumbled "Don't be an asshole. *"After all, she did cook breakfast!"* I thought, as the hot water beat down on my tired body.

Before going down, I dressed for work. My black Liz Claiborne suit was hitting me just right along with my stylish Liz boots.

Karen, showing off her domestic skills, had cooked one hell of a breakfast. It was complete with eggs, hash browns, French toast, juice and grits.

"Um Grits, everybody can't cook em!" I thought, looking at the steamy mixture.

Being straight from the Deep South, breakfast wasn't really breakfast to me without a nice helping of grits. I was impressed and pleasantly surprised to find the Karen knew how. Still admiring the table, I complimented a proud Karen on the beautiful meal she had put together. Secretly I wondered if I had told her how much I craved a big breakfast after a night of hot sex. Either way the gesture was nice and very much appreciated.

When Love Aint Enough

After breakfast Karen went upstairs to shower and I went out on the balcony to look at the ocean. The bay was empty except for seagulls flying in an out in search of food. I walked to the ledge and leaned against it.

As I looked down, I saw my neighbor running with her dog. They played carefree in the sand, taking turns chasing each other. Sensing my presence, she looked up and waved. I waved back smiling. Sometimes it was still hard to believe that I was really apart of all this.

"Was this really me? Had I made it?" I thought.

"I'm ready"

I turned to find Karen standing in the doorway.

"Okay, let's go"

As we walked to the door, I grabbed my keys and jacket.

MY GIRL RONNI

Morning traffic on I-64 was always a mess for commuters trying to bully their way back into the city after eight. So I took the Hampton Expressway trying to make up for time after taken Karen home to get her car.

When I walked into the office I said my usual hellos and went into my office. As I sat down, Ronnie walked in.

"Good morning Ronni" I said looking over the stack of papers she'd placed on my desk.

"Good morning, how are you this morning?"

"Fine and you?"

"I'm good. A Marty Feldman from EarthTel called for you several times this morning. He would like to meet with you today at your earliest convenience. Your calendar says you're free after lunch, what do you say" asked Veronica as she scribbled something on the small pad she held in her hand.

"I don't have any plans thus far but let's hold on before committing to that," I said still eyeing the file on my desk.

"I need you to contact Monica and Alexander and remind them of our meeting scheduled for ten to wrap up the Joshua file."

240

"Alex isn't in today, he called saying he had a family emergency".

"Oh?! Did he say what was wrong?"

"No," said she said shrugging her shoulders.

"I see"

The Joshua Case was due for a final hearing on Monday. The company was trying to avoid a possible take over by one of its rivals. Projected earnings had been down by twenty five percent for three consecutive quarters and the stockholders were getting antsy. It looked like a rival competitor was making an unwanted bid and Joshua Financial was trying to ward them off. Monica and Alexander were the two paralegals working with me to preempt the motion.

"Well we still need to meet. Get with Monica maybe she has his files. I'll push the meeting back to eleven"

"It looks like I'll be free after two. Give Mr. Feldman a call to confirm we can meet at three. It can be my last appointment of the day."

"Ok boss I'll take care of it," said Veronica as she turned to leave.

"Also can you order lunch for the three us today? We will probably have to work through lunch since we're short a person, I'm sorry."

"It's not a problem. What would you like for lunch?" She asked.

"I'll have whatever you get, I'm not picky today, I had a big breakfast."

Veronica, turned away frowning. Then returned to her desk, to make some calls.

Ronni, as I liked to call her, and I had been working together for a couple of years now. We first met in the bathroom of a mutual friend's party a couple of years ago. We'd both sought refuge there trying to escape all the boojey wanna-be's that had flooded the place. I was reluctant to talk to her at first thinking she was one of "them."

In the bathroom, she sat on the sofa and I on the sink, talking shit about the guests. We totally clicked from the moment we met. I soon found out she wasn't your typical straight sista. She was about 5' 4" with coca brown skin. She looked like she weighed a buck –fifteen soaking wet. Her hair was jet black and traveled down her back past her shoulder blades. When she smiled it revealed a set of perfectly straight teeth with a little gap in the front.

After about thirty minutes of talking in the bathroom, we decided to give the party one more try. It was of no avail. We soon found we enjoyed talking to each other more so than mingling with the crowd.

As we talked I was very careful not to flirt. I did not want this beautiful sista to put me in the same ole stereotypical bag most people put gays, in that they were always after sex. In fact, I really wondered if she knew. I assumed she did because after all, the host was notoriously gay and for the most part, most of the guests were too.

Either way, it didn't really matter because I wasn't interested in her in that way. Not that she was unattractive or anything like that, she was fine as wine. It's just that I was taking a sabbatical from love. But on the other hand, I actually found her conversation quite stimulating. She had a radiant smile and when she laughed her eyes grew smaller. I could definitely see why she joked her man was constantly checking up on her. She was gorgeous.

As the night went on we found ourselves inquisitively entranced with each other, each learning more of the others life style.

Conversation on lifestyle choices was always a sticky subject with me because I knew being gay was no more a choice than my being able to choose the color of my skin. It was something I was endowed with by my creator. And whether people liked it or not, it was normal.

It is as natural to me to see a pretty woman and want to know her name, as it is for a so-called straight person to look at the opposite sex admiringly. But for some odd reason Veronica and I could talk of this. And that was refreshing. I made it abundantly clear that my sexual preference was the least important thing about me.

Vivian M Kelly

We talked for hours about judgmental and absurd attitudes of not just straight people but gays as well. She found it funny that I refused to align myself with either.

"I'm Casey!" I said. "I don't like labels it's too restrictive." I stated proudly.

I even explained to her how I came to develop that philosophy. It was years ago after I had finished college that I had returned from a trip to New Orleans, Louisiana. I had bought a sticker with a gay pride symbol on it and proudly placed it on my car tag. One day as we stood in the driveway my mom noticed it. She asked what it meant. Since I had come out to her years prior, I felt comfortable saying, "It's a gay pride symbol."

"Oh really" she said appearing puzzled. She looked at it a minute more and turned to me and said,

"If it doesn't say gay pride who will know"

"Other gay people" I said confidently

"How can you be proud if no one knows what it is but you and someone else who is gay" she asked confused but making her point very clear.

I thought about it and realized the sticker was dumb. It didn't stand for pride at all. It was just clever advertisement. Needless to say I threw it away.

Veronica and I laughed.

"The things you do when you're trying to find yourself," I joked.

"You too" she pointed still laughing" "I thought I was the only one who went looking."

For the rest of the night, we chilled with the amply supplied liquor and talked. Before leaving we exchanged numbers.

After the party we'd call each other and would occasionally meet for coffee or a movie. One night Veronica called me very upset. I'd just finished a hellafied work out at the gym and anxiously rushed home to shower and rest. The light on the answering machine was flashing. It was Veronica and she sounded as if she was crying. I picked up the phone and called her back. After about the fifth ring she answered.

"Hello" she whispered.

"Ronnie?"

"Yes"

"Hey girl, what's wrong?" I said.

"Can I come over?" she asked.

"Sure, do you want me to come get you?"

"No, no, I can drive. I'm leaving now if that's okay."

"Sure," I said, wondering what the heck was up.

"Okay, I'll see you in a minute."

"Drive carefully", I instructed before we hung up.

Ronnie didn't bother to say bye. I stood holding the receiver, entranced by the dial tone and the sadness in her voice.

At the time, I had a loft apartment downtown on Gransby. Ronnie and her finance lived in Portsmouth. So I had a good 45 minutes to get cleaned up before she arrived. It was autumn, my favorite time of the year, but this night was particularly cold so I lit the fireplace to take the chill out of the air. After showering I threw on a pair sweats and a tee shirt.

My apartment was on the ninth floor, high enough to have a view of the city but not good enough to see the Atlantic Ocean, which was only a few miles away. As I stood looking out onto the streets, I asked myself if I would miss the convenience of downtown once I moved to my new house overlooking the bay.

"Nah-h-h" I responded aloud

A single star had escaped from behind the cloud and shone brightly in the dark sky. As I watched it, the doorbell rang. I went inside leaving the door cracked so the crisp cool air could filter in to mix with the dry heat from the fireplace. When I opened the door, there stood Veronica, looking smaller than usual. She'd been crying.

"Hey, come on in."

She walked over to the sofa and plopped down on the overstuffed pillows as if she wanted to be swallowed in. I sat opposite her in a brown leather chair pushing the ottoman away with my feet so I could sit up straight because Ronni looked as if she needed my undivided attention.

"What's wrong?"

Veronica, fighting back tears, told me of the argument she'd had with her fiancé Raymond. I'd known her to talk about they're arguments before but I'd never seen her react this way. She sobbingly told me how Raymond had met her at the door of their apartment in a jealous rage. He'd accused of her of being out with another man because she was late coming home from work. They fought and he'd stormed out.

Although the scene she described made me mad as hell, I didn't show it. I'd learned a long time ago not to get in the middle of things like that. Because the fight between them was temporary, if I got it, I ran the risk of one if not both being pissed at me for taking sides. So I chilled and took it all. As Veronica, continued describing the fight, tears streamed down her face. For the first time in their relation she found herself scared of the man she loved! My soul ached with hers. I thought back to when Matt and I had our one and only drag out fight. I immediately wanted to comfort her, but I was unsure how.

Though we'd become very close, I was always on guard when it came to straight women. I didn't want any misunderstandings! My heart went out to her but I couldn't bring myself to comfort her with a hug. Instead, I went to get a box of tissues and gave'em to her. When she reached up for them our eyes met and my heart sank even farther. I hated seeing her like that. In fact, I was really shocked. She'd always seemed so strong. When she and I talked of relationships, it was always me who seemed to be the weaker of the two.

I went back to my chair and tried to lighten the moment by telling her of my weight lifting fiasco earlier. She looked up, flashed a smile, but continued to cry. Unable to take her crying I said,

"To *hell with it, shit she's my friend!"* I thought.

I went over to sit beside her and offered her my shoulder to cry. I put my arm around her shoulder and she gently laid her head on my chest.

As the soft sensual smell of her perfume filled my nostrils, I wondered how Raymond could be so stupid. Didn't he know that was the quickest way to push a person away!

Veronica and I sat there for a while with me holding her like that. All about us was quiet except from the little whimpers and the blowing of her nose every so often.

"Casey wake up"

"Huh"

"Wake up, it's getting late. I'm fixing to go"

"What, what time is it" I asked wiping the sleep from my eyes.

"It's a little after midnight, go to bed, I'm leaving" she said getting up to leave.

But it was late so insisted that she stay. I think she wanted to anyway. Neither of us knew what she could expect if she went home this late.

"He's at work now. He don't get off until 8 in the morning"

"That's all the more reason to stay. Besides, if you go there you'll probably stay up half the night, thinking."

"Probably so..." she agreed.

So we went to bed. Her in the bedroom and me on the sofa.

The next morning around 6:30am I was awakened by the smell of bacon and Mocha coffee. Veronica was busing herself in the kitchen as I walked in to get my morning cup of Java.

"Morning"

"Good morning," she replied. "I hope you don't mind me cooking breakfast. I would have asked you but were sleeping so good I didn't want to wake you."

I smiled at her bashfulness. But she wasn't lying, I'd slept like a log all night long. I poured a cup of coffee and leaned back on the counter to take a sip. It tasted a hell of a lot better than the stuff I normally made.

As I pulled the cup down from my lips, my eyes shifted to the butt before me. Ronni was leaning over, removing croissants from the oven. The little tee shirt I'd given her last night did nothing to hide the fabulous ass she had half hidden under it. I felt a little butterfly try to make its way into my stomach but I managed to shake it off by quickly looking away. Ronni stood up holding a tray of croissants and placed them on the counter. I took two plates from the cabinets to set the table.

Ronni appeared very comfortable wandering about the kitchen getting our breakfast together.

"So, how did you sleep last night?"
Without looking up she said,

"It was okay"

"That's good" I said, still envisioning her round butt in my head.

"How do you like your eggs? She asked.

"Sunny side up"

"Oh you're one of those huh" she kidded, flashing me a smile as she proceeded to fix my eggs.

After she finished cooking we sat down to eat. Everything looked and smelled great. I bowed my head to say grace and when I'd finished looked up at Ronni. Her head was still down. I waited until she'd finished before speaking.

"Everything looks delicious!" I said digging into the food before me.

She flashed a weak smile.

"I like to eat a big breakfast when I'm depressed"

"I normally only eat one after a night of wild passion," I smirked.

Ronnie looked at me then back into her plate.

"I'm sorry Ronni I didn't mean to be insensitive"

"Its okay girl, come to think of it me too! I guess we both be working up an appetite, huh?!"

I laughed.

"I guess so"

That morning I was full of conversation. Ronni added what she could but she still had other issues on her mind. After breakfast I showered and got dressed for work while Ronnie did the dishes. When I was ready, we walked out together. I gave her a big hug when we reached her car. I asked her to call me later and she promised she would. Her normal confident manner had taken a back seat and all was left was a little girl who didn't know which way to turn.

I got into my truck and turned on the radio. Erika Badu was playing. I listened to the soothing lyrics as I drove out of the parking lot and into the traffic. The thought of Ronni going back home bothered me. I wondered if Raymond would be there and if so, would he try to start another fight since she didn't go home last night. I made a mental note to call her when I got to work. Silently I asked God to protect and keep her safe. I had seen men like Raymond before and the worst thing she could do was underestimate his potential for violence.

After that night, we grew even closer. It was the defining moment of a true friendship for both of us. Ronni eventually left Raymond. But it wasn't until she they had reached rock bottom in their relationship. The last straw for her was when she caught

251

Vivian M Kelly

him with another woman at their apartment. Even though he swore he'd never done it before and would never do it again, Ronni wouldn't forgive his transgression. By leaving she threw away everything old to find something new. She began a new job, found a new apartment and redefined her sense of self. It was as though she had been walking in the dark and someone had finally turned on the lights. She saw life through a different perspective. This time everything was new and people were just that, people. There was no sense of high ideals of what a person would add or subtract from her.

Her inner calm came not from those who came into her life but what she exuded out of it. Ronni learned her happiness depended upon herself and not others. And her attitude showed it. She went back to school and began working toward her masters. When I got my big promotion I offered her a position as my assistant. It proved to be a winning situation for both us.

KNEE DEEP

We accomplished a lot by working through lunch that day. By all estimations we were ahead of schedule and I was looking forward to the sit down with our clients on Monday. While tying up some loose ends o'l girl called. I politely dismissed Ronni and Monica to take the call.

"Hey babe"

"Hey you, what's up?" I replied.

"You baby, definitely!"

I smiled and paused.

"I've been thinking about you too," I lied.

I turned around slowly in my chair to look out the big picture window behind me and adjusted my headset.

"So how's your day going? Are you very busy?" asked Karen

"Well at one point I was, but it's gotten progressively better. What about yourself?"

"I'm on my lunch break right now. Jason has been cracking the whip all day up here. I'm sick of him!"

"I thought you two were cool?"

"Sometimes, but today he's got his panties in a wad!"

253

"Girl you're a trip," I said laughing at the thought of Jason wearing panties, and in a wad at that!

"No really, he gets like that sometime. Most times I ignore it since normally it isn't directed toward me but today he's been tripping!

"Well just try to stay out of his way."

"That's what I've been doing but he has gotten on my last nerve! I had to take an early lunch to get out of there. But as luck would have it, the little fart saw me leaving and told me he needed to speak with me when I get back. I don't know what the hell it could be but if it's some mess I'm damn sho going to straighten his ass!"

"Calm down, I'm sure it's nothing."

"Anyway!"

"Anyway" I repeated, mimicking her. "Sounds like y'all need to sit down and talk if things are that serious. Shit last night you said he was cool now today this…just tell him how you feel."

"Talking won't do any good," she sighed. "He has been like this every since I told him I wasn't interested in going out with him. Now he is doing everything possibly to make my life miserable."

Now, if I hadn't been so damn slow I would have noticed what she was telling me wasn't adding up. But as usual, when Jade and I were on the outs I rarely thought clearly. Because if I had, I would have thought it odd she was cool with ol boy last night and today he was harassing her, that was some shit to make you say 'Humm' but I didn't and instead I went into my legal beagle mode.

"Have you spoken with anyone else about this?"

"Not really, I was kind of hoping it would blow over. But today he's on a rampage. He mentioned he'd page me last night and asked why I didn't return his call. I told him I was out on a date and didn't take the pager and he went off! He told me that the pager was given to us so we would be accessible! Shit I said I was sorry. Then he wouldn't say nothing…just stood there staring at me like he'd lost his damn mind or some shit!"

"Hump"

"He just kept going on and on about the damn pager. He acted like he wanted to hit me or something. Shit besides suing his ass, I'd lay his light ass out! 'Cause I'm grown!"

"Sounds serious. Have you thought about going to HR?"

"What, Human Resource, hell no, I'd really be out of a job then"

"Well if it's affecting you like that you need to do something. And quite frankly I think HR should be made aware of the situation. They can advise you on your options."

"I don't know Casey, HR?! They might try to flip the script on me or some shit! I'm not trying to lose my job."

"It's not like that. They'll investigate it then go from there." I said reassuringly.

I went on to explain how the HR process worked to assure her of its confidentiality and commitment to the employee.

"Girl you don't know Jason like I do.   He can be ruthless."
I pondered her statement for a minute, "Well if you don't want to involve HR you should start documenting things like this any way."

"Well maybe, I can do that." She said, sounding as if she didn't want to push her luck.

"Listen I didn't mean to bother you with my problems but I am just tired of this. But a girl gotta work, ya know?"

"I know, like my grandmother would say, ya' can't cut off your head to spite your neck."

"You damn sho' right about that! Anyway, that's not why I called you. I called because I wanted to tell you again how nice last night was and to invite you over to my place tonight. I'm cooking."

The invitation caught me off guard. I had been so busy I hadn't had time to think about last night. Or maybe I'd subconsciously suppressed. Never the less, I wasn't going to make it a habit. I mean, she was cool and her body was definitely banging but Jade was my heart.

"Well…" I said, trying to think of a way to decline the invitation without hurt her feelings.
But she sensed my reluctance.

"It's no biggy or nothing. If you have other plans I can understand that. I was just extending the invitation. It's open. So whenever…."she said apologetically.

"It's not that" realizing she knew I was brushing her off, I decided to come clean, "It's like I told you, I'm involved with someone and even though things aren't on track with us right now, I don't want to send out the wrong signals or impression."

"Oh I guess you're just out there slanging and banging huh?" Karen said with a jittery laugher.

"No, no it's not like that at all. Last night was really nice for me too and actually the first time I've stepped out of the relationship. But for now, I'm just chilling just trying to enjoy the moment.

"Well I guess I can appreciate your honesty," said Karen somberly. "Maybe some other time, I need to make some notes on what happened with Jason today anyway. And you would be a distraction, a welcome one, but a distraction nevertheless."

"That's right," I agreed. "Let's see" I said still trying not to burn my bridges on this new found wealth of good loving and companionship, "I'm going to the gym for an hour or so but afterward that I'll give you a call to see how everything is going"

"That'll work, she said. Well… I guess I'd better get off this phone and go back to my desk. Thanks for listening. I feel a lot better now."

"No problem…I'll talk to ya later."

Karen hung up. I continued looking out the window over the misty gray city. I thought of Karen's comment about Jason, "H*e's ruthless?!"* I knew he was sleazy but to go so far as saying ruthless you would have to give the boy some credit for having some type of intelligence. And of that, I sensed he had none. Not even common sense it seemed. Then I thought about her dinner invitation.

 "Man w*hat's wrong with me*?" I wondered to myself. *"T*his *beautiful woman wants to spend time with me, something Jade won't do but I'm too busy racing home to watch a telephone that won't ring. Have I lost my mind! Who am I trying to be loyal too? She hasn't shown me any loyalty."*

Still, I felt bad about having slept with Karen. I reflected sadly on the fact that Jade and I hadn't talked in four agonizing weeks. She and I had disagreements all the time about her thing with Richard but we'd never stopped talking to each other for this long.

New Orleans was an eye opener, but I was still stuck on stupid. For over two years I'd been at Jade's beck and call. But she only made time for me when it was convenient for her not when I wanted to see her. But after the trip, I learned Sir Richard had a key to her place! Hell, I felt like I was dating a married woman! The times we spent together was done behind closed doors at my house. But like a champ I had hung in there offering her unconditional love, which she mistook as weakness.

I loved that woman's dirty draws and deep down held on to the hope that one day we would be a family.

To give up on that was to admit she didn't love me and to do that would be to deny myself the air I breathed. It would kill me and I knew it. I was hopelessly and pitifully in love with her and she knew it! Looking back on it, I wasn't a fool, I was a damn fool.

The last time we talked she'd cursed me out like I was some nigga on the street!

"Hell!" What was the reason she gave for our break up this time?" I mumbled aloud still looking out over the city.

"It had to be about Richard! Somehow, no matter what we argued about it always comes back to the mighty Richard. But in all actuality why am I getting mad at him? It's not him, it's her! And her refusal to make a fucking choice! Hell yeah, I remember, Ms. Jade didn't like being questioned about her relationship with Richard. The first thing that flies out of her mouth is "Why you worrying about him. See you worrying about the wrong thing."

Yeah, I remembered it clearly now. Said I was stressing her out over shit I'd agreed to from jump!" The nerve of that lil *motherfucker! Talking to me like she's a pimp or some shit*! I thought. *"Shit I aint stressing her. If anything she's been stressing the fuck out of me with that wanna- be- player shit. What the hell do I look like, Chop Liver?!"*

I snapped back to reality when the phone rang!

   "Yes" I answered startled, readjusting myself in my seat.

   Mr. Feldman is here for your appointment.

   "Ok, great...give me a minute to freshen up"

   "Sure thing, " replied Ronni.

   I got up from my desk and walked into my bathroom. Being an associate partner allowed me certain luxuries. One of them was a beautifully furnished office with an awesome view, my own private bathroom and completely stocked wet bar. Though I seldom found any personal use for the wet bar, it came in handy for jittery clients who occasionally needed something to steady their nerves.

   Mr. Feldman was seated in the waiting area clutching his battered briefcase. I walked over and extended my hand. He stood up and shook it eagerly. As he and I turned to walk inside my office I motioned to Ronnie to hold my calls. She smiled and nodded her head in acknowledgement.

   Mr. Feldman, the Chief Accountant for one of our largest clients EarthTel, was a short man, around five foot nine with a slender build. He looked like he was in his late fifties by his receding hairline. He gave off a humble presence almost to the point of groveling. He was dressed in a traditional grey flannel suit, black wingtip shoes and smelled of mothballs. As Mr.

Feldman nervously positioned himself in his chair he started to speak right away. He spoke of the pending merger my firm was currently in charge of. He said he had some information he felt was vital to that merger.

He began by stating that the information he was giving me was of a secure nature and asked me about attorney client privilege. I explained my attorney client privilege to his company and officers thereof. Mr. Feldman asked candidly,

"What if the information gathered is deemed not within the interest of the company but more so one of its employees?'

"I don't quite understand what you're asking me."
Mr. Feldman readjusted himself in his chair and leaned forward.

"I don't know, maybe I made a mistake," he said looking way and shaking his head.

"Made a mistake about what?"

"I'm unsure myself" he said.
Now it was my turn to sit up in my chair. I took a deep breath and asked,

"Mr. Feldman if I might ask, what is this all about?"
He took a moment to speak as he gazed out the window behind me. He seemed to be entranced with something. I was tired and becoming impatient with his behavior. I crossed my hands on my desk and tried to exhibit patience with his curious behavior. Finally he began speaking again.

"Ms. Banks, I am between a rock and a hard place right now. I have been with EarthTel for twenty years. During that time I

261

have seen a lot of people come and go, some for the better and some for the worst. I have a wife and three beautiful children at home. My oldest is in college and the other two are in a private academy."

Mr. Feldman reached into his coat pocket and pulled out a white crumpled handkerchief. He unfolded it then refolded it before dabbing at his forehead and his mouth.

I looked at him intently not daring to disturb him so that he would go on and get to the reason for this meeting. After placing the handkerchief back in his coat pocket he continued to talk all the while looking out of the window behind me.

"I have come here today for my life."

I was surprised and my expression showed it. He looked at me and smiled wearily.

"Yes I'm afraid I'm trying to regain what's left of my life, what's left of me for that matter."

Now, I was intrigued. Up until that moment I thought his ravings were that of a man highly stressed and on the verge of a breakdown. While I still hadn't dismissed the idea completely, at this point I wondered if there could possibly be some sanity to his madness.

Mr. Feldman went on to tell me of what he had been directed to do by his firm. In the past five years EarthTel had acquired a substantial piece of the telecommunications pie by purchasing several small telecommunication firms that were in trouble but yet profitable companies. Business was booming! So much so that they were recently listed as one of the top up and coming corporations to watch.

Mr. Feldman told me of a directive he'd received to manipulate the books of several of its subsidiaries for a sell off. This was not the first directive he'd receive directing him to play with the company's numbers. In fact he spun a tale that went back as far as seven years. He gave an estimate of the corruption to be in the billion-dollar range. My head started reeling so I stopped him!

"Mr. Feldman, do you understand what you are doing here?" I cautioned sternly.

He nodded his head solemnly.

"Like I said, I am asking for my life back. When I met at the first board meeting at EarthTel something about you immediately drew me to you. And though I don't know you from Adam, I had a good feeling about you. And the more we interacted at meetings, the more certain I became that you were the one who could help me get out of this!"

"But my firm represents your company. It would be a definite conflict of interest!" I said incredulous that he would even think I would betray my company or his for that matter.

"You represent the company and its employees, correct?"

"Well yeah but not in that manner, only when it's within the interest of the company"

"Well it-is within the interest of the company" he said in an insistent manner that he all most sound like a growl.

"I fail to understand how so. What you've been telling me for the past 10 minutes is a tale of alleged corporate corruption that spans back over seven years."

"That's correct" he nodded.

"Well how is that within the best interest of the company?"

"If this thing isn't resolved we are talking about thousands of people losing their jobs and pensions"

"Okay and I understand. But my firm represents EarthTel. I would be legally bound to defend my client not prosecute them. Your coming here today poses a big risk in itself. First, I could take your allegations and make them known to both my firm and EarthTel's senior management" I said looking Mr. Feldman square in the face.

"But you wont" he said calmly.

"And what makes you think that?"

"Because I can tell you are a person of high moral integrity and it shows. And it's going to take someone with that quality if I am ever going to be able to expose what's going on with that company!"

After leaving the office I could hardly concentrate. My first thought was to go to the gym like I normally did and get my work out on. But I had too much on my mind. I needed to relax and a cocktail was definitely in order. So I went home. The moment I got there I walked straight to the phone to check the

answering machine. Jade hadn't called as usual. I kicked my
shoes off and made my way upstairs to take a shower.

The water was good and hot, beating down on my tired body
like rain on a hot summer day. Last night Karen had really done
a number on me. Besides riding me until the cows came home,
she had me sore as hell from all the wild bouncing around she
had done on top of me. I lathered myself with body wash and let
the water beat every speck of soap off me until my body was
thoroughly massaged.

My mind drifted back to the revelation of the day, Mr.
Feldman's allegation against EarthTel.

"What the hell?!" I mumbled aloud.

He was asking me to save his life at the risk of losing mine! The
thought sent a chill running down my spin. It was too much to
think about. I got out of the shower, grabbed a towel from the
rack and walked into the bedroom. I threw on a pair of sweats
and a hoody. I made myself a stiff cocktail of then retired to my
safe place, the balcony. It was a little windy out, pneumonia
winds as my grandmother would say, but it felt good blowing
through my hair. I lit a Chimenea and grabbed the throw off the
chaise.

I sat down in the nearby lounger and looked out over the
beach. It was empty except for the seagulls. The ocean helped
to sooth me. Once in a while the sun would make an appearance
from behind one of the steel cloud and warm things up. I lay

back in my chair covered with my throw rethinking the events of the day.

That Mr. Feldman had surprised the hell out of me.

"*Was he for real? And if he was could he really prove it as he claimed?*" I pondered whether I should have informed the senior officers of his allegations. I knew it was my responsibility to do so but something deep down told me to wait. My mind played through all the possible scenarios. One thing for sure, this thing was so much bigger than Mr. Feldman that it chilled me to my bones to think where it could lead. The fallout could be very costly if I were to become involved. Hell, I was comfortable with Carruthers, Sims and Nash. Something like this could make waves for everyone involved. I was reminded of what Mr. Feldman had said,

"This could affect thousand of people and their families!"

"Damn sure could, with me included!" I said aloud.

"*I needed to get some advice. And it has to be from someone I can trust with my life…*"

I sat looking out over the darkening sky trying to decide whose advice I should seek. Then I remembered Old Granite. Professor Granite Lawrence, my third year law professor. He had been my staunchest supporter while in school and had even gotten me my position with Legal Aide back in Gulfport.

"Old Granite will know what to do" I'll call him tomorrow and talk with him about it. If anybody knows how I should handle this it'll be him."

Then the phone rang.

It was Karen.

"Not now..."

"Hello"

"Hey baby" sang Karen happily.

Before I could say anything else she went into a long speech about being bored and having thought about me all day. She wanted to know if I'd decided to come over or not. I told her something had come up and I kind of wanted to chill. The tone of voice told me she was more than just a little disappointed.

She wasn't trying to hear it. Instead she tried to lay a guilt trip telling me she'd made a special dish in hopes that I would join her for dinner.

Since I really wasn't feeling it, I begged off again. But she threw me for a loop when she said she'd put it in a container and bring it to work.

"Ah hell naw!" I thought.

As Karen continued to talk all I could picture was her coming into my office, holding up a doggie bag, making a big production out of the fact she'd brought me lunch.

"I definitely can't have that," I thought.

Interrupting Karen's non stop babble, I told her I'd changed my mind and would come over after all. She was ecstatic. She asked if I wanted anything special to drink or smoke. I declined on both and told her I'd be there in an hour.

I hung up and I continued to absorb the hazy sky with its gray sun as it slowly decesended down over the calm ocean. After a while the cold became a bit much. I reluctantly put out the fireplace and went inside. I changed into a wind suit and slipped on a pair K-Swiss, grabbed my keys and left for Karen's place.

WHO'S YOUR DADDY

Karen answered the door wearing a sheer red teddy. I took one look at her and knew more than dinner was waiting for me. As she leaned over and kissed me, her sweet perfume permeated my nostrils. Seductively she took me by the hand and led me through the foyer and into the living room. A Lil Kim CD was blasting away on the stereo. As I sat down on the sofa, I looked around trying unsuccessfully to sniff out the meal she'd cook. Without warning she straddled my lap facing me. She smiled slyly as she preoccupied herself with the zipper on my jacket.

"So I take it you've been productive tonight," I said allowing her to push me back on the sofa with her head.

Karen raised her head and giggled still trying to pry my zipper loose.

When she'd succeeded she reached inside and groped under my sports bra for my breast. A bit uncomfortable with the overture I rose up and tried to pull her hand out but she had a good hold on it. She quickly dipped down and buried her head into my chest and started sucking on my breast. I had no choice but to fall back on the sofa as she tried to coax me into sexual excitement. As she bobbed her head sucking and licking

269

sensually on my breast I kept comparing her actions with those of Jade.

I couldn't help but think that by no means would Jade ever do something like that, not because I didn't want her too but because she just didn't get down like that. She was uptight about a lot of things. And aside from the time in New Orleans, she just didn't do that type of thing. Deep down though, I believed her lust for bumping and grinding was so strong that she would do just about anything given the right situation. I just hadn't found that situation yet, to my disappointment.

Finally Karen came up for air and flashed me a big grin. The look on her face made me uncomfortable but I didn't know why. Seductively she licked her lips and was about to go down for seconds before I stopped her. I held her hands in mine and tried to start up a conversation. Reluctantly I asked her how the rest of her day had gone.

"I don't feel like thinking about that asshole"

Since I wasn't really interested anyway, I dropped it. Still straddling me, Karen ran her hands up to my neck and shoulders and gently massaged my tight muscles. Now this was just what the doctor ordered. The girl was go-ood. She was anticipating my needs instead of me trying to figure out hers. My eyes rolled back in my head as I took in every stroke of her warm hands on my tired body. But soon my whipped-ass mind drifted back to Jade. Try as I might, I couldn't get the image of her out of my head. I felt as though I was betraying her by enjoying myself. I leaned back on the sofa and wondered how long was she going to keep all this up. In those moments between wanting to embrace the ecstasy of her tantalizing touch and the agony of thinking Jade could be enjoying the same pleasure, I squinted through my partially opened my eyes at the muted the television show. My throat grew dry as an uneasiness crept into my soul pricking and prying at me like a jagged knife being raked across my heart. I thought back to years gone by and couldn't remember it being this hard to let go of a relationship and get on with doing my own thing.

Karen's face was buried on my neck now, kissing and teasing me with her tongue. I put my arms around her and ran my hands up and down her back pulling and squeezing her close to me, still fighting the urge to push her away. I was intoxicated with the emotions I was feeling. My joy was bittersweet as I moved and grind with her wishing that the woman who was moving and grinding in my lap was my beloved.

My heart was welling up with tears with each gentle touch. She leaned her chest on me and whispered in my ear,

"Are you hungry baby?"

Relieved for the distraction I lied.

"Yes"

Slowly she stood up still holding my hand. I attempted to stand as well but she stood in my way and glared down at me. So I leaned back again. She smiled broadly and reached down and

271

pulled off her panties, exaggerating her movements allowing me to look deep into the well of her teddy at her firm round breast.

"Shit!" I thought to myself. "Is this what she cooked?"
As though reading my mind she answered,

"Soups on" and moved even closer to me allowing the sweet aroma of her body to fill the air I breathed.

"But baby..." I attempted to say, licking my lips self-consciously.

"What?" she purred as she stepped up on the sofa cushions and placed a foot on each side of me and squatted, putting her mound directly in the line of fire with my mouth. I was like the hotdog and she was the bun.

"Girl you are something" I mumbled, trying to breathe with her muff in my face.

"Really, show me!"
She had done it! She'd worn me down and I couldn't for the life of me rationalize why I should not be enjoying myself like I was damn sure Jade was probably doing with her married man. The thought of her in his arms weakened me. I didn't have liquor or the false safety of a joint to boost me up tonight. Now, there was only Karen, giving me strength, pushing aside my insecurities and making me feel damn desirable. It was refreshing to feel desired by someone again. In that brief moment I abandoned all my unjustified loyalty and pride.

"What the hell? If she's giving it away and she wants ME to have it, I'm going to take it! Hell, I aint no punk or no shit like that!" I laughingly thought to myself.

I grabbed the back of her butt and pulled her closer and slid my tongue up and down her slit.

"Ooh baby damn!" She moaned.

"Is this what you want" I asked with my tongue still caressing her, mastering the art of tickling her button as I looked up to check her expressions.

"Oh yes baby, yes!" She said, grabbing my head with both hands pulling me deeper into her crotch.

We continued in this position until she was too weak to stand. Trembling and shaking, she pushed my head away and climbed down, automatically pulling me to my feet as she tried to regain her composure. Again she led me by the hand, this time to the bedroom.

Once inside the room she peeled the Teddy off and let it fall seductively to the hardwood floors.

"I have something for you," she said.

"More?" I growled in a husky voice.

"Yeah a lot more"

"Bring it on!" I said grabbing her by the crotch. She laughed and wiggled out of my reach and disappeared into the bathroom. I quickly stripped off all my clothes and laid down on the cool silk sheets to wait for her return. As I watched the ceiling fan spin around, again I thought of Jade.

Vivian M Kelly

My mind raced to the last time we'd made love. I wished I could taste her on my lips. Gently I massaged my crotch thinking of her. Had I not been in someone else's house I would have cried because I missed her so much.

In the nick of time Karen stepped into the bathroom doorway and called my name. I rose up on my elbow and looked over to her. There she stood wearing a red leather cowboy hat and red cowboy boots. In one hand she held a whip in the other dangled a black nine-inch strap on.

"Which one do you want" she asked playfully.

I jumped up from the bed and walked over to her. Brushing my body up against hers I reached for the strap on.

"Whose is it" I said examining it carefully.

"Who do you think?"

"Yours?

"Naw Baby, I don't do girls. I bought it for you today. Only rule is when you leave, it stays. I don't want no shit"

I looked at her and laughed. This chick had thought of everything. I wouldn't have been surprised if exotic dancers came out the closet and started feeding me grapes!

As I slipped it on, Karen circled me with the whip in her hand.

"I hope you don't think you're gonna use that thang on me" I said, watching her carefully as I positioned my weapon to fit snuggly.

"Naw baby" she said slyly, "I want you to use it on me."

274

"Just because I'm from the south doesn't mean I know how to use a whip" I joked.

"It's easy," she said. "I want you to do me from behind and stick the end of the whip up my ass while you do it," she explained calmly.

"What!!" I said incredulous.

"Yeah, I want you to work my ass off with this while you stuff my pussy with your cock."

"Un-huh" I said more than just a little surprised at the kinky side she was showing to me.

Though I wasn't the type to do all that, watching Karen prancing around in that hot red outfit was making me horny as hell. And right about then I needed to fuck, suck or lick something for damn sure!
Cat like, Karen crawled onto the bed and positioned herself on her hands and knees spreading her legs wide apart, inviting me in.

I walked up behind her stroking and pulling my weapon getting turned on my damn self, from what was about to do down. I rubbed my hand across her voluptuous ass and smacked it hard causing her booty to jiggle with pleasure. Karen reached back and pulled me closer by my cock. Purring like a kitten, she whined for me to spank her with the whip. I obliged her and spanked her on the ass with the handle. She cried out in pure ecstasy.

I rubbed the head of my rod up and down her pussy before penetrating it making her wiggle in anticipation. Karen purred and moaned begging me to put it in. Turned on like crazy, I jammed my love stick into her tight hole and nibbled on her back. Then stoking her gently, I slid the whip handle up into her tight ass.

Karen began to buck wildly. I held her waist with one hand as I continued to slam into her pussy and ass. Karen jerked back and forth moaning wildly calling me daddy. Her juices made a sloshing sound as I pumped inside her. Aside from the sounds her body made as I went and out the only other sounds was her repeatedly whispering,

"Oh daddy! Fuck me daddy!"

Exhilarated by the control, I grew wet as hell and weak from all the excitement. Lost in a sea of lust, she and I both fell forward on to the bed when she came, shaking and creaming all over my dick. I climbed onto the bed and straddled myself over her face. Sweat was pouring down my face. I brushed her hair back and lifted her head to meet my cock. Gliding it gently it in her mouth I leaned back and watched as she sucked it like candy, licking every drop of her juice off its head and shaft.

When she had cleaned it, she buried her head between my legs as I hovered over her and stuck her long tongue up inside me. Chills surged through my body as I pulled her head closer while she ate me out with fierceness. Soon I grew weak from the tongue-lashing she was giving me and gently rolled over onto my back in the bed. Karen slid down between my legs and lay on her stomach with her legs bent up in the air and giving me terrific head. My butt cheeks squeezed together involuntarily as she ran her tongue in and out of me sucking and licking me all over. I should have known from the way she licked me that she was falling. But I didn't. I couldn't. My only thoughts were of Jade. Even though the sex sessions with Karen were hot as hell it did little to take my mind off of Jade. In fact the entire time we were fucking I wished it were Jade.

Afterwards we showered together and played around some more. When I told her I had to leave, she grew upset. She'd already formulated the notion that I would be spending the night. Though I didn't feel I had to justify my reasons for wanting to go home and irritated at her insistent that I stay, I told her the obvious, I had work in the morning. This seemed to satisfy her, though she was still pouting when I left with my doggy bag of shrimp fettuccine she'd prepared for me.

As I got in the truck I was still shocked about all that had transpired that night. My button still tingled from the way Karen had gnawed on it. It was sore as hell, it almost felt like she had bit my ass. To any avail I'd had fun. It was refreshing to be served instead of serving all the time.

Then my thoughts turned to Ms Jade again. My conscious was whooping my ass. I rationalized I was only reacting that way out of some sort of weird guilt and that fucking Karen was perfectly okay. But deep down it wasn't.

It seemed the more time I spent with Karen, the more I wandered what the hell Jade was doing. I was becoming frantic, wandering if my suspicions were true and someone was knocking a hole in that thang. I had to find out what the hell was going on with her. And the sooner the better!

One night, about a week after Karen and I had been messing around, I fell week. I'd just left Karen's house and as usual, we had fucked like rabbits. It had become a nightly thang with us, still I insisted we were only enjoying the moment and Karen even agreed. But this night was different. Karen had really put it on me and I was tired as hell. But at every turn Jade was jumping in and out of my mind. After showering I gave my standard excuse of needing to get home to go to work and left. Karen, of course, pouted as usually.

When I got home I fixed a cocktail and turned on the radio. Our song by Brian McKnight was playing. An emptiness so strong hit me that I wanted to jump into my truck and race over to her place and beg her to love me again! As the music filtered through every fiber of my being, I decided to call her.

When Love Aint Enough

Jade was still at the office when I finally reached her. I could tell from the tone of her tone voice that she was definitely surprised to hear from me. In my excitement at hearing her voice I divulged that I'd been thinking about her and was calling to see if she was still alive and kicking. I could sense that she was genuinely happy to hear from me. We talked idly updating each other on what was going on in our lives. I asked her about my baby Jas and was happy to learn that she was doing great.

Then the conversation turned to our personal lives. Jade wanted to know if I'd been dating. I quickly replied no. Because in actuality, I wasn't, Karen was nothing more to me than a fuck buddy. A good fuck buddy but a fuck buddy no less.

Nervously I posed the same question to her. I wanted her to tell shed she'd been alone for weeks and missed me as much as I was missing her. But she didn't. Instead she reported that nothing had changed.

"So you're still with o'boy?!"

"Why do you always have to go there?" she asked annoyed.

"Because I must!" I said indignantly.

"But he doesn't have anything to do with us, can't you see that?"

"No Jade I guess I can't" I said pausing trying to choose my next words carefully but knowing deep down what her response would be regardless of how tactfully I put it.

"Haven't you realized it yet, as long as there is a him there can be no us or don't you care?"

279

"Well Casey you knew my situation when we started this thing"

"That's a lie! You said you were single. The bull about him came months later, or don't you remember?"

"It doesn't matter because I don't want to live my life out in the open like that."

"Oh I guess it's better to date a married man huh?! Yeah that's a helluva lot more respectable than being called a dyke or something!" I said sarcastically.

"Now you're being stupid", Jade snapped back.

"I just bet! I regret I even bothered to call you now!"

"I'm not going to argue with you. This is foolish!"

"Yeah, that's me, the fool" I said sarcastically.

"I didn't say that Casey. I just don't want to argue."

It really wasn't my intention to start an argument but the mere mention of his name always pushed my buttons. But, I missed her and we were talking, so I tried to chill.

"I'm sorry baby. It's just that I miss you so much. I love you girl"

"I love you too baby" she said softly.

"I can't tell," I blurted out before I knew it.

"See there you go with that mess again"

"You're right, I'm sorry" I said.

"Is this why you called, to argue with me?"

"No, I told you why I called, I miss you"

"I miss you too baby. Maybe we should be having this conversation face to face, can I come over?"

"It's late and I have a big day tomorrow," I said playing as hard as I could possibly muster knowing damn well I wanted nothing more than to see her.

"Oh, really now, well I thought maybe we could talk and maybe spend the night"

"Spend the night?!" I exclaimed

"Yeah spend the night. Jasmene is at my mother's so I'm free tonight."

"What about…" I began.

"I said I'm free baby" she interrupted.

"Okay"

"I will be there in an hour, okay"

"Okay"

"I love you Casey"

"I love you too baby"

"Aint this some shit! She actually wants to spend the night! Here! With me" I yelled out into the quiet house. I smiled in jubilation as I jumped up and down in ecstasy. Though I was happy as hell to know she wanted to see me I was even more shocked at her telling me she was going to spend the night. I would have pinched myself to see if I was dreaming for fear I was so instead I decided to let the dream play out. I jogged up the stairs to my bedroom pulling off my clothes as I went, so that I could jump in the shower, yet again.

281

An hour later the doorbell rang. I opened the door and there stood Jade. She was draped in a Burberry trench coat wearing three inch black boots that seemed to go up forever. Her sandy brown hair danced softly on her shoulders. She was breathtakingly beautiful as I stood in the doorway looking down at her. She smiled coyly at me for what seemed like eternity, waiting for me to let her in. Catching my faux paux, I stepped aside, allowing her to enter. As she walked past me she handed me a small Burberry bag. I gladly took it and placed it on the coffee table in the foyer.

Silently I walked up to her and took her into my arms and kissed her. Her body melted onto mine as I swept her into my arms and carried her down into the living room. Gently I laid her on the sofa and positioned myself along side of her small frame. My heart was beating out of control at the joy or seeing her and having her with me. Softly I leaned over and kissed her lips savoring every inch of her mouth. I moaned in delight as she ran her hands gently through my hair. Our kisses consumed me leaving me light headed as she gently pushed me aside. Obligingly I rolled over and allowed her to rise up from the sofa and stand before me. Jade blew me a kiss and disappeared into the hall bathroom.

I lay there silent, confused as to what was going on. My mind flashed to Karen. That shit had been a mistake.

"Man if I had only known that Jade and I were going to get back together I would have never...." I thought to myself before being interrupted by her reentry into the room.

Jade had a curious look on her face. One I couldn't quite pin point. My mind shot to the bathroom.

"Damn! I hope Karen didn't leave any of her stuff in there" I thought.

Watching my every move, Jade walked over to where I lay and stood over me. Slowly she untied the belt to her coat allowing it to slip off her shoulders and fall to the floor, revealing her beautiful tan body draped in a black satin bra and black satin panties!

It seemed as if a thousand butterflies had gathered in my stomach at one time, making me weak, forcing me to moan out loud.

This was the woman my soul ached for. This was the woman who made my heart race by the mere mention of her name. This was the woman I wanted to spend the rest of my life loving. I was dangerously in love and for the first time I knew it!

Jade's eyes became misty and she blushed as I stared at her in adoration. I felt suspended in time as the her words fell softly from her lips,

"Baby I have missed you more than words can say. And I need you to know that I've realized that you are the love of my life. Casey"

Her declaration of love for me melted my heart making me love her all the more. My body trembled with anticipation of holding her, touching her, and making love to her. Slowly I reached out to her. I tried not to let my trembling show as I anxiously waited to feel her touch. Gently I pulled her down on top of me and held on to her for dear life. Our bodies melted into each other, she with her light tanned body and me with and my coca brown skin formed a delicious melting pot of sensuous caramel.

"I love you baby" she whispered in my ear as I smothered her neck with kisses.

"I love you, I love you, I love you" I moaned happily.

The sound of the seagulls woke me from a perfectly blissful sleep the next morning. I anxiously rolled over and looked at the beautiful woman beside me.

"So it wasn't a dream" I whispered aloud. *"She's really here. She's with me!"* I said relaxing back onto the mattress allowing myself to breathe again.

Quietly I propped up on my elbow and reached out to touch her hair but she looked so peaceful, so angelic that I didn't want to risk waking her. I soon gave into temptation and I slid up to her, spooning her body with mine and wrapped my arms neatly around her. I took a deep breath inhaling her scent as the smell of her White Linen perfume filled my nostrils.

When Love Aint Enough

I leaned over and kissed her lightly on her back and traced the small strawberry tattoo on her shoulder. When I'd first asked how she gotten her tattoo she said it was something she'd done one night while out drinking with college friends, on a dare. She hated it when I kidded her about it and talked of having it removed.

I continued to explore her body tracing its outline with my finger being careful not to wake her but secretly wanting her to wake up to play with me. I was like a kid anxious to get up and get going. In my case I was anxious to get up and get in her.

Finally I couldn't restrain myself any longer and I began hunching her and squeezing her breast. For her back, I kissed and licked it tenderly while grinding into her nice round butt.

I never wanted to let her go. I still couldn't believe that she had finally spent the night with me. It was something other couples did all the time. But not us. This was our first time doing an overnighter at my house and I was in heaven.

Time was whisking by fast as it always did when one is attempting to savor every moment and make time stand still. Finally she began to move with my rhythm, pushing her ass deep into me. She turned her face around slightly to meet mine and we kissed, long and hard.

"Ooh how I love this woman" I thought to myself as I sucked her tongue deeper and deeper into my hungry mouth.
We lay entangled in each other's arm as our foreplay soon turned into passionate lovemaking. And though she and I had

285

made love until the wee hours of the morning my desire for her was overwhelming. I lay on my back and watched in anticipation as she mounted me. Her hair swayed with her movements as she moved up and down, back and forth, riding me, kissing me, making love to me. I pushed up in her with delight and held her butt firmly with my hands squeezing it tight. The sound of her sliding up and down on my stick made me want to scream. I pulled her down to me and continued to penetrate her forcefully. She moaned, calling my name as I rolled her over onto her back and climbed on top of her. We looked deep into each other's eyes as I continued to force myself deeper and deeper into her. I trembled slightly as I slid my cock in and out of her. Jade moaned and frantically turned her head from side to side,

"Oh baby you're going so deep" she moaned, clawing my butt, pulling me deeper inside her.

"I know, I know," I whispered momentarily releasing her small breast from the hostage of my hot mouth. Hearing her voice only worked to excite me more as I pumped harder into her love mound,

"I want you to have my baby" I whispered huskily in her ear.

"Oh yes baby I will" she said grinding hard beneath me. The juices from her canal ran down my leg as I attempted to devour both her breasts in my mouth, teasing each nipple with the tip of my tongue. Jade's moan grew louder as I pumped deeper into the wells of her canal. Sensing an explosion of monumental proportion she began pushing me downward. I knew what that meant. Carefully I pulled out of her and started making my way down to her pussy. The steam from her passion filled my nostrils arousing me more. Carefully I parted her lips with my tongue as she reached down and grabbed my head with her hands. I licked the inside of her pussy with my tongue like it was melted ice cream. The strokes of my tongue were strong and deliberate as I moved about. Jade jolted her torso high in the air while I tongue fucked her forcing her legs high over her head. Unable to take the pleasure I was giving her she pushed her hand down between her legs and began feeling around for my lips.

I withdrew my tongue from her nest and allowed her to stick her fingers in my mouth. I sucked them softly as she moved about the bed still grinding her pelvis. Anxiously I made my way to her mound again and sucked her clitoris into my mouth. I increasingly sucked and teased it with the tip of my tongue as Jade screamed my name.

"Ok its time" I thought.

Jade flailed around in the bed to get away from my mouth without success. I had her pinned and there was no escape. I continued to attack her clit without mercy driving her to contort and heave violently until her body exploded!

Jade screamed out in ecstasy burying my face in her pussy with her hands and wrapping her hips around my head. Still enjoying the taste of her I continued to softly lick her pussy but was stopped abruptly as Jade cried out she couldn't take it any more. I looked at her in silent amusement. And thought to myself,

"Damn I love this woman!"

Making love all day and night has a funny way of exhausting a person! And we were no different. So we both decided to play hooky from work. Ronni could handle things at the office for me. I was busy celebrating my reunion with my baby. Still I had one thing I needed to do that had procrastinated on all week and that was contact Professor Lawrence about my dilemma.

When I called the school and his secretary trying to give me the two step. She kept saying he was busy and would call me back. But I was persistent. Time was of the essence. It took some convincing but she finally gave me a number to reach him. And it was just in the nick of time too because he was about to go away on vacation. After a few minutes of playing catch up, I told him why I called. He asked a few questions, most of which I could answer and some I hadn't even thought about. But he was being honest and that's what I needed to hear. He told me he knew of an Attorney that could possibly be of help to me. But he wanted to check some things out first.

"We have to be very careful as to who we divulge any of this to" he warned.

"I know, that's why I called you."

When Love Aint Enough

"Well that's flattering Casey. I tell you what, I'm going to do some things on my end and when I know that the person I have in mind is the right one I'll have him to call you."

"Okay"

"Mind you, I want tell him all that you've told me but I will tell him enough to make sure his head is on straight."

"I understand, I trust your judgment."

We continued to talk a little while longer then I let him go. Talking to him had taken me back to a moment in time when all I thought about was another beautiful woman that I loved dearly, Nahdia. The moment was bittersweet as I looked over at Jade who was patiently watching TV, waiting for me to end my call.

For the better part of the day we stayed in bed. We ate breakfast in bed, watched TV in bed and made more love in bed. Around 4pm my phone rang. I didn't want any interruptions so I allowed the answering machine to pick up. I didn't recognize the voice at first but soon realized it was Karen!

As luck would have it, Jade had just walked downstairs to the kitchen for more refreshments so I quickly picked it up.

"Hey what's up?"

"Oh nothing, I called your office and your assistant told me you were out today. Are you sick?"

"Naw just a little tired." I lied.

"Umph, I was kind of tired myself this morning, I guess we must have worn each other out last night, huh?" said Karen

I laughed anxiously wanting the conversation to end.

289

"I waited on you to call last night but you never did" Karen blurted out.

"Oh, I didn't know you wanted me to."

"It would have been nice don't ya think? After making love like that, shit, I thought I'd get flowers!"

I took the phone down from my ear and looked at it. *"Yeah right"* I thought to myself.

"I didn't know, I guess I wasn't thinking, I'm sorry."

"Well, I'm sure you'll find a way to make it up to me. What cha' doing tonight?"

Now I was growing anxious to get off of the phone. I could hear the faint sound of Jade humming as she came down the hallway.

"I was about to walk out the door can I call back later?" I asked calmly.

"Sure. So does that mean you want to hook up later or what?"

"I don't think I'll be able to but I will call you and let you know."

"Oh, okay" She said sounding disappointed.

Jade entered the room carrying a bowl strawberries and a bottle of wine. She let out a big grin and walked over and kissed me lightly on the lips, I silently kissed her back.

"Okay, I will give you a call later then," I said silently playing with my baby.

"Bye…", Karen managed to get out before I hung up.

Jade fed me a strawberry and smiled. Awkwardly I dabbed at my mouth with my fingertip. I wasn't use to anyone feeding me, much less Jade doing it. I smiled coyly as I wiped away the juice that trickled down my chin.

"Who was that?" She asked curiously staring into my eyes.

"No one" I answered as I pulled her up to me to lay my head on her stomach.

Jade and I spent the remainder of the evening playing in bed. I didn't know it but she'd made arrangements to spend yet another night with me.

"Don't wake me, I must be dreaming!"

That night I didn't get a chance to call Karen. I told myself she'd understand and charged it to the game. Jade and I took a long hot bath together and climbed in bed early. That night we talked more about our relationship and where it was going. I made it clear to Jade that though I needed more from her, I was willing to be patient. She seemed pleased with it and repeatedly declared her love for me as I declared mine for her. We talked for hours. We had a lot to catch up on. Most of all I wanted to get her opinion about Feldman. Telling her was like a weight being pushed from my shoulders. I'd missed having someone to confide in. And this was definitely a biggie.

The next day was Saturday. Having gone to bed so early the previous night we rose at the crack of dawn. Jade suggested we go down on the beach for a morning walk since we hadn't been outside the house since she arrived.

The air outside was crisp. The seagulls flew in and out in search of their morning meal as we strolled up the beach side by side through the dampened sand watching nature awakening around us. I could still smell her perfume on my skin lulling me into a state of perfect euphoria. From time to time I would glance at her to make sure I wasn't dreaming.

As the reality of our being together set in, my mood lightened. I began chasing her up the beach with fists full of sand intent on stuffing it down her tee shirt. Like carefree children, we raced up and down the shore playing tag and throwing sand at each other. At one point during the chase, I tripped over my own feet and fell on top of her. We lay silent, both shocked it had happened. Then Jade broke out in a hysterical laughter. I watched her curiously not knowing what to make of her knew found attitude. The old Jade would have had a fit about anything that remotely resembled any type of public displays of affection as she called it. But not today, not Jade.

She grabbed at me and we rolled around in the sand until she was on top of me and I was begging for mercy. Tenderly she leaned down and kissed me. I was floored! The tables had turned, now I was the one who was self-conscious. I quickly looked to see if anybody was around, then looked back at her. She was smiling softly.

292

Sweaty and grimy from the sand, we decided to go home. As we walked back, Jade took my hand in hers and held it without saying a word. I almost fainted.

When we got to the house a race began, this time for the shower. Pushing and shoving playfully, we stormed into the house full throttle trying to be the first one to get to the bathroom. Jade got the upper hand when she threw her dirty tee shirt at me, hitting me in the face as we raced up the stairs.

As I ran through the bedroom peeling off my clothes, I couldn't help but notice the red light on the answering machine blinking. Deciding to check it later, I ran in the bathroom behind Jade, who was already damn near butt naked. She was in rare form. Because when I bent over to pull off my shorts she popped me on the naked butt with a wet towel. I jumped up and shot her a look of disbelief.

"Ooh I bet that's gonna leave a mark," she said laughing hysterically.

I snatched the towel from her and guardedly took off the rest of my clothes while she lit some candles. When she was done, we slipped into the steamy shower and lathered each other's body and coping cheap feels.

Then the phone started ringing. I reached for the shower door to go answer it but Jade asked me to let it ring. So I did.

After showering we got dressed to go out for breakfast and do some shopping.

293

"Baby I was thinking, I would like to take Jas shopping with us today. Is that okay with you?" she asked.

I got up from my chair and walked up behind her as she stood in the mirror fixing her hair. I slipped my arms around her waist and kissed her gently on the back on her neck.

"Of course it is. I think it would be great" I said amazed she'd even suggested it knowing how hard in the past she had worked to keep our relationship away from Jas. Looking back now I realize it wasn't the big things that impressed me that day but the most trivial and insignificant things that people take for granted, that touched me. Any normal couple would already have introduced their lovers to their children. As a matter of fact, most women say,

"To love me you must love my children.

But it hadn't been that way for Jade and I. For us, everything had been one big secret. On occasions she would ask me to meet her and Jas at a restaurant or store and pretend it was an accidental meeting. At first I thought it was cute and that it was her way of breaking the ice. So I did so willingly. In my efforts to be supportive of her feelings I was disregarding the hell out of my own. I had unknowingly become and enabler of her avoidance.

But now she was daring to peep out the closet and would soon see things weren't as bad as she'd once imagined. And even though my bruised ego had weathered the storm and was still sensitive to its aftershocks, I happily accepted her validation of our relationship without question.

Anxiously, Jade and I walked arm in arm to the front door to leave. As I closed the door behind me I heard the phone ring again. This time I felt too unnerved to let it go unanswered so I told Jade to go ahead. I ran back inside and grabbed it but the caller had hung up. When I looked at the machine and it showed that I had fifteen new messages! As I listened to them, to my astonishment, I found they were all from Karen! She was going off saying all kinds of shit. Most of the messages were too lengthy for me to listen all the way through, so I decided to check them later. But from what I did hear she was mad that I hadn't called and for some ungodly reason she seemed to think I'd stood her up.

"Is she crazy?!" I thought shaking my head in disbelief. I tried to put the messages out of my mind as I walked out into the garage to where Jade was patiently waiting for me.

"Is everything alright?" She asked.

"Yeah" I reassured her "Everything's fine."

HELLO! MY NAME'S DRAMA!

Sunday, I'd gotten up early to go to church with Jade and Jasmene, who were at their condo downtown. I was supposed to pick them up at 11am. It was 10:15 when I walked out to my truck. It had been late when I came home from our day out together. A day, I might add, that was filled with some serious shopping and more serious go-carting.

Anyway, I'd parked in the driveway instead of the garage to walk down to the beach for some air and to think.

That morning when I walked out I noticed my truck seemed to be sitting lower than usual to the ground. I made a mental note to check the tire pressure when I got in it. As I got closer to the truck I saw the tire wasn't low at all, it was flat.

"Damn!"

I was wearing a skirt suit and heels and by no means was I able to change a tire in that outfit. I clicked the remote opening the passenger side door and plopped down on the seat. I leaned over and pressed the button for roadside assistance and grabbed the phone. As I waited for someone to answer, I got out and walked to the back of the truck to look at the spare. That's when I saw the back tire on the driver side was flat too. In shock I circled the truck and found to my astonishment that all of my damn tires were flat!

"What the fuck!"

Just then an attendant came on line. I got myself together and reported my problem. The young lady on the other end asked if I thought it could be vandalism.

"Vandalism! In this neighborhood, of course not!"

"I understand ma'am but I would recommend you also call your local authorities to report it. It couldn't hurt." She said.

"Yeah you're right"

Still, I was mad as hell. Besides the fact it was going to cost me an arm and a leg to replace all my tires, I felt violated. I looked around the quiet neighborhood to see if anyone was standing outside that I could question.

"Vandalism?! I mumbled aloud angrily.

After giving all my information to young lady I hung up and called the police. They suggested the same damn thing, vandalism!

In the midst of the chaos, I remembered Jade and Jasmene were waiting. It was now five minutes till eleven. If they waited on me any longer they wouldn't get there on time. But what could I tell Jade? I didn't want her worrying and something like this would definitely do it. Things were finally getting on track with us and I didn't like having to lie to her but since I didn't know what was going on, I had to take my chances. I took a deep breath and dialed her number. She answered on the first ring.

Before I could say anything she was all over me,

"Casey where are you?" she asked anxiously.

"Hey baby"

"Hey yourself! Did you forget you were taking us to church this morning?"

"No baby I didn't forget. But as I was walking out a client called. I won't be able to go. I'm sorry for telling you at the last minute. But this is an emergency"

Jade sounded suspicious but she accepted my lie. Still, she didn't try to disguise her irritation with my last minute cancellation. Sensing it, I offered to take them to dinner afterwards and she graciously accepted.

The police arrived about 10 minutes after the service truck had gotten there. They dusted the truck for fingerprints and examined the tires. They reluctantly told me they couldn't find any prints good enough to use for a match. They filled out a report and gave me instructions for filing it with my insurance company. Roadside towed me to the nearest dealership they could find, some 35 miles beyond the Chesapeake to have my tires replaced.   An hour and a half later, I was writing out a healthy check, of which pissed me off to no end. Somberly I drove home mad as a motherfucker and parked it securely in the garage.

When Love Aint Enough

For the first thirty minutes I continually peeped out the window looking for anyone suspicious lurking around. I kicked myself for having been so careless to leave it in driveway in the first place. Still pissed to the highest piss temperature, I took off my suit and threw on a pair of jeans and a sweater. Then the phone rang. Thinking it was Jade I answered it on the first ring.

"Hello" I answered.

"Hey you!"

It was Karen.

"Oh, hey" I said annoyed.

"You sound disappointed."

"Naw it's not that. I'm waiting on a phone call" I lied.

"Well, I thought you'd be glad to hear from me since I haven't heard from you all weekend" she said sarcastically.

"I'm sorry. I've been a little busy"

"With what?"

"Just busy," becoming increasingly annoyed with the tone of her voice.

"Well, I didn't mean to bother you. I was wondering if I could see you today?"

"I'm sorry but I've already made plans"

"Oh?"

"Yeah, what's with the twenty questions?" I asked defensively.

"Damn you're sure in a bad mood!"

"I'm sorry. I don't mean to be. I just walked out to my truck and found all my damn tires cut."

"Girl you lying?!"

"Yep! Some fucking lunatic cut all my damn tires!"

"I can't believe someone would do something like that? Are you sure you didn't run over some glass or something?"

"Hell no I didn't run over no damn glass! Glass wouldn't tear up all your tires I don't think. Besides the police say there were knife punctures on the sides of the tire."

"You called the police?!"

"Hell yeah I called them!"

"So what else did they say, what did they do?" she asked

"They took finger prints and everything."

"Really?"

"Yeah"

"Well, they'll probably catch who ever did it then," she said confidently.

"Maybe, I don't know."

"Well, I see why you're in such a bad mood then."

"Yeah"

"Do you need a ride or anything?"

"Naw I've replaced em already. It cost sixty hundred and fifty fucking dollars though."

"Ouch!"

"Yeah damn right! I hope I get my hands on the motherfucker who did it. I'm going to put my foot so deep in their ass they'll be able to tell me my shoe size!"

"Girl I don't blame you. I would too."

There was a pause in the conversation then Karen asked,

"Well I still would like to see you tonight, what about later?"

"I don't know, I don't think I'd be very good company."

"Ahhhh come on, it would do you good to get out for a minute."

"Well actually, like I said, I do have plans.

"Oh? Do I have competition?"

"Jade and I are talking again."

There was a brief silence.

"Really now, well that's good. Everybody needs friends."

"Yeah but I don't know about the friends part but…"

"Oh well, I don't want to intrude."

"Thanks Karen. Look, I'll give you a call next week okay."

"Sure" she answered dryly.

"Alright, see ya."

"Bye"

Over the next couple of weeks Jade and I worked hard on rebuilding our relationship. We had many long talks and discovered a little more about each other than we knew before our breakup. The relationship was better than it had been in months. Meanwhile, I was working to distance myself from Karen. She was becoming a pest. Finally I had to stop talking to her at all. One day she left me a message saying she'd fallen in love with me.

"In love! With me! Yeah right!" I thought as I dialed her number to put an end to the bullshit.

After a heated argument Karen started crying and told me I was being mean. But I wasn't trying to hear it. Her mood changed constantly as we talked and it was irritating the hell out of me. It took everything in me to be patient with her and hear what she had to say.

Karen poured out a long sob story about how she had been having trouble sleeping. She even had the nerve to accuse me of disrespecting her!

"You been fucking the shit out of me, then tossed me away as soon as Miss Thang was willing to take to your black ass back!" she said angrily.

I snapped. I couldn't take it anymore. I was tired of pacifying her and she needed to be brought back to reality. After all we were both grown women!

"What the hell are you talking about?! You knew what was up from jump now you want to play dumb?! It aint my fault that you're feeling like you're feeling. You wanted it just as much as I did."

"I know," she said trying to stifle her tears on the other end but I could still hear sobbing.

I felt shitty having to break it down like that but it had to be done. I'd been there and done that and I knew it wasn't no good beating around the bush.

She told me how much our lovemaking had meant to her and asked me if we could sleep together one last time.

"No Karen I don't think that would be a good idea."

"Why not baby, I miss you. I just want to feel you on me one last time. Please, pretty please." She begged seductively

I took a deep breath. The girl was killing me with the mood swings. Yeah, the sex had been wonderful and I told her that. But it was something we both needed at the time. I searched desperately for the right words to say to make her understand,

"Karen you're a beautiful woman. You deserve someone who can commit to you because I can't. Maybe if things were different you and I could have given it a try" I lied, stroking her feelings. "But reality is, I love Jade and she loves me too. That's who I am and what I'm all about right now," I said as tactfully as possible.

Karen was quite. She seemed to be studying what I'd just said. I waited patiently to see what, if anything, she had to say.

Finally I was able to breathe a sigh of relief when she reluctantly admitted she knew I loved Jade.

"Maybe we can be friends," she said defeated.

Before hanging up she told me she appreciated my honesty and thought I was good person.

"Maybe some of your goodness will rub off on me" she joked.

It was Monday. Clouds were looming overhead as I drove up the interstate to work. The weatherman had forecasted snow and I was ready for it. I was on top of the world. Several weeks had passed since Jade and I had reconciled and I was happier than I had been in years. On that day I wore a black leather slacks with a black mock turtleneck. A girl was cleaner than a lean dick dog. When I walked into the office it was apparent to all that a new Casey was on the horizon. The reviews to my wardrobe were dramatic.

"Well good morning!" she smiled.

"Good morning Ronni", I smiled back

"My, my, aren't you glowing?" she kidded.

"It's just a little something-something" I replied with grin.

As I walked into my office the phone rang. I grabbed it. It was Ronni.

"What's up?"

"Marty Feldman has left three messages for you this morning. He's requesting that you call him asap.

"Is he in his office?"

"I'm not sure but he left a number."

"Okay send it to me, I'll call him."

Now that wasn't the way I wanted to start my day, I thought. This whole thing with Marty kind of bothered me. I was still very concerned why he had chosen to confide in me about his allegations. Still, I was mildly interested in whether in his claims of fraud were true.

When Love Aint Enough

I made myself comfortable and signed onto my desktop. Just
like clockwork, I got Ronni's email with Marty's number in it.

I dialed it. He answered on the second ring sounding very
excited. He wanted to set up a meeting because he had
something to show me that could prove his allegations against
EarthTel. With the turn of events in my personal life I hadn't
made a decision about him. I had pretty much pushed it to the
side in hopes that he would somehow go away. After talking
with Jade I knew I needed to hear him out but I was still
reluctant. I'd decided I'd let him make the next move to get
together. Now he was doing it. So I had to follow through.

I offered to meet him in the lobby. I chose there because if I
found this was a strategic move on his part to undermine the
takeover, I would not have compromised myself by appearing to
be sneaking around with him. Beside the best place to be
discreet was in public. So we agreed to meet there then walk to
a restaurant down the street for our meeting.

My day was pretty much routine. First I attended the
Monday morning roundtable. It was routine. Jason Andrews
was there to give us our quarterly projections. It was bonus time
and he was here to tell us just how much. He presented us with
our quarterly financial report package. We discussed the status
of our on going cases, then wrapped it up with new assignments.
The meeting ended around noon, which was a good thing
because my mind had been drifting to the upcoming meeting

with Marty. I was anxious to see the so called proof he claimed to have.

After chatting with co-workers I jumped into the elevator and was joined by Jason. He was a short man, of small build. His hair seemed to be thinning and looked as if he was balding prematurely. He mentioned the package he'd given out in the meeting and I remarked it was probably going to be some good reading. Jason smiled curtly and remarked he was going to get him a bite to eat. When we stepped off the elevator into the lobby I saw Marty standing near the door. I smiled as I walked up to greet him. Jason said goodbye and glanced over at Marty.

Marty's demeanor today was different. There was color in his cheeks and he looked like a man on a mission. We decided to go to a nearby restaurant for a bite to eat. As we waited for our order I decided to go ahead and start the meeting.

"Okay, Mr. Feldman," I began. "What do you have?"
Marty looked at me suspiciously then reached down beside him. His look made me a little leery so I rearranged myself in my chair. He reached inside his brief case and pulled out a manila file and handed it to me. He watched intently as I opened it. Inside it were copies of emails and memorandums. They were from the Chief Financial Officer of his company.

I read each one carefully. A debate was going on between Marty and the CFO, Carlton Braggs. At one point Marty seemed to be openly defying a direct order by the CFO in reporting some irregularities in the company books. The emails dated back as far the past two years. I read silently looking up only when the waitress came over to bring our food. Then I put the materials aside.

"What does all this mean?"

"You read it. What do you think it means?"

Now I looked at him suspiciously. *Was he being condescending or what? I couldn't quite pinpoint his attitude.*

"Well, it looks to me as if you are being directed to overlook an accounting mistake of some sort"

"Yeah, go on" he said anxiously.

"Ah, and maybe this was an ongoing thing"

"Exactly!" Marty exclaimed.

I was surprised at this show of excitement by him and looked around to see if others were watching.

"But what does it all mean Marty?"

"What does it mean?! Its clear cut proof that Braggs has been changing the numbers."

"Changing the numbers?"

"Yes changing the numbers to make the company look more profitable than it actually is."

I sat in silence. Up until this point I hadn't realized the full scope of what Marty Feldman was trying to tell me. Now I understood. If my understanding was correct it meant the CFO of EarthTel was engaged in some seriously damaging corruption.

"How much?" I asked.

"To the tune of over 5 billion dollars!"

"Billion?!!"

"Yes billion!"

"You're going to need more than a few emails to prove an allegation of that magnitude."

"I know and I do," he said confidently

"What is it?"

"No, Ms Banks, now its time for me to ask you some questions?"

I leaned back in my seat and tried to get a fix on him.

"Go ahead," I responded.

"After seeing this do you think you will be able to represent me?"

I thought for a minute. I was well aware of the fact that my representing Marty could be deemed a conflict of interest since our firm did represent the company he worked for and was making this allegation against. But if this all this panned out to be true this case could rock the financial world. And it could be promising to the lawyer who was able to successfully represent the facts. Since the beginning of my career in law my goal had never been to acquire fame. I was quite comfortable with my six figure salary. But this could case could mean millions. Then again, it could be explosive and cause irreparable damage for the person who dared go against this corporate giant.

"Marty, I'll be straight with you. I have definite reservations. Aside from my firm's legal responsibilities to your company this is really not my area, I'm not a prosecutor. I think our first step should be to collect all of the proof and then weigh our options then. If it were found that the evidence overwhelmingly substantiates what you're alleging then contacting the SEC would be in order. But that's a call that's too early to make at this stage."

"So you will help me then."

"For now let's say I'm in it until we find out which road is best traveled. I may not be the best person for the job. I'll definitely have to do some research. We both will."
Marty nodded his head in agreement. He insisted I keep the file, stating the originals had been put up for safekeeping. After our lunch I returned to my office. Ronnie was still out on her lunch break so I walked inside my office and sat down. I turned around in my chair to look out the window. My little visitors were busy pecking on the ledges and fluttering around. I was mesmerized by their sense of calmness and carefree agenda. I was entranced in the way they flew in, landing perfectly as though guided by God himself. Then the phone rang.

It was Jade. She mentioned that she'd called several times that morning. When I asked her how her day was going and she said great. It seemed we both were feeling the positive effects of a revitalized relationship. Before hanging up we made plans to meet later. Jasmene had dance rehearsal, which would free up sometime for us to be together. I was all for it. When I hung up the phone I thought to myself,

"Now that's how I want to end everyday, by spending sometime with my baby."

After a long day I left the office around six. While driving home my thoughts went to the police report I had filed weeks ago. I still didn't have a clue as to why the vandals had chosen my vehicle. I had checked with several of the neighbors and no one else seemed to have had that problem. But then again everyone else had parked in the garage.

"But why cut the tires and not steal the truck?" I wondered aloud.

It was dark now. The sun had gone down as I drove down coastline home. When I got there I pulled into the garage and jumped out. Since my tires had been cut, I was very cognizant of my surroundings. I looked cautiously around me as I made my way into my house.

I resented this new feeling of apprehension that had taken over me. But like my mom always said, "You can never be too careful."

I had been home about two hours when Jade arrived. She brought over some take out from Claude's. It was a welcomed break since I'd been working on a brief since I got home.

After eating, we retired to the living room. And though she'd already asked me this the first night we'd gotten back together she asked me again tonight,

"Casey, while we were apart did you see any one else?"

When Love Aint Enough

The first time she'd asked me I quickly told her no. But now since Karen had been acting so damn unpredictable I wondered whether I should tell Jade about her. I weighed the pros and cons silently and decided not to. Still, the question bothered me. I wondered if she'd forgotten we'd already been down that road or had some new revelation come up. I looked at her and told her there was no one special in my life during that time as I leaned over to kiss her. Jade kissed me back.

"I was sick without you."

"Oohhhh really " she moaned and kissed me again.

I honestly didn't feel I was lying because I wasn't involved with Karen or anybody else for that matter. And I was damn sure sick over the breakup. Still, I wasn't quite sure why she continued to ask me about it so I decided to flip the script and bring up her relationship with Richard. Deep down I really didn't want to know the answer because it was always the same but I asked anyway to get the spotlight off of me.

"Its over."

I couldn't believe what I was hearing. I looked away and then back again. Jade sat there poised with this sheepish grin on her face. I wanted to pinch myself to see if I was dreaming but I felt silly enough as it was with the look of surprise I imagined plastered across my face.

Jade said she was tired of loving one person but being with someone else for appearance sake. I was floored! Incredulous I pointed toward myself and she nodded her head.

311

Never in my wildest dreams did I ever think she would be making such a move. Of course it was what I wanted but the idea of it ever materializing seemed a distant fantasy when it came to her. I didn't know whether to be overjoyed or to cry. I looked at Jade and took her hand in mind. At that moment I felt we were the only two people in the world.

I wanted to tell her that she'd made the right choice and that I would love her always. I wanted to alleviate her all too familiar doubts, that our love was okay. I wanted to tell her there would be times when she would wonder if she'd made the right decision by choosing me. And reaffirm that she had, but the fact of the matter was, I was scared to death.

Yeah, I loved Jade but I also knew how frightening stepping out of the closet could be. I wanted to shield her from the negativity but realistically I knew some would come. The thought of this made me pull my lover close to me. I wanted to hold her, protect her, and reaffirm that no matter what, my love was unconditional. Though I searched my heart of hearts for the perfect words to say on that momentous occasion the only ones I could muster was,

"Are you okay?"

Jade raised her head up from my shoulder and whispered,

"Yes."

I held her tight swaying back and forth wanting to protect the woman that I loved more than life.

I'd stepped out of the shower and was sitting on the edge of my bed lotioning my damp body when the doorbell rang. Jade had just left thirty minutes ago. I snatched my robe off the chair and threw it on. I jogged downstairs and flung the door open assuming Jade had returned.

"Alright what did you forget..." I asked, stopping abruptly when I saw it wasn't Jade but Karen instead.

"Nothing! I brought it all" she said holding a fifth of Cognac high in the air.

"Karen, I thought..."

"What? That I was Jade maybe?"

I pulled my robe together awkwardly,

"Yeah, what's up?"

"Oh I was in the neighborhood and thought I'd stop by to see an old friend." She said as she walked past me and into the house. "Since an old friend doesn't seem to ever call anymore. You aint acting funny are you?"

"Well actually I have been pretty busy lately."

"Yeah I bet. I guessed as much that's why I decided to surprise you."

Karen walked over to the sofa and sat down. Hesitant and more than a little confused, I followed.

"So what's been up?"

"You"

"Me? What do you mean?"

"I've been thinking about you"

313

"That's nice" I said wondering if I had tripped and hit my head in the shower to account for this twilight zone – like moment.

"I brought you something to eat" she smiled.

"I don't see anything but Cognac."

Karen stood up in front of me and allowed her coat to fall to the floor. She was wearing absolutely nothing beneath the coat. I looked down and shook my head in disbelief.

"Karen what is this about?"

"Oh, like you don't know"

"No, I don't know."

"I miss you babe. I miss your touch. I miss your tongue…"

"We have been through this already" I said, shaking my head in disbelief as a nagging headache crept its way up to between my eyes.

"Through what?" she asked innocently

"Through this!" I said, as I reached down for her coat lying at my feet.

"Here, put it back on."

"No, I want to be with you tonight!" she purred stubbornly.

"I'm sorry but I can't do that," I said, annoyed at her insistence on forcing her way into my life.

"But Casey I love you."

I handed her the coat.

"No, you don't!"

"How can you tell me what I feel?"

"Because I've been there - done that Karen! What you're feeling isn't real and you need to know that!"

"Cause you felt that way doesn't make you an authority on me. I do love you! I can't stop thinking about you babe. Don't you want me?" Karen said, moving closer.

"Karen this is wild. I'm with Jade!"

"I don't care that's how I feel."

She moved a step closer and started running her hands across my chest. Startled, I jumped and grabbed her hand as it was making its way down to my crotch. She snatched it away as if I had struck her!

"Look, I'm not trying to hurt you, but this has got to stop and I mean it," I pleaded. "You don't love me and I don't love you!"

"You don't know shit about what I'm feeling. All you know is Jade!"

"And that's all I want to know," I blurted out.

Karen turned to me and shot me a look that made chills run up the back of my neck. And for a brief moment, I actually feared her.

"You're in love with a woman who's got a man!"

"You don't know anything about our relationship!"

"I know what you told me."

"Well if you know what I told you then you know I love her and I aint going no damn where!"

"I know she is a dick-taking dyke!!"

"Girl, get the fuck up out of my damn house. It's time for you to go!"

I walked to the door and snatched it open. Karen raced over to me with tears streaming down her face. Tension filled the air like smoke. I was shaking from my anger and I didn't know how much longer I could control it without telling the psychotic bitch where to get off. Silently I counted to myself trying calm down as I waited for her to leave. Karen threw on her coat and walked toward the door. Then suddenly she stopped, seemingly pondering something, turned and walked back to the sofa. She picked up the bottle of Cognac she'd brought and walked toward the door again. When she reached me she stopped.

"You WILL regret this!"

"I doubt it!!"

Karen walked out and I slammed the door behind her. Shaken by the whole thing, I paced the floor anxiously regretting the day I ever met the nut!

"What did she mean I would regret it" "What the hell could she possibly do to me?" I thought.

HITTING THE FAN

I had been in the bed for hours when the phone rang.

"Hello" I said sluggishly.

"Hey babe can we talk?" It was Karen. I glanced at the clock. It was 2:30am!

"What is it!?"

"I want to apologize for the way I acted earlier."

"Its cool," I said hurriedly wanting to avoid a long conversation.

"Do you mean that boo?" she asked

"Yeah I mean it" I said groggy with sleep.

"Baby I know you don't believe me when I say this but I honest to God love you."

I took a deep breath and sighed. It had taken a long time for me to calm down to the point where I could drift off into a still very agitated sleep, so I wasn't in the mood to hear any more of her shit. But I realized anger wasn't going to get me anywhere with this fool. So I tried something different,

"We both knew the deal when we first started. You said you were cool with that. Now you going somewhere totally different and I don't understand your rationale"

317

"Things change. Yeah, I was down at first. But now my feelings are all tied up in it."

"I understand that but I am with someone else Karen."

"But how could you choose her over me anyway?"

"It's not about that Karen, I was with her when I met you, remember? I told you I loved her then."

"I know, I know," she insisted.

"Well if you know then why are you acting like this?"

"Because you're making me feel so bad man. You act like I'm nothing to you"

"That's not true"

"Yes it is true," she said crying "Don't you think I know it was only a fuck to you. But you don't have to treat me like I aint shit!"

"If that's how I've been acting then I apologize but this has got to stop"

"Stop, I haven't done anything to you." She exclaimed. "I'm the one having to take pills to sleep, after you treated me like the shit on your shoes!"

"Look Karen…"

"No you look, I'll be damned if I'm going to let a woman do to me what a man has always done!"

"Are you threatening me?" I asked struggling to sit up in the bed.

"Of course not! Who am I to threaten the mighty Casey Banks!"

"I'm not the mighty anybody but I'd advise you to think twice before you fuck with me though!"

"Yeah right, I am so scared!"

"I'm hanging up now. Don't call my house anymore"

"Fuck you!"

"Naw, Fuck you bitch!" I said slamming the phone down. For the rest of the night I tossed and turned. And when I did drift off to sleep, I dreamed about the bitch!

Things were getting out of hand and I was at a loss as to what the hell to do. Again I pondered whether I should tell Jade about Karen. I couldn't imagine how she would ever find out about her. They didn't travel in the same circles or anything but when Karen was in the equation anything could happen. But still, I resisted. There had to be another way out of this mess and I was damn determined to find it!

The next morning I was awakened again by the phone. I instinctively jumped with anxiety.

"If it's that crazy bitch again I'm gonna kill her!" I thought as I rolled over to answer it.

"Wake up sleepy head"

I quietly breathed a sigh of relief and rolled over onto my back. I lay watching the ceiling fan twirl above me and became entranced in the sound of her sultry voice though I was tired as hell!

"What time is it?" I asked.

"Time for you to get up chick"

I glanced over at the clock at again and saw it was 7:10am. I sat up on the edge of the bed and stretched my tired body until my feet rested comfortably on the floor.

"Can you meet me for lunch today?" she asked.

"Sure what time?"

"Around noon"

"Cool"

"Okay" I will meet you at your office," she replied.

"I'll be waiting babe"

"Bye" she said.

I sat on the edge of the bed for a moment then dragged myself to my feet. Slowly I made my way into the bathroom and stood looking into the oval vanity mirror. I looked like I shit and felt even worse! My mind flashed to Karen's call. I shook my head in disgust and I pulled off the silk scarf that was wrapped loosely around my head.

"Crazy bitch!" I mumbled aloud. "Good thing I found out in time!"

When I stepped off the elevator that morning the office was all a-buzz. There was a young lady who I recognized from downstairs, in deep conversation with Ronni. I greeted them with as much warmth as I could muster considering how tired I was, then walked into my office. I dropped my briefcase on the loveseat and walked over to the bar to get a cup of the coffee.

Ronnie made a fresh pot for me every morning. I'd been sitting at my desk for only a brief while when Ronnie came rushing in.

"Good morning boss"

"Good morning"

"You'll never guess what happened this morning"

"Probably not, so tell me" I said peeping at her over the rim of coffee mug.

"A girl downstairs tried to kill herself in the bathroom!"

"What!"

Ronnie stood with her arms outstretched nodding her head up and down.

"Yep"

"Who was it?"

"Some chick named Carolyn."

I immediately felt all the blood leave my face and I went blank. My heart was racing furiously in my chest as I tried to think. Cautiously I leaned back in my chair and tried not to look as shaken as I felt. Ronnie continued to talk, oblivious that with each word, my strength was seeping out of me. I sat quietly, listening to the details of how it happened. Ronnie spun the tale like a soothsayer.

She told me a cleaning woman found Karen lying face down on the bathroom floor. At first they thought she was sick or had fainted. But the paramedics confirmed it was an overdose of some sort.

"Well I'll be damned! Does anyone know why she did it?"

321

"From what I hear she's married but she's been having an affair"

"Oh really?"

"Yeah" Ronni continued. "I don't know if it's that or the fact she and her boss don't get along"

"It could be a number of things," I added.

"Man if it is about a nigga she's a damn fool. I've been there-done that! And it aint worth it. Nine times out of ten, the guy doesn't give a dam, so she aint hurting nobody but her damn self!"

I thought how ironic Ronni's word were, "Been there done that!' I had used the same phrase when Karen and I argued last night.

"You're probably right," I said, looking up at Ronnie still trying to participate fully in the conversation without betraying myself.

Ronni was talking a mile a minute when she suddenly stopped, and stared at me with a funny look on her face. One I couldn't quite place but made me feel uncomfortable just the same. Avoiding eye contact, I tried to change the subject without arousing her suspicion. But it was too late. She was on my ass like white on rice.

"Well I hope she's alright." I said finally.

"Yeah she's probably going to be fine" Ronni said still appraising me.

"What?" I asked.

"I don't know, you tell me," she said.

"Tell you what!" Suddenly Ronni clasped her hands to her mouth and exclaimed,

"No!"

"What are you talking about?!"

"Casey tell me its not you?"

"It's not me what?!" I said.

"Casey no! You know who I'm talking about don't you?" I sat in silence.

Ronni was my girl. I could trust her and I knew it. But this thing about Karen required more than trust. Shit I needed some hellafied discretion! After all, wasn't I responsible for this entire mess? Whether intentional or not, this nut had flipped her lid and now my black ass was in deep trouble. I didn't dare look up. Sensing she would see the shame and guilt smeared all over my face, so I dropped my head.

"What in the world have you been up to?" she said grabbing the arm of a nearby chair to sit down without taking her eyes off of me.

"Girl this whole thing is crazy"

"I'm sure it is but from the way you're looking your gonna explode if you don't tell somebody," she said trying to sound reassuring.

For the first time in days I took a deep breathe, exhaled and spilled my guts. Ronnie listened patiently as I told of my first encounter with Karen. When I'd finally finished Ronni sat quietly staring at me. Filled with embarrassment at my lapse in

323

judgment I turned to look out the window. All of my little feathery friends were off flying about other places now. There was only the open space an overcast grey sky.

"I am so sorry," Ronni said finally.

Flushed with shame I turned around to face her.

"You don't have to feel sorry for me Ronni"

"I'm not sure I do. But I do know what you and Jade have been going thru and now this!"

For the first time I thought of Jade.

"*Oh my God,*" I thought.

My eyes widen as my heart began to race again.

"Jade's meeting me here for lunch today. What am I going to do?"

"There's nothing for you to do. How many people knew you were dating this girl?" asked Ronni.

"I wasn't dating her!" I insisted.

"Well seeing her, sleeping with her, what ever?" Ronni added quickly.

"I sure as hell didn't tell anybody and I don't think she did either"

"Well I can check that out. And if it is the big secret you think it is, you'll probably be okay. Are you gonna tell Jade"

"Hell no!!"

"See, just like a nigga! Why not?!"

"Why should I? It was nothing!"

Ronnie looked at me shaking her head disapprovingly.

"I bet but your nothing and Jade's nothing are two totally different things. You gotta tell her Casey"

"You're probably right but I can't run the risk of loosing her again. Things are perfect with us now"

Yeah right, perfect" I thought to myself. I looked off into space deeply disturbed by feelings of impending doom.

"I just can't risk it," I whispered. "Not now."

"Well I think it'll be better if she hears it from you rather than someone else, don't you think?"

"But how would she if no one knows about it"

"Because shit happens that's how!"

"Yeah don't I know it…" I said sadly.

Ronni gave me some words of encouragement then returned to her desk, leaving me to contend with my own thoughts of persecution and apprehension.

Noon came before I knew it and I hadn't accomplished a damn thing. Ronnie buzzed me to tell me Jade was outside. I jumped up from my chair and walked over to the door to meet her. When I opened it, there stood my baby looking more beautiful than ever, smiling broadly as she walked in. I quickly locked the door behind us.

The crème cashmere sweater and tight fitting brown leather skirt couldn't do her sexy body justice as she walked past me, exciting me with the smell of her sweet perfume. Her hair was pinned up off her neck giving her a more than studious appearance. I reached out and grabbed her by the arm and pulled her back to me. My mouth quickly found hers and I tried to devour her with kisses. My kiss was one mixed with feelings of love, fear and dread. Tears welled up in my throat as I tasted her lips and I felt her body pressed up against mine. Jade, caught up in the moment allowed her jacket and purse to fall to the floor as I pressed my body closer and closer to mine in my attempt to make us disappear to some far away land, a place where no one knew us or cared that we were two women who absolutely loved each other. A place where there were no Karens or Richards, where we could be free of the ever present feeling of danger that filled my consciousness. Sensing my urgency she gently pushed me back and took a quick inventory,

"Down boy"

"I laughed nervously, still holding her close, gazing into her hazel eyes. Slowly I loosed my hold on her and led her to my desk where I sat down and pulled her onto my lap. I held her snug and buried my face into her bosom as I sniffed her perfume that radiated from it.

"What brought all this on?" she asked, lifting my head to look into my eyes."

"All what? This is everyday stuff."

"Alright everyday stuff" she laughed.

I slid down in my chair pulling her down with me. Again I kissed her. For an eternity we sat there kissing and holding each other, not daring to let go.

When Love Aint Enough

Because of all the commotion going on in the building that day, I decided not to risk walking about the offices, not even to for lunch. Instead I convinced her that we should stay in and order food from the restaurant downstairs. She reluctantly agreed when I ran my hand up her skirt, pretending it as my ulterior motive for wanting to stay in. For now I was safe, it was just the two us and all was well.

The week seemed to stretch on forever as each agonizing day I waited to see if I would be associated with Karen's attempted suicide. It was only at the end of that week that I learned she'd been placed on an indefinite leave. I weighed the thought of calling her to see if she was okay but each time figured that would only add to my problems. For now she was quite so I breathed and went on.

When Saturday came, Jade surprised me by telling me she wanted me to go out. We hadn't been to a gay club since we left New Orleans. Before that Jade claimed she had never set foot in one before. This was to be her first endeavor at stepping out of the closet in our fair city. Even though I was perfectly fine with staying at home and doing something around the house she insisted we go out and party. It was a pleasant and definitely unforeseen change, so hey, I was game.

"Things were definitely on the way up," I thought as I soaked in the spa tub, anticipating our night out together. It was rare that I got the opportunity to show off my beautiful lady. And I wasn't

going to miss it. So off to the club we went. Wearing matching outfits, she with form fitting and mine baggy, chocolate leather pants and chocolate mock turtleneck. We were hot talent!

Crossover's was a gay and lesbian club located on the waterfront. It had been a seafood warehouse in the early 60's and transformed into a mega disco in the late 80'. Since that time it had gone thru a variety of owners and was now one of the largest gay and lesbian clubs on the whole eastern seaboards. Three clubs all rolled into one nice and neat package. The main attraction inside it was the Palace. The Palace is where the drag queens performed extravagant shows for its hundreds of patrons. The shows normally lasted about two hours with an hour intermission in between each show. In the middle of the Palace was a gigantic theatrical stage with curtains that hung from the twenty feet high ceilings to the wooden stage floor that stood five feet off the floor. The seating was arranged similar to that of a 1920's ballroom, with tables and chairs strategically placed about the floor. On each side of the stage were large white stone columns adorned with ivy vines from the top to the bottom. On the stage in each corner stood a two, five foot high candle operas adorned with white taper candles.

For your drinking pleasure there were four cash bars that served alcoholic and non-alcoholic beverages placed in all four corners of the thirty-five foot square room. And if you were too tired or preoccupied with the scenes to move around there were beautiful waitresses and waiters moving about constantly waiting to tend to your drinking needs.

Just outside the swing doors of the Palace was a lobby where people could sit in little alcoves to socialize. There was a large bar that sold everything from condoms to zigzags and also more liquor. Just to the rear of it was an open stage area where live bands played and teased the patrons into frenzy.

To the right of its stage was a swing door that led to the second club that played hip-hop and techno music. The fifty-foot high walls were lined with ladders ascending to cages where you could dance high above the dance floor if the desire should arise. The air in the club was filled with smoky fruity mist that lulled the senses and induced patrons to gyrate their bodies out of control. The crowd there was normally younger patrons or old heads trying to pick up one.

Then there was my spot, a small quaint club in the back with a small dance area and private entrance and exit. Its seating area was lined with plush loveseats and overstuffed chairs giving off the feelings of home. It had an enclosed patio equipped with a cash bar, waiters and waitress and limo service. The music varied from jazz to reggae. Its patrons in there were more of a professional crowd who enjoyed the bar scene but didn't want to be seen doing it. This area was strictly members only.

Since it was Jade's first time I took her to the Palace first. She'd never seen a drag show. I figured it was probably the best way to break her in. When we arrived the show was about to start. Luckily we noticed a couple getting up to leave who had perfect seats near the stage so I sent Jade over to grab them while I raced to the bar for some drinks. As I waited in line, I peeked over at Jade to make sure she was okay. She was captivated by the scene of the Mistress of Ceremonies being carried in on top of a white leather chaise lounger, by four muscular male Adonis wearing only a towel and a smile. At the same time being fanned on each side, by two more men with 6 feet long palm branches.

The first performer to come out entered the stage by way of a Harley Davidson motorcycle. She was perfectly clad in white leather biker chaps, a white leather jacket, turned up collar, exposing a leather bra beneath it. The crowd roared and clamored toward the stage to get a better view and toss money at her feet. Security, rushed over to make sure no one got out of hand or loitered around the stage. It was like, "Pass the money please and go on." Even Jade got excited and wanted to get into the act.

"Come on" she said.

I smiled and stood up at her command. When we got to the performer, he winked and did a little shimmy to Jades delight. She turned to me smiling. I smiled back happy to see that she was genuinely enjoying herself.

The show was great as usual. The performer's sizes ranged from minute' to gregarious. Not only did men perform, or queens as we affectionately call them, but there were women who were dragging too. It was a hot combination. And we were having a beautiful time.

At the end of the show people got up to move about and socialize. We decided to do the same. Crossroads was packed wall to wall. Bodies upon bodies must have been the theme. The line for the women's bathroom ran outside the door. People of all nationalities were representing. As I gave her the grand tour of the house we were entertained by a variety of nationalities. The girls were definitely out!

As we toured Crossovers she marveled at the people who looked like her, straight. I wondered to myself if she'd expected to see biker women and sissy boys or some other stereotypical thing. But after reminding myself of her virgin status to the gay scene I dismissed her remark and concentrated on finding a spot where we could chill.

We finally decided kick it in the hip-hop club. We found an empty love seat in the far corner and grabbed it. After a while we danced. Jade received rave reviews. People stared at the two of us as we delighted in each other's latest dance move. It was hilarious. Me with my "uptight, no can dance but I'm gonna try anyway" moves and Jade with her fashionable chic renditions of all the popular dances but just a "little off" when it came to serious boogying.

Then came the slow jams of the night. I pulled my baby close and whirled her around the floor. I raised my head from

331

her shoulder only long enough to look deep into her eyes and whisper

"I love you"

She whispered it back and I resumed floating on air.

Around 4am we left and went to a local coffeehouse.

"I really enjoyed myself"

"I'm glad. I did too"

"Were gonna have to do that again" she said

We spent the night at my place and made love until the sun began to filter through the skylight.

Around noon I woke up hungry as hell and remembered I was out of breakfast food. Impetuously I threw on a wind suit and drove down to the local grocery store. Jade complained of the cold so I let her stay in bed.

When I returned from the store Jade was sitting in the living room. I was surprised to see her up since she'd complained about getting up but I didn't really think anything of it, I began telling her about what I'd bought. Still talking, I took the groceries into the kitchen and came back out still high from last night. I called to Jade, but she didn't answer. I walked over to where she sat and stood in front of her. Her eyes were red and her face was flushed. She'd been crying. I got down to my knees beside her and asked what was wrong.

The look she gave me sent chills through my body! We stared at each other, then she abruptly ran upstairs. I stumbled to my feet trying to catch her, calling out her name as I went.

When I reached the bedroom I found her lying face down in the bed. I sat down cautiously beside her hoping she wouldn't jump up and run again.

"Baby what's wrong?"

She didn't respond. I touched her lightly. This time she flung around and glared at me.

"Who is Karen?"

"Who?!"

"Who is Karen, Casey"

"Karen…."

"Yeah, your bitch, she called while you were out. We had a long conversation."

I sat dumbfounded. *Was this some kind of miserable nightmare? Was I still asleep? If I am oh Lord please let me awake up soon!"* I thought.

"Jade, there is nothing going on with me and…."

"Don't lie to me she told me everything. She even knows all about me!"

"No baby no, she's not telling it right!"

"Telling it right?! Suppose you tell me then! Are you involved with this woman?"

"No, of course not!"

"Well according to her you are, and that's not the half of it!" She yelled. Jade proceeded to recant the tale Karen had told her. First she claimed that we'd been lovers for months. She claimed I'd told her of Jade but said the relationship was over. She even went so far as to describe the way we'd had sex! After finishing her fairytale, Karen pretended to be sorry for having called, claiming she was just as much a victim as Jade was.

"Baby I swear she's lying!"

Jade listened patiently for me to tell my side of the story. I began with the booty call and ended with the attempted suicide. After I'd finished Jade sat looking at me as if she didn't know me. I tried to get her to talk to me but she wouldn't. I pleaded with her to say something but she just sat there. I broke down in tears as I watched her put on her clothes and gather her things. Frantic to make her stay and understand, I stood blocked the doorway. The next thing I saw was light, dancing about my head, after she'd slapped the shit out of me and walked out the door.

My first thought was to call Karen and make her take the lie back. But I knew if I talked to her I would end up going to her house to put my foot in her ass. Right now I needed to concentrate. My thinking was going wild. I couldn't concentrate. All I knew was time was not on my side. Things with Jade and I were fragile. Shit, she'd just decided to trust me by coming out of the closet, now this shit!

I didn't trust her emotions right now and I damn sure couldn't trust mine. I reached for the phone and called her cell phone. There was no answer. I left a message then called right back. After repeating this ritual about fifteen times I decided to call her at home. Though I knew she wasn't there I wanted my voice to be the first one she heard when she walked through her door. I couldn't lose her now. I refused! She was my life and without her I'd die!

I paced the floor for hours waiting on her to call me back. Then the phone rang. I rushed over and picked it up. It was an attorney named Taylor Collins he'd called to schedule a meeting as was suggested by Professor Lawrence. Though I was desperately preoccupied with the events of the day, this was important. I gathered my thoughts together as best I could and made a date for Tuesday. Taylor told me he would be flying in from Maryland to conduct some business anyway so it was a win-win situation for both of us. I declined to discuss any specifics over the phone and sensing the sensitivity of the matter, he didn't press.

After hanging up with Taylor my mind turned to Marty. I hadn't spoken with him in a couple of weeks. Last time we met we agreed that he would be gathering more concrete evidence in order to decide in which direction we should proceed. I grabbed my Blueberry and sent myself a memo to touch bases with him. Thoughts of the case were short lived when the phone rang again. This time it was Jade.

Remix

If you can beat me rocking, you can have my chair!

When Karen and I spoke we agreed to meet at Buckets, a restaurant on Fifth Street. She claimed she wanted to clear the air and tell me everything that happened between her and Casey. The bitch made a point of adding she wasn't trying to be messy but that she had invested a lot in their relationship and she wanted to know where Casey and I stood. Although it was against my better judgment, I decided to meet her. After all, she claimed she wanted to clear the air. And I wanted to meet the bitch and tell her to stay the fuck away from my baby!

I knew my motives for meeting this woman weren't right but I had to do something. My head ached terribly and worst yet I felt physically ill. My entire body was weak from what this bitch had told me. I know women can be messy and I know they lie, but the shit she said to me was some serious shit. And if Casey and I were to have any type of future I needed to handle my business. Even if that meant meeting Karen's ass in public! Then I thought about Casey's ass. *She actually had the nerve to be crying.*

 "How could she do this to me?

I was pretty sure we discussed her seeing other people and I remember her telling me she hadn't. Now this!

337

Well, I don't know which one is telling the truth but I am damn sure gonna find out.

When I arrived at the restaurant I sat outside in my car for about thirty minutes wondering if I actually had the nerve to go through with it or not. After all, Casey did say she'd told me everything.

"What was left to say"

Still I knew I had to meet her. I needed something visual to make sense of this mess. To hopefully understand what about her had my baby's attention. I resolved to myself that even though it was a less than tasteful move, it wasn't out of the ordinary. Regardless of what happened I would not allow my emotions to cloud my judgment.

This meeting is to clear the air and clear the air only!

I reached into my purse and pulled out my lipstick and fixed my face. I stepped out of my 645ci BMW and proceeded to walk through the parking lot and into the restaurant. There was a nice crowd. Most of the people looked as if they'd just come from church with their freshly done hairdos, starched shirts and children all around. I immediately felt embarrassed.

"I should have had my butt in church today! But instead I'm here to meet some broad to discuss my lover, who happens to be a female!"

The thought infuriated me as I looked around the room to see if I saw any familiar faces. I sighed in relief when I didn't notice anyone in particular and hoped to God that no one noticed me!

Then my thoughts turned to Karen.

"How will I know her? I feel like a sitting duck"

Then I remembered, she said she would find me. That thought made the hair on the back of neck stand at attention.

"How in the hell does this broad know what I look like?"

A young woman approached me wearing khakis and a polo shirt. As she did, I tensed up feeling butterflies collect in my stomach. My palms grew sweaty and I grew stiff with anxiety. Then I saw the menu she was carrying, and I allowed myself to breathe.

"Hello, table for one ma'am?" she asked.

I was about to answer when a voice from behind answered

"No, for two"

I immediately turned around to see a woman, about 5ft 5in with caramel colored skin. Her hair came to her shoulders under the horrible church hat she wore. I examined her quickly from head to toe, taking in soberly the pair of last year's three inch Versace heels that had enough dust on them to bake a cake, matching her too tight, shiny red blouse. Her black skirt was wrinkled from what appeared to be a long period of sitting or …lying. I finished my appraisal and asked,

"Karen?"

"Yes" she replied "And you're Jade right?"

I nodded my head confidently even though my nerves were doing cartwheels. I felt weak but I'd damned if I let her know it! Karen led the way, following the hostess.

To my relief, we were seated near the back of the restaurant. After all, I didn't need anyone seeing me if I decided to slap this bitch in her mouth. When we were seated we sat silently appraising each other. A couple of times Karen let out an audible "Umph" as she looked at her menu. Since I didn't come there to eat, I waited while she placed her order to the smiling waitress. When the waitress walked away Karen remarked,

"Yeah, you are definitely everything I thought you would be. I like your hair by the way"

"What the hell is this," I thought.

I cleared my throat and began to speak.

"Let's get to the bottom of this. I didn't come here to hear about my hair"

Karen who had been leaning on the table with her arms folded, sprang to attention and bucked her eyes as if she was surprised to hear me speak.

"You said you had something you wanted to tell me so what is it?!" I asked calmly.

"I can see why Casey likes you. You definitely got that umph about yourself!"

I grabbed at my purse. I hadn't come all this way for this. This broad was playing some sort of sick game and she obviously thought I was her entertainment. I proceeded to stand up and turned to walk away.

"Hold on girlfriend, not so fast. You didn't come all the way down here not to hear what I had to say, so sit your boojey ass down and listen"

"Bitch I know you don't think you're talking to me." I whispered insistently.

"I don't see no other boojey-wanna be bitches around, do you?"

"You better be glad we up here cause I'd kick your ass!" I snarled.

Karen laughed.

"Yeah right, you and who's army"

"I don't have time for this! You're not going to get me to stoop to your level! You asked me to meet you so I did. Personally I wanted to see what you looked like. Now I've done that and I'm not im-pressed! My baby was just fucking around and got caught up in the mix. It-will-be-all right! You have a good day!" I stated and began walking away.

"Which baby! Casey or that woman's husband you been fucking?"

I spun around again! This time I was fuming.

"I know Casey didn't tell this bitch my business!" I thought.

"Bitch you don't know me. You – know – nothing – about – me!" I whispered angrily.

"I know you don't deserve Casey! I know that! I know you could never love her like I love her. I know that!"

I refused to give her the satisfaction of debating a damn thing with her.

"You really are crazy aren't you!"

"You don't know crazy bitch! Would you think I'm crazy if I told you I know not only where you live but where you're man lives as well! Is that crazy enough for you!"

"I have had enough of this bitch. My coming here was a definite mistake. To think, I actually thought she and I could sit down like adults and talk this thing out!"

The sound of her voice was echoing in my head as well as my own thoughts. I felt as though I was in a tunnel and sounds were bouncing all about. I looked around and saw the other customers were looking in astonishment at the spectacle she was making of herself. I wanted to walk away but I was frozen. Next I saw my bag high in the air and it was coming down with a ferocious force as I slammed it into her face. The gasp from the onlookers did nothing to sway me from hitting her a second and third time. She held her hands up screaming obscenities at me as I swung at her the fourth time. But to my dismay a waiter, who had been standing nearby, intercepted it. Karen took the opportunity to scurry up out of the booth to hit me back. Her arms were flailing around in a windmill-like motion, as another waiter rushed over and grabbed her by the waist.

"You don't want any of this bitch!" I screamed.

When Love Aint Enough

"You dick taking dyke!" She screamed, as the waiter held her back.

I could hear the faint whispers of the crowd as she repeatedly screamed the obscenity at me. I was thoroughly embarrassed but would not be outdone by this slut. I spit at her and it landed on the cheap red blouse she was wearing.

She pretended to struggle even harder to get to me. I knew it was only an act as I dared her to fuck up and touch me. Finally she was ushered out of the restaurant kicking and screaming. Another waiter took me to the back of the restaurant where I waited until Karen was escorted off the parking lot. Afterwards I left for home.

I was furious. Casey obviously had spilled her guts to this bitch! There was no telling what she had told this nut. I decided to call Casey and confront her with what had happened. Tears rolled down my face as I thought of what the bitch had called me a "Dick taking dyke. A damn dyke! *Me of all people! Shit I aint gay!*"

Shivering with anger I walked to my car. My thoughts were racing as I fumbled in my purse to find my keys.

"Had there been anyone inside who knew me" I wondered.

Finally I got into the safety of my car and picked up the phone. My hands trembled as I dialed Casey's number. It rang only once and before she answered.

"Hey Baby, where are you?" she asked.

"I just met your Bitch!"

"What!"

"Yeah I just met that crazy hoe you been fucking!"

"What are you talking about? Where are you?"

I proceeded to tell her of my meeting with Karen and the fight that followed.

"Ohhh baby, I am so sorry"

"No it was my fault for coming"

Casey was silent.

I loved Casey, but now I was beginning to question whether she really loved me. And if so would it be enough to get us through all this.

"That crazy fool threatened me," I continued. "Casey you know I can't afford that. What about my family? What about Jasmene? It's not just me and you, you know. I have a child to think about!"

"I can't believe this is happening," said Casey. "You do believe me when I say there was nothing to all that don't you?" she said.

I was silent.

"Please baby, tell me you believe me" she begged.

"I really don't know what to believe anymore. But I do know this, that bitch is stupid!"

I hung up the phone. I needed to think and I couldn't do it with her on the line. I turned onto the freeway and drove to my apartment. Jasmene was still at her grandmother's and I was

glad. The last thing I needed was for her to see me like this.
No, I needed some quiet time to think.

The past few months had been beautiful. My love for Casey
seemed to have grown by leaps and bounds. I could finally see
myself in a monogamous relationship with her. A woman of all
things! That was something I never would have contemplated
just a year ago. I thought I could do it and that I didn't care
about what others thought of me. But today was a rude reminder
that I did. I cringed at the thought of the names she called me. I
knew who I was and she didn't! But still the name calling was
very unsettling. And suppose she's serious and those weren't
just idle threats she made. Suppose she does know where I live
and where he lives. What then? This was some mess. I
couldn't help but think it was all Casey's fault. And I wasn't
prepared for it. Somberly, I walked into my condo and went
straight into the bathroom to take a bath. I needed to relax
terribly and a hot spa bath would surely do the trick.

The water was hot and sudsy just like me and Casey like it.
The tub always seemed to relax me when I was especially tense.
And I needed desperately for it to work its magic now. I turned
off the lights and lit a candle. The light danced off the mirrors in
the bathroom giving the room a mystic glow. Desperately I tried
to relax. I lowered my body deep beneath the water and tried to
wash the pain away.

My arms felt heavy and were awfully sore from all the
pulling in the restaurant. Gently I allowed the water to pulsate

over my body. I laid my head back on my bath pillow and closed my eyes. I could feel my heart breaking. Images of Karen and Casey filled my every thought.

"Did she make love to her the way she makes love to me?" I wondered.

I thought of the last kiss Casey and I shared. It made me weak. It made me cry. Tears burned at my pupils as a torrential rainstorm came gushing down my cheeks. I sat in the tub holding on for dear life. I cried out to God to please stop the overwhelming pain that was filtrating it's way through every inch of my body.

Karen The Shocker

"That bitch definitely don't know who the hell she's fuckin with!" I screamed, as I beat my already bruised hand on the steering wheel of my Mazda 626.

"I will fuck her ass up!"

My face was hot and my hair was all over my head.

"The nerve of that bitch to hit me with that fake as Burberry purse. I should have brought my gun. I bet the bitch wouldn't have been so willing to jump then! But I'll show her and that weak ass Casey too. They don't know who they fucking with when the fuck with Karen James. Hell naw!"

I was madder than a mother fucker! Out of the goodness of my heart I decided to tell the hoe the truth about Casey and me and she wants to fight! I should have known she wasn't a real woman anyway! A real woman would have known how to keep her lover at the house, instead she was lapping up between my legs!

A tingle surged through my pelvis as I thought about Casey licking my cat like she was licking ice cream.

"Damn!"

Vivian M Kelly

"But I'll show 'em who not to fuck with. Nye!" I said out
into space as I started up my raggedy-ass car and drove off
Bucket's parking lot, and into the streets to go home.

As soon as I got home I grabbed the phone. I wanted to call
Casey and curse her stupid ass out. But by this time I'm sure
she knows I've talked to that stupid bitch of hers! And I'd hate
to have to whoop her fucking ass if she try to get sporty with me.
Stupid bitch!"

How can she not see how much I love her and truly want to
be with her? But no, instead she wants Jade. Hell Jade aint gay.
She takes more dick than I do! But you can't tell Casey's stupid
ass shit. She thinks the sun rises and sets on that golden cunt!
I continued to pace the floor with the phone in my hand.

When I think about it, it makes me mad how stupid Casey
can be, that's why I cut her fucking tires. Damn straight I cut
them! The bitch shouldn't have played with my fucking
emotions! Here she is over here fucking the shit out of me then
laying up with another bitch! Hell yeah I did it and should do it
again, with her stupid ass. Gonna come telling me this simple
ass lie, talking about she was busy or some shit! Then next thing
I know her and the little family come driving up. I thought them
bitches were going to stay all night as I sat in that tight as car,
waiting on 'em to come out. When they did come out they were
all happy and shit like they were some kind of family. And
Casey with her stupid ass looked like she was in heaven.

"How- in the hell could- she do that to me?!" I screamed, as I continued to pace the floor, reliving that night.

So I followed that whore and that's how I found out where Miss Priss lives. She thinks she some shit living in that high priced ass apartment downtown like she somebody. And Casey, man it aint no words to describe how dumb one sister can be. As soon as she drops off Ms Priss and the baby, a nigga comes in right behind her. I figured out later it was that married man she's been fucking. That's what saved Jade's ass the first time.

I was just about to park when this nigga come flying out of nowhere and cuts me off to the parking space in front of the building. I didn't even sweat it. I parked behind him and got out anyway. Turns out he was going inside too. He was a fine ass brother too. 6 foot tall, chocolate with a clean-cut haircut. I started to holla at the nigga my damn self but I'm glad I didn't. If I had I probably would have missed him in the lobby talking to Miss Priss and that baby of hers. I watched all three as they got on the elevator. Jade was acting all stuck up, pulling away when the nigga tried to touch her and shit.

"Bitch! You aint shit!" I screamed. "You ought to be glad anybody wants your narrow ass!

But still, I felt for Casey when I saw that cause I knew she didn't have a clue. Hell, if he had sniffed hard enough he could have probably smelled Casey's pussy on her breath. But he was stupid too. Talking to her like she was a child or some shit. *" Man slap that bitch!" I thought.*

349

But he didn't, he just followed her upstairs like a damn puppy. I wonder what she's putting on them motherfuckers to make em act like that. It must be some powerful shit cause him and Casey both act stupid as hell around her. Anyway, after seeing all that I went back to my car. I knew, with him up there, I wasn't going to be able to talk to her so I decided to leave. Yep! I'd just catch her on another day. She wasn't going anywhere.

Then it hit me! As I walked back outside and was getting into my car, I glanced at his Jaguar. That nigga got to have some dust! I bet his wife don't know he over here banging Ms Thang! Well, somebody ought to tell her, I figured. And why not me?! I took the brother's tag number down and later phoned it in to a friend who works at the DMV. And bingo baby! I got the nigga's telephone number, address and every damn thang! Yeah, I knew that shit would come in handy."

"Yeah, I knew it would come in handy." I yelled out into the quiet house.

I ran over to the sofa where I'd thrown my purse. As I bent over to pick it up my head throbbed like crazy. I put my hand up to my head and held it as I looked through the purse with the other hand and the phone.

"Shit, I think that bitch broke something" I muttered aloud as my head continued to ache and I got dizzy from looking down. So I sat down and poured the stuff in it out on the sofa cushion beside me. I was looking for that paper I'd scribbled all of Mr. Richard Patterson's information on.

350

"Ah ha, I found it!" I said pulling the paper out of all the rubble.

"Okay girl, now let's see how we gonna work this…" I thought, thinking of how I would word my revelation to his old lady!"

Then I dialed the number.

Shit, the phone rang so long I almost hung the damn thing up when finally someone answered,

"The Patterson's residence"

I was so startled someone finally answered I almost forgot what I'd plan to say. But you know a bitch baby, in the end, I rattled it off like clockwork!

"May I speak with Mrs. Patterson please" I said in my most quaint southern drawl.

"May I tell her whose calling?" the lady on the other end of the phone asked.

"I'm calling from the Antebellum Society" I reported.

"One moment please" the lady said.

There was silence for about 30 seconds before another voice came to the line.

"This is Gloria Patterson how can I help you?" she said

"Ah, Mrs. Patterson you don't know me but I am calling on behalf of Hoes Anonymous and it is my sad obligation to inform you that not only is your husband cheating on you with a HOE but she is a dyke as well! Yep that's right! She is a Dick taking

Dyke! Now of course all of us hoes are very upset about this because we take pride in our business and….."

"Who in the hell is this?"

"Never mind who I am. Jade Monroe is the hoe fucking your husband! I'm sure you can find her at the Channel 9 television station!"

Click!

I hung up.

"Nye! Take that bitch!" I said throwing the phone down as I walked into the kitchen for some ice to put on my damn head!

Jaded

The hot bath did nothing to comfort me. I was mentally and physically exhausted. I toweled dry and slipped on a night gown. All I wanted to do was sleep and pretend this day never happened. I called my mom and asked her if Jas could stay the night. I could hear the concern in my mom's voice when she asked if everything was ok. How could I possibly tell her that I'd just learned my lover, a woman, had cheated on me. And I had actually gotten into a fight at a public restaurant with the other woman.

How could I make her understand why my heart was breaking when even I didn't know why? All I could say was that I wasn't feeling well and needed someone to look after Jas for tonight. Mom offered to come over and take care of me too but I wouldn't hear of it.

See these are the things that Casey doesn't think about, the responsibilities I have to other people in my life. No, all she wants to acknowledge is "I love you don't you love me." She thinks love is the answer for everything, when it's not.

353

Sure love is great when its good but when it's bad it's like a jagged knife being pulled out of an open wound. Right now I was bleeding and felt like I was dying. Sure, I told her to see other people. At the time I didn't really care what she did. I had somebody. I thought maybe it would take the pressure off me. Now she blames me for her indiscretion.

What she doesn't understand is it's not so much the cheating but the fact that it involved me. Sure, that's selfish, but I told Casey all along, I didn't want to live my life out in the open like that. Yes she waited for me to come around but I didn't ask her to do that. It was a decision she made, alone. She doesn't understand I am going against everything I am and all that I know in order to be with her. When it is so much easier to simply do what I have been brought up to do, be with a man. I do like men. I'm not like her! I actually enjoy being with a man but I love her and I don't understand why.

I'm a thirty year old woman with a young daughter and I'm damn proud of it! I have to do what's best for her. I'm all she's got and I'll be damned if I let the world take anything away from her.

As I lay in my bed the phone rang.

"It's probably Casey," I thought.

I didn't bother to answer it. It rang four times and then the answering machine picked it up. As I settled back and tried to remember where I'd left off in my thoughts, the phone rang again. This time I checked the caller ID. It was Richard. I didn't want to but I went ahead and answered it because he's the type if he doesn't get you on the line he'll be out looking for you and I didn't want that.

"Hello"

"Hey, this Richard"

"Hello Richard"

"Jade we need to talk" he said anxiously

"Richard I'm tired. As a matter of fact I am already in bed" I said

"It won't take but a minute. I'll be there in 15 minutes"

"Richard what is this…" he hung up

"Damn, I am not in the mood for this!" I said aloud as I placed the phone beside me in the bed.

Like clockwork, fifteen minutes later my doorbell rang. I'd slipped off my gown and put on some sweats and a tee shirt. I reluctantly went to the door and peeped out. It was him alright. I opened it slowly. Richard rushed past me into the apartment. He seemed agitated. I looked after him and closed the door agitated as well. I didn't have to wait long to learn what was on his mind.

"Someone called my wife today," he began.

"Really" I said not understanding why that would concern me.

"Yeah really! They told her that I was dating a hoe that happened to be a dick taking-dyke!"

355

The blood rushed to head so fast I thought I'd faint! I had to steady myself on the wall as the words "Dick taking Dyke ran through my head"

"They said what!" I yelled

"They told my wife that I was fucking you and you were a dyke!" he said angrily as he paced the floor.

I was incredulous. When he made the statement I knew who made the call. I was at a loss for words. My mouth went dry and my hands began to shake. I told myself to get it together. I glanced at Richard. He was fuming and pacing the floor like a caged animal ready to pounce at any minute. I had never seen that side of him before and I wasn't prepared for it now. Quietly I summoned to the courage to go on the offensive. When I felt the strength seeping back in me I lashed out

"I know you didn't come over here to tell me some crap like that!" I said faking all the indignation I could muster.

Richard stopped pacing and stared at me.

"So are you saying it aint true?"

"What? Which one, I'm fucking you or that I'm a dyke? Which one because I'm confused?!"

"Are you a dyke damn it?!"

"Hell no! Are you?"

Richard rushed toward me. I took a step back and glared at him. He froze in place.

"Richard, I am not in the mood for this shit so if you don't mind I would like you to leave"

"I'm not going nowhere until I get to the bottom of this" he said defiantly.

"Oh yes the hell you are, Jas and my mother are on their way back and I don't want...."

"What?! You don't want what?"

"You are acting like a madman coming over here with this insane accusation about me being gay or something!" I yelled at him

"Well why would someone say it if it aint true?"

"How in the hell would I know! People lie all the time am I'm supposed to know the reason why?!"

Richard continued to stare at me. I could tell I had cast some doubt in his otherwise already made of mind as to my sexuality. So I continued.

"If I had known this is what you wanted to discuss I would have never allowed you to come over. It's crazy. You act like you don't know me. Shit you've only been fucking me for the last four years. Did I seem like a dyke to you then? Huh? Did I?!" I screamed at him.

Richard rushed over to console me but I wasn't having it.

"Don't touch me!" I warned placing my hands up as he walked toward me.

"Baby I'm sorry...I don't know what came over me" he said apologetically

357

Vivian M Kelly

I turned my back to him and walked toward the door to open it.
I could hear the patter of his feet rushing toward me. As I turned
around I could feel his hot breath on the back of my neck.

"Can we meet later tonight?" he asked, hovering over me with
a wild look in his eyes.

"No Richard. It's over. It's been over."

"Who's the lucky guy?" he said wryly

"No one. And with shit like this to look forward to, I'm
satisfied with being by my damn self!" I said glaring back at
him.

Richard looked down toward the floor. I opened the door and
watched him walk out. After he left I leaned on the door and
peeped out.

I exhaled. "This bullshit has gone too far!"

Now,
Back to our
original
Program...

Blue Monday

It was a blue Monday. Jade and I hadn't spoken since her last phone call. I dreaded going into the office but knew I had to. I dragged myself out of bed and stumbled into the shower so the water could wake me up. I was exhausted. I'd tossed and turned all night. After my second call to Jade without an answer, I'd decided to give it a rest. I decided to give her the time she needed to process everything. Besides, I didn't want to alienate her any further.

I lathered my self down and allowed the piercing water to work on my exhausted frame.

Ronni was sitting at her desk when I arrived. She was smiling. I wasn't in the mood to talk so I put forth my best, "Good morning I'll talk to you later" look. I stopped in my tracks when I saw a bouquet of flowers sitting on my desk. I turned around and found Ronnie behind me.

"What's this?"

"They're for you! She beamed.

"But who sent them?" I asked as my heart raced hoping foolishly they were from Jade.

"Read the card silly!"

I did. They were from Ronni. It was bosses day. She never forgot a birthday, anniversary or anything. I smiled and gave her a hug.

"Thanks Ronni" I added genuinely.

"You're welcome boss"

"Yeah right, boss" I said. "If anything I should be giving them to you, Boss"

She laughed. But I was being sincere. Ronni made my job easy. She was very proficient and dedicated. I thanked God for such a valued employee who was also my friend.

"Well I'll leave you to your work. I saw that 'I don't want to be bothered look' you gave me a minute ago" she said kidding me.

"You're the best! Thanks again"

"You're welcome" she said as she exited the room.

Ronni had given me an idea. It was bosses day for Jade too so I sent her flower arrangement to brighten her day. After all it had done the trick for me. I called my florist and ordered a dozen lilacs and roses to match. She loved lilacs and the roses would be a reaffirmation of our love. It was my tactful way of saying I love you.

Later, I remembered I needed to call Marty. He and I had not spoken since we met for lunch that day. I wanted to tell him about my impending meeting with Taylor Collins. When I originally called he wasn't in his office. The secretary was sketchy as to his whereabouts. Then I remembered the number Ronni had given me. I called it. He answered. He was still at home.

"Hello Marty this is Casey Banks"

"Good morning Casey"

"I'm sorry to bother you this morning but I felt it was imperative that I speak with you as soon as possible"

"I understand"

"How is the collection of evidence coming?"

"I think I have what we need"

"Sounds good. Listen I've scheduled a meeting with Taylor Collins on tomorrow. He's an attorney out of Maryland. I will be discussing our matter with him and getting his input"

"Taylor Collins, I've never heard of him. How well do you know him?" asked Marty.

"Well I don't. But my professor does and I know my professor pretty darn well. I would trust him with my life" I could sense the hesitation on Marty's part as we spoke. He was very deliberate in his words and sounded very apprehensive. I tried to reassure him of my dedication to him and reminded him I had a lot at stake as well. Since it was my first meeting with Taylor, I explained, I thought it best if only Taylor and I was present. Marty and I both agreed this was best for now. I promised to call him after my meeting to give him an update. And the call ended.

When Love Aint Enough

Around 2pm I realized I hadn't had lunch. I called the deli downstairs and had them to send up a roast beef on rye sandwich. Ronni, who also hadn't bothered to eat, joined me.

After work, I went home. Despite the fact I'd sent Jade flowers, she hadn't bothered to call me. I tried to stay positive about it but sadness was taking over me fast. I continued telling myself she needed time and things would eventually be ok as I tried to keep busy around the house. Later I went for a jog on the beach running up the coastline with wild abandonment. Jogging was like a drug for me. It was invigorating and always left me quite satisfied with myself. But tonight was different. The farther I ran, the farther I wanted to run. I ran for miles until finally I found myself in an area I had never been before. Exhausted, I stopped.

I searched around for a familiar landmark but found nothing. Anxiety began to overwhelm me as I searched for something I could find refuge in. I sat down in the sand and looked out over the ocean. Its pulse was beating fast too. The waves came rushing in madly as if on the attack but retreated as soon as they reached shore. I sat mesmerized for what seemed like minutes but was actually hours. My mind drifted back and forth just as the waves did. I thought of Jade and Karen.

I hated Karen for what she'd done. From the door she knew the deal! I told her I had a woman now she's acting like I didn't say shit! Then there was Jade.

363

"Was I so wrong in getting involved with someone else" I thought. After all, by all indications that she'd given me, we were threw. I thought I had lost her. And all I could do to handle the pain was to turn to Karen. How could Jade expect me to know she didn't mean it. How can she fault me for turning to someone one when her whole conversation before that was that I needed to live my life. A life that included her but not restricted to her. Hell, she even told me I should see other people since she was seeing Richard.

I felt tricked by both women. Karen, because she said she could handle it and didn't. And Jade, by telling me it was okay for me to see other people when actually it wasn't. Either way, neither situation was fair.

I sat silently looking out into nowhere. Wishing I could wake up from this nightmare…

It was getting late. So I decided to go home. I got up from my seat, shook off the sand and raced down the beach frantically trying to get home.

"Maybe Jade's called," I prayed.

When I got home there was nothing. She hadn't called. I battled my desire to dial her number. But I wasn't in the mood for more rejection. Instead I decided to treat myself to a movie. I searched through my collection of DVDs and found my favorite, "Imitation of Life." It was a tearjerker but I felt I was all cried out and could take it. My favorite part was the ending when Mahalia Jackson sang at the Annie's funeral.

I showered and threw on my favorite pajama bottoms and a tank top. I raced into the kitchen and grabbed a bottle of water and some pretzels. I came back into the living room and lowered the TV. I turned off all the lights and anxiously positioned myself in my favorite overstuffed leather chair. I took the remote and pointed it at the blinds leading to the balcony. I opened them slightly to keep from feeling closed in.

I turned on the DVD and got ready to be lost in wonderland. Anxiously I watched the trials and tribulations of the characters. Tears came to my eyes as I watched the young girl deny her mother while her mother allowed it. I sobbed as I watched the weary woman on her death bed give out the plans for her soon to be funeral. Then it came. The grand finale of Mahalia Jackson singing her solo. Just as the tears welled in her eyes so they did in mine. I wept terribly. I cried for the mother. I cried for the daughter. I cried for everyone. Mostly I just cried.

Tuesday was a big day for me. I still hadn't spoken with Jade but I was determined not to let that get me down. I had an important meeting with Taylor Collins and I was anxious to meet with him. Before doing so, one of the senior partners, Joseph Maxwell dropped by my office.

I found it to be a pleasant surprise. Attorney Maxwell wanted to present me with my quarterly commission statement.

The figure was massive. He and I talked idly for a short while then the conversation turned to business. He told me things were looking very promising for me and encouraged me to stay dutiful and that I would someday make full partner. I was on top of the world. Maxwell returned to his office and I was again alone in the office.

I pondered the statements he had made. How ironic, I thought that he should come in on today and give such a strong speech regarding company loyalty and dedication. Though I was elated over the special attention, I was taken aback. I couldn't quite put my finger on it but in many ways it seemed as if Maxwell was attempting to warn me of something. The more I thought of what he said the more uneasy I felt.

"What the hell am I doing? Am I betraying the company by getting involved with Marty?"

I remembered a conversation Marty and I had months ago. He told me he was trying to save the jobs of thousands. I'd prayed and searched my soul for the right thing to do. I loved my job. The company had been good to me. And I felt I was good for the company. Up until now I had never doubted my loyalty. As I would a cool chill, I shook it off. I knew who I was and I was aware of my obligations. I thought about something Old Granite had told me years ago, when he asked a prominent lawyer how he felt about defending a lady who killed her husband after learning he'd been sexually assaulting their daughter. The lawyer replied the real question for me is did the person deserve to die." And just like that I picked up my coat and left to meet with Taylor.

The restaurant wasn't very crowded when I arrived. In fact, I arrived about ten minutes before Taylor. The waitress seated me in a booth beside a window. I told her who I was expecting and waited for him to arrive.

Taylor was a very attractive man. He kind of reminded me of Matt. As the waitress escorted him to the table I quickly gave him the once over. He wore a grey wool Versace suit with shoes to match. He stood 6'5" inches tall and weighed about 230 lbs. His skin was a perfect coca brown. His head was bald and he had a dimple in his left cheek. His teeth were perfectly straight and gave off an alluring smile of confidence when he flashed them. I stood to greet him as he approached and we shook hands. His hands were large and swallowed mine. I blushed and he smiled back warmly.

Lunch was cordial. We talked of the professor. As it turns out, Taylor and I had a lot in common. We both had attended the same law school and were mentored by the professor. Taylor was from Alabama and had moved to Maryland in the early 90's. He was married but didn't have any children. We talked of the many nights in the law library and the professors demanding pace. It was great to meet someone from the old stomping grounds.

After we'd eaten we settled down and got to the issue at hand. I explained all about Marty and the information he'd presented to me and the representation my firm provided for EarthTel. I handed him the folder from my briefcase and studied his face as he read through the information.

After reading it he leaned back in his seat and spoke,

"Wow!"

"My sentiments exactly." I said

"How much revenue are we talking here?" he asked

"By Mr. Feldman's accounts is could be in the billions!"

"Whewwww!" he whistled

"So are you asking me to ride second chair on this?"

"Not exactly. Its more like it's yours if you want it."

"I hear what you're saying but this case, if it can be proven, will blow the lid off world trade and possibly be a landmark" he said.

"I understand that."

"And you're still willing to let it pass?"

"As I see it. I really don't have a choice."

"Well it's your call. But I've got to tell you I don't think I could pass it up myself" he grinned.

"Then you'll take it?"

"I would like to meet with Mr. Feldman first, of course"

"Yes of course."

"I'll have to do some investigation of my own regarding his credibility and so on."

"Yes, I understand."

"Well when all is said and done, looks like you've got me."

"Great" I smiled. "That's just what I hoped you'd say."

I told Taylor I'd arrange a meeting with him and Marty on Friday. That would give him three days to check out Mr. Feldman. I was certain he'd check out and reassured Taylor of this. After our meeting ended, I drove back to the office.

When I arrived, I learned Jade had called. I quickly called her back. My heart raced in anticipation as I dialed her number and waited for her to answer.

Finally she did.

"Hey you" I said.

"Hey" she replied.

She sounded dry but I didn't let that deter me.

"I got your message, what's up"

"Are you busy later?"

"I'm never too busy for you sweetheart"

"Good. I'd like to come over to your place around eight"

"Sounds good to me" I said elated.

"Ok see you then"

"Okay babe, I'll be waiting"

She hung up.

I didn't like the way she sounded but never the less I was glad she'd finally called me. "This calls for a celebration" I thought.

I picked up the phone again and called Tiffany's. I asked for the store manager. I explained what I needed and asked if he could have it ready by six. He said it'd be a push, but he'd try his best. That's all I could ask for.

It was 4 o'clock. I had four hours to make things perfect for Jade. I called Ronni and told her I was leaving for the day. She was surprised but happy to see me smiling. I raced down to my truck and drove to the liquor store. I grabbed a bottle of DOM off the shelf and went to the counter.

"Yeah this is my chance." I thought. *"We're gonna get past this!"*

I paid for my champagne and headed to Tiffany's. Traffic was terrible. I was stuck on the freeway for over an hour. Anxiously I watched the time. It was now five-thirty. I called the jeweler again. I explained my dilemma and pleaded with them to stay until I arrived.

Finally the traffic began to move again. It was six-fifteen when I pulled in to the stores parking lot. I jumped out of my truck and ran to the door. It was locked. Anxiously I banged on it until a man came from the back. As he opened the door and I rushed inside. We walked over to the counter and he pulled it out and placed it on the counter.

"It's beautiful!" I whispered. "This is good. This is very good" I said handing him my platinum Visa.

I arrived home shortly after seven. I showered and dressed in my best fitting jeans and threw on a nice crème cashmere sweater. As I walked thru the house I dimmed the lights and lit candles to set the mood. The champagne was chilling nicely in the bucket. I grabbed two champagne flutes and put them in the fridge.

"Yes!" I said aloud as I walked back into the living room, very pleased with myself.

Then the doorbell rang. My heart quickened. Calmly I walked to the door, before opening it, I ran back upstairs the bedroom and grabbed her gift and slipped it into my pocket. I doorbell rang a second time. I yelled out,

"I'm coming…"

I skipped down the stairs and opened the door. And there she stood.

"Hey Babe," I said nervously.

"Hey," she answered as she walked past me into the house. I closed the door and followed her admiring the pretty jean skirt she was wearing.

She walked over to the sofa and stood. I walked up to her and looked at her trying to get a feel of where her head was. She sat down on the sofa, so I sat beside her. She stood up and moved to the chair. I was alarmed. This was definitely a bad sign.

"No matter what we always sat beside each other," I thought. I tried desperately to shake the ill thoughts from my head but it must have shown on my face.

371

"I came here to talk Casey" she explained apologetically.

I nodded my head in acceptance.

"What's up?" I asked

"Have you spoken to Karen?"

"Hell no! Why do you ask" I answered defensively.

"Richard paid me a visit Sunday"

"Why?"

"Well, he was very upset. He came over to tell me about a call his wife had received"

"Yeah right."

"Yeah that's right! I don't have to lie to you!"

"I'm not saying that. It just funny he has to come over to tell you about a phone call."

Jade shot me a look of aggravation and I sat quietly waiting on her to continue.

Jade went on to explain the reason for Richard's visit. She told me of the call his wife had received. I was floored! Silently I listened as she told how his demeanor threatened her and how she was finally able to convince him to leave.

After she'd finished she sat quietly and stared at me.

I didn't know what to say. I knew all to well how Jade felt about her privacy and the fears she faced about coming out of the closet. I knew it must have been devastating to hear what Richard had to say.

"Babe I am so sorry" I said as I got up and went over to her. I tried to kiss her but she turned her head.

"No Casey."

"No?"

"Not now."

I sat dejected on the floor beside her.

"Who do you think did it?"

"Karen of course!"

"I don't know Jade. I know she's crazy as hell but how would she get Richard's number to make such a call?"

"I've been asking myself the same question. But she obviously did."

I jumped from the floor and went over to the phone. I picked it up to dial Karen's number.

"Well I'll find out that's for dam sure!"

Jade called out to me,

"No, don't!"

"Why not?"

"If she did she will never admit it! It's only going to stir up more shit!"

I hesitated then place the phone back on its cradle. I walked back over to Jade and got on my knees before her.

"Babe, I can imagine how you must feel. And believe it or not I've been where you are now"

"No Casey, you couldn't know. I have a child to think of and what about my family? If this gets out I don't know what I'll do"

"If we're going to be together we will have to deal with it at some point." I explained

Jade turned her head and stared out into space.

"You do still plan to be with me don't you?"

"I don't know Casey"

I sat back on my legs and stared at her.

"Are you saying it's over?"

Jade was silent.

"Jade look at me" I said touching her for the first time since she'd arrived. "Look at me!"

Reluctantly she turned to face me.

"I love you" I began. You are my world babe. We can get pass this" I pleaded

"Casey, with you its easy, you've been gay all your life. I haven't"

"I know but…"

"No, listen to me" she interrupted. "Yes I love you. I never thought I could but I do. But sometimes love aint enough"

"Love aint enough?!" After two years of waiting you tell me love aint enough!"

"Sometimes it isn't" Jade said apologetically

"Babe look, I know you're scared. I'm scared too. I wonder sometimes if I can be all that you need. Yes, that thought has occurred to me. Then there's Jas, I want to be a good parent for her. I love that little girl. I know this shit with Karen has been a bit much but I believe we can get past it. Together. The thought of you not in my life is like telling me to breathe without oxygen. I can't do it!"

Tears began to run down Jades cheeks. I wiped them away and continued.

"Girl, I don't want to beg and I can't make you any promises that it will be easy but I can vow that my love is unconditional. I will never leave you. You can gain a hundred pounds and I will still be in awe of you. I love you Jade."

Jade let out a small smile and bent forward laying her head on my shoulder. I hugged her softly and lifted her face to mine and kissed her. This time she didn't avoid me. We kissed passionately stopping only to get some air. I looked into her hazel eyes and reached into my pocket. I pulled out her gift and handed it to her. She was surprised and began to cry again.

"No baby, don't cry. This is a good thing" I kidded.

She opened the packaging to expose a small wooden mahogany box. As she opened the box she glanced at me and then back at the box.

"Ohhhhhh babe," she gasped as she opened it.

"You like?"

"Yes definitely. Oh babe, this is pressure!"

"No babe this is you and me, together always."

I took the ring from the box and placed it on her finger. The only thing that glimmered brighter than the three karat Lucinda diamond was her eyes, as she fought back the tears. I stood up and reached down for her hand. I pulled her up and kissed her on the cheek. Quietly I led my love to the bedroom. Once inside we slowly undressed each other. Then we made love. Love like we had never made it before.

After our ferocious lovemaking, I was lulled into a deep sleep. When I awoke, Jade was gone. Frantically I looked about the house to find her. Then I walked back into the bedroom. Lying on the floor was a note she'd left for me. I picked it up and sat on the bed as I read it:

My dearest Casey,

I do love you. But what you are asking me to do is too much. I don't want to live my life like this. I have more than myself and you to think about. I know you won't understand this but I am doing you a favor. Everything that has happened in the past couple of weeks has made me realize I can't do this. Sometimes love just isn't enough.

Jade

My hands trembled and I dropped the note. My entire body was shaking. I reached for the phone. On the nightstand beside the phone, lay her ring. I picked it up and stared at it. The pain was becoming overwhelming now. I couldn't hold back my tears. My body convulsed as I shriveled up into the fetal position in my bed.

"I've lost her!" I cried. "I've lost everything!"

The next morning the phone rang, it was Ronni.

"Hello," I said wearily

"Hello to you too" she said quizzically. "Is everything ok?"
For a moment I thought she knew of Jade's and I breakup. My
head was spinning wildly and I wondered if I'd called her last
night during my drunken stupor.

"What cha mean" I said clumsily

"Well, its 1pm and I hadn't heard from you so I decided to
call and see what's up?'

"What time did you say" I asked attempting to pull myself up
from the chair of which I'd slept.

"Its 1'oclock in the afternoon"

"Damn!" I yelled.

"Casey is everything alright?"

"Yeah Ronni everything is fine. Has anyone been looking for
me?"

"No not really. You had a couple of phone calls but that's
about it. Your calendar is pretty empty today."

"Good" I whispered slowly as my brain throbbed to the tune
of 'the little drummer boy' in my head.

"Ronni I'm sorry I didn't call you. I had a late night last night
and I guess I over did it."

"Its okay, I understand. I called because it's not like you not
to call or anything."

"Yeah and I apologize for that."

"Are you planning on coming in or will you be out for the rest
of the day"

377

"I think I will go ahead and make a day of it. I have some things I need to get done today aside from work."

"Okay well don't worry about things here. I've got it."

"Thanks Ronni, you're a life saver."

"It's not a problem."

I clicked the phone off and lay back in my recliner. As I looked about the room I saw the empty Dom Perignon bottle lying on the carpet. Sitting beside me was a half-empty bottle of cognac. I could taste all of that and more in my mouth as I attempted to get up from my makeshift bed. Clumsily, I stumbled to my feet and walked through the hall and into the bathroom.

Last night I had done more drinking than crying. I was tired of crying over Jade. I was tired of feeling sorry for myself. Hell, Jade knew I loved her and it had become obvious to me that my love definitely wasn't enough for her. This whole thing was like a bad dream. Thoughts of what happened came fluttering back to me. I was pissed. I was hurt and I was pissed again. I remembered the ring I'd given her. She had left it behind. I went up to my bedroom to see if I could find it. I searched about the room wearily.

"Yeah, you're going back to the store bitch!" I yelled as I searched feverishly for it.

I sat on the bed and tried to retrace my steps from last night. I remembered having the ring in my hand but I couldn't remember what the hell I had done with it. Just when I was about to give up my search I saw it peeking from under the covers. It was beautiful. I picked it up and stared at it. It was more beautiful than I remembered.

It was a ring she and I'd first seen at Tiffany's in New Orleans and she'd fallen in love with it. The Lucida diamond, a square shaped diamond set atop of a platinum band. I clutched the diamond in the palm of my hand and held it up to my lips. My phone rang again. This time I didn't answer. My head was still spinning and I needed to lie down. As I did, the liquor from the night before came spiraling back up my throat. I rolled out of bed and crawled to the bathroom. I flung my head over the toilet and held on for dear life as I began puking my guts out, still clutching Jade's ring the entire time.

After the bathroom episode I showered and put on some pajamas. I got into my bed and lay tucked away watching a blue television screen. The phone rang again. This time I answered it.

"Hey Babe"

"Hey" I answered methodically

"Why aren't you at work today?"

That voice. It wasn't Jade. I yelled out,

"Karen?!"

"What's the matter babe?"

"Bitch you've got some nerve calling my house."

"I got your bitch, bitch. I see you still stuck on stupid."

"Whatever or whoever I'm stuck on is none of your damn business!"

"Temper, temper. Calm down it's not that serious!"

"Someone should be telling that to your crazy ass! You fucking psycho!"

"I didn't call you to get cursed out…"
I interrupted.

"Why in the hell did you call then? What you got some more shit up your crazy ass sleeve that you want to throw at me.? Bitch I will beat your ass…"

"Naw none of that sweetie. You ain't in no position to be throwing out threats."

"Fuck you bitch and the horse you rode in on!"

"Fuck you too!" she screamed

"Bitch if you ever call me or anybody I know again I will put my foot so deep in your ass that you will know my shoe size!"

"Fuck you bitch!"

"You wish!" I yelled as I threw the phone across the room.

I lay there fuming. I wanted to call Jade but I was tired. I was tired of begging and tired of hearing the same ol excuses. This merry go round had gotten buck wild and it was time for me to slow my role. My thoughts went to the office.

"Hell, I got shit to do," I thought. I sat up on the edge of the bed and tried to get myself together. Standing up was a chore with my head spinning like it was doing. I made my first

attempt but felt queasy and sat back down. I took a deep breath and exhaled.

"Even if I don't go in today I need to make a move and do something," I thought

Slowly I tried standing again. My head was spinning and my stomach was queasy but I managed to make it to my dressing room.

"It will take a better bitch than Karen to defeat me!" I thought, as I looked through my closet for something to put on.

There, I'd made it. I was in my truck driving down the highway. I didn't know where I was going but I knew I needed to do something. My cell phone rang. I checked the caller ID it was Kris. "What the hell…" I wondered.

"Hello?"

"What's up man?"

"Shit"

"Uh okay", Kris laughed.

She loved my vain attempts to kick a little slang. She thought it was nerdy but cute.

"Where are you"

"Just turning some blocks man" I answered

"Come by the restaurant maybe I can sneak out and turn some with you"

"Bet, I can do that." I said, in my deepest of urban slang drawl.

Kris laughed and I laughed too.

"Cool, give me thirty minutes" I said

Kris hung up. That call was definitely a surprise. Kris and I hadn't kicked it in a minute. Since Jade and I had reconciled I really hadn't had any time for anyone but her. The call from Kris made me realize how isolated I had made myself lately. I looked forward to hanging with my buddy. That nigga was definitely crazy and would help me to get into a better mood. I turned on Hwy 60 and headed to Claude's.

It had been snowing all morning and the traffic was going kind of slow. I bypassed a few cars that had pulled to the side of the road and had their hoods up. I always liked the snow. It was a far different climate from the hot and muggy conditions of Mississippi. As I drove to the restaurant I marveled at the beauty all around me. When I had first arrived in Virginia, Kris had suggested I get all season tires for weather such as this. She was definitely right. My first couple of winter seasons I had been at a lost for driving. I was timid of the streets whenever the snow came. Now, I wheeled through the streets like an old pro. As I sat back in my truck and tried desperately to throw my mind deep into the scene around me, I couldn't help but reflect on the night before.

I hadn't spoken with Jade since she left. She hadn't called me nor I her. My pride would not allow me to go begging her again.

"Yeah what had happened to her was foul. But shit happens!"

"I thought we were better than this! If I was a man, yeah she'd be mad, but it wouldn't stop nothing! We'd still be together! Probably closer than before cause she wouldn't want to lose her man to another woman" I mumbled aloud. Naw this wasn't nothing but a double standard!

"That girl don't love me! She don't love me!!" I yelled out into nowhere.

"I would never do this to her. Hell she had a man, told me to get me somebody, now she tripping! Hell I can't read fucking minds" I yelled as I changed the station on the radio.

Fervently I scanned the radio stations to find something to sooth me. Then I heard it. It was near the end. But the end of this song was damn near better than hearing some songs in its entirety. It was Lenny Williams singing, "I love you." I chimed right in and sang along with him. I could feel where he was coming from. The man was hurt. He was broken and all because he dared to fall in love. Now he was crying. But I refused to cry. I was mad as hell and damn tired of crying.

I continued to sing every song that came on the radio, whether I knew the lyrics or not. I refused to let this beat me. I had been beaten up enough this month.

It was too soon for the evening crowd so the parking lot was pretty empty. I parked my truck at the front of the door and jumped out. My stomach was still queasy from last night so I decided to have some more of the dog that bit me. I opened the

383

big wooden door and walked through the foyer. The hostess wasn't at her station so I decided to seat myself at the bar. I greeted the bartender and ordered a Margarita. As I waited for my drink, I looked around the place for Kris. She was no where in sight. I let out a sigh, hoping I wouldn't have to wait long. I had things to do and people to see. And I wasn't in the mood to sit up at a bar all day, whether I was waiting for my dawg or not.

"An idle mind is the devils play toy," as my mom always said. And at that moment the devil was trying to have his way with me.

I turned my attention to the plasma screen over the bar. Sports Center was on. Normally, I loved watching it but now nothing but thoughts of Jade kept my attention for any length of time. Anxiously, I looked around the restaurant again, this time turning on my stool to give the place a good look. There she was! Sitting in a booth talking with one of the waitresses. She must have felt me looking because she instantly looked up at me. I waived and smiled. She nodded and held up a finger. I took the queue and swung back around on my stool to face the drink the bartender had placed before me. I picked it up and took a deep gulp and glanced at the television again.

I had finished my first drink and waiting on the second one when Kris came over.

"You finally made it, huh," she grinned.

"Finally, did I take long?"

"Man I talked to you over two hours ago!"

I raised my arm and pushed back my sleeve to look at my Platinum Gucci.

"Hell she's right! It did take me a while!"

"You know what the weather's like out there don't you?" I asked making excuses for my tardiness. "I must have been driving slower than I thought"

"Its no big deal, I'm just fucking with you" she kidded.

"Yeah right," I said not amused.

"Are you ok?"

"What do you mean?" I asked suspiciously.

"Jade called me and told me about what happened"

"Oh really, what did she say happened?" I asked annoyed.

"She said some chick name Karen told her ya'll was kicking it and that ya'll broke up over it" Kris said apologetically.

"Oh, no shit! Mighty damn funny she can tell people shit about us but I am suppose to keep every damn thing to myself!" I said angrily.

"Man it's just me" Kris said, throwing her hands up.

"I know and I 'm not saying I have a problem with her telling you because I don't. It's just that Jade has a double standard when it comes to telling people about what's going on with me and her. And I guess I'm seeing it for the first time."

"I hear what you saying. It's cool," Kris said taking a seat beside me.

"So, how are you holding up" she asked sincerely, looking me in my eyes for clues.

"Man its kind of funny. You know how much I love that woman right!"

"Yeah I know, she's your dream girl" Kris answered.

"Last night after I realized she'd left me, I got pissy drunk and missed work because I overslept. I probably couldn't have made it anyway because I was sick as a dog and vomiting all over the place"

"Man you can't do it like that dawg" Kris interrupted shaking her head disapprovingly. "I know you're hurt but is it really worth it?"

I looked at Kris incredulous.

"What do you mean is it worth it? Don't ask me no shit like that. You've been where I am!"

"And in the end it wasn't worth it"

I stared at Kris. People sure could be cold when it wasn't about them."

"When your woman left you and went back to her husband I thought I was going to have to put you in an asylum of something."

Kris reflected back and nodded her head in agreement.

"Then please don't forget the time that girl from Maryland flew down to surprise you and caught you doing the do with another chick. You hollered for damn near a month and ya'll were just fuck buddies, so you told me! So yeah, she's worth it!"

"I get ya man. But even though you're hurt, you still have to take care of self. 'Cause you can bet your last dollar she is! See you got to be able to go thru, without going thru. Know what I mean?" Kris said lowering her voice as the bartender approached with my drink.

"Yeah I know. But I'm not good at that."

"I know but you have to try" Kris reasoned.

"What else did she say?" I asked, hoping to hear something to give me hope.

"She asked me to check on you and that was about it"

"Oh" I mumbled disappointed she hadn't said anything about loving me.

I picked up my drink and gulped it down.

"Slow down man" Tracey warned as I killed the last of my third margarita.

"I'm cool."

"Have you eaten" Kris asked as she beckoned for the waiter to come over.

"Naw I thought I'd get something here."

"Good and while you at it, try to lay off the liquor. You live to damn far for me to have to take your ass home."

I forced out a laugh and picked up my empty glass to slurp out it last remnants.

Sole Searching

I sat in my truck, outside of Claude's, trying to gather my thoughts as the still of the night surrounded me. I convinced myself that when I got back home I would call her. I knew I ran the risk of more rejection but I needed to try. My thoughts were consumed with her. I rehearsed aloud what I would say when she answered the phone.

I would make my case and convince her that things weren't as bad as she thought. I would tell her of my feelings of insecurity when I first came into the life. I would reaffirm the fact that she was the only woman I wanted or needed and together we could conquer anything. And finally if all else failed I would ask her to take more time to think about her decision before deciding something that would effect both of us for the rest our lives. Then I stopped.

"The rest of our lives," I said aloud, shocked by the finality of it. "I could loose her for the rest of my life"

The thought sent chills through my body. Startled, I shook my head in disbelief trying to drive the thought as far away from me as possible. Surely she couldn't imagine life without me nor I her. That was madness.

"Not because of this," I said aloud to myself.

The idea pained me to my very core. I began to realize the desperation of the situation and it seemed overwhelming. Whenever Jade and I had argued in the past I'd always comforted myself in knowing that she would never go far. I never dreamed that it could possibly end. The feelings I felt for her were so strong that a permanent separation never entered my mind. When we argued I would give her the space she needed knowing that she was only away in body but never in spirit.

Yes, I had lied. But now it was time for me to get real. I told her I'd thought it was over when I slept with Karen. I pounced on her words in my defense to justify my actions of having slept with another woman. Now I was left with the painful truth. Karen was there when I desperately needed someone to be. Though I hadn't heard from Jade in weeks, I didn't believe our bond was truly broken. I was hopelessly in love with Jade. My hope for our future couldn't be dismissed so easily. When I reached out to Karen, somewhere in the depths of my heart I held on to the hope that Jade and I would get through our differences.

Yeah, there were moments when I doubted her love for me. That was natural, given her involvement with someone else. But for some inexplicable reason I'd accepted her infidelity hoping she would realize that it doesn't matter so much who you love but that it's more important that you love.

My insecurities would set in on those lonely nights when all I thought about was where she was or worse yet, who she was with. My mind teased me constantly with thoughts of her making love to someone else while I lay in my bed alone. I couldn't help feeling the weight of the world on my shoulders whenever we allowed our disagreements to separate us. I guess I resented her for making me endure the pain of missing her. So that time I did something about it, I turned to someone else to help heal my battered soul. Whether I wanted to admit it or not, my sleeping with Karen had saved my sanity, momentarily.

When I got home that night my answering machine showed I had received two calls. Anxiously I listened hoping Jade had called. The first call was from Kris. She asked me to call her to make sure I'd gotten home safely and the other was from Taylor Collins. With all that had happened I had forgotten to arrange the meeting with Marty. I kicked myself for forgetting something so important. Hopelessly I searched my Blueberry for his number but was unable to find it. Reluctantly I decided to call Ronni to see is she still had it. I dreaded calling her because I didn't want to get the third degree about not coming into the office.

She was perceptive as hell and knew it was unlike me to miss coming in. I also knew she worried about me at times and I didn't want to bother her with my problems. It was 9pm and I guessed I could probably catch at her home. Reluctantly I sat down at the bar and dialed her number.

"Hello"

"Hey Ronni" I answered casually.

"What's up?"

"This is probably a long shot, but I was wondering if you had Marty Feldman's home number, you know the one you gave me earlier this?"

"I'm sure I do. You know I keep everything in my palm pilot" she said hopefully.

"Yeah I know."

"What happened to you today?" she asked as she looked for the number.

"I guess I had one too many last night" I answered praying that she'd end it there.

"Well I know that silly. You told me that earlier. What happened? It's not like you to drink during the week like that?

"Yeah I know," I said searching for a convincing enough reason to give her so she could let it drop.

"Oh I get it. Was Jade with you?" she added quizzically. That name struck a cord with me. I hoped it wasn't noticeable. I realized if I didn't say something quick we would go off into Jade-land.

"Actually, I was alone. I'd bought a bottle of liquor and drank without eating, you know the rest"

"Oh" she said, sounding unconvinced.

"Man it tore me down too. I thought I was never going to stop hugging that toilet" I kidded ignoring the fact that I didn't think she believe a word I was saying.

"What were you drinking?" she asked

I sighed, "*Damn let it go*" I thought.

"Dom" I answered, tired of lying and anxious to end the call. "What about that number" I asked

"Oh, its here somewhere. You know me I just have to look for it."

"I tell you what, you go ahead and look for it and when you find it give me a call back" I suggested.

"Hold your horses. I'm still checking my palm pilot."

"Ok, I'm good " I mumbled.

There silence for about a minute then her voice rang out "Here it is. See!"

I faked a small laugh.

Ronni gave me the number and went on to tell me about her day at the office.

I listened intently conveying the customary "oh really's" and "sounds good" as she rattled the events of the day off to me.

Next I called Marty. He was home. I told him about my meeting with Taylor. Still he was apprehensive. As time went on he seemed more relaxed and even seemed anxious about the impending meeting. I suggested he bring all of the information he'd gathered to the meeting. I suggested we meet on Friday at the Green Room. I was a member and it would give us the privacy we needed to discuss matters.

Next I called Taylor. I reconfirmed our meeting with Marty and told him of the place and time. He was excited. Then I got off the phone. I needed to get myself together, quick.

"A lot is riding on this meeting tomorrow," I thought. "I need to be mentally alert because time is of the essence."

It was then I decided to go ahead and call Jade. I needed closure. I needed to tell her what I was feeling and find out how she was doing. But first I needed to relax.

Somberly I went into the bathroom and got into my spa tub. The bubbles danced across my skin like ants. I thought back to the first time Jade and I had shared it together. She'd loved it so much she had insisted on getting one for herself.

It was almost eleven when I got out. I knew Jade would be up cause she never went to bed before midnight. I threw on some boxers and a robe then grabbed the phone. Before dialing her number a case of the jitters hit me, so I started pacing the floor trying to build up my nerve.

"Can I really take anymore rejection from her" I wondered to myself.

Then I did it. I dialed her number and waited patiently for her to answer. The phone rang four times before she picked up.

"Hello" she said lazily.

"Hey this is Casey" I offered timidly.

"Hey" she answered.

393

"I know it's late but I really need to talk to you"

"Well I can't right now" she insisted.

"It'll only take a minute" I pleaded softly.

"I have company," she said.

The words cut through me like a knife.

"Company, who, your mom?" knowing already it wasn't.

"No" she answered flatly.

"Well who then?" I asked feeling the heat accumulate in my cheeks as I spoke.

"It doesn't matter," she said calmly

"Maybe not to you but it does to me" I countered still trying to contain my anger. Then I heard a male's voice in the background call to her. I was there now, mad as hell and wondering what the fuck was going on.

"You have a man over there?!"

"I've got to go"

"I don't believe you! Just last night you were here with me now you doing this!" I screamed.

"Doing what! You don't know what the hell I'm doing that's why you're mad!"

"Oh baby I'm not mad. You haven't seen me mad"

"Well you sound mad to me!" she stated flatly.

"I'm over here going out of my mind and you're over there parlaying! Ain't this some shit!"

"What ever! I've got to go!"

"Well go then!" I screamed back clicking the phone off and tossing it to the floor.

"This bitch!" I said aloud as I paced the floor.

My damn spot wasn't even got cold yet and she's already got another nigga up in the house!
I was furious. I knew I needed to calm down but I couldn't. My self control had taken flight and my mind was off to the races.

"Who the hell is it" I wondered. If it had been Richard she would have said so. I couldn't stand it anymore. I grabbed some jeans off the rack and jumped in 'em. I was going over there!

I drove like a bat out of hell to get to Jades condo, I figured after our conversation she'd probably told the nigga to leave. I figured it would be a missed opportunity to see who he was. But I knew it was probably best. That way she and I could talk and try to clear the air.

Twenty minutes later I pulled up in front of her building. I parked on the street and jumped out running toward the doorman. He greeted me and as I rushed passed him into the lobby and to the elevators.

Jade lived on the 10th floor. It seemed to take ages for an elevator to arrive and even longer for it to climb the 10 floors to her condo. I paced inside the tiny elevator rehearsing again what I would say to her. It was imperative that I not appear to be mad

395

when I arrived. That would only add fuel to a flame that was already spiraling out of control.

The doors of the elevator opened and not a minute too soon. If it had taken any longer I felt I would have climbed out and taken the stairs. Nervously I walked up the corridor to her door. This was only my third or fourth time at her place. Normally I never came over. Jade had long decided it would be best in an effort to keep down all the gossip that goes on around the complex.

I always attributed it to her closeted ass personality. At first it had been the subject of many disagreements. But I'd long since given up that fight, deciding I would be more comfortable at my own place instead of hers anyway. Still, I felt remised at times when she would talk of the little gatherings she would host for co workers and friends knowing I was never invited. But I loved her and tried desperately to respect her privacy when it came to our relationship. Like she always said,

"It's nobody's business what we do."

"Yeah right!" I mumbled aloud as I rang her doorbell. Moments later, she opened the door. We stood looking at each other. Slowly she began to shake her head in disbelief.

"At least she's fully dressed. That's a good thing," I thought.

"Can I come in" I asked softly.

"Casey why are you doing this?" she pleaded.

"What am I doing that's so wrong Jade?"

"Coming over here like this for one. I told you I had company"

"Company, so the motherfucker is still here!" I thought.

"You had no right to show up on my door step like this" she continued.

"Listen to what you're saying. I have every right to be here!" I said pointing past her into the condo.

"Who ever you got up there is the one that has no right to be here!!"

Jade continued to shake her head in exasperation. I shoved my hands in my pockets and stood stubbornly waiting for her response.

"Casey go home, its over" she said finally.

"How in the hell can you do this Jade! I've come all the way over here the least you can do is take a moment to hear what I've got to say."

"Now is not the time."

"Well when is the time?" I asked growing furious over her turning me away.

"I don't know. But now definitely isn't."

"I'm not going no damn where so you can tell that motherfucker to leave!" I demanded.

"Casey please" she whispered. "Lower your voice someone might hear you."

"Oh yeah, well guess what, I can get louder."

397

All of a sudden, the door opened wider and there stood Brooks. I looked at him and back at Jade. Trevaire was the guy she was engaged to marry before she found out he had cheated on her with damn near everyone in town. Jade dropped her head and my heart sank.

"*What the hell*" I screamed to myself. "*No she don't have this weak bitch up in here at damn near 1 o'clock in the morning!*"

"Is everything alright Jay?" he asked still looking down at me and I at him.

"Yeah Tre I'm just talking to a friend".

"*A friend!!*" I repeated her words in my head. "*A damn friend!!*" I was livid and it showed.

"Go back inside I will be there in a minute" she turned and asked of him as he towered over both she and I.

"*Ah hell no it ain't going down like this*" I thought. Before I knew it I had stepped forward and said,

"What are you doing here?!"

Trevaire looked at Jade and then back at me.

"You talking to me!"

"I don't see another tree trunk motherfucker around here! Hell yes I'm talking to you!" I yelled back.

"Jade you'd better get your little friend," he said half laughing still glaring at me.

Jade hurriedly interrupted,

"Tre please, go back inside I will be there in a minute"

Tre held fast and didn't move. We glared at each other fiercely. I was about to step closer to Tre when Jade abruptly stepped out the doorway and in front of me.

"Casey!" she whispered insistently, "You're making a scene!"

"Fuck that! You got some big-footed bitch up in there at 1 am in the morning and you want to say I'm making a scene! Hell naw! Where's Jasmene! Where's Jasmene?" I yelled.

"Casey please, please don't do this to me" she begged. Tre reached out to grab her arm. She pulled away with tears rolling down her cheeks. The sight of her pain pained me but I refused to allow what was happening to happen.

"I think you'd better leave" Tre announced in a stern voice.

"And I think you'd better kiss my ass bitch! You don't know me and don't want too!" I growled. Tre threw up his hands, in disbelief. He looked at Jade then back at me. Finally he went back inside the condo leaving us alone in the hallway.

"How in the fuck can you have this nigga over here like this Jade? What in the hell is wrong with you?!" Jade looked away as tears streamed down her face.

"Are you fucking him now?!" I demanded. She didn't say anything. I grabbed her and shook her forcing her to look at me.

"What does it matter?" she screamed. My head began to spin.

"What does it matter! What kind of fucking answer is that?!'

399

Jade turned her attention to the apartments down the corridor. One her neighbors was peeping out of his door. She quickly glared back at me.

"See what you've done!" she hissed at me, waiving her hand, signaling everything was okay. Then she turned to go back inside.

"How can you do this to me?!" I asked.
Jade turned around coldly, still holding the door knob and looked me dead in the face.

"You did it to me didn't you!"
And that was it. She walked inside and slammed the door behind her. I stood staring at the door, numb as I listened to the tumblers click into place from the lock on the door.

I banged on the door but she didn't answer it. The guy down the hall opened his though. I waved him off and left. I was worn out.

The drive back home was one of the longest in my life. With each turn of the tire, I was moving further and further away from the woman I loved. Tears clouded my vision as I fought to see out the front windshield. Thoughts of her making love with him flooded my brain. I was being swept away in a sea of pain. My heart hurt and my soul grieved.

"All of this over some bullshit!

I couldn't make any sense of the situation and at this point I was too tired to try.

When I got home, I knew I wouldn't be able to sleep. I tried reading to take my mind off it but it was no use. Over and over, thoughts of him enjoying her body began to fill my head. I cried out to God to help me. I pleaded with him to have mercy on me and to make me strong. My head throbbed terribly.

"I've got to be strong!" I said over and over again until finally I drifted off to sleep. As I slept I dreamed. I dreamed of him and her making love. I dreamed of him and her laughing hysterically at me as I cried. I woke up abruptly to find that I had drifted off for only a short while. I dragged myself up from my chair and went upstairs. Exhausted I climbed in bed fully clothed and pulled the covers over my head as I prayed for peace of mind. I felt I was losing it. And there was nothing anyone here on earth could do to stop it. I prayed for sleep, a peaceful sleep. And finally, I prayed for death.

When it Rains it Damn Sho Pours!

It was Friday. I had barely slept all night. Waking up was a shock considering I had prayed not to. Exhausted, I got up and showered. My meeting with Taylor and Marty was today. I grabbed a suit out of the closet and worked to get my tired ass together. I couldn't afford to make a mess out of things for everybody else just because my life was in the toilet.

When I arrived at the office Ronni eyed me suspiciously. I greeted her and walked into my office. There was a shit load of papers on my desk and I let out a sigh of exasperation at the sight of it all. I put down my brief and went to the bathroom.

When I came out Ronni was there. She'd brought me a pastry and was at the coffee pot making me a cup of coffee. I quickly went over to the bookcase pretending to look for something, giving her time to finish what she was doing so she could leave. But she didn't. Instead she took a seat and waited for me to sit down.

"Casey we need to talk" Ronni announced.
I pulled book after book off the shelf, looking through them, hoping to give the appearance of being damn busy.

"What about?" I asked casually, still looking into the book.

When Love Aint Enough

"You" she said defiantly.

I sneaked a glance at her. Her back was turned and she was waiting patiently.

I was too tired play cat and mouse so I gave up.

"Okay what's up Ronni?" I asked as I went over to sit down at my desk.

"I'm worried about you. You didn't come in yesterday and now today you come in looking like something the cat dragged in. What in the world is going on with you?"

"Nothing, I'm just a little tired that's all"

"I don't believe you" she said defiantly.

I looked at her sternly, becoming increasingly aggravated with the conversation hoping to bully her into leaving me alone.

"Don't give me that look! I know you! I know when something is wrong with you. Now, what is it?! What's got you so down?"

"I really don't want to go into it Ronni"

"Well I do," she said. "I've been watching you for weeks now and you look like you're carrying the weight of the whole world on your shoulders. I thought we were more than boss and employee. I thought we were friends," she said disappointedly.

"We are Ronni. I just don't want to bother anyone with it. This is something I have handle myself" I explained.

"But you're not alone. I care about you. I'm not some Joe-blow off the street trying to get into your business! Whatever it is that's got you like this, needs to be addressed!"

403

"Hump! I've had enough of addressing shit" I said sarcastically.

"Now what does that mean?" she asked.

"Nothing, nothing at all" I said immediately regretting I'd made the comment.

Ronni got up and walked over to me. I looked up at her hoping she'd leave before I broke down and told her all my business.

She reached out her hand to me and mechanically I took it.

"Casey, I love you" she whispered.

I choked back tears as they tightened in my throat. Her words were comforting to hear but did little to relieve the awful feeling of abandonment I was feeling.

"I love you too Ronni" I said, still fighting to hold on to my pride.

"No, Casey. I LOVE YOU!"

I looked up at her.

"What does she mean by that?" I wondered. I searched her face for an explanation but there was none. And as quite as she said it, she just as quietly let go of my hand and walked out, closing the door behind her.

My meeting with Taylor and Marty turned out better than expected. Just as he'd promised, Marty produced documents showing EarthTel had doctored their books for years hiding losses of monumental proportions. Marty had delivered the goods and boy was it good! The facts were undeniable.

So it was decided. Taylor agreed to represent Marty and Marty was more than please with my selection of representation. I, on the other hand abdicated any legal responsibility. It was my duty to stand by my firm. Marty told me he understood my reasoning and thanked me for the part I'd played in all of this. Taylor offered to keep me abreast of what was going on with the case. But again I abdicated knowing my moral obligation to the company and by no means wanting this transference of information to cause any legal ramifications for them or myself if the knowledge of my involvement were to get into the wrong hands.

Thus we were all in agreement. I would walk silently into the night as they proceeded to pursue a case of landmark proportions. Besides, I knew I was in no position to take on case of that magnitude even if I wanted to, my life had become too complex and I didn't feel it would be fair to either of them.

Since there was still some good daylight left in the day I decided to go back to the office after my meeting. When I arrived I found a note to call the Director of Human Resource, Pam Smart.
I immediately called her. Her secretary told me she was in meetings for the rest of the day. I left a message and hung up. I sat back in my chair and turned around to look out the window behind me. My mind was racing. I couldn't imagine why I

would be contacted by Human Resource. My mind drifted to the meeting I'd just left with Taylor and Marty.

"*Oh, my God*" I thought.

Rather than drive myself crazy with assumptions, I decided to go home. This turn of events made me mentally fatigued. Trying to get anything done with this looming over my head would be useless.

"*Damn*," I thought, "Things are going from sugar to shit, fast!"

Though I'd attempted to contact Mrs. Smart after receiving her note I wasn't able to speak with her for another two weeks due to a death in her family. The human resource person who had been left in charge was not apprised of the situation, which only aided in my speculation that something of dire circumstances was involved requiring only the head person. I lay awake countless nights fretting over what she wanted and why it was so urgent.

I talked myself into believing that it was nothing and if it was something the only thing I could do at this point was hurry up and wait for her return. Still the suspense was a more than I could take given my involvement with Marty and Taylor regarding EarthTel. It was all too much of a coincidence. And on top of it all, Jade and I still had not spoken. I was beginning to believe this was all some supreme plot to drive me out of my fucking mind! The tension was mounting. I wasn't sleeping well and times I wasn't thinking straight either.

When Love Aint Enough

Since I was stuck in a state of limbo at work as well as with my personal life, I decided to get some relief from somewhere.

It was Friday. I left around noon and drove to the television station to see if Jade would have lunch with me. I didn't bother to call since she wasn't bothering to return any of them anyway. When I arrived, her secretary told me she was out. I was reluctant to believe her of course because I'd been given the run around for weeks. When I asked when she'd be back she told me Jade was gone for the rest of the day. I asked to use the receptionist phone and called Jade at home. When it rang she answered. I hung up without saying anything and drove to her place.

That was a big mistake! Because like my mom always says,

"If you look for trouble you're sure to find it."

Nervously I parked my truck and walked in. As I did, I noticed her co worker getting off the elevator. He was an extremely tall, light skinned dude looked like he weighed about a buck fifteen soaking wet! He was one of the few people I'd met at her job, one day as we had lunch in her office. He was currier or some shit. I jokingly called him a Snoop dog wanna be. She'd agreed, only to add that somebody must like him since he was screwing half the office! When I saw him our eyes met and I was about to speak but he looked away. It was an odd reaction that made me take a second look as he walked off. He must have sensed it because he glanced back too.

407

As I approached Jade's floor the man's odd behavior continued to bother me. By the time I reached her floor I'd dismissed it and was concentrating on the chore before me, getting Jade to talk to me. When I got to her door I became apprehensive but I summoned all my courage and rang the doorbell. Almost immediately she opened the door. To her surprise and mine as well, she flung the door open wearing only a man's tee shirt and panties. I was shocked at the sight of her and she was shocked to find it wasn't whom ever she'd thought it was. We stood looking at each other in amazement. Then it hit me. The guy I'd just seen exiting the elevator had obviously just left Jade's apartment.

My mind was reeling at the idea of him and her doing the nasty only moments before I arrived. The scowl on my face revealed everything I was thinking. Jade tried to explain, which was a sure-fire sign my calculations were on point, because she didn't explain shit! I walked numbly through the lobby and back to my truck.

My embarrassment overwhelmed me. I felt betrayed, yet again. My heart was beating so fast I thought I'd faint. I slumped back on the seat and stared out the window. My cell phone started ringing. I checked it. It was Jade. I didn't bother to answer it the first two times but the continuous ringing aggravated the hell out of me. I pushed the phone up to my ear and spoke my name.

"That wasn't what you thought" She said immediately.

I listened wanting desperately for her to explain away the terrible thoughts going through my mind. She admitted the man I saw in the lobby was the same one from her job and stated he'd come over to bring her some papers. She said she'd thought it was him returning when she answered the door and found me standing there.

"If you thought it was him then why did you come to the door dressed like that?
She didn't answer.

"That's what I figured!" I yelled at her. "I have been making myself sick! Physically sick over the thought of having betrayed you when actually you've been buck wild from the door. How many more nigga's are you fucking Jade? Huh! Tell me, because I'm damn sure that bastard aint the only one!" I yelled into the phone

"Casey listen to me!"

"Listen to what? More lies. You obviously have no respect for me whatsoever and me with my dumb ass actually thought you loved me. I have been kicking myself for fucking Karen!"

"If it wasn't for her..." she began attempting to change the tone of the conversation.

"If it wasn't for her what! If it wasn't for her what the hell would you be doing, fucking less?!"

"I don't owe you any explanations! You never believe anything I say anyway!" she screamed.

409

"And whose fault is that? Everything is about games with you!"

"If you feel like that then leave me alone! I didn't ask you to come here!"

"No you didn't! And guess what, I didn't ask you to make a damn fool out of me but you did! So we are tit for tat"

"I've never lied to you Casey?"

"So are you saying you and that guy aren't fucking?" I asked calmly

"You and I aren't together! I'm not your woman!" She yelled

"Thanks for answering my question!" I said as I disconnected the call.

Well I'd gone looking for it and damn sure found it. As I drove back to the office I cried out to God to please save me, this time from my damn self! I was beginning to see a different side of Jade and I didn't like it. She was proving to me how selfish and uncaring she could be. I thought our love stood for something and was being rudely awakened to the fact that it didn't mean shit!

I'd been in bad relationships before, enough to make me want to settle down with that special someone. Now I was in something, I could not for the life of me, understand. Every fiber of my being told me she loved me but how could I refute evidence being placed squarely before me. Was I that naïve to people, to women? Was everybody so oblivious to others that

When Love Aint Enough

the wrong they did to other people was justified as long as the other person was unable to see that wrong?

I was deeply concerned, was I losing my sanity along with everything else? Since all this craziness began I had been strong in the knowledge of who I was and what I wanted. But now it was as if I was in a battle for my soul. A soul that grieved the loss of Jade and the ideals I'd held for so long. I decided if anything was to materialize between Jade and myself she would have to initiate it. I was beaten. My pride had been smashed and my heart was torn in a million places. I wouldn't know how to begin the repair work on it were I given instructions and a visual guide.

When I arrived back at the office there were several messages from Jade. They were all justifying her actions by my having slept with Karen.

The next morning at work I received yet another note from Mrs. Smart of Human Resource to attend a 10am meeting. I took a deep breath after reading the memo and worked to prepare myself mentally for whatever it was they chose to throw at me. The meeting was set for the main conference room. That in itself was a warning to me that it was something big for us to meet there instead of her office. This meant that she and I wouldn't be the only ones there. In a way it took a load off my shoulders knowing I could soon put an end to the mystery.

411

As I walked into the room, my eyes met those of the senior partners, Anderson, Carruthers, Jones and Maxwell, of whom I had just received praised from, only weeks ago. The conference room in itself was frightening if you found yourself on the wrong side of the table. It was filled with conferencing equipment and a table that seated forty people. Four senior partners were assembled there along with our human resource agent and a stenographer. I immediately began to sweat.

My underarms grew moist and I could feel the perspiration beading up on my forehead. This didn't look good. All that morning, as I had prepared for work, I'd experienced an ominous feeling of dread. I'd assumed it was due to the encounter with Jade the previous day and tried unsuccessfully to dismiss it. As I walked into the room, the same sense of dread overwhelmed me again. I looked about the room uneasily trying to find a warm face but could not. Though they weren't frowning they gave no illusion of being happy either. I took a seat in the chair pointed out by Mitchell. I positioned myself in the chair confidently. I folded my hands in my lap calmly and waited for someone to explain the reason for the meeting. Mitchell began by saying that this was not an indictment but rather an investigation. I held on as my mind began scrambling and went immediately to EarthTel.

Mitchell dutifully explained the charges leveled against me. Karen had charged me with sexual harassment.

"This crazy bitch is trying to make good on her threat to destroy me," I screamed to myself.

I tried unsuccessfully to listen to every word but was distracted by my own thoughts. Finally, Julia Smart, Human Resource representative asked me if I wanted to make a statement. I shook my head.

"I need time to think," I thought.

It was all coming at me too fast! My eyes attempted to focus on the faces of those around me as I gathered my thoughts. Mitchell seemed to be watching my every move. I felt like a trapped animal! They all glared at me like I was some sort of pervert. I tried vainly to dismiss the uncomfortable feeling of being judged by making eye contact with them. My voice trembled as I made an effort to speak.

"First of all, I want to assure you of my innocence. The charges are absurd. But since this was only brought to my attention today, I will need some time to ingest it all. To be honest, I really am quite confused to what's going on here." I said calmly

"Casey, we are not here to judge you. Its like Mitchell stated earlier, we're simply investigating a charge. You are well aware of the policies and procedures of this company so you know that we are obligated to investigate any allegation reported to us," said Mr. Carruthers.

I looked at him briefly as he spoke. I could feel the steam coming from my face now. It grew hotter as I sat looking out

413

the window beyond them. Tears fought ferociously to gain their
way into my eyes but I fought back! I wasn't about to allow
anyone to know how utterly helpless I was feeling. And with all
of my heart, I cursed the day I'd ever met Karen!

"That low life drunk," I thought to myself. *"I tried to be her
friend and this is how she chose to repay me. She wants to
destroy me! End my career! And for what?! For what?"* I
thought. *Because I don't want her! Ain't this some shit!"* I
thought.

"The *first time I try to do the right thing and be up front with a
hoe and she wants to trip like this. I could kill that bitch!"* I
screamed to myself.

After a lengthy and thorough explanation of the review process I
was given the opportunity of forwarding my statement to them
via email. Finally, they suggested, in light of the charges that I
refrain from any contact with Karen to ward any further
retribution on her part. Then the meeting was adjourned and I
was excused from the room. As I got up to leave, I tried to
exude an air of self confidence. But deep down I felt like a dog,
with its tail tucked between it legs!

I returned to my office and asked Ronni to hold all my calls.
She asked if I was okay but I could only nod my head. I entered
my office and closed the door behind me. I sought refuge in my
chair and spun around to look out the window. I sat there
silently watching the birds as they flew on and off the window

ledge. I was transfixed by the grace of their movements. It was comforting to watch them waddle carefree along the ledge.

As I sat looking out the window the impact of all I had just experienced came crashing down on me. Yes the bottom had fallen out of it!

"I had met my mammy drunk," as my mom would say.

A subordinate had accused me of harassment. And now my integrity was being called into question. I was furious! The thought of Karen insinuating that I would harass her nasty ass for sex made me sick. But even more sickening was having to discuss my personal life with my superiors. I was in a corner and was desperate to put the matter to rest. It was humiliating to hear those charges coming from the mouths of people who once held me in such high esteem. Now they wanted me to give sorted details of my relationship with Karen in order to clear myself of the bullshit!

"This is the last fucking straw!"

And thought they'd had suggested I not contact her, I decided to do it anyway. After all, it was just a suggestion not a direct order. And this woman was no longer just fucking with my heart she was fucking with my lively hood. And I needed to put an end to this shit fast!

So I decided to pay her a visit at home. Last I'd heard she'd been out on leave since her near miss with the pills in the ladies

415

bathroom. I got up from my chair and grabbed my jacket. I told Ronni I'd be out for the rest of the day.

When I got into my truck I debated whether to call her from my cell but decided not to. The dirty bitch might try to use it as proof to say I was harassing her or some shit! As I drove onto the street I decided to stop at a payphone to call her. If she was there I would hang up and pop in to surprise her. I nervously dialed her number, but there was one answer. I tried it again, same thing, no answer. I slammed the receiver down and got back in my truck. I tried to calm down and think.

"Maybe it's a sign I should leave it alone and hope for the best when I give my statement." I reasoned aloud. At this rate if I did find Karen I would only make things worse because I was so pissed. I sat in parked truck weighing the pro's and cons.

Finally, I decided what the hell! My ass was already in the sling. This passive aggressive shit hadn't gotten me nothing but walked over by the woman I love and fucked over by the bitch I dumped. It's time I took back control of things. So come what may, I was going to find her ass.

I knew Karen liked to drink. She went to happy hour dam near every day. I looked at my watch. It was five after two. "*Too early for happy hour*" I thought, but knowing that lush she was probably sitting up waiting for it. It was a long shot but I had to do something. This shit had gone too far and I was damned determined to end it today. Once when she and I talked she'd told me of a seedy sports bar over by the river called Spanker's.

I jumped on the freeway and felt my way around to find the exit. After stopping for directions several times, I finally pulled up into "Spanker's parking lot. But it was empty except for a couple of trucks and a scooter. Karen's Mazda 626 was no where to be found. I pulled off the lot and drove to the light. I decided to make the block and check all the little pubs for Karen's car. I was casing the street like an undercover cop looking for bad guys. In that area my truck stuck out like a sore thumb. At one point the police were actually following me. I looked damn suspicious driving in an out of the parking lots and jumping in and out of my truck looking up and down alleys.

I had driven to about twenty clubs in that little area when I decided to call it a day. I was disgusted! I kicked myself for thinking it was going to be that easy to find her. Looking for a drunk in this part of town was like trying to find a needle in a haystack. Aggravated like a mug, I stopped at a Seven Eleven for some gum and a bottle of water. As I was walking out of the store, I saw something. I stopped in my tracks. Across the street from me was a small hole in the wall. You could barely tell it was a club because it had a little greasy spoon attached. Beside it, was an alley. And in the alley was a Mazda, same make, style and color as Karen's.

"Well I'll be damned!" I said aloud.

I ran across the street and went into the alley to make sure it was her car. I looked inside and saw her badge hanging off the rearview mirror. I ran back across the street, parked my car on the side of the building. I jumped out and I jogged across the street to the little club. The place was called Radars. There was a little blinking sign in the window announcing happy hour.

"It figures!" I thought.

Cautiously I walked in. Darkness slapped me in the face as I entered the foyer. Awkwardly I felt for the wall. My eyes quickly began adjusting themselves to the lighting as I rounded the corner and saw three older men sitting at the bar. Two of them turned around and looked in my direction as I entered the room. B. B. King was playing on the jukebox. I listened trying to appear casual as I walked into the open area and over to the bar.

I felt as out of place as a sheet wearing sheet clansman at a SWAC football game, all eyes were on me. I opened my jacket and asked the bartender for a Long Island Ice Tea. He told me that wasn't on the happy hour menu.

"That's fine"

I smiled at the two guys staring and looked away. They in turn, returned to their conversation. Casually I looked around the dark room for Karen. There were some couples sitting at some tables in the corner but neither of the women was Karen. The bartender brought my drink over and I paid him. I took a sip and continued to look around. Half way between my drink, I'd begin to think I'd chosen the wrong club when I heard a familiar laugh. It was coming from the hallway. The music had died down and the laughter seemed to be getting louder. Then Karen walked out. She was done. Her hair was frizzy and she wore a wrinkled blue wool coat. She looked a hot mess! She was hanging on the arm of some guy. They walked over to the jukebox and started looking through the selections. I turned my back hoping she didn't see me and sipped on my drink. I soon realized that I hadn't really thought this whole thing out!

I never anticipated her being with anybody. My mind raced on what I should say or if I should say anything. I inconspicuously watched thru the bar mirror. She still hadn't noticed me yet. The bartender came over and asked if I needed anything else. I hadn't realized it but I had gone though the drink and now was sucking air through the straw. I nodded my head and asked for another one. I looked into the mirror again to see what Karen was doing and this time she wasn't there.

I turned around on my stool and saw she was no longer in the room. Instinctively I got up and walked down the hall from where she'd come. It was even darker and led to a unisex bathroom. Further down was a room whose door was slightly ajar. I peeped in to see if she was there. The small musky room was empty except for a worn out pool table and a couple of wooden chairs. Hurriedly I walked back out into the club and went over to the bar. My drink was waiting for me. I asked the bartender if he had seen where the lady in the blue coat had gone. After some memory jogging, he said she'd left out. I paid him and left too.

I ran out and peeped into the alley and spotted her again. She was seated in the car. The guy was standing outside the passenger side leaning in through the window, talking to her. I ran around to my truck and waited for her to drive down the one way street.

I decided to follow her back to her place. A couple of minutes later, her car came rolling by. I ducked down and allowed her to get up the street then I pulled out to follow her, careful not to get to close.

She drove for about twenty minutes and then pulled over at a diner called Buckets. I pulled in behind her. She parked her car and got out. I waited, then did the same. I walked inside and peeked over the crowd to find her. She was seated at the bar smoking a cigarette. I decided to approach her. As I walked in her direction I saw someone was beside her. They were talking. I wondered how close I could get without her seeing me. I decided not to chance it. I couldn't afford to have her calling this person to as a witness. I had to be smart.

So I turned and walked out. When I got inside my truck I slammed my fist onto the steering wheel. I was starting to doubt myself again. The whole thing had me acting a damn fool.

"Here I am following o'l girl like I-Spy trying to talk to her. Hell I don't even know what to say when I do get a chance to talk to her. The whole thing might just blow up in my face. If

When Love Aint Enough

the broad is that vindictive to make up shit there's no telling what she'll do if I say something to her crazy ass," I thought.

I started up my truck and put it in gear to leave. As I looked up to pull off, I saw Jason Andrews walk from the dinner. Seconds later Karen walked out behind him.

I put the truck in park and lowered myself in the seat. They stood talking in the parking lot and then went to their individual cars.

"What the hell were they doing together? Supposedly they can't stand each other!" I said aloud as I watched Jason drive off and Karen followed. I waited, then fell in line behind them both.

I didn't have to drive for long. They drove to a little motel located not far from the diner. When she arrived she jumped out of her car, swinging her purse over her shoulders and walked through the semi crowded parking lot to one of the cottages, room 304. She knocked on the door and it opened. And there stood Jason, his tie was loose and he'd taken off his jacket. They exchanged words as she walked past him into the dark room. He lingered a moment surveying the parking lot then closed the door.

I sat in my truck across the street, hidden by brush. I was still incredulous of what I had stumbled upon and tried to make some sense of the whole thing.

"Jason and Karen are having an affair," I thought. *"What else would they be meeting at this little dingy roach motel?*

421

I debated whether I should wait in my truck or go knock on the door. I was fuming at the thought of being played by the hussy and I wanted her and Jason both to know I knew their dirty little secret. But a little voice deep inside told me to chill. So I waited hoping my next move would come to me just as this gold mine of information had fallen into my lap. I reclined my seat and patiently went through my CD collection, all the time watching room 304.

Their little thrist didn't last as long as I thought it would. Though it seemed like hours it was only about twenty minutes before the door opened. I watched through the steering wheel as Karen came rushing out looking disheveled and pulling her coat tightly around her body. She staggered through the pothole filled parking back to her car. As she fumbled with her keys, Jason peeped out the door, surveying the lot again, and then made a quick exit to the side of the building where he'd parked his car.

Both cars pull off at the same time. I thought quickly as to which one I should follow. After a minute, I decided to follow Jason. Jason led me back to the office. I parked my truck in the garage and went back into the office building.

Since Jason was the son in law of one of the senior partners, Albert Carruthers he had an impressive office located on the 12th floor. Anxiously I paced the floor of the lobby. My mind carefully calculated what my next move should be. Karen was a thorn in my side and the longer I allowed this investigation to pry into my personal life the more problems it might create for me in the long run. I could ill afford that kind of notoriety around the office. But the question remained, what should I do with this information that had miraculously fell into my lap. Like my mom always said

"What's done in the dark always comes to light" and about that she'd never lied. I decided to go for it. I was going to confront Jason.

I jumped in the elevator and began my ascension to the 12th floor. The Muzac bubbled through the speakers of the elevator walls, seeping softly in my ears as I tried to assimilate everything I'd witnessed, wondering how I would approach Jason. The elevator jerked to a stop jarring me back to reality as the doors opened, announcing my destination. I stepped off looking around carefully at my surroundings. Jason's office was straight ahead to left.

The outer office where his secretary sat was empty. She'd left for the day.

Slowly I walked up to his office door. It was slightly ajar but still I knocked and waited. A deep voice from within beckoned me inside. I pushed the door open and cautiously walked inside. Jason was seated behind his desk, deep in thought reading something. I looked around casually as the heavy smell of cigar floated up my nostrils. Jason's office wasn't huge. The lights from the streets danced through the open blinds and reflecting off the cattycornered windows that gave a panoramic view of the city. An antique mahogany desk with brass trim gracefully stood before the twelve foot high windows. The desk was decorated with an antique brass lamp and pictures of his wife and kids. Hundreds of leather bound books filled the shelves that stretched from one end of his office to the next. The books gave off a light hint of musk, that when mixed with the cigars, made the office feel stuffy. That accounted for the Hepa filter that hummed in a nearby corner struggling to rid the office of its fumes. Two leather chairs were placed meticulously in front of his desk on each end. And a leather love seat sat off to the right of the office.

Jason looked as I walked inside. From the look on his face, he was definitely surprised to see me.

"Hi Jason, do you have a minute?" I asked calmly.

"Hello Casey. To what do I owe the pleasure?" he asked as he returned his attention to the papers he was reading.

"We need to talk, are you busy?" I asked dryly.

"Well actually I'm in the middle of something can it wait until ..." he asked as he began to search through his desk drawer.

"I'm afraid not. It's an urgent matter" I insisted

Jason stopped his search and looked up at me. I stood rigidly watching his every move. He closed the drawer he'd been rummaging through and clasped his hands, resting them on the desk before him.

"I see...In that case how can I help you?" he asked staring at me curiously.

"Its concerning Karen James" I said.

Jason became visibly nervous. He unfolded his hands and sat upright in his chair.

"Really, what about her?" he asked staring at me defensively like an animal about to be attacked.

"I saw the two of you together today over on Preston." I said calmly.

The weight of my statement hit him like a ton of bricks. The dim light from his desk lamp shimmered off the beads of sweat that instantly appeared on his forehead. Though he tried not to show it, it was evident the mere mention of Karen's name unnerved him.

"Casey you must be mistaken. I've been here all day..." he began.

"No I don't think so." I said in matter of factly sort of way. "But that's of no consequence to me really!" I said flatly.

Jason watched me intently as I told him of my chance encounter with him and Karen at the diner and later the motel. I was reluctant to tell why I was looking for Karen in the first place but figured since she reported to him, I was certain he was already aware of the harassment charges she'd filed against me. After I'd finished we were both silent. Jason glared at me vengefully. The look was intended to ward me off but instead it

425

was laughable to me. I was in no mood to be fucked with. If he wanted to battle,

 "It was on!" I thought. But like my mom always said, "You get more flies with honey than vinegar" so I stayed calm.
After staring me down and it not working, he broke.

"Look I can explain" Jason offered.

"Jason I'm really not interested. You do what you do. Fine! That's between you and your wife and maybe some other interested parties if you get my drift. But me I'm the innocent party in all this," I said flatly.

"I understand. But it's not what you think" he insisted.

"Look, my thing is this, I want her off my back and out of my life. And that's where you come in. This whole thing could get very ugly and I'm not talking about just for me" I threatened, certain he understood exactly what I was alluding too.

"I can't help you," he said, lowering head in defeat.

"So you're willing to risk everything for this tramp?" I asked amazed.

"It's not as simple as you think," He said still looking down.

"Seems simple to me! You either tell you're girl to lay off me or I'll tell Carruthers that you're fucking over his daughter, again! I know your reputation and I'm sure it won't go down quite as well as you think!"
Jason slammed his fist down on the desk.

"I can't do it Casey. My hands are tied!"

His attitude surprised me but by no means was I going to back down!

Since I'd walked into his office I had been standing. Now I took the opportunity to sit down. Things weren't going as I'd planned.

"Why in the hell is he being stubborn about it. Doesn't he realize I'm not making idle threats?" I thought.

"Jason, I don't know if you just don't give a damn no more or whatever the hell is your problem but I mean it when I say I'm not going down alone!"

Jason looked up at me. Stress was written all over his face. He got up and walked over to the door that was still ajar. He pushed it close and locked it, returning to his seat.

"Casey, I can't do anything because Karen is blackmailing me," Jason said firmly.

My mind reeled.

"Wh-a-t?!" I thought.

I sat quietly and allowed Jason to continue.

"A couple of months ago Karen and I had an affair. It was innocent enough in the beginning but her constant talk of you began to concern me. She said she wanted to be with you but you were too demanding. She said you had other women but wanted her to be at your beck and call. Her whole talk was about you constantly. She even told me how you'd cheated on her then jumped on her when she confronted you about it. She was determined to get even with you!"

"That's a damn lie!" I blurted out

"Maybe, I don't know. I just know I couldn't take her unpredictability. Hell, I felt like if she hated you like this and could plot on you the way she was doing she wouldn't blink and eye when it came to canceling my ass. So I began to distance myself from her. I figured since she was so caught up with you that she wouldn't miss me. I figured I was in the clear until one day, out of the blue, she informed me she was pregnant!"
I shook my head slowly in disbelief.

"This can't be happening" I mumbled aloud.

"That's what I said," said Jason regretfully.

"So what then?" I asked

"We talked and she said she wanted to have an abortion. She said it would be the best thing for everyone involved. I was so relieved to hear it, I not only paid for the abortion but gave her and extra thousand as a show of good will."
I shook my head uneasily. I knew the rest. The taste of money made her want more, I was sure.
Jason continued,

"That was a month ago, last night she called me and asked me to meet her at the Diner. When I got there she told me she didn't have the abortion and that she planned to keep the child. On top of that she is demanding I give her twenty thousand dollars or she'll go public with the whole damn thing!"
My heart sank.

"What are you going to do?" I asked.

428

"I don't know! What can I do? If I don't give her what she wants my life and probably my career here with the firm is over.

"And if I you do who's to say that will be the end of it!" I added

"I know! I'm damned if I do and damned if I don't!" he snapped.

"Yep" I said, agreeing with him. "Damn she's a busy bitch! Hell, before you and her met today I saw her at a bar over off the reef!"

"Was she was drinking?" asked Jason surprised.

"I don't know, when I saw her she was coming from the back with some guy, but what's she doing in a bar if she aint?" Jason pondered my statement.

"Women are supposed to drink if they're pregnant are they?" he asked

"I don't think so. Did she give you any proof she's pregnant!"

"Yeah she showed me papers that were supposed to be test results verifying her pregnancy" said Jason still puzzled.

"Well how do you know it's yours Jason?" I asked.

"That's just it. I don't! All I know is I can't afford to have her go public with this. Not right now! My wife would leave me for sure! I'd be ruined!"

"So basically you took her word for it. And you and I both know Karen isn't the most trustworthy mother-fucker in the world!" I said

"Of course I had my reservations but when she told me she was going to have the abortion there was nothing to question. I just wanted it over. So I tried to do the right thing by giving her the money she needed."

"Pardon me for saying this but I think she might be putting the fuck to you!"

"I thought that too but today when we meet her stomach looked bigger."

"Did she take her clothes off?" I asked.

"No, that wasn't our reason for meeting. We only went there for more privacy after she dropped the bomb on me at the diner" he explained.

"It still sounds strange to me," I said.

"Do you think she's lying" he asked hopefully

"Don't know, but there's one way to find out, get her tested"

"Oh no, that might make her crazy ass mad. No, she's already told me if I do anything to piss her off, she's going straight to my wife! And I can't afford that!"

"Well how are you going to know for sure? You can't just take her word for it. That's crazy!" I argued.

Jason rubbed his hand across his eyes. He was visibly worn. But he had no one to blame for his predicament but himself. Even so, I felt for him. I knew how manipulating Karen could be. I was a definitely a witness to that. And to hear Jason tell me how she talked of me and seemed to be obsessed with me was unsettling. But it gave me an idea.

"Jason" I said calmly as I steadied my thoughts,

"Maybe we can I can get her to talk"

"I would love it if you could but she's crazy..."

"Yeah crazy about my ass"

"Well yeah..."

"Maybe that could be a good thang" I said still thinking.

Up until now, I'd thought confronting Karen would be dangerous. Now I wasn't so sure. If she was that obsessed with me I was sure she wouldn't be able resist getting together one last time. It was a long shot but at this point neither of us had very much to lose.

"So you think she'll come clean about the pregnancy"

"Hopefully, she'll come clean about something"

"What about me...what do I do"

"I need you to swear that if I can prove she aint pregnant you'll stand up for me with the partners and tell them how this psycho bitch has been casing me"

"What will I say when they ask why I didn't come forward when she pressed the charges"

"Who told you about it?"

"She did"

"Well there you go, you didn't know."

"I don't know Casey it seems weak to me"

"Well Jason do you have anything better"

"Well...."

"Okay then, we'll do it my way for now"

"Seems we damned if we do and damned if we don't"

"You damn right" I agreed.

Jason was scared it would backfire and Karen would make good on her threat to rock his world. I knew Karen. And I didn't believe she was pregnant by a long shot and if she was it wasn't Jason. I was damned sure of it. Once he found out she wasn't pregnant it would give him more leverage to deal with her. And by the same token he could go testify on my behalf that she was obsessed with me. That along with my explanation might be enough to get ass out of hot water. And better yet, once he found out she wasn't really pregnant he could us that as leverage to make her back off of me. I didn't tell Jason, but in the end he might have to admit he'd slept with her, but I would deal with that when the time came.

So we devised a plan to hopefully trip up the "mighty Karen." Jason told me Karen's leave of absence was officially up today and that he expected her to be back in the office tomorrow, Tuesday. He said she had given him until Friday to get the money together. He thought he could possibly talk her into extending the deadline to the following Monday if needed. We sat in his office for hours fine tuning our plan. We had to work quickly because time was definitely not on our side. I needed to submit my official statement to HR ASAP. And Karen wanted the money from Jason, like yesterday.

I knew the company, and unless this thing was totally disproved, there would always be a shadow over me. And a

432

shadow possible guilt was as disastrous as being found guilty. So it was settled. We would proceed as planned and hoped for the best. It was an unlikely alliance but at that point we were all we had.

The plans were laid out. First, I would try to make contact with Karen and entice her to see me. Then Jason would meet with her afterwards. If all went well we would both have what we wanted by the next week. I was anxious to get started. It would require an Oscar winning performance to trick that old dog. But I was prepared to give it my best shot.

The next day our plan rolled into action. Since Karen and I hadn't exactly talked in a while our plan depended upon an accidental meeting. Jason called me and confirmed Karen had reported to work as scheduled. I was to go to the Grill, where she normally ate lunch and hope for the best. If she was there it would turn into a cat and mouse game, with her as the cat and me the mouse. Knowing Karen, she wouldn't miss the opportunity to try to rub what she'd done in my face. And I was obliged to let her do so. Eagerly I went down to the first floor and walked into the Grill. I placed my order and casually looked around to see if she was there. But she wasn't. I took a seat by the window in full view of the counter hoping if I didn't see her she would at least see me. But it was to no avail. She never showed up. Disappointed, I returned to my office and called Jason with my report. He was disappointed too.

We both knew this thing was a long shot but in order for it to be convincing we needed to make it look like it was an accident as well as any interaction being her idea, not mine. During the course of the day I continued to try to different places I thought she would be. But as chances would have it she was nowhere to be found aside from her desk. But I refused to get discouraged. I was convinced if I could run into her it would all work out. It had to. Everything was riding on it.

On Wednesday, I tried again. Still there was no sign of her. Then came Thursday, reluctantly I went down to the Grill. This time I hit pay dirt. She was there. And she was alone. I walked inside and went directly to the counter. Because I'd eaten there for the past couple of days, I'd become somewhat of a regular. The cashier greeted me with a big hello and smile,

"Your usual" she asked, referring to the chef salad with Dijon dressing I always ordered.

"Yes please" I replied smiling back broadly at the waitress. I figured that played well, after all, Karen wasn't stupid. I wanted it to look as if this was my new hang out and it did. I stood at the counter laughing and talking with the waitress until my order arrived. As I did so I noticed Karen watching me out of the corner of my eye. I really began to play it up then. Her interest energized me. The waitress finally gave me my order and I took it and looked around for a table. As I walked past her table I glanced at her but looked away quickly not bothering to speak. Karen was a glutton for punishment.

She craved attention like babies craved milk. I could feel her eyes on my back as I walked over to a small table by the window. Casually, I sat down and prepared to eat my lunch. Then my cell phone rang. I reached over and pulled it from my jacket. It was Jason. I told him she was there and hung up. As I sat eating my salad and looking out onto the sidewalk at the busy pedestrians passing by, I could still feel her watching me. Soon I was genuinely consumed by the passersby wondering what their lives were like, wondering if they were as carefree as they looked. It didn't take long before she took the bait.

"Hey Casey" she said curiously as she stood at my table with her coat draped over her arm.

I looked up briefly to see her standing there in a dark wool suit with a string of pearls around her neck. For a moment I was upset at the sight of her and my heart began to quicken. I fought back the urge to be nasty and gave a polite,

"Hey how you doing?"

"Umph, I'm surprised!" she said

"About what" I asked focusing all of my attention on the salad that sat before me.

"That you didn't bite my head off!" she said looking at me suspiciously.

"Oh really! Well I'm surprised you spoke considering I've been harassing you"

"Ok here we go," she said.

"Well what did you expect, flowers?" I asked carefully.

"No!" she said defensively. "I mean, I don't hate you or anything. I simply don't like the way you handled things."

"Oh so you're admitting I didn't harass you? I asked as I looked into her eyes.

"I'm not going there. All I know is I don't like the way things went down with us. You knew how I felt about you," she whispered as she looked around to see if anyone could hear her. Instinctively I took a quick survey of my surroundings then looked back at her.

"I thought I did. But I guess I was wrong!" I said flatly as I returned my attention to my plate.

"No you weren't wrong. I do love you Casey! You know that"

"Well sweetie if that's love, I certainly don't want to know what it would be like if you hated me." I mumbled with a mouth full of salad.

Karen stood there pondering her next statement. I could tell my last statement had hooked her. She was simple like that.

"How's your girl"

"What girl!"

"Oh don't pretend you don't know who I'm talking about!" She snapped.

I laid my fork down and rested my hands in my lap.

"Well if you referring to Jade, I wouldn't know. We're not together"

"Oh really?!" she said looking at me in disbelief.

"Yes really" I said determined not to show any emotion.
Karen took the opportunity to sit down in one of the chairs at my table. I glanced over at her and prepared to leave.

"Casey! Wait! Don't go." She pleaded.

"I don't have time for this. We don't have anything to talk about!"

"I think we do!"

"About what! First you try to destroy me now you pretend we're cool. Naw lady, you must have me confused with some other fool! Anyway aint you afraid somebody might see you talking to your harasser. That blow your whole case right out of the water!" I whispered annoyed.

"Casey plea-se, things got out of hand, I'm sorry. Can we talk?" she pleaded.

"Yeah" I said to myself. *"That's all I wanted to hear"* continuing to gather my things.

"Maybe here's not the place but I do want to talk with you. I've been sick about the whole thing. You've got to believe me!" she insisted.

"Yeah right," I said sarcastically.

"Please Casey, please." She pleaded.

"When?" I asked reluctantly.

"What's good for you?" she asked staring at me intently.

"I'm free all the time. I sure as hell don't have a social life anymore!" I said
This seemed to refuel her.

"Maybe you can come by my place later," she asked hopefully.

I shook my head. I wasn't going to make it easier. She wasn't stupid and I hope she didn't think I was.

"Naw, it might be a set up" I said. You can come by my house" I suggested.

"When?" she asked excited as she moved about in her seat eagerly.

"I don't know, I'm flying out tomorrow to Maryland and I'll be gone for a couple of days. Tonight is the only night I have free this weekend. Maybe next week." I said waiting again for her to take the bait.

"Tonight is fine for me. I can be there by 8 if it's okay with you" she said

I pretended to think about the suggestion, "Well, I don't know…I don't need any more shit," I said cautiously.

Karen threw up her left hand and said,

"I promise no mess. I'll be there at 8, okay" she said excited.

I looked at her left hand in the air and thought to myself,

"Dummy it's your right hand!"

"Fine" I said as I picked up my jacket and walked out.

When I got back I eagerly called Jason. I told him of my conversation with Karen and our plans to meet tonight. He was ecstatic. He cautioned me to be careful and I assured him I would.

Eight o'clock had come and gone and Karen was a no call-no show so far. Normally she was very prompt. I grew nervous thinking she'd changed her mind. I didn't want to look overly anxious by calling so I was forced to be patient and wait. Around eight-twenty three the doorbell rang. I peeped out and saw Karen standing on the landing. I took a deep breath and opened it.

"Hey" waived Karen.

"What's up" I replied. "Come in" I ushered.

Karen walked in and stood. I took her coat and placed it in the closet.

We walked into the living room with me leading the way. I promptly sat down on the sofa and grabbed the remote. Nervously I flicked through the channels on TV allowing Karen time to start the conversation. But she didn't. Instead she sat quietly watching me. The silence permeated the room like a thick musk. Finally we both began to speak. I stopped, apologized and allowed her to continue.

"So how are you doing Casey?" She asked sincerely.

I continued to flick through the channels on the TV as I replied,

"Please ask another question" I mumbled.

"I'm serious, you've been on my mind constantly."

"Umph"

"I know you must hate me and I really can't blame you but you can at least try to see my side of things..."

439

"See, this is what I didn't want to happened" I interrupted. "But then again I don't know what I expected. Naw, I don't hate you. I don't hate anyone. But I can't say I respect what you did. Because you lied"

Karen was silent, almost too silent. I wondered if I'd blown it by telling her off so quickly but nevertheless, the deed was done, if she didn't leave I would try harder to keep from snapping when she made stupid remarks.

I could feel Karen's eyes on me. I refused to look at her, afraid my resentment would be overwhelming obvious. Slowly she began to speak,

"Casey you don't know how much you really hurt me" she whispered faintly as though wincing from the pain.

"But you knew the deal Karen I don't understand why you're making it seem as though I deceived you?!" I reasoned.

"Yeah you were straight with me" she whimpered.

"Well why then" I asked turning to look in her direction for the first time.

"Why what?" she asked as our eyes met.

"Why did you say those horrible things about me trying to ruin me at work?"

Karen was silent.

The cat and mouse game was beginning to irritate me. I had to make her admit she had lied on me and that I was innocent. Forget about Jason. Shit I was fighting for my life!

But each time we got to the truth she avoided it or said nothing. This was beginning to weigh on my already limited patience.

"Can I have something to drink?" she asked.

"What would you like?" I said.

"Cognac maybe?" she said.

I got up from my seat and walked to the bar. I mixed us both a drink. I returned shortly with two cocktails. I passed one to her and sat back down. She took a long sip and held what was left in her glass daintily. Things were getting tense. I decided to revert back to game plan and get her to talking about Jason. Then maybe she would do some talking.

"So how are things at work?" I asked.

"It's cool" she replied as she took another long gulp of her drink.

"Is your boss still hassling you?" I asked cautiously.

"No I took care of that," She said with a smirk.

Karen finished off her drink and asked for another one. Again I went to the bar, this time I grabbed the bottle of cognac and brought it back to the sofa. I handed it to her. She poured another drink as I continued to sip on my original one. Karen was drinking like a sailor. We sat in silence as Karen continued to drink devoutly.

After a while she started talking again.

"Are you dating anyone?" she asked abruptly.

"No" I said calmly.

"Still waiting on Jade huh?" she said sarcastically.

"No! I'm not waiting on anyone. She's gone on with her life and I'm doing the same. I simply don't want to date right now" I explained becoming increasingly agitated.

"Have you talked to her?" she stumbled.

"No and I don't want to talk about Jade"

"Hump" she grunted.

I ignored her and continued to watch the screen.

"Well I can see you haven't gotten over her," she said.

Again I ignored her. The conversation was like a pinched nerve, aggravating as hell! I figured she was trying to push my buttons but I refused to let her. I took another sip of my drink and watched her dig into her purse. Victoriously, she pulled out a small case and opened it. Inside it were some hand rolled joints. She took one out and asked if it was okay to for her to smoke. I said she could, hoping the combination of liquor and weed would make her open up. Karen lit the joint and took a couple deep pulls on it. She offered it to me but I declined. I had finished my drink and was about to pour me another one.

"Come on" she insisted "Maybe it will lighten you up a bit" she said.

"No, I'm good." I assured her.

An hour had elapsed since she'd arrived and still she hadn't confessed to anything. Things were not going well at all. The more she sat beside me the more I wanted to wrap my hands around her scrawny neck and choke the shit out of her! I tried keeping my cool by concentrating on my objective, exposing her to be the fanatical liar I knew she was.

The drinking and smoking was taking its toll on Karen. After a while she was high as a kite. I, on the other hand, was sober as a rock and becoming increasingly more irritated by the minute.

"So, what's up Karen?" I asked

"Nothing" she replied

"When we talked earlier you made it seem as though you wanted to clear the air, now you have nothing to say, what's up" I asked sternly.

Karen looked over at me lazily with glazed eyes.

"Baby I just wanted to spend time with you" she said softly I sighed and said,

"Karen, look," I sighed again, "What you're doing to me at the office could cost me my career with the firm. Now I want to know if you are going to correct it or what?"

Karen seemed to think about it and then said,

"Nope"

My body was tingling. My throat grew dry and I thought I would explode.

"What?!" I said

"You heard me. I'm not stupid. I know the only reason I'm here is for you to dick me down and so I can change my mind but I aint having it"

I put my drink down and slowly stood up. Standing with my hands on my hips I looked Karen in the eye and said,

"I wouldn't fuck you with your own damn dick! You make me sick. You are an evil manipulating little bitch who has no sense of decency and couldn't spell morals if it was written on a piece of paper and tattooed on your ass. You aint shit! You never will be shit and I regret the day I ever met your trifling ass!"

My body shook with anger waiting for her response. It was about to get ugly and if I had to I would slay this hoe for real and she could tell any damn body she wanted to cause I was sick of her shit!

Karen looked at me calmly and fell out laughing.

"You are so damn full of yourself it's amazing!" she yelled

"Get out!" I said calmly.

"Not before I say what I have to say!" she said stubbornly.

"I don't want to hear shit you have to say, now get out of my house before I throw you out!" I insisted.

"I came here to tell you how I feel and I'm not leaving until I do so," she said calmly, still seated on the sofa.

I was furious. I began to pace the floor trying to regain my composure.

"Karen, I'm so sick of motherfuckers telling me what they aint gonna do, its sickening. Now you can leave of your own volition or…"

"Or what? What you gonna do? Whoop my ass or something"

"No I'm not going to put my hands on you…"

"You right about that! But like I said, I came here to get some things off my chest and damn it I'm going to"

"Go ahead and say what you have to say then get out!" I barked as I continued to pace the floor in front of her.

"Okay I will. I came over tonight hoping to find that after all this time you'd realized that Ms. Thang was no good for you and to make you realize how much I cared for you"

"First of all, it's none of your damn business what I think about Jade and please don't try to tell me you care for me..." I began

"Op, let me finish," she interrupted. "Now like I was saying, I do care for you, I care for you very deeply. I love you Casey. Lord knows I have tried not too. And it kills me that you are willing to settle for the bullshit Jade is dishing out!"

"There you go again, in my business thinking you know what's best for me"

"Look at you! Just look at you. You're pacing the floor like a maniac mad as hell at me 'cause she dumped your silly ass when the truth is if she loved you nothing I or anybody else could have done would have mattered. Not nothing! The only person miss thang cared about was herself and her precious image! She didn't care about you. But I did! And you probably won't believe me when I say this but it's true, you really hurt me.! You

445

fucked me, used me and then tossed me away like a bad habit when she came back into the picture!

Now she had my attention. I stopped pacing the floor and for the first time since the whole thing started, listened to what she had to say. I looked at her as she rehashed the events of our brief affair. As she poured out her heart to me I began to realize something. I realized that she was just as much a victim in this whole thing as I was. Sure, it wasn't my intention to use her but I did. And she was right, I dropped her ass with a quickness when I learned Jade was coming back.

The expression on her face said it all. I believed she cared for me. She may have even loved me. One thing for sure, she didn't deserve to be treated like yesterday's garbage. Nobody did.

And for the first time, I accepted my part in all of this. I could have handled things different. But no, I acted like I was the only one who had feelings. It never dawned on me that she might actually be offended by the cold and callous way I treated her. Suddenly I was ashamed of myself. I'd acted like hypocrite when I demanded that she be a grown woman about things when I, myself was acting like a spoiled child. I was selfish and thought only of myself, not her, not anybody. It was all about what Casey wanted!

The revelation hit me like a ton of bricks. I felt like a damn fool when I realized I'd brought it all on myself. The heaviness of the punch made me sit down in the nearby lounger. I realized most of the hell I'd been through in recent months could have been avoided.

I wanted what I wanted and to hell with anyone who got in my way. In my heart I could hear my mom just as plain as day,

"You know I didn't raise you like that Casey. You gotta treat people the way you want to be treated."

"Who is this person I've become?" I thought

Tears welled up in my eyes. Karen, seeing my anguish, walked over to comfort me. She stood over me quietly rubbing my back in solace. I didn't deserve her sympathy.

"I'm so sorry" I whispered to her.

"I'm sorry too Casey. I never meant for things to go this far. Like I said, I was hurt. I needed you to feel the pain I felt. And I knew if I attacked your job it would do the trick."

I began to cry even more. I felt ashamed for having created this elaborate trap to catch her when all I really had to do in the first place was listen. She'd been crying out to me for months but I was blinded by my own desires and saw her as nothing but an obstruction to Jade and I being together. She stood there rubbing my back and confessed she had lied about me harassing her. She confessed to having spied on Jade and me on several occasions and even told me she was the person who had cut my tires so many months ago. Finally, she said she loved me and asked me to forgive her. I did.

447

I stood up and hugged her. Her body felt good against mine. For the first time I noticed what she was wearing. It was the same outfit she'd worn the first night we were together. I thought about telling her I'd noticed but decided to leave it alone. I whispered in her ear how very sorry I was for having hurt her. She leaned back in my arms and looked deep into my eyes. She gave me a light kiss on the lips and looked at me again before turning and walking back to the sofa. She picked up her purse and walked to the door. Mechanically I followed. When she reached the door she stopped and turned to me.

"Everything will work out Casey, I promise" she whispered as she planted one last kiss on my cheek.

I nodded my head realizing deep in my heart that it would.

"Are you okay to drive" I asked

"Girl you know me, it takes a lot more than a little Cognac to rock my boat" she kidded. "I'll be fine"

With that she grabbed the doorknob and walked out of my life. I watched as she walked down the walkway to her car. I closed the door behind me and went back into the living room. I plopped down on the sofa and reached under the sofa. I felt around for a couple of seconds before pulling out the voice-activated recorder I'd hidden under the sofa. I pushed rewind and listened to the conversation that Karen and I had just had. I pushed the stop button and laid the recorder on the sofa beside me. In the minutes that followed I did something that surprised even me. I got up from my seat and walked to the patio. I

When Love Aint Enough

opened the door and walked out into the cool crisp air. The ocean was rustling wildly. I ejected the tape from the tiny machine, kissed it and hurled it out into the darkness. I stood there transfixed on the sight and sounds of the ocean before me. In my attempts to save my life or what I thought my life consisted of, I realized I had been dying a slow death for a while. I walked back into the house, turned off the lights and went to bed.

The Beginning of the End

The television came on at six fifteen, awakening me from the best sleep I'd had in months. Lazily I rolled over in bed and pulled the covers over my head, hoping to get ten more minutes of sleep. The news was on. The reporter was talking about EarthTel. I snatched the covers down from my head to see what was going on. A press conference was ending as the news reporter spoke in the background,

"Now here's a recap of recent tumultuous events. Late Thursday night a high ranking official at EarthTel unveiled alleged corporate espionage exceeding two billion dollars in EarthTel's attempts to hide critical losses. It is highly speculated that the dollar amount may increase, as investigations required by the SEC probe into their books for the past five years. These allegations, according to industry watchers, are likely to force the Norfolk based telecommunications giant into a tailspin."

The news hit me hard! I sat straight up and stared at the TV. "Oh my God, oh my God, they've done it! They've done it!" I screamed rolling wildly across the bed. My face felt flushed and my mouth grew dry as I listened to the news reporter describe the near chaotic state of one of Norfolk's most renowned corporations. I could hardly believe what I was hearing. I grabbed the remote and began flipping through the channels to see the impact the news was having on the rest of the world. The story was on almost every channel, CNN, CSPAN, MSNBC, local affiliates, everywhere! Anxiously I jumped out of bed and ran to the closet. As I rummaged through it looking for something to wear, it hit me,

"I bet they are scrambling around like chickens at the office," I said incredulously.

I didn't have to wait long for my answer because the phone began ringing off the hook. I ran over and grabbed it.

"Hello" I answered breathless.

"So I guess you've heard, huh?" asked Ronni

"Yeah, a minute a go," I answered, still trying to catch my breath.

"On one channel they mentioned Marty's name" she said

"They did?" I said incredulously. This whole thing was like a dream. Although I hadn't spoken to either Marty or Taylor in weeks, never in my wildest dreams had I expected things to transpire so quickly!

"What do you think he has to do with it?" she asked.

"Well, I'm sure we'll learn more as the day progresses" I reassured her.

We hung up and I raced back to my closet. I pulled out a gray flannel suit guessing it was going to be a gray flannel day.

451

As I entered the parking garage, it was apparent the news of the day had made its way through the ranks, disturbing everyone in its path, which was evident by all the cars parked on the normally empty and private level. Eagerly I parked my truck and jumped out almost running as I made my way to the elevator. As though sensing my urgency, it swiftly whisked me to my floor without stopping. As the doors opened I was greeted by a sea of people, some I knew and most I didn't, making their way through the corridors collectively talking and whispering. Even Ronni had a slew of people huddled at her desk ranting away about the scandal. I took a quick survey of the group, cordially spoke and rushed into my office.

Ronni soon followed, closing the door behind her as she informed me of hectic agenda for the morning. She told me a meeting was currently underway in the war room for all senior staff members and another one was scheduled for 9:30 for the associates and CFO.

Ronni briefed me on the reporters who had been asked to leave by Carruthers under the cautious escort of building security, just prior to my arrival and of the uproar it had caused through out the building. I sat in my chair listening intently as she described the mayhem she had encountered when she arrived an hour ago. Vividly she described the beleaguered looking attorneys as they raced back and forth through the hallways, as waves of gossip floated throughout the building about EarthTel's trouble. Out of breath, she stopped for a moment to allow everything she'd told me to sink in and get my reaction.

Neither of us waited for long as my cell phone began to ring. Ronni waited as I answered it.

"This is Casey" I announced to the caller. There was a slight hesitation then an old familiar voice sang out.

"No doubt you've heard the news" the voice on the other end asked.

Calmly I pulled the receiver down from my ear and motioned to Ronni to give me some privacy. She nodded her head obediently and quietly walked out, closing the door behind her. I waited until she was gone, then returned the phone to my ear.

"Who hasn't? I asked eagerly of Marty who was waiting on the other end.

"Casey I never dreamed it would be like this! In many ways it's a bit overwhelming," he said.

"I can imagine. What happens now?" I asked, thinking of the ramifications of Marty's courageously bold actions.

"I'm not sure. Right now I'm calling you from a hotel that Taylor set me up in. He thought it would be better to get me away from the news media.

"Are you going into the office today? I asked curiously.

"Yes ma'am! I'll be there like I've been there for the past twenty years, wild horses couldn't keep me away!"

I turned around in my chair to look out the window behind me and glanced down at my watch, it was eight thirty-five.

"I have a meeting in forty-five minutes. I don't know the agenda but I am pretty sure it's about EarthTel."

"I'm sure it is. Listen Casey, you will never know how much your assistance has meant to me."

"I didn't do anything" I insisted.

"Yeah you did! And I want you to know that I'm glad I wasn't wrong about you. Hell I don't know if I'll have a job when I get to work but I do know I will have my life back and without you I don't think I would have. Thank you. From the bottom of my soul I thank you Ms Banks"

I exhaled deeply and sighed,

"No, thank you Marty, you're a hell of a man. Take care now."

"I will and you do the same. I'll keep in touch," he said.

"Please do," I said pulling the phone down from my ear as I clicked it off.

I laid the phone down on the desk and turned my attention to the birds on the ledge. The phone rang again. This time it was my office line. I turned around and grabbed the receiver. It was Jason.

"Did you get it" He asked eagerly

"Get what" I said confused.

"How did the meeting go with Karen" he asked anxiously.

"Oh that, it was a bust," I replied.

"What?!" he said

"Yeah, she came over, we argued, and then she left."

"You've got to be kidding me!"

"Nope! She tried to come on to me and when I refused she got upset," I lied.

"I don't believe this shit! You had her Casey! How could you mess it up like that!" he exclaimed.

"Look, I'm not compromising my principles for no one, not even to save my own ass!"

"That's not what I'm saying. I just think you could have been a little more accommodating."

"Yeah maybe, but I wasn't in an accommodating mood. The whole thing was a bad idea," I said cautiously.

I knew Jason was depending on me to help him get out his jam but I was tired. Last night's confrontation with Karen had generated a tidal wave of emotions that left me craving the simple things. Yes, I wanted more than anything to put the whole fiasco of cheating on Jade behind me. Yes, I valued my job and desperately wanted to save it but no, I was no longer willing to spin a web of deceit in my vain efforts to save myself. If this whole thing had taught me anything it was that I couldn't control anybody but myself. And after all I'd been through, it was a lesson well learned.

There was an awkward silence on the other end of the phone. Then he finally spoke,

"Well, maybe you're giving up but I can't afford to. I'll lose everything if she follows through with her threat. She hasn't come in yet. So I'll give her until noon then I'm going to give her a call my damn self" he said optimistically.

"Well I wish you good luck on it!"

"Right!" he said before slamming the phone down abruptly. I held the receiver out, looked at it and placed it back on the cradle.

It was ten after nine, I decided to head to the War room for our meeting. When I got there, it was it was just like I knew it would be, chaotic! It was apparent that all the other associates had decided to get there early too. As I walked into the room I was greeted by several of my peers, while most stood collectively huddled, discussing the events of the morning. I carefully chose a seat that would allow me maximum observation of the senior partners. I didn't want to miss a thing. Outlandish implications swirled around the room like buzzards for prey. Casually I listened to wolf tales varying from espionage to the possibility of insider trading. Though none of the scenarios mentioned could be substantiated, everyone seemed convince their theory was correct. I smiled inside thinking it odd how hysterical this collection of corporate wizards appeared.

But there were other perplexing thoughts on my mind as well. I couldn't help but be plagued with thoughts of my own disloyalty. Though I had chosen not to represent Marty, I had been instrumental in finding someone who was more than capable of doing the job. In addition, after learning of EarthTel's fraudulent activity I didn't bother to tell the firm, a firm that had been a good to me when I really needed it. Try as I might, my part in this mess did not set well with me. I tried to rationalize why I had chosen the path I'd chosen, growing increasingly uncomfortable as my mind raced over my options until a little voice inside me whispered,

"Let go and let God," comforted by the thought, I took a deep breath, exhaled slowly and poised myself for the meeting.

Moments later, a hush fell over the room as Attorney Carruthers and the other senior partners walked in with grim looks on their faces. The people who were standing idly, quickly took their seats as did the senior partners and the meeting began.

Carruthers opened the meeting explaining the events as reported to him by EarthTel. EarthTel had received a formal request from the SEC regarding its previous years earning statement last Friday. Due to its sensitive nature it had not been disclosed. EarthTel was now prepared to provide the documents requested but prior to being able to do so the media got wind of it. Now the objective of the firm would be not only to provide damage control for news releases but also prepare for the statement, which was due. EarthTel's Audit Committee would be reviewing the company's financial records for not only the past year but the two prior to that. As a part of their efforts to be forthcoming, EarthTel requested the assistance of a New York accounting firm for the review process. If, after review, the company believes additional actions are required, it would make an announcement promptly.

The meeting continued as other partners expressed our commitment and allegiance to the global giant and reminded us of our duties and obligations to the company. We were told over the next couple of days committees would be formed for various representation needs of EarthTel. We were not given the objective but instead told it would be of the highest security level. The floor was then opened for discussion. Normally, this is where I stepped in with a solidifying statement or two, but I didn't. I could see the partners watching inconspicuously for my comments. But I had none. I was content to listen as the others zealously questioned and proposed antidotes smelling the opportunity to stand out and get ahead of the pack. I did, however, wonder if the committees had already been selected.

Although EarthTel was a client I'd worked with over the past year, I thought it unlikely in light of my current caseload and the impending investigation by HR that I would have any major part in it. The thought normally would have concerned me. But for some reason it didn't. A peace that knew no understanding had come over me. My quest to be in the limelight was overshadowed by my desire for EarthTel to do the right thing. As I drifted off in a sea of my own thoughts I was jostled back to reality by the vibration of cell phone. I reached down discreetly to unsnap it from my slacks. It was Jade. She was paging me 911.

"What the hell?!" My mind searched for a reason why she might be calling. She and I hadn't talked in weeks. Though I tried not to let her page excite me, it did.

The meeting ended an hour later. It would have ended sooner but like I said, we had a lot of people trying to outshine each other. Before dismissing us, Carruthers instructed us to be mindful of the media. Quietly I gathered my things and walked out of the conference room with the rest of my associates.

When I returned to my office I could not help but run to my desk to return Jades called. As I lifted the receiver to call her I couldn't help but reflect on how odd it was that this woman still possessed such power over me that even though she had abandoned me in the manner that she did then slept with her co-worker, I was still at her beck and call just like ever before. Dismayed by my thoughts, I placed the phone back on its cradle and sat down at my desk. I was tired. Mentally, I was drained. The thought of calling Jade make me feel weak and frightened. I wasn't prepared for more bad news and I couldn't fathom her wanting to talk to me about anything on a positive level. I bowed my head and closed my eyes. I didn't like what I was feeling. The pain of her rejection began filtrating through me as if it were the first day she'd left me that awful letter. Suddenly I opened my eyes and reached for the phone. Before I could dial and call came in. I switched over to the incoming line.

"Casey Banks" I answered dryly.

"Hi Casey, this is Jade"

My heart began pounding wildly in my chest. I could feel my pulse on the side of my neck jumping to get out. My palms grew sweaty and I didn't know if I could utter a word out of my mouth.

I sat there holding the phone as though transfixed.

"Hello?" she repeated through the receiver.

"Hey" I finally managed to say with a little confidence.

"How are you?" she asked.

"I'm fine and you?" I asked trying to conceal my nervousness.

"I'm fine," she said calmly.

There was another pause.

"Did I catch you at a bad time" she asked

"No, I'm just returning from a meeting" I explained.

"Oh, I bet. I heard the news about EarthTel. How did it go?" she asked.

"It was pretty standard, damage control and all that."

"Well you guys definitely have your hands full now."

"I'm sure," I said dryly

"Casey, I was wondering if you and I could get together tonight to talk." She said

"Talk?"

"Yeah talk. I think we need to. What do you think?" she asked

"I've been trying to talk to you for a minute now......" I began before she interrupted me.

"I know, I know. I wasn't ready then, but I am now."

"Umph...where" I asked more than a little irritated with her apparent confidence and my lack of it.

"Well I could come by your place if it's not a problem." She asked

"I don't see why not." I said, "To talk right?"

"Yeah Casey to talk. Jas has a skating party tonight so she will be with her friends at the rink and there will be plenty of chaperones there so I can come by after I drop her off at seven if that's ok with you?"

"Sure, no problem" I said hoping not to sound too accommodating.

"Good, it's settled. I'll be there around seven thirty ok?"

"Is this why you paged me 911?" I asked curiously

"Yes, I figured you wouldn't answer it otherwise since last time we saw each you were furious with me," she answered.

I reflected back to the last time I saw her standing in her door way wearing a tee shirt and panties. I had to sigh to keep from cursing. It had definitely been payback! My heart wanted to meet with her but my head was against it. In the end my heart won out.

"So it's not an emergency then?"

"No, I didn't think you'd call me back unless I said that."

"I see." I mumbled

"Okay, so I'll see you tonight right?"

"Sure," I agreed and hung up.

I didn't have time to think about the implications of Jade's call because Ronni burst into the office smiling broadly waving a memo at me.

"What's going on?" I asked smiling back at her.

"Oh a little birdie just brought this over," she said still waving the paper in the air.

"Damn it must be good! The way you're acting someone would think you just won the lottery or something."

"Nope but you did," she said.

"What?" I asked, extending my hand for the piece of paper Ronni kept dangling before me.

Ronni danced closer to me and handed it to me. As I took the note from her and began to read it I saw it was from Karen. The moment I read her name I looked back up at Ronni angrily.

"Go ahead read it!" she insisted.

"Wasn't this addressed to me?" I asked irritated.

"Yes it is but..."

"No Ronni, no buts, it was addressed to me not you! Did you read it?!"

"I was only trying to make sure..."

"Make sure of what?! Damn!" I said angrily.

"I wanted to make sure she wasn't trying to make anymore trouble for you."

"But what could you do about it if she was? Huh, what?" I demanded

Ronni dropped her head, embarrassed by the way I was talking to her.

"I'm sorry Casey, it's just that when she gave it to me and asked me to give it to you I didn't know if you'd be upset or not so I tried to intercede, I'm sorry," she whimpered.

"Karen gave this you?!" I asked astonished.

"Yeah, she just left," Ronni answered still looking down at the floor.

"Oh, I didn't know, I'm sorry Ronni. Things are crazy for me right now and my nerves are on edge"

"There's no need to apologize, you're right. I don't have the right to read anything addressed to you," she blurted out before turning and walking toward the door.

"Hey Ronni, hold on a minute" I said standing up from my seat.

She stopped and turned in my direction but avoided eye contact.

"I'm sorry I lost my temper, I know you meant well. Will you forgive me?" I asked earnestly.

Ronni nodded and looked up at me sheepishly

"Now will you read the damn thing," she mumbled.

I smiled warmly at her and replied,

"Yes, I'll read the DAMN thing!"

I began reading the typed letter again. It was addressed to our Human Resource Department head, Julia Smart. It read:

Vivian M Kelly

Dear Ms. Smart,

This letter is to formally inform you of my desires to drop all charges brought against Casey Banks by me. In further reflection of the facts I admit that the charge of Sexual Harassment was a gross overstatement. Ms. Banks did not, nor has she ever, approached me in a manner that was either unprofessional or inappropriate. I apologize for any inconvenience this may have caused you and your department and especially Ms. Banks. It is my sincere desire that this case be dropped. I extend my deepest apologizes to Ms Banks for the terrible wrong I've done her. I can only hope that my coming forward now with the truth will right the terrible wrong I've done. Please contact me if you have any further questions. With that said, I do hereby submit my letter of resignation effective immediately.

Sincerely,

Karen Campbell

I looked up from the letter in amazement. I couldn't believe what I'd read. I quickly read it again and looked over at Ronni. She was smiling broadly awaiting my reaction. At that moment it was if the weight of the world had been lifted up off my shoulders. Gently I placed it down on the desk and let out a deep breath as I reflected on the words I'd read. Karen had done it. She'd exonerated me! Sure, I had hoped beyond hope that she would do the right thing but last night I'd decided to give up the fight. The past couple of months had been terrible. In them I'd witnessed a part of human character that I never acknowledged truly existed in my seemingly perfect world. Yeah, before now, I had been naïve, so naïve that when faced with the reality of it I found myself very disillusioned and saddened with its prospects. This letter and Marty's bold stance at EarthTel was a small reaffirmation that people were still human and ultimately the good in most people prevailed.

My attention went back to Ronni who was standing quietly at the door watching me for a sign. I didn't know what to give her. Of course I was happy that the truth had come out, but still I was very much aware of how my own actions had caused most of my problems. I was by no means an innocent bystander in the whole situation. I was simply blessed.

On queue, Ronnie spoke out,

"It's over," she said quietly

"Yeah, it is," I said leaning back deeper into my chair, folding my arms on my chest.

"Well, congratulations. I'm happy for you," she said, as she turned and opened the door to leave.

"Thanks Ronnie, I appreciate it," I said solemnly.

It was only noon, but for me it had been a full day. Thoughts of Karen ran rampant through my head. For a moment I'd even forgotten about meeting Jade later.

465

"Jade," I mumbled aloud.

Though I hated to admit it, I was anxious to see what she wanted to talk with me about. I couldn't help but harbor the hope that she'd realized that love was more important than anything else and wanted to reconcile. Though I tried to pace myself and not let my thoughts get ahead of me, I knew deep down I wanted her to tell me she loved me and this breakup was over. I wanted her to confess her love and desire for us to be a family. I was ready. Hell, I was more than ready, I was feening for it. The rest of the day I immersed myself into my work. It wasn't hard considering everything that was going on at the firm that day. Before leaving I got a call from Human Resource, it was Mrs. Smart. She told me of the letter Karen had written and offered to send me a copy via office mail. I thanked her and called it a day.

I got home that evening around six-fifteen. I had roughly little over an hour before Jade would arrive and it seemed like an eternity. I tried to busy myself around the house, by straightening up to take my mind off of her. But it was no use, regardless of where I tried to channel my thoughts they always seemed to come back to Jade. Finally, it was seven-thirty and she wasn't there yet. I was beginning get panicky.

"Maybe she changed her mind," I wondered aloud.

Anxiously I paced the floor trying to keep myself from calling her to see what was going on. I walked to the bar and took out a glass to pour myself a stiff drink of Cognac. As the soothing liquid slid down my throat, the doorbell rang. I quickly put the glass aside and walked to the door. Every nerve in my body was jumping. Abruptly I stopped, ran back to the bar and poured myself another drink. This time I allowed it to accompany me to the door.

So, with drink in hand, I opened the door to see Jade standing there. As usual, she looked beautiful. Silently I ushered her in. I walked quietly behind her as she headed for the living. She sat down on the sofa, softly slung her hair back and spoke,

"Hi Casey."

"Hey," I said softly.

My voice trembled and I silently hoped she hadn't detected it. Awkwardly, I walked over to the chair and took a seat, then grabbed the remote to mute the television.

"Why are you sitting way over there?" she asked.

"Oh, no reason," I said awkwardly.

"Well come over here then," She said

Quietly I got up and walked over to the sofa. I put my drink down on the coffee table and made myself comfortable. I was careful not to sit too close, just far enough away that I could still smell a hint of her perfume.

"So what's up?" I asked

"You, maybe me," she said coyly.

"Really," I said softly, still in awe that she was sitting there beside me once again.

"Yeah really," she teased, smiling softly at my awkwardness.

"Okay…" I said, waiting for her to explain.

Jade began by telling me she loved me. She said during the past weeks she'd realized how much I meant to her and missed me. She spoke passionately about what had happened between Karen and me, reliving her hurt in every word. Then quietly, she told me she had finally put it behind her. She admitted she'd done some things to get back at me. Like ol boy I saw leaving her condo that day. She swore that she'd only flirted with him though and that they didn't do anything else. I wanted to argue the point but there was no need.

"Two wrongs don't make a right," like my grand momma used to say. What's done was done. So if she was willing to forgive my indiscretions. I had to be willing to forgive hers. Right was right!

Needless to say, her words were music to my ears yet there was some nagging doubt inside me, preventing me from realizing the joy I truly felt. She continued on to say she missed "us." Now, I began to breathe!

I watched her intently as she reminisced over the last night we'd spent together. Every time she mentioned Karen's name I would hold my breath and wait for the axe to fall. I so wanted to put Karen behind me and I felt the more she discussed her, the slimmer my chances were becoming of actually having her back in my life.

When Love Aint Enough

"Jade, I've truly come to understand how much I hurt you. And I would give anything to take back that moment in time. But I can't."

"I know you would baby, I know that. And I guess if I had made it easier for you to tell me and not been Ms. Bitch all the time you might have felt comfortable telling me. That's why I'm here," she explained.

Again, I began to breathe.

"I want to know if we can go back to how it was in the beginning?" she said.

"The beginning? Which one?" I asked.

"The one before all this mess started. The one where we were both happy!"

"Are you talking about before Karen did all this and you had left Richard?" I asked cautiously.

"I'm talking about the way things were when we first met," she said calmly

"Jade, when we first met you was with someone!" I said as the blood began to race fiercely through the vein in my neck.

"Casey I'm not gay. I've realized that. I do like men. But I happen to love you" she said shifting on the sofa to face me.

"You mean to tell me you came all the way over her to ask me if I would go back to being second or third to some nigga you just met?!"

"No I came all the way over here to see if you wanted to get things back like they were!"

"Ah hell nawh! Hell nawh!" I exclaimed.

"Casey listen to me, this time it would be different…"

"No you listen to me! I refuse to allow you to cultivate your new relationship with some nigga after I've been waiting on you to come around for over two years. Hell nawh! Would you ask him to do the same for me, huh, would you?"

"That's different he's a man!"

"It ain't no damn different. No, if you want to be with me you leave him the hell alone, that's it!"

"Casey that would mean I'm gay and I'm not"

"No that would mean you love me! This other mess is bullshit!"

"I do love you!" She insisted.

"Oh, just not enough to be with me without some dick in the background I guess!"

"Casey you're not being fair. You know I have a child. You know if I was with you it could never be beyond these four walls. I am not gay!"

"Well what would be different? The fact that it's a new guy. Is that the difference? Shit when we were together at first we never went beyond these four walls. Hell, we hardly ever did shit beside go to New Orleans and then you fucked the nigga before you came to be with me!"

"Casey you're not being fair. I never lied to you. I have always told you the way things were, now haven't I?"

"Yeah, you sure did, but things change, people change! Don't you understand what it does to me to know I am sharing the woman I love with someone else? It doesn't matter that it's a man. It's the fact that it's someone other than me!"

"But I love you Casey!"

"Yeah right, and I bet you tell him the same thing!"

"No, I don't love him."

I grabbed my head in disbelief, "Well in hell are you with him?!"

Jade was silent. I continued to ask the same question but she refused to answer. We sat in silence.

"Will you think about it Casey, I don't want to loose you."

"No, you think about this, leave him alone and be with me. With me Jade, after all you say you love me right?" I questioned

"Yes I do love you," she said.

"Well if you love me then leave him. I can take care of you and Jas. Just leave him baby," I pleaded.

Again Jade was quiet. I stared at her intently trying to figure out what was going on in her head. Her face gave me no clue. I resigned myself to picking up my drink and leaning back to study the ceiling.

Before leaving Jade agreed to think about what I had said. It was an insult she could even part her lips to ask me some shit like that! I loved Jade but she had gone too far. What was I supposed to be, the pussy licker while the man at home was the

pussy sticker? Hell nawh, I wasn't going to do it! It was the
same ol shit again just a different nigga. In my anticipation of
seeing her I hadn't bothered to eat, now I wasn't hungry. Instead
I was outraged as I busily walked about the house preparing to
go to bed. All I wanted to do was to sleep. My heart raced as I
thought of how the woman I loved with all my heart could forget
so easily all I had endured to be with her. I grew sick thinking
of how long I'd patiently waited for her to be mine and mine
alone. Sure we argued but hell, most times our arguments were
about him and her failure to spend any quality time with me. No
she didn't understand. She was too busy cultivating a
relationship with a married man. And I had endured it. And in
spite of it all, I had loved her like I'd never loved anyone in my
life. I was certain she had to know this and wouldn't risk losing
the love of a lifetime. Jade loved me, I was sure of it. In fact,
had someone asked me prior to today, I would have bet my life
on it! Yet the uneasiness of it all was beginning to weigh on my
heart.

This woman had to love me. Sure she was scared of what
people might say and sure she loved her child but I was also an
important part of her life. What ever was going on with
whomever she was with at the moment, was

"Just something to do!"

I wouldn't last. It couldn't!

"Not if she loved me. Not if she- loved -me!" I repeated
aloud to myself as I fell on my knees before my bed. I bowed

my head and prayed for strength. I asked God to help me through all I was going through and protect me. I raised my head up from my tear soaked mattress and climbed wearily into my bed.

"Jade loves me, she'll do the right thing. I'll give her a couple of days to think and she'll choose me. She'll choose me." I whispered as I drifted off into a turbulent sleep.

The next day was Saturday. I'd barely slept all night. Groggily, I lay in bed as the television came on at six-fifteen. In my anguish the night before, I had forgotten to turn off the alarm. The news was on. The news stations were still talking about the EarthTel debacle. I grabbed the remote off of the nightstand and began channeling through the networks. Exhausted and unable to find anything interesting to watch, I turned it off and lay quietly. It wasn't very long before my thoughts turned to Jade. It was making me sick as she consumed my every thought.

As I lay in bed, I tried to plan my day and fill it with work but it was to no avail. My mind continued to wander back to the conversation she and I had the night before. In frustration, I grabbed a pillow, smashed it down over my face in hopes of smashing away the thoughts of her. But it didn't do any good. Frustrated, I threw the pillow to the floor and rolled out of bed. If I was up this time of the morning, I might as well make the best of it. I stumbled to my closet and looked inside for a pair of sweats and grabbed a sweatshirt from the drawer.

I decided to go out for a jog on the beach. It was early; my only company would be other joggers and maybe the seagulls. As I stepped out into the chilled air, the breeze from the ocean filled my nostrils. I breathed in deeply attempting to extract all that was good from the air as if it were medicine for my troubled soul. Slowly I began my decent unto the sandy beaches looking about for anyone, not caring if I saw no one. My soul was hurting. And though I tried to reassure it Jade would choose me, it still grieved.

I spent the rest of the day like that, jumping from one thing to the next, in a futile attempt to wipe the memory of Jade from my mind. Later that evening, I decided to treat myself to dinner at Claude's. It was around eight when I arrived. I hadn't seen Kris in a while and I was certain the change in atmosphere would do me good. Plus, I was looking cute if I did say so myself. My linen slacks hung loosely around my waist as a result of the 22 pounds I'd lost since Jade and I'd broken up. I felt good about the way I looked, though I knew the way I'd lost it wasn't the best way to do it. Sill it was a good thing. Hell, Jade had loved it when my clothes sagged off me. She often remarked it was my subtle boyishness that initially attracted her to me.

As I arrived in the parking lot of Claude's, I thought it was great that Kris had such a large crowd. Normally I shied away from a lot of people when I was down but tonight was different.

474

When Love Aint Enough

My soul was craving some attention. It had been shut up too long and I was only happy to oblige. I think I would have driven back home to Mississippi if it meant I could stop thinking about Jade for a minute.

Enthusiastically, I jumped out of my truck and made my way to the entrance of the restaurant. As I entered the busy foyer I smiled at the thought of seeing Kris. Cautiously I walked over to the hostess who greeted me with a big smile. She remarked she hadn't seen me in a while and I in turn I smiled back and asked her to tell Kris I was in the house. As the Hostess departed her station, I took an inventory of the crowd. Casually I skimmed the room filled with customers as they laughed and talked joyfully. Then I heard it, it was a brief faint laugh, but I would have known it anywhere. My body stiffened as my heart started to beat faster. I looked around but I didn't see anyone. I took a deep breath, convincing myself I must have been mistaken. Then I heard it again, that laugh. I started walking around in a daze, straining desperately to hear from which direction it came. Then I saw her. It was Jade. She was sitting at a large table surrounded by people. Then I saw him, Trevaire looking at her adoringly with his arm around her.

I was dumb struck! I stood motionless for what seemed an eternity, staring until she finally looked up, feeling my piercing gaze on her face. Her glance was brief but it too, seemed to take an eternity. My heart beat heavily in my throat as I attempted to open my mouth, but as if struck by some unforeseen force, I could only watch. Abruptly she turned back to face her companions. I stood frozen in place as the music and chatter began to drift back into my ears and the realization of what had just happened pierced my soul like a dagger! In a dizzy frenzy, I stumbled and turned away making my way through the seemingly endless ea of people who had now encased me. Frantically I pushed my way through to the foyer and out onto the deck. When the blast of the cold air hit me I began to walk. As the chill of the night seeped through my sweater, so did the harsh and cold reality of what I'd just seen. My paces quickened as I anxiously made my way through the parking lot. Soon I was running. When I reached my truck I was soaking in perspiration. Awkwardly I fumbled in my pockets for the key. The faint voice of someone calling my name drifted over to me. More frantic than ever now, I desperately began patting my pockets in search of the keys. When the warmth of a hand touched me on the shoulder, I froze. I didn't want to turn around. To turn around now would be to acknowledge my existence at that moment and I didn't want to. Not to myself and definitely not to Jade.

"Are you all right man?"
Still facing my truck, I whispered,
"Yeah"
"Where are you going?" she asked
"Home," I replied.

"Let me fix you something first," she said.

"Nah man, you too busy to be fixing me something. Go back in there, you've got a full house," I said still facing the door of my truck.

"Man I aint never too busy for my friends, now come on," she said pulling at me.

"Nawh dog, I'm gonna go home. It's cool. I'll be okay" I said

"You sure?" asked Kris.

"Yeah, I'm sure" I said turning slightly to see the look of concern in her eyes as she stood watching me.

"Well can you do me a favor?" She asked, staring at me intently.

"Sure, what?"

"Will you call me when you get there?"

"Sure"

"I mean it. Call me and let me know you got home safe."

"I will dog. I'll call you," I said reassuringly.

"Alright"

"Later," I said.

Kris waited patiently as I finally found my keys and opened the door. Under a watchful eye, I put on my seatbelts and waved goodbye. As I pulled out of the parking lot I saw her still watching me.

Nervously I pushed the CD button. There was an old one in there, Mariah Cary. As Mariah wailed out her notes, I withered in my seat. I tried to tell myself it meant nothing, that there was

477

a good reason for her looking away and maybe, just maybe, she didn't look away at all. Maybe she was out telling him it was over. I told myself anything and everything except what I knew to be true. Jade was out with her man, and she had totally dissed me!

The ride home was silent except for Mariah's singing. The words of her songs seemed to sooth me. And I definitely needed soothing. When I made it home, I popped out the CD and slipped it in my jacket. I needed her. I needed her to sooth my soul some more. I milled around in the house as though in a trance. My heart kept shouting out to me to call her but I couldn't. I didn't know why but I knew I couldn't. Instead I remembered to call Kris. It took a moment but she finally came to the line. She asked if I was home and I told her I was. She asked how long would I be up and I told her I wasn't sure. I listened as Kris tried uneasily to make idle conversation. Something in her voice was wrong. My blood ran cold through my veins as she finally came out with what she'd been keeping from me.

Kris told me that Jade and Trevaire had announced their plans to be married. The blood was rushing to my head now, I felt dizzy. Tears stained my cheeks as I listened to Kris tell me why Jade and her man had come Claude's.

"Look man, I'm coming over," insisted Kris.

"No!" I yelled firmly.

"Man I don't know what to say. All I know is I didn't want you hearing it from anybody else. I could tell by the look on your face tonight that you didn't have any idea. And neither did I until I went back inside."

"Yeah man, I understand. It's not your fault!"

"Man, I know you probably don't want to hear this but it's going to be alright. You got to keep strong!"

"Yeah I know man. It's gonna be alright," I repeated mechanically.

"Man look, I can be over there in an hour if you want me too." I was full fledge crying now and I couldn't hide it anymore. I stifled back the tears as I begged Kris not to come. I promised her I would be fine. I asked her to give me a minute and I would be fine.

"Man, she didn't have to do it like this I know. But you'll see. It will be fine. You got to concentrate on you right now. You're strong dog, kick rocks on that shit!" Kris demanded

"I know man," I cried. "Listen I'm going to call you back okay"

"I'm here for you man."

"I know it."

"Call me back, okay."

"No doubt. I'll call you later," I lied

I hung up the phone with Kris and let out a weary laugh.

"She's right I need to kick rocks on this and keep kicking."

From day one I have made sacrifices for Jade. I sacrificed my pride, my principles and myself. I changed all there was about me to accommodate a lifestyle I didn't believe in, her dating a married man with the topper being me dating her and devoting myself to a woman who couldn't and wouldn't devote herself to me. She was a selfish bitch. She can scream all day long until her tonsils fall out that she's not gay. She can holla till the cows come home that I was the one exception. But when the day is done and the damn drop falls, she's a liar. She lied to me. She lied to others and most of all she lied to herself. Hell, I don't care if she's gay or straight, my thing is out of all the shit she'd let slip out of her mouth, the one thing I had believed was that she loved me. That was the one thing keeping me there for all those years, that Jade loved Casey. I was mad, no, I was furious! I didn't know what to do or what to think. I didn't know if I should call and confront her ass or wait.

Constantly I paced the floor. I walked over to the liquor cabinet and flung open the doors. I looked inside to see if I had enough liquor in stock, because a nigga was drinking tonight. I grabbed the first bottle I saw and popped the cork. It was Cognac.

"Cognac's been a good friend to me lately," I thought. Instead of getting a glass I turned it up from the bottle. I needed to drink and I didn't have time to get a glass or a chaser. I gulped the smooth stuff until my throat burned from its harshness. Then I pulled the bottle down from my lips and

wiped my mouth with my sleeve. And instant buzz rushed to my head. I held the bottle tight and went up to my bedroom. I tore off my clothes and grabbed a tee shirt and a pair of pajama bottoms Jade had bought me one Christmas. As I slipped into the bottoms I thought of what Jade had said when we were exchanging gifts that year.

"I got you something to get into when I'm not around." I laughed out loud. I laughed so hard I started crying. The pain of it all was becoming too much for me to handle. My lips were trembling as my soul spent out of control crying out to anyone to help me endure this terrible heart ache. I fell to the floor and laid there in the fetal position crying and rocking to sooth the wrenching pain that was tearing through my body like a knife. My thoughts raced through my mind as I shook my head wildly trying to rid myself of the thought of her with him and not with me. I wondered how she made love to him. I thought of all the positions and wondered which ones satisfied her. I was tormented! Soon I blamed myself for everything that had happened. I cursed myself for having been vulnerable to Karen. I loathed the things I'd done and the arguments I had started for no apparent reason. I wanted to take back every harsh word I had ever said to her and make her see how much I loved and needed her with me. My head ached violently as I lay there on the floor in the midst of my own torment, crying erratically and calling Jade's name.

That was me two days ago.

481

I was a mess then and I'm still a mess. Slowly I rose up from my chair. It was Monday, and I'd called in sick. I walked past the bottle of unopened Cognac sitting in the middle of the floor and saluted it. My mouth tasted like cotton balls. I dragged myself into the kitchen to get some water as Luther Vandross sang on. As I entered the kitchen the phone rang. I raced over to the counter to answer it.

"Hello," I said anxiously not bothering to check the caller ID.

"Hey, what's up?" Asked Ronni

"Oh, hey," I said showing my disappointment that it wasn't someone else.

"Well good morning to you too," Ronni answered cheerily.

"What's up," I said dryly

"Carruthers asked me to call you. He wants to see you."

"For what?!" I said agitated

"Dah, we are kind of busy around here, remember EarthTel!" said Ronni sarcastically

" I know that but what does he want with me…"

"Well you are one of the top associates so it's only natural he'd want you in on this, don't you think?"

"No, I don't think!" I snapped.

"No you sure don't!" Ronni snapped back

"What did you say?!" I asked incredulous.

"I said, no you don't think!" Ronni repeated.

"Look Ronni I am not in the mood for this today…."

"And neither am I. Now get off your ass and get in here to see your boss. The pity party is fucking over!" She said before hanging up in my face.

I pulled the phone down from my ear and stared at it incredulous.

"Who in the hell did she think she was talking to like that! I will fire her ass so fast it'll make my head spin!" I screamed.

I paused for a second then called her back.

The phone rang twice and then she answered.

"Casey Banks office" she answered.

"You damn right! Its Casey Banks office and I'm wondering what gives you the right to talk to me like that!" I yelled.

"You give me the right Casey. I am sick of this." She responded

"Sick of what? What do you have to be sick of?" I screamed

"You're acting a damn fool over a broad who don't give a damn about you!"

I was shocked. What is going on? Has everybody fell the off or what?!"

Ronni continued,

"Kris called this morning looking for you."

"For what?"

"You know why, because you didn't answer at home when she called you!"

"Kris hasn't called here!" I screamed.

483

"Yeah she did Casey and each time she's gotten your answering machine. I tried a couple of times myself this weekend also.

"Well it rang when you called this morning," I said quizzically.

"Well maybe you weren't on it this morning I don't know! But it's time Casey!"

"For what?!"

"For you to get on with your life!" she said raising her voice. The words ran through my head like wind. I refused to dignify her remarks with answer. *"Who was she to tell me what to do or how to do it,"* I thought angrily.

"Ronni, I appreciate your concern, but I..."

"It's more than concern Casey…"

"What else is it?"

"I care about what happens to you Casey."

"Well thanks, but I can take care of myself if you don't mind."

"It doesn't look like it to me."

"Ronni I am not in the mood for this today okay. I'm not feeling this."

I could hear Ronni breathing hard on the other end of the phone. I didn't want to hurt her but I was going through something and the only feelings I could concentrate on were my own. After another heavy sigh, Ronni spoke again,

"I love you."

"And I love you too." I said, still agitated like hell and wanting very much to end the conversation.

Ronni sighed yet again.

"No, I'm in love with you Casey."

The words came out of no where. Months ago when she and I were talking she had made a similar remark. I didn't bother to ask her to elaborate because I thought I understood what she meant. Now today she was saying the same thing again. I walked over to the table and sat down.

"Was this, her way of validating me so I'd feel better about being dumped!"

"You don't love me Ronni."

"I do."

"No, you don't." I insisted

"How would you know?! You're so busy with your head up Jade's butt! You wouldn't see me if I was standing in front of your face butt naked, waving a red flag and dancing a flamingo!

"But why Ronni, how…" I began

"You know I've asked myself that same question for over a year now." She sighed

"An entire year," I repeated incredulously as I leaned against the wall.

"Yeah, a whole year Casey."

"I don't know what to say…"

"There's nothing for you to say. I know how you feel about Jade. But losing Jade isn't the end of the world is what I'm trying to get you to see."

"It just feels like it."

"I know, been there, done that."

"Then why are you so hard on me?" I whined, my eyes tearing up again.

"I'm not trying to be. But somebody has to tell you. So why shouldn't it be someone who genuinely cares for you."

"I see"

"You see what?"

"You're saying all of this because you think I've flipped or something," I said softly.

"Earth to Casey! Listen woman, I am saying this because I do love you. You're a beautiful, thoughtful person, I love your smile, your cocky attitude and you have a great sense of humor when you're not tripping. I don't know what else to say, I love Casey Banks!"

I was really tripping now, one of my best friends and employees was telling me she loved me and I was too far gone to know what to say. I wanted to cry but I was tired. The weekend had taken everything from me. I just sat holding the phone to my ear, ashamed that deep down inside I still wished it was Jade saying those words to me.

"So?" Asked Ronni, interrupting my thoughts.

"So what?"

"Are you coming in today?'

"I need to take a shower."

"Okay ... then take one."

"Ronni I've been drinking all weekend I 'm a mess."

"Well I tell you what, go jump in the shower and I'll come over there to help you get ready."

"That's too much trouble."

"It's no trouble. I'll be there in thirty minutes."

Tears were welling up in my throat again. I needed Ronni but I was too embarrassed to admit it. I was broken and I didn't want anyone to see me like that, not even my girl Ronni. Silently I prayed for words to say to make her understand but in the end all I could muster was,

"Are you sure?"

"Yes, I'm sure," she whispered back to me.

"Okay"

Ronni hung up and so did I. I leaned over the table and stared out the bay window. I didn't know what to think. I jogged the recesses of my mind to remember if I'd ever led her on or flirted with her. I didn't believe so, but most straight women assumed you wanted them even when that's the farthest thing from your mind.

"Shit you can't rape the willing," I thought.

In any case, she'd be here soon, and I needed to take a shower, no better yet, I needed to soak. When I told Ronni I looked a mess, I wasn't exaggerating, I really did. I got up from the table and walked upstairs.

For the first time in two days, I picked up a comb to fix my hair that was damned near matted. I took the curling irons from the cabinet and plugged them up. Then I got in the tub to take a hot bath.

Ronnie arrived just as I was drying off. The doorbell rang three times before I was able to answer it. When I snatched the door open there stood my girl Ronni. She was wearing a black button front DKNY suit with black DKNY heels to match. I hadn't noticed until now that she'd cut her hair. It looked nice, giving her a Halley Barry sort of look. I don't think I'd ever noticed how brightly her eyes glistened before, as I did that day. She smiled warmly at me then walked inside. I closed the door and pulled my robe together. There was brief silence as I watched her walk through the foyer and into the living room, placing her DNKY bag down on a nearby table. She took a brief inventory of the battered room then turned to me and asked,

"So, what would you like for breakfast?"

About the Author

Vivian M. Kelly was born in Edwards,
Mississippi. She attended Tougaloo College before
enlisting in the United States Navy. After
traveling abroad, she returned to Mississippi and
now works for a Fortune 500 company. She is
currently working on her second novel.

Printed in the United States
68482LVS00001B/4-12

9 781597 440516